D1095724

Once
A Bride

ALSO BY SHARI ANTON

The Ideal Husband

Once A Bride

Shari Anton

WARNER
FOREVER

NEW YORK   BOSTON

Warner Forever is a registered trademark of Warner Books

Cover design by Diane Luger
Cover illustration by Jon Paul
Hand lettering by David Gatti
Book design by Giorgetta Bell McRee

Warner Books

Time Warner Book Group
1271 Avenue of the Americas
New York, NY 10020
ISBN 0-7394-4138-8

Printed in the United States of America

To Ross and Ruth Foley
who are courageously giving
love a second chance. Here's
a toast to your success!

Acknowledgments

An author is part of a team. Mine is excellent.

My agent, Pamela Hopkins, who has never lost faith in me.

My editor, Karen Kosztolnyik, who challenges me to write the best story possible.

And you, the readers, whom we all strive to please.

My sincerest thanks to all of you!

Once A Bride

Chapter One

Autumn 1333

THE SUMMONS was delivered by a nervous squire in Sir John Hamelin's pointed manner. Father wished to see her in his accounting room *now*.

Eloise Hamelin's boot heels clicked briskly over the passageway's plank floor, confident she could defend each of her recent purchases.

Maintaining a castle as huge and well manned as Lelleford required certain purchases. Eloise spared her father the task of buying mundane items, like spices and kegs of ale, sacks of various grains, barrels of salted fish—staples of the winter food supply—and other necessities. For her trouble he didn't begrudge her the occasional trinket.

Yesterday, merchants from all over England had attended the yearly village fair, making their goods readily available for her inspection and she'd taken full advantage. Her trinket consisted of several ells of utterly lovely, finely woven wool, a purchase that she'd deemed vital, and likely the reason for this morning's abrupt summons.

Most of the wool would be sewn into winter tunics for

her father. Even under ordinary circumstances she would be remiss to send the lord of Lelleford back to Westminster—to enjoy the grand festivities of the king's Christmas court—garbed in less than elegant fashion.

The remaining wool was for her own gowns, suitably styled and elegantly trimmed. She hadn't yet told her father of her desire to accompany him to court, waiting for the right moment to make her request without risking outright denial.

He simply *must* let her accompany him.

Eloise didn't doubt Father intended to contract another betrothal for her while at court. What better time to negotiate a marriage bargain than while mingling among the highborn men of the kingdom? 'Twas her destiny to marry well, and she accepted the duty.

Except this time she wanted a look at her intended husband first, to ensure him healthy and strong—unlike Hugh St. Marten, who'd fallen dead at her feet on the church steps before he could utter his marriage vows.

The horror had left her numb for days. Even now, two months later, the sorrow over Hugh's death lingered. She'd not known him well, but he'd been too likable a man not to feel saddened that one so young should die so suddenly and ignobly.

People tried not to remind her of Hugh's death, but occasionally she'd see pity in their eyes and hear them mutter "poor Lady Eloise" when they thought she didn't hear, and she abhorred being pitied.

She paused outside the accounting room's door. With a flight of hands over her emerald velvet gown and a quick tuck of a rebellious strand of long hair back into her braid, she ensured her appearance without fault.

Spine straight, chin set, she rapped on the heavy oak door.

"Eloise?"

Her father's voice held a sharp edge, even though muffled through the door. Perhaps this wasn't the right time to make her request.

"Aye, Father."

She heard the bolt slide. The door flew open into a small chamber that smelled of crisp parchment, pungent ink, and beeswax candles. Before she could blink, he pulled her into the chamber.

Eloise gasped at the carnage, unable to comprehend why parchment scrolls littered the dark oak desk, or why an overturned bottle dripped indigo ink onto the brown robe of unconscious Brother Walter, who sprawled facedown beside the desk.

Ye, gods! Was the monk dead? Nay. The young cleric breathed, though shallowly. Her hand trembled as she bent toward the bloody gash at his temple.

The door slammed, making her flinch.

"Leave him be!"

Too confused to do aught else, Eloise withdrew at her father's sharp command. Fury darkened his dove gray eyes to pewter, a near match to his thinning hair. Never before had she seen his barrel chest heave so rapidly, nor felt so fragile in his imposing shadow.

Desperate to make sense of the senseless, she ventured to ask, "What happened?"

He waved a meaty hand at the monk recently retained as his clerk. "Yon dolt proved unworthy of my trust. You can do what you will with him after I am gone."

"Gone where? Why?"

He strode toward the desk and shoved several scrolls into a black leather pouch.

"Best you do not know of my whereabouts." He glared at Brother Walter. "I have been declared a rebel, Eloise. Even now the earl of Kenworth comes to make the arrest."

Stunned, she could only stare at her father. Surely there must be some mistake, but for the life of her she knew not where to place the blame.

He closed the flap on the pouch. "Show Kenworth no resistance. Allow him through the gate. Give him free roam of the castle. Feed him. Serve him our finest wine. By all the saints, give him no reason to seize Lelleford by force!"

Eloise snapped out of her stupor.

"Dear God, Father, what precisely have you been accused of?"

"Treason."

Her stomach roiled, her knees nearly buckled. A conviction on such a high crime demanded gruesome punishment. Hanged, drawn and quartered.

From a trunk in the corner he hefted a gold chest encrusted with rubies and set it on the desk. From the coffin he scooped two handfuls of coins into his money purse, then pulled the string taut.

"Sew some coins into the hems of your gowns and cloaks in the unlikely event you are forced to abandon Lelleford. By the grace of God, perhaps Julius is on his way home and can take charge on his return."

Julius, her eldest brother, had gone to Italy on pilgrimage. Useless to wish he'd walk through the door _now_.

"Father, there must be some way to resolve—"

"There is, but not with the earl of Kenworth. He and I have been at odds for too long. Do not send to Jeanne or Geoffrey for aid. There is naught either can do to assist me and the fewer of my children involved the better." He snapped up the leather pouch bulging with scrolls. "I will take Edgar with me. He should be readying horses."

Eloise now understood the squire's nervousness when he delivered her father's summons. Edgar must have witnessed whatever had occurred between John Hamelin and Brother Walter, possibly knew how the monk had been injured.

"What of Brother Walter?"

"The wretch will live. 'Tis probably best not to restrain him. All you need do is feign ignorance of my affairs and all should be well."

She'd never felt more ignorant or frightened in her entire ten and seven years. Panic battled with anger over his abandoning her to this perilous predicament.

Eloise wanted him to stay, but if he didn't go, he could very well be hanged in his own bailey with his own rope.

A lump formed in her throat, tears welled in her eyes. Damn. Now was no time for sentiment. Sir John Hamelin, a knight of the realm, a heretofore trusted advisor to the king, would find a way to dispute the charge and avoid hanging.

'Twas on her part in this calamity she must concentrate, fulfill her duty.

"Do you know when the earl will arrive?"

"Likely before evening meal."

Only a few hours away. Not enough time to prepare, but all the time given her.

"You had best hurry, then."

"I shall send word when I deem it safe. Do as I have told you and all will be well. I place great trust in you, Eloise. Do not fail me."

"Have I ever?"

He tilted his head; his expression softened. "Nay. Of all my children only you have shown unfailing loyalty. Have a care, Daughter."

Eloise knew her father disliked overt shows of affection, didn't often reveal his softer side, and she would never do anything to embarrass him. But they were alone, and she might not see him for a very long while. She wrapped her arms around his barrel chest and squeezed hard.

Even before his arms came around her and pulled her in tight she could hear his heart thud rapidly.

"Do not despair, Eloise," he whispered into her hair. "All will come out right in the end."

Desperately wanting to believe him, holding back tears, Eloise reluctantly backed away. "Godspeed, Father."

He flipped up the latch and slowly opened the door, peering up and then down the passageway before he strode out.

Eloise leaned against the desk and took several deep breaths. She lacked time for either outrage or self-pity. What to do first?

Brother Walter sprawled on the floor, unconscious, the blood on his temple drying dark and garish against his pale skin. An untrustworthy man according to her father. The monk deserved whatever misfortune befell him for whatever part he'd played in her father's downfall.

Nay, not downfall. Merely a misunderstanding her father must put to rights. Treason? Unthinkable! Too often Father praised young King Edward's policies, and been effusive over Edward's military prowess. 'Twas against all sense for her father to betray the young sovereign he admired.

Do nothing. Feign ignorance.

Sweet mercy, did Father know what he asked of her?

Likely, because he'd seen fit to issue pointed instructions for her behavior.

The monk stirred, moaning.

The churl didn't deserve any show of concern, but show it she must if he were to believe she'd simply come upon him, found him wounded—didn't know he'd somehow betrayed her father.

She knelt and put a hand to his shoulder. "Brother Walter, can you hear me? Can you awaken?"

He opened his eyes, dazed. "L-lady . . . Eloise, I—"

"Do not try to speak yet. You must have tripped and hit your head on the desk. Can you sit up?"

He braced on an arm and eased upright, shaking his head as if settling his brain into its rightful place.

Once he seemed balanced, Eloise moved away from the monk she'd dearly love to toss in the dungeon.

Brother Walter glanced around the room. Looking for Father?

She righted the ink bottle. "Tsk. Such a mess you made. I daresay Father will not be pleased if he sees his possessions in such disarray. But come, I will take you down to the hall and tend your injury before we attempt to tidy the room."

"Where is . . . Sir John?"

"I know not." She swallowed the lump threatening to choke off her air. "Are you able to walk?"

The monk sighed. "I believe so."

Eloise watched him struggle to his feet, unable to muster any compassion. She'd ease his aches and stitch the gash if need be. Then needle information out of him? *Do nothing.*

'Twould be the hardest command to obey. Truly, she didn't understand why her father deemed it best to run from a confrontation. Why not secure the castle, place additional guards on the crenellated battlements, deny the earl entry?

From the time of the Conquest, Lelleford had withstood both outright attack and long sieges. With winter coming on, the earl couldn't keep his force in the field long without suffering many hardships. Lelleford's storage rooms bulged from the recently completed harvest; both wells were deep and flowing. 'Twould be the perfect time to take a defensive stance.

Even with the threat of hanging, running away seemed cowardly, and she'd never known her father not to stand his ground.

Eloise eased toward the door, giving the monk time to find his legs, deciding her father must be taking the right course of action. She had to trust he knew the best way to deal not only with the earl but with the charges against him.

So she'd feed the invaders, serve them wine, be the most gracious of hostesses—and pray she would give the earl of Kenworth no reason to take Lelleford by force.

*   *   *

Traveling with the earl of Kenworth compared favorably to traveling with the king—both liked their comforts and provided commendably for those in their retinue.

Sir Roland St. Marten ate his midday repast in the large tent in the company of William, earl of Kenworth, and his knights. Outside, the squires and men-at-arms dined on hearty if less sumptuous fare.

One would think the company traveled for pleasure, not on serious business. Kenworth seemed in no hurry to reach Lelleford, take Sir John Hamelin into custody, and haul him off to Westminster for judgment.

Roland thought Kenworth misguided in his belief that, with surprise in his favor, the knight would allow the earl to enter the stronghold and give over peaceably to the arrest.

John Hamelin wasn't the type of man to roll over and whimper like a beaten dog. Having spent several days at Lelleford, Roland knew the fortress was strong and well manned. Sir John could avoid seizure for months if he chose.

But capturing Sir John was the earl's problem, not his.

Roland was entrusted with taking charge of Lelleford in the king's name, to ensure the holding suffered no setback while its lord answered to the charge of treason.

He intended to remain neutral in this whole affair, the only sane position to take.

The earl popped the last bit of lamprey into his mouth and washed it down with a healthy swallow of wine. The ensuing belch complimented the cook and signaled the end of the meal.

Kenworth set his goblet on the table and grinned at the

knights attending him. "Let us hope Lelleford's cook compares favorably to mine own. I should hate to come so far only to be forced to endure thinned stew and meek wine. Tell me, St. Marten, do the cooks at Lelleford make good use of spices?"

Since he was the only one of the company who'd been inside the keep, such inane questions were usually directed Roland's way. Would that the earl were more concerned with the keep's defenses, the size of the storage rooms, or the number of men Sir John could send onto the field.

Roland had learned immediately upon joining the retinue that Kenworth harbored no concerns over possible obstacles and didn't take kindly to people who did.

Keeping his opinion to himself when among the magnates had been among Roland's first lessons upon entering the king's service. The dukes and earls of the kingdom took counsel from only their trusted advisors and each other—and then did what they pleased anyway.

It pleased the earl to dismiss Sir John as no more than a thorn in his paw, easily plucked out and tossed aside.

"I found no lack in Lelleford's hospitality, either in the comfort of the beds or quality of the victuals served." At a hint of the earl's displeasure, he quickly amended. "You must remember I was at Lelleford when the Hamelins wished to make a grand impression on my family. No doubt the meals and company are not always so excellent and gracious as are your lordship's."

"I should say not." Kenworth leaned back in his armed chair. "A near miss, that. If Hugh—rest his soul—had lived, you would now be related to the traitor."

The shiver of revulsion Roland allowed to show was

genuine. "I praise God for his intervention, though I wish He had done so in less mortal fashion."

To this day he could envision his half brother's death, see Hugh's enchantment with his bride dim to pain, his eyes roll back in his head just before he collapsed. Hugh St. Marten had died an ignoble death, sprawled facedown on the church steps at his bride's feet.

And the bride, Lady Eloise Hamelin, hadn't shed a tear over the man who worshiped her, who would heed no argument against his betrothed. Roland had tried to convince Hugh to reconsider the marriage, to no avail.

The earl's fingers drummed the chair's arm. "One might wonder if a scoundrel of unsavory character and low morals, not God, intervened."

Given the suddenness and timing of Hugh's death, Roland had suspected treachery, too, but been disproved to his satisfaction. "My father's physicians assured us 'twas Hugh's weak heart at fault, not villainy of any kind."

For a villain, Roland had only to look to himself. That last heated confrontation with Hugh still haunted him. He couldn't help suspect their argument had overtaxed Hugh, contributed to damaging a failing heart. Hastened his death.

"A shame, that. Had villainy occurred, you would now be in a position to avenge Hugh's death. Such an opportunity does not come often."

Wary of the earl's tone, Roland sought to make his position clear. "I have no personal quarrel with Sir John other than his treachery toward our beloved sovereign."

"Ah, but personal quarrels are the most satisfying to settle." Kenworth abruptly rose. "If we are to sample

Lelleford's hospitality this eve, we must be off. Ready the men."

Roland shook off the bad memories and traces of guilt as he followed the other knights out of the tent, their exit a signal to all to break camp. He headed for the horses — his particular assignment on this journey — to ensure them properly cared for. Not a hard job due to the efficiency of squires who knew their knights' horses were their most highly prized possessions. Even now the squires and grooms scrambled for saddles, including Timothy, Roland's own squire.

Odd that, to have a young man at his beck and call, doing those tasks Roland had always done for himself until recently.

So much had happened in the two months since Hugh's death.

Soon after the ill-fated wedding, Roland had gone to the Scottish wars with Sir Damian, the knight with whom he'd fostered for most of his life, and who he afterward served as a trusted squire. All had changed in the flash of a sword. He'd been in the wrong place at the right time on Halidon Hill, guarding a king's back when it was most needed.

A year older than the two and twenty king of England and a bit taller and broader in the shoulder, Roland had earned King Edward's admiration for his prowess on the battlefield and his timely intervention between the king and a Scot's claymore.

Rewards followed. During his few weeks in the king's service, he'd been dubbed a knight, been granted several horses right out of the king's own stable, received all the weapons and armor necessary for the rank, and taken

Timothy as his squire. Now all he required was an income rich enough to support his new rank and gifts.

Which was why, Roland was sure, King Edward set him to this task. Kings could be extremely generous to those who served them well.

Roland planned to begin his upward rise by faithfully following royal orders, even if the damn earl of Kenworth took it into his head to cause mischief—or worse.

The earl's tent tumbled to the ground. Soon tent, poles, furniture, and foodstuffs were being loaded into the baggage carts. Knights and men-at-arms prepared to take their places in line.

Swiftly, Roland completed his final inspection of bridles, bits, and straps. When sure neither the knights nor the earl would lose his seat from a squire's carelessness, he approached his own horse and squire.

"All is ready, Timothy?"

With a toothy grin, the tow headed lad of ten and six bowed at the waist. "Aye, Sir Roland. You can tug all you wish and not find a loose or misfit piece anywhere. 'Twould not do for the knight in charge of the horses to fall off his own, now, would it?"

Roland couldn't withhold a smile. "Impudent imp. What news?"

Timothy furtively peered around Roland's huge black stallion to locate the earl's squire.

"There is something afoot," the lad said just above a whisper. "Gregory knows, but he is not saying, just smiling like he hoards a secret. Could be the rest of us are wrong, and I dislike speaking ill of my fellow squire, but . . ."

"Then speak no more. Speculation does us no good."

"My apology, milord, for falling short of my task."

Roland grasped the squire's spindly shoulder, still amazed a lad so slight, though tall for his age, could heft a saddle to such a great height as a stallion's back.

"You did not fall short, Timothy. You cannot inform me of those things you do not know. Keep a sharp eye and ear. 'Tis all I ask."

With his chin set in determination, the squire nodded, then bowed off to see to his own mount.

Roland swung up into the saddle and nudged the stallion forward. Near where the line began to form, the earl spoke earnestly to the two men assigned to ride ahead and beg a night's hospitality at Lelleford for the earl and his retinue.

Would John Hamelin open the gate or tell Kenworth to go to the devil? Given an open gate, would the earl arrest Sir John with the dignity due his stature, or do mischief?

Roland wished he knew, but he'd learned no more over a meal with the knights and earl than Timothy had from the squires and grooms.

Perhaps there was nothing to learn. Perhaps he feared treachery when none was forthcoming.

Perhaps cows gave wine and sheep gave linen.

His instincts hadn't failed him yet. The prickling on the back of his neck yet nagged. The earl of Kenworth intended to torment Sir John Hamelin just as surely as that man's daughter had intended to rule Hugh.

Truly, 'twas a mercy Hugh had escaped that particular noose, wrapped in silk and gently tightened, but a stout rope all the same. Her sunny smile disguised a heart of ice; her courtly manner concealed a will of steel. Behind her beautiful face lurked a shrewd, cunning mind.

He'd gone to Lelleford hoping to like the woman who would be his sister-by-marriage. And he had, perhaps too much.

Unfortunately, he'd also determined she was an unsuitable wife for his half brother.

Roland smiled, looking forward to the moment when Lady Eloise Hamelin learned that Hugh St. Marten's "disgusting toad of a brother" had been given royal authority over her home.

'Twould be an interesting test of wills to see who prevailed over the weeks ahead. A contest he had no intention of losing.

Chapter Two

ELOISE SAT Brother Walter down on a bench near the huge stone hearth, which cast flickering light and welcome warmth into the cavernous room. If forced to declare a favorite spot in the entire castle, this would be the place.

Here, as a young girl, she'd sat on the rush-covered floor at her mother's feet and learned how to work wool. From here she could see the various colorful banners hanging from the high beams and the assortment of ancient weapons displayed on the walls, each with its own tale of her family's renowned, proud heritage.

And here, on most evenings, her parents had settled in, surrounded by their children and her father's favorite hunting hounds. They'd talked of the day's trials and joys, played quiet games, made plans for the future.

One by one they'd left her. Mother had died, Jeanne given away in marriage. Geoffrey's self-imposed exile in Paris, Julius's pilgrimage to Italy. And now her father.

She'd endured each disappearance in its time, accepting the reasons. All but the last.

She glanced down at the huge deerhound that spent most of her days lolling near the fire, now too old for the fields but too dear for her father to be rid of as he'd dispensed of other animals no longer able to work. The bitch wouldn't understand why her master no longer took a moment during his day to scratch her behind the ears, just as Eloise couldn't understand why the lord of the castle chose to desert his daughter.

Determined to shake off the self-pity, an indulgence she couldn't afford, she sent one of the serving wenches to fetch a basin of water and strips of linen for bandaging, then nudged the monk's blood-sticky, coarse brown hair away from the ugly gash.

He winced. She felt no remorse for hurting the monk her father considered untrustworthy. The cleric likely knew why her father deemed it necessary to leave Lelleford, might even be the cause. And she dared not inquire or risk giving away her knowledge of her father's escape.

Where were her father and Edgar now? Had they passed through the gate? Where would they go once clear of Lelleford's lands?

She struggled to keep her voice light. "'Tis not deep enough to need stitches, I warrant. I shall clean the blood away to make sure, but I believe you came away from your mishap with no lasting harm done."

Still pale, Brother Walter mumbled, "Praise be the Lord."

"Praise be," Eloise responded, mostly from habit, but also grateful the monk retained his senses.

Except his senses seemed muddled. He stared at some spot across the expanse of the hall, as if his thoughts roamed far from the cut on his head, too. Did he feel guilt for his part in her father's predicament? She hoped so.

At the sight of blood, several of the castle folk gathered

around to satisfy their morbid curiosity. The serving wench approached with careful steps, heeding the water in the basin she carried. Beside her shuffled Isolde, Eloise's handmaiden, clutching towels, favoring her disfigured foot.

Did Isolde know her beloved older brother, Edgar, had left Lelleford with its lord? Had Edgar informed Isolde that Sir John Hamelin required the young squire's attendance in a heedless dash from home?

Eloise took the towel Isolde held out, noting no worry in the curve of the maid's bow mouth, no concern in her brown doelike eyes. Concluding Isolde either didn't know of her brother's peril or hid her concern very well, Eloise dipped a corner of the towel into the basin.

She gently dabbed at the monk's wound. "As I thought. 'Tis ugly but not deep. No need for needle and thread."

Isolde tilted her head to get a better look. "Aye, ugly. How did you come by such a cut, good monk?"

Brother Walter yet stared across the hall. His continued silence bothered Eloise.

Since coming to Lelleford near winter's end from Evesham Abbey, a monastery to which her father generously contributed, Brother Walter had kept mostly to himself. He either tended her father's accounts or prayed in the chapel. He rarely spoke unless addressed, but he always acknowledged a question or comment. Had the bump on his head done more damage than she thought?

"Brother Walter?"

He jerked at the sound of his name. "My lady?"

"Isolde asked how you came by your wound."

His hand rose to touch the gash. "I must have hit my

head on the desk when . . ." His daze began to clear as he glanced around the hall. "Lady Eloise, your father, I must speak with him."

He is gone, and you know why.

"I know not where my father is right now. Surely whatever you have to say to him can wait until after we patch your head."

"No time." He slid off the bench, becoming agitated. "I must find him forthwith."

She grabbed the wide sleeve of his brown cleric's robe. "You yet bleed. Pray sit before you fall over."

He glared at her with uncharacteristic ire, then tugged his sleeve from her grasp and called out, "Has anyone seen his lordship in the past few minutes?"

He was answered with silence and shaking heads.

"Saints preserve us!" Brother Walter hustled to the stairs and then disappeared up them. Cries of "Sir John!" echoed back into the hall.

Isolde giggled. "How odd. I did not know the monk could move so fast or shout so loud. 'Tis as if a bee got up beneath his robes and threatens his privates."

Eloise couldn't withhold a smile at the maid's irreverence, or from thinking Brother Walter deserved to get stung.

She shook her head at her foolish musings. Soon an earl would arrive, seeking to arrest her father, and she should be preparing somehow. Except how did one prepare when one wasn't supposed to know? She wasn't even sure she should allow Brother Walter to run about the castle shouting for Sir John.

Eloise turned to the serving wench. "You may empty

the basin. 'Twould seem the good monk's head wound is the least of his concerns."

With the dismissal, the other observers wandered off, too—except Isolde, who stared at the stairs, puzzled. The sound of leather sandals slapping stone preceded the return of the monk, who made a quick perusal of the hall before scurrying out the door that opened to the bailey.

Isolde sighed. "He must have something right important to tell his lordship. What do you think it might be?"

"I have no notion."

Likely she'd find out soon enough, though. When Brother Walter didn't find Sir John, he'd likely come to her—she hoped—though she wasn't sure she wanted to hear what he had to say.

'Twas unsettling being torn between wanting to know the worst of her father's troubles and fearing to learn the details. She certainly wasn't about to make an undignified dash after the monk. Until he came to her, all she could do was carry on as if her world hadn't been flipped up into the air, threatening to land with a horrible thud.

Eloise put a hand on Isolde's shoulder. Three years separated them in age—mistress and maid. Right now Eloise felt as old as the towering oaks in Lelleford's woodlands.

"Have you finished your chores for the day?"

"Almost, milady. If you have no further need of me, I will go up to your bedchamber and mend the rip in your gray dress."

Trips up or down stairs were painful for the maid, Eloise knew. A lass of ten and four, Isolde never complained about pain or belabored her hardship. She stoically carried on as if her foot were normally shaped, doing everything required of her. To reward the maid's bravery and spare her pride, Eloise tried not to treat Isolde differently from other servants of the same age with similar duties.

"As long as you go up, take a bucket of coals. If tonight brings the same chill as last night, we may light the brazier."

The girl bobbed her head. A few strands of her blond hair tugged loose from her braid to curl impudently about her forehead. So pretty. So sweet. So unfortunate.

Needing a task to keep her hands and mind occupied, Eloise headed for the stairs, intending to straighten the mess in her father's accounting room. Not that she knew where all those scrolls belonged other than scattered on the desk and floor.

Before she reached the stairway, one of the gatehouse guards entered the hall and came straight at her.

"Lady Eloise, your presence is requested at the gate."

A chill slithered up her spine. The earl couldn't be here already, could he?

"For what purpose?"

"Two messengers wait without. They seek hospitality for the night for the earl of Kenworth and his retinue. Since his lordship rode out to hunt, Sir Marcus thought the messengers should make the request of you."

A household knight of long-standing, Sir Marcus served as captain of Lelleford's guard. "My father went hunting?"

"Aye, milady. He and Edgar had a falcon with them when they rode out the gate." The guard smiled. "We placed wagers on whether or not his lordship brings down the big heron that has harried the trout pond."

Then as far as anyone knew, the lord of Lelleford was out flying his falcon. Her father had possessed the presence—or perhaps deviousness—of mind to give her a credible explanation for his absence.

Eloise followed the guard out the door and down the slope of the dusty yard that served as a buffer between the keep and the gatehouse at the inner curtain wall. 'Twas the closest anyone was allowed near the keep without permission. In times of dire trouble, visitors were halted and questioned before being allowed over the drawbridge at the outer curtain wall. Both thick, high stone walls, manned by highly trained guards, served to defend against an invading force.

She was tempted to order the drawbridge raised and the iron portcullis lowered. Unfortunately, her father had ordered her to allow the enemy inside. Which still felt wrong, unwise.

Near the gatehouse Sir Marcus stood beside Sir Simon, her father's steward. Both burly warriors had served her father since beyond Eloise's memory.

Had Father told either of them of his predicament? 'Twould make sense for him to take his knights into his confidence.

Feign ignorance.

Gads, how her father's orders grated, especially those that concerned feeding and entertaining the earl. To have the enemy in the hall, drinking her father's wine. But that wasn't the worst of it. Obliged by customs of hospitality, she'd have to offer Kenworth the best bed in the keep—her father's.

Eloise halted before the knights. "I understand we are to have visitors."

Simon nodded, his gray eyes narrowing. "Unwelcome visitors. The earl of Kenworth brings several knights and men-at-arms with him."

Armed knights and men-at-arms wielding pikes. Invaders, not guests. She struggled for calm.

"Not unusual for an earl's retinue, is it?"

"Nay, but Kenworth is no friend of Sir John's. I sent a patrol out to find his lordship. 'Twould be prudent to await his return before granting the earl hospitality. Unfortunately, 'tis also not prudent to delay an answer to a man of so high a rank."

From his comments, Eloise deduced that Father hadn't told Simon he wasn't truly out hunting. Indeed, except for the monk, only she knew the reason for the earl's visit, and she'd been ordered to let the bastard through the gates.

"Do you think my father would deny the earl's request?"

The corner of Simon's mouth quirked upward. "His lordship might be tempted, but I doubt he would deliver such an insult."

Damn. She'd hoped for the opposite answer as an excuse to delay. Eloise glanced at Marcus. "You agree?"

Marcus shrugged a shoulder. "I fear Simon is right. We must allow Kenworth and his knights into the keep, but his retinue can make camp outside of our walls. The fewer men inside to guard, the better."

"Will the earl find the arrangement acceptable?"

Simon huffed. "He will not be allowed the choice, my lady. If he wants a decent meal and soft bed for the night, he accepts the condition or does without. 'Tis a common arrangement and should pose no difficulty."

The knights' easy manner calmed her nervousness. They would carry out their duties and see to the protection of the castle, at least until after they learned the reason for the earl's visit. And after they knew their lord was suspected of treason? Eloise hoped they'd be shocked and disbelieving, but loyally stand behind Sir John Hamelin, and thus his daughter.

"Where are the messengers?"

Simon waved a hand to indicate the gate. "Beyond."

Flanked by the knights, Eloise passed through the inner gate to the outer bailey. Two men-at-arms, garbed in black and gold livery, waited beside their mounts. Both wore the staid expressions of soldiers, giving no hint to the disagreeable purpose of their lord's visit, which she allowed they might not be aware of. She took a calming breath before addressing them.

"You may inform the earl of Kenworth we are pleased to offer hospitality for tonight. When might we expect his arrival?"

The tallest of them bowed slightly. "Your graciousness is welcome, Lady Eloise. I expect his lordship will arrive shortly after none."

Midafternoon, then. Not much time.

"Pray give the earl our regards."

The messengers mounted and departed, picking up speed and kicking up dust as they approached the outer gate.

Simon crossed his arms and muttered, "Reckless."

"Just like the earl," Marcus commented.

And sometimes like my father, Eloise thought, but kept the observation to herself.

She turned to go back to the keep—and saw Brother

Walter headed toward her, his eyes wide and wild, dried blood yet clinging to the side of his face and neck. The man might collapse if he didn't halt his senseless running about. She sighed, wondering if that might not be for the best.

Marcus leaned toward her. "What the devil happened to the monk?"

"He hit his head and broke it open. The dolt refuses to have the cut tended."

Marcus raised an eyebrow at her insult to a man of the cloth and exchanged an amused glance with Simon. "Shall we force his cooperation, milady?"

"Only if I cannot make him see sense."

Eloise left the knights behind and strode toward the cleric, still unsure of what to do with him. Lock him in his chamber? Send him out the gate? Leave him to his own devices?

He halted. "Have you seen his lordship, milady?"

"I am told he went hunting. Come back—"

"Nay! He cannot have left the castle!"

"I assure you he did!" Eloise put a hand on his forearm, hoping to calm him. "Allow me to bandage your head, and you can tell me why you so desperately seek my father."

The monk's eyes closed. His shoulders drooped and chin hit his chest. "Heaven preserve us. If his lordship has left Lelleford, I fear we shall require a miracle to save us."

His desolation chilled Eloise clear through.

"Brother Walter, you had best explain yourself."

His chin rose slightly. "Prayer. Only the Lord's

intervention—I am to the chapel, my lady, there to remain on my knees in supplication until the storm passes."

Then he was off, his robes billowing in his flight. Eloise bit back a reprimand and reluctantly let him go, knowing where he'd be.

"Milady?"

Eloise glanced over her shoulder to see Simon yet standing where she'd left him.

He unsuccessfully tried to hide a smile. "I gather the monk has not yet come to his senses. Shall I go after him, sit him down to be tended?"

Eloise waved a dismissive hand. "Nay, leave him be. He goes to pray. Mayhap the Lord will see fit to heal his head." And perhaps he'd simply keel over someplace and stay out of her way. "Tell me, Simon, do you know Kenworth well?"

"Well enough, and most of his knights, too."

Most of the knights, barons, and magnates of the kingdom were acquainted with each other, having fought together over the years in various wars, or against each other in tournaments. Simon likely knew how to treat the earl better than she did.

"What do I feed the earl of Kenworth to ensure his good humor?"

Simon thought for a moment, then answered, "Eel."

Eel. The one dish sure to sour her stomach at a whiff of the odor. Still, she'd order the eel served, hoping an upset stomach was the worst indignity she would suffer tonight.

With her eyes closed, Eloise sat quietly and breathed evenly, gratefully submitting to having her hair combed with long, soothing strokes. Isolde seemed to sense her mistress's need for peace, performing her task without her usual chatter.

The past two hours had gone by in a blur.

Cook had grumbled about the addition of eel to this evening's meal because she didn't like abrupt changes to her plans, not even when a peer of the realm was to be the unexpected guest. Eloise had listened patiently to the old woman's muttering. If she hadn't, a disaster of cold or wrongly spiced food might be the result.

Straightening her father's accounting room proved disheartening. All the while she put the room to rights, found places to neatly tuck away the scrolls, she couldn't help wonder why her father had taken several scrolls with him. Did they contain proof of his guilt or innocence? If innocence, then why hadn't he stayed to confront the earl?

She'd been telling herself all along that her father admired young King Edward too much to betray him. Still, John Hamelin had fled with possibly condemning evidence in his possession. So she'd reluctantly removed a handful of coins from the coffin to hide in her bedchamber, in the event she decided to sew them into the hems of her garments.

Then there was Brother Walter who, as far as Eloise knew, still lay prone on the chapel floor engaged in fervent prayer. One glance at him had so dismayed and annoyed her that she'd quietly left the chapel without disturbing him.

The stroke of the comb obviously hadn't quieted her questions and worries, but at least her jaw no longer hurt from clenching her teeth. She might be able to greet the earl without scowling or snapping at him. To give her father as much time as she could to get as far away from Lelleford as he was able, she had no choice but to be pleasant to Kenworth.

"Ribbons?" Isolde asked.

"Aye. Both the crimson and gold."

While Isolde fetched the long ribbons, Eloise brushed away broken strands of hair from the gold-trimmed, crimson velvet gown she wore. 'Twas the richest and newest gown she owned, made up for her wedding day, the only time she'd worn it.

Isolde's deft hands wound the ribbons and hair into a thick braid. "You look fine enough to greet royalty, milady."

Fine enough to distract an earl for another hour or two while her father and Isolde's brother put time and distance between them and Lelleford?

"I hope so. Isolde, did you talk to Edgar before he and my father . . . went hunting?"

"Last I had a word with Edgar was early this morn. Why?"

Eloise battled her conscience. Refraining from forewarning Isolde of the adversity to come didn't sit well. If anything horrible happened to Edgar, his sister would suffer mightily.

"I merely wondered if he said where he and my father intended to go."

"Not to me." Isolde tied off the ribbon, then chuckled. "If I had me an extra coin or two, I might wager on them bringing down that big heron. Sure is taking them long enough, though. Or perhaps his lordship thinks bagging the heron of more import than waitin' on an earl."

Isolde assumed the patrol had found his lordship and informed him of the earl's impending arrival. Eloise knew those men must be confused and worried by now, had likely checked all of her father's favorite hunting spots and not found him.

"Perhaps." Eloise rose from the stool and adjusted the gold-link girdle that wound about her twice to rest lightly on her hips. "Think you I need more adornment? A gold amulet or brooch?"

"Nay, milady. 'Twould be a waste. Once men fix on your face they do not notice all the rest anyway."

"You flatter me, Isolde."

"'Tis no more than the truth."

Eloise knew men noted far more about a woman than her face. Too many times she'd been inspected from head to toe, her form and assets judged. Some lingered over-long on her bosom, some tarried at her hips. She'd learned how to distinguish appreciation from lust. Some men's looks revolted her, while others invoked a delicious tingle of response.

She tugged lightly on her sleeve to smooth the velvet, memories of the disastrous wedding coming to the fore. Hugh St. Marten and several members of his family had arrived two days before the ceremony. In the spare moments they'd managed to find time alone, she'd tried in vain to conjure delicious tingles for her betrothed.

In his eyes she'd perceived a mingling of affection and desire. As a dutiful wife, she'd have lain with Hugh and borne his children. Perhaps, in time, she might have come to care deeply for him.

Unfortunately, at the time she'd been distracted by another, wholly unsuitable, irritating, and compelling man who inspired not tingles but deep, burning heat. With a shiver she again thanked the Fates that she'd unwittingly discovered his disdain of her before she'd made an utter fool of herself over her betrothed's half brother. To her chagrin, she could still envision Roland St. Marten's face more sharply than Hugh's.

A rap on the door brought Eloise out of her disturbing thoughts. Isolde admitted a page.

"Sir Simon says to fetch you, my lady. The earl has arrived."

"I will be down in a moment."

The page scurried off. Eloise took a deep, calming breath.

"Must be a fearsome one, this earl," Isolde commented. "'Tis rare to see you uneasy."

"Does it show so much?"

"You rub your hands together. A sure sign."

Eloise stilled her hands. "I wish my father were here to greet him. High nobility can be troublesome guests."

With that nasty thought in mind, she made her way down to the great hall. Just inside the doorway stood Simon with a group of chain mail-clad knights and a bevy of squires. Eloise guessed the oldest and most richly garbed man must be William, earl of Kenworth.

Chin high, spine straight, Eloise sallied forth to perform her duty—and nearly tripped over her own feet when one knight stepped apart from the others.

Roland St. Marten. Clad in armor. Now a knight and obviously in service to the earl of Kenworth. He listened to whatever Simon was telling the earl with brooding intensity, which she hoped meant he hadn't noticed her momentary hesitation.

Of goodly height and solid warrior's build, Roland's raven hair was long enough to brush atop his wide shoulders. His hazel eyes were no less sharp, his jawline no less rugged. On their first meeting, she'd been instantly aware of his potent charms, but utterly fascinated by his aura of strength and power.

He'd warned Hugh against marrying her, declared her an unsuitable bride. The wretch. Never, in her entire life, had anyone dared insult her so.

Concentrate on the earl.

She fixed a pleasant, welcoming smile on her face. Then Roland seemed to sense her presence and turned those intense hazel eyes in her direction. Her knees went weak and her mouth dry. Eloise gathered every shard of willpower to ignore her body's stirring and force aside her wanton awareness of the man who should be, if fate hadn't intervened, her brother-by-marriage.

The man who'd called her brazen, and who she now considered no better than a lowly, disgusting toad.

With her ire piqued, Eloise managed to turn her attention back where it belonged, on the earl who'd come to arrest her father for treason.

The earl of Kenworth had noticed her, too. He inspected her with narrowed eyes and thinned mouth. Short. Balding. Well fed. A mean boar in human form.

Simon looked relieved to see her. "My lady, our guest, William, earl of Kenworth."

Eloise dipped into a deep curtsy before the earl, low enough to give a royal personage proper respect. "My lord. You do us honor with your visit. We welcome you and your knights."

" 'Twas you who gave the order for my retinue to remain beyond the walls?"

She rose to face his sharp disapproval squarely. "I approved our knights' recommendation, my lord. We shall leave the final decision regarding the encampment to my father."

"Who I understand is not here."

Nor would he be.

"Thus our decision to exercise prudence." She turned to Simon. "Any word on my father's whereabouts as yet?"

"Nay, milady. I explained to his lordship that Sir John had gone hunting, unaware we were to have visitors. I expect our patrol and Sir John to return shortly."

Eloise strained to reclaim her smile. "My lord, might I offer you and your knights goblets of our finest wine and a hearty repast to make the time pass more quickly?"

The earl spun to his knights. "Take out patrols. Find him!"

Father needs more time!

"Surely that is not necessary. If naught else, Father will be home for evening meal."

"I suspect not." The earl took a menacing step toward her, glanced at Simon. "I swear, if Hamelin is not found quickly, I shall hold you both accountable for aiding a traitor!"

Eloise nearly choked on an ill-advised, strangling gasp.

Simon drew his sword, the rasp of steel from his leather scabbard a call to battle, answered swiftly by the earl's knights.

"Sir John a traitor?" Simon asked fiercely. "Never!

How dare you insult his lordship in his own hall, with him not here to defend against your base accusation!"

The earl waved a dismissing hand. "Hamelin has been duly charged! And how dare you draw your sword on a peer of the realm! Seize him!"

A last sword whipped from its scabbard. Roland's.

"We seize no one except Sir John. Sheathe your swords." The earl's hands clenched, his anger now focused on Roland. "I gave an order I expect to be obeyed."

"And I am under the king's orders, which I intend to obey. Attempt to seize Sir Simon and I will stand with him."

"You are a fool. The king will hear of your insolence."

The corner of Roland's mouth quirked. "Pray inform him, my lord, for then Edward shall know I followed his wishes to perfection. If you intend to send your knights on patrol, do so. I am for Lady Eloise's gracious offer of wine."

Eloise remembered to breathe when Roland sheathed his sword, taking it as a sign the worst danger past, noting to whom he owed allegiance—King Edward, not Kenworth. She didn't know if she should be relieved or not.

The earl waved at his knights. "Go. Before you leave set guards at the drawbridge. No one of Lelleford is allowed outside the gates until Hamelin is firmly within my grasp."

The knights' swords slid home and Eloise stilled her hands.

Before she could once more offer wine, the earl glared at Simon and Roland. "Bring Lelleford's knights into the hall. I want you all within my sight. Be aware that aiding a traitor is cause for hanging, and I will not hesitate to so punish anyone who interferes with Hamelin's arrest."

With that, Kenworth stomped off toward the table where a servant had set out flagons and goblets.

Simon lowered his sword. "What goes on here, Roland? This makes no sense. Is Sir John truly charged with treason?"

"I fear so. Kenworth is to seize Sir John and take him to Westminster for trial. The king will sit as judge."

Eloise forced herself to look into Roland's hazel eyes. She saw no contempt for her father, no sign he thought any better of her. Still, she had to make her belief known.

"My father would not betray King Edward, I am sure of it."

"Then he has naught to fear."

"Does he not?" Eloise wasn't so sure anymore. Kenworth struck her as a man out for blood, her father's blood.

"'Tis for the king to decide on his guilt, milady, and Edward is a man of both intelligence and honor."

So she'd heard—more than once—from the man accused of betraying the king.

"You serve Edward, not the earl. What do you here?"

Roland glanced around the hall before he looked at her again. "By the king's order, I am to oversee Lelleford until after your father's fate is decided."

Stunned, Eloise managed to withhold a squeal of denial and displeasure. Roland St. Marten oversee Lelleford? Unthinkable!

Chapter Three

INDIGNATION SHIMMERED in the lady's sapphire eyes, deep pools of blue a man could drown in if he weren't careful.

Roland never questioned why Hugh had been instantly smitten with his intended bride. Eloise's beauty would capture any man's attention. Fair of skin, bold of mouth, lithe of form, and possessed of a royal bearing, the woman deserved every tribute paid to her lovely face, curvaceous figure, and effortless grace.

Even knowing Eloise Hamelin was betrothed to his half brother, Roland hadn't been immune to her beauty. From the moment of their introduction, he'd felt the natural stirring a healthy male feels for a desirable female, had envied Hugh the marriage bed with so delectable a woman.

Unfortunately, during the two days before the wedding, he'd watched Hugh become so enamored of his betrothed he neglected to note her presumption. Out of her bold mouth spewed bold words. Those sapphire eyes flashed with ire at the slightest provocation. He'd never encountered a less docile woman.

Still, if Eloise had given any sign of admiring Hugh to

a high degree, Roland might not have taken his brother aside to warn him of his betrothed's strong will. He should have realized Hugh was too besotted to listen. Nor had he counted on the lady overhearing and adding her opinion to an already heated argument.

So Hugh died angry at Roland for speaking ill of Eloise, who dressed today in the crimson and gold gown she'd worn on her wedding day. The velvet molded against her body as enticingly now as then. Inviting a man's admiration, and worse, his hands.

"Insufferable," she blurted out. "Surely you misunderstood the king's intentions. He cannot have meant to give such an insult."

"I assure you, my lady, the king meant no insult to you personally. He merely strives to ensure Lelleford is under sound management in your father's absence."

Her nostrils flared. Then, as quickly as her ire ignited, she doused the fire with the ice of her will. He'd never met a woman who could alter her emotions so quickly, so completely. Once again she appeared calm, regal, in control.

"You may inform the king we have no need of an overseer," she finally said in that sublime manner that demanded immediate obedience.

He didn't mind disappointing her in the least. "I fear neither of us is given a choice in the matter."

She looked to Simon in an appeal for assistance the steward couldn't possibly grant, his answer a shaking head.

"Milady, if the king so orders then we must yield. I grant you, 'tis insulting, this whole business. But better

Sir Roland as overseer than others the king might have assigned the duty."

Simon's acceptance of the inevitable didn't sit well with her, and Roland didn't doubt she'd accept most anyone else's authority over Lelleford with less distaste. That bothered him, but he didn't need Eloise's approval or support. The knights' cooperation was far more important to his success.

Lelleford boasted a grand great hall, fit for the residence of a royal personage, a tribute to the Hamelins' heritage, wealth, and high position. So, too, was it an impressive fortress, with solid defenses and a highly trained garrison. Should the household knights band together against him, they could easily toss Roland out the gate and lower the portcullis.

A man accustomed to following orders, Sir Simon seemed resigned to accepting what his mistress dreaded. Roland could only hope Sir Marcus and the others would be sensible, too.

Roland glanced at Kenworth, still standing by a trestle table, currently content to pour himself a second goblet of what was sure to be fine wine.

"We had best gather the others," he told Simon. "And quickly. I do not wish to leave Kenworth to his own devices overlong."

Simon leaned slightly toward Eloise. "Be wary of Kenworth, milady. The earl is easily provoked into foul temper. We shall return as soon as we can."

Eloise crossed her arms and shot them both a scathing glance. Whatever biting comment she longed to make she withheld, uttering only a mild, "Very well."

Simon headed for the door. Roland hesitated before

following, concerned over leaving Eloise alone with Kenworth. But the earl had ordered him to accompany Simon, and he'd already provoked the earl enough for one day. Surely, she'd be safe enough in the hall for a short time—if she didn't state her opinions to Kenworth.

"Simon is right about the earl. Have a care."

Her chin rose, tilting her nose to a haughty angle. Without a word she spun around and headed for the man he'd just cautioned her against.

Well, she'd been warned. Perhaps she would heed the caution if only because Simon told her to be wary, too.

Out in the bailey, Roland fell into step beside Simon, who marched toward the inner gate.

"What precisely is Sir John accused of?" Simon asked, his voice rough, his jaw set in a hard line.

The worst charge against an English lord that Roland could imagine in this time of unrest.

"He stands charged with conspiring with the Scots."

"Ha! John? Never. The king believes this idiocy?"

"I know neither all the details nor who brought the charge against Sir John, only that the king is in possession of a condemning missive."

Simon struggled to absorb the news, then declared, "Sir John is no traitor."

Roland admired the steward's steadfast loyalty, even if misplaced.

"That is for the king to decide. My duty is to ensure Lelleford and its people suffer no undue hardship until the matter is resolved one way or the other."

"Why you?"

Why him, indeed? Roland hoped the king considered

him trustworthy and sought to give him the chance to prove himself. But it was a weak reason to give Simon.

"Perhaps the king just wants me out from underfoot."

Simon seemed amused. "So he sends you here to irritate us."

"Lady Eloise certainly is not pleased to see me again."

"Given what happened . . . before, and the shock of hearing the charges against her father, I cannot blame her. I thought she handled the news rather well."

So Simon noticed her uncharacteristically mild outburst, too. 'Twasn't like Eloise to not fully speak her mind. Perhaps the earl's presence had subdued her volatile nature. Still, he didn't doubt a storm brewed, 'twas only a matter of time before thunder roared.

As they approached the inner gate, Sir Marcus strode toward them, frowning mightily. "Is it true?"

Roland didn't doubt by now everyone in the castle knew why the outer gate was closed.

Simon gave Marcus a brief explanation of what occurred, then ordered him into the hall with the admonition to keep a close eye on Eloise. He obeyed, but only after grumbling that the earl went too far in lowering the portcullis, that surely Sir John would return from hunting shortly and set all to rights.

Roland admitted 'twas possible John had truly gone hunting. Several people had seen him ride out the gate with a squire at his side and a falcon on his arm. 'Twas also nigh impossible to believe John would go far from Lelleford without telling either Simon or Marcus, men he trusted implicitly, about why he left and where he was going.

As they made the rounds of the bailey, gathering up

the other knights, it became clear that everyone truly believed Sir John was out chasing a heron. Still, though he
had no firm reason to disbelieve the tale, Roland couldn't
shake the feeling that John had known the earl was coming for him and taken flight.

His musings ended upon entering the hall.

No earl. No Marcus. No Eloise.

The hair on the back of his neck itched.

Simon waved forward a page. "Where is Lady
Eloise?"

The page glanced at the stairs leading to the upper
floor. "She took the earl up to his lordship's accounting
room."

Simon's countenance turned stormy. "Is Marcus with
her?"

"Nay. The earl sent Marcus to find Brother Walter."

Roland headed for the stairs, Simon right behind him,
wishing Eloise had taken his warning to heart. But then,
if Kenworth ordered her to show him John's accounting
room, she would have no choice but to obey. If he didn't
already know where the accounting room was located,
Roland would have found it by following the sound of
Kenworth's raised voice.

"I have every right! 'Tis your father, the traitor, who
no longer has rights!"

Roland turned into the small room. Kenworth sat behind the oak desk, scrolls scattered across it. Eloise stood
with her back to the door, her arms crossed and spine
rigid.

"My father is no traitor," she stated.

"I have proof otherwise, and if there is more proof
among your father's documents, I intend to find it."

Kenworth looked around Eloise. "Ah, St. Marten. Has Hamelin been found?"

Eloise spun around, her ire fading to concern.

"Not as yet. At least none of the patrols have returned that I know of."

Eloise's relief contrasted sharply with Kenworth's frustration. The earl waved a dismissive hand.

"Go. Roland, her ladyship and the knights are to be placed under guard in the hall. The next piece of news I want to hear is that John Hamelin is captured."

"As you say, my lord." Wanting nothing more than to get Eloise out of Kenworth's reach, he extended a hand, palm up. "Come, milady."

She stared at his outstretched hand, then with a look of loathing walked right past him. The slight stung, but he let it pass without reaction. To Eloise he must seem the enemy, a usurper of her father's authority over her home. That she resented his mission wasn't unexpected.

'Struth, he'd been sent here to oversee the holding in the king's name, not to pamper or befriend Eloise Hamelin—not that he wanted to. The less he must deal with the woman, the better.

Roland left the accounting room and closed the door behind him. He strode toward where Simon stood near the end of the passageway, Eloise pacing nearby. The gold trim on her crimson gown flashed in the light beaming in from an arrow slit.

"No one is allowed to touch Father's private documents without permission," she petulantly told the steward. "Must we allow this affront?"

"From an earl, I fear so," Simon answered. "No matter that I share your distaste for his presence and mission, we cannot hinder Kenworth without putting our own necks, and your father's, at further risk. What does he want with Brother Walter?"

"He believes Father's clerk can help him find whatever he searches for in more timely a manner. Truly, if I thought we could toss the earl out the gate without causing my father more difficulty, I would."

Then she turned to face him, her ire high yet carefully controlled. "If we must suffer this outrageous invasion of our home, I wish to know what your intentions are as overseer."

He didn't have to explain anything to the daughter of the household, but given the presence of the steward, whose cooperation he needed for a peaceful surrender to his authority, he decided courtesy was in order.

"The king gives me full charge over Lelleford. Sir John's arrest puts the holding at risk, both from attack from without and turmoil from within. 'Tis my duty to see neither happens."

"You have proof of this grant of authority?"

"I do, which I will give to Sir John as soon as he presents himself. Perhaps we should now retire to the hall to await his return."

"Giving orders already?"

"Not an order, merely a suggestion. I see no sense in standing up here in the hallway when we might sit on a bench in the hall."

Eloise pursed her lips and turned to descend the tightly winding stairway. He and Simon followed in her regal wake across the hall to the table where flagons and goblets yet sat.

She served her knights first, an unsubtle violation of

the rules of hospitality, letting him know she didn't consider him a guest but an intruder—as if he weren't already aware. When she finally handed him a full goblet of the ruby wine, she did so with a look that suggested she'd rather toss the drink in his face.

He took a sip and forced himself to appreciate the full body and rich aroma. Unfortunately, he couldn't block out the fragrance of the woman who now stood so close to reluctantly serve him.

Where other women wore flowery, cloying scents that merely hinted of their presence, Eloise smelled of a tangy exotic spice that flooded him with erotic thoughts, luring him to taste the delicacy so appealingly presented.

He lifted the goblet in a slight salute. "Divine, as always."

Her lips curved up in a tight, false smile. "I am delighted you approve. You will be sure to let me know if this evening's meal meets your particular standard."

"The earl once asked me if I had found any fault with Lelleford's hospitality. In all sincerity I informed him I had not. I suspect he will find I told him true."

"Had I a choice . . ."

"But you do not. Besides, even given the unfortunate circumstances, I doubt your pride would allow you to present less than Lelleford's best."

"You believe you know me so well?"

He'd taken her measure two months ago and hadn't yet seen any reason to change his opinion. Prideful. Brazen. Too damn forward and outspoken.

"Well enough."

She leaned forward and whispered, "You know nothing."

Her scent and nearness muddled his senses. With great effort he countered her move, bringing them nearly nose to nose.

"Think you? We shall see, milady."

Simon cleared his throat.

Roland snapped his attention back to where it belonged. God's wounds, he'd been so engrossed in sparring with Eloise he'd forgotten that others stood nearby, and had allowed his mind to wander from his duty. He'd not let it happen again.

From the doorway strode a grim-faced Marcus, beside him a man-at-arms upon whose forearm perched a peregrine falcon.

"We have two problems," Marcus said. "I cannot find Brother Walter. As you suggested, milady, I first looked in the chapel. He is not in his quarters. No one seems to have seen him of late. But that is not the worst of it." He nodded to the soldier. "Report."

The soldier addressed Simon. "We did as you ordered, first searching the trout pond, then Sir John's other favorite hunting spots. We found no sign of either his lordship or Edgar until about an hour ago." The soldier glanced at the falcon. "She was tethered in a tree near the old mill, sitting in plain sight, like she were waiting for someone to come get her and bring her home."

In the ensuing stunned silence, Roland set his goblet on the table. Surely no one now believed Sir John Hamelin had merely gone hunting. He'd left the falcon in a spot he'd known would be searched, and then fled.

The earl wouldn't be pleased, and Roland dreaded being the one to tell him. Still, the man must be told.

"I will inform Kenworth." He glanced around at the

half-dozen grim-faced knights. "I ask for your pledge to remain in the hall of your own accord."

To a man they gave agreement.

Eloise turned glistening sapphire eyes his way. "We will do naught to give the earl reason to do Lelleford or its people harm. I ask you have a care to do the same."

Roland made his way to the accounting room, mindful of both her unnecessary caution and the disturbing sight of Eloise's unshed tears.

Nothing in her experience had prepared Eloise for dealing with a peer of the realm in high temper.

Seated at the dais, with the earl occupying her father's chair next to her, Eloise struggled to keep her stomach calm. But with Kenworth's surly disposition and the sickening smell of eel, she was fighting a losing battle. For all he appreciated the effort she'd made to have one of his favorite foods prepared, she might as well have served him thinned stew.

Then her stomach wouldn't now be as sour as Kenworth's mood.

If being seated next to the churlish earl weren't bothersome enough, on her other side sat Roland St. Marten. A man whose physical presence made her heart beat a bit faster, a little harder, every time she got too close to him. Not a good reaction at all.

And right now she was much too close to him, seated on the same bench, mere inches apart. So close his heady male scent almost overpowered the odor of the eel. Almost.

'Struth, she'd been glad of Roland's presence during the long afternoon as the patrols came in and the earl's knights reported their lack of success. Though she was loathe to admit it, only Roland's calm manner and firm stance had kept the earl's wrath under restraint.

Without question, Lelleford was now firmly controlled by William, earl of Kenworth. His guards manned the gates, with orders to allow no one outside the walls without permission. Neither she nor Lelleford's knights were allowed out of the great hall because of Kenworth's fear they might attempt to escape and go to their lord's aid.

He'd taken control of the castle, but not by force, and for that Eloise gave thanks to the Lord and, grudgingly, to Roland St. Marten.

Truly, she should have taken a stronger role in dealing with the earl, not let Roland assume most of the task. Undeniably, the man possessed a core of strength and purpose, cast forth an aura of power mingled with intelligence. While Roland used courtly manners, she didn't doubt he, too, would be dangerous if crossed. The man certainly hadn't hesitated to draw his sword against the earl's knights in defense of Simon, a good sign.

Still, she'd accepted his assistance too easily. So, too, to her way of thinking, did Lelleford's knights accept his authority. Simon hadn't argued about giving up his usual seat at table to Roland, had merely slid down a place to accommodate the arrangement. Marcus also accepted Roland's authority as unavoidable, not worth the effort of a protest.

Her whole being rebelled at the thought of having anyone but her father, or she in her father's absence, holding sway over her home. 'Twas insulting, galling—and unavoidable. But damn, she didn't have to like it or even pretend she did.

At least not to Roland St. Marten.

Kenworth was another matter altogether.

She wanted the earl gone, but not too soon. Wherever her father was going, she wanted him to reach a safe haven without worrying about pursuit and capture. Surely there must be a way to keep the earl and his knights at Lelleford for a day or two to give her father more time.

Kenworth dearly loved his wine. Was it possible to keep a man intoxicated for several days? Drunk, he wouldn't be able to think clearly, much less sit a horse and chase after her father.

Unfortunately, she doubted Kenworth would fall for the ploy. She'd only get herself into further trouble.

The earl reached for his goblet. When he frowned into the empty vessel, Eloise immediately signaled for a page.

"Bring another flagon of wine for his lordship," she told the boy, who scurried to obey.

Kenworth slammed the goblet onto the table, causing her to flinch and bump shoulders with Roland.

Hard and rock-steady, he didn't move. She straightened almost immediately, but not before his warmth seeped into her and his solid presence reassured her. She held on to both under the earl's disapproving scowl.

"Your servants are lax, Lady Eloise. That lad is not suited to serve the high table."

Eloise immediately took offense. The lad had earned the right to serve the high table, had done nothing wrong this eve—except not realize the earl attempted to empty an entire keg of wine all by himself. However, 'twould do no good to inform Kenworth of his error.

"The fault is mine, my lord. I should have ensured the more experienced servants served you, not a lad who might be overawed by the honor of attending an earl. 'Tis not often we entertain such a grand personage in our humble hall."

The honeyed words tasted foul in her mouth, but seemed to placate Kenworth somewhat. He leaned back in the chair, his scowl easing into contemplation. Of her. She wished she could read the thoughts in those narrowed eyes.

"No grand personages of late?" he asked.

"Nay, my lord."

"No lairds?"

Eloise twisted her hands in her lap.

"No Scottish laird has ever visited Lelleford."

"You will pardon me if I do not believe you. Your lie only puts you in collusion with your treacherous father. Not a surprise, I suppose. Indeed, I suspect an entire flock of traitors reside within these walls."

God's wounds, but she was tired of this odious earl and his horrid accusations.

"Then you would be mistaken, my lord."

"I think not, but we shall see."

Eloise quietly seethed as the page returned with the wine. She stretched out her hand, grabbed the flagon, and waved the boy off. Wishing she had the courage to poison the bastard, she filled the earl's goblet.

"I believe you are mistaken about my father as well."

"As for Sir John, I harbor no doubts of his guilt and should have further proof shortly." He glanced about the hall. "I would likely have the proof in hand by now if that infernal cleric had not disappeared."

Eloise put down the flagon. While irked that Brother Walter seemed to have disappeared, she was relieved he couldn't be called upon to assist in the search through her father's documents.

"The last I saw Brother Walter, shortly before your arrival, he was in the chapel. Where he went after, I know not."

"St. Marten, come dawn, I expect you to flush out the elusive monk."

Roland leaned forward to look around her. "As you wish, my lord. If he is within the walls, we will find him."

'Twasn't fair that even the man's voice affected her, the deep rumble reverberating along her spine.

Now the earl leaned forward and Eloise, trapped between the two, tried to make herself small, with little success.

"He had *best* be within the walls or those who aided his escape will suffer."

She nearly shivered at the threat.

"Perhaps the monk will appear of his own accord," Roland answered in a voice Eloise decided lacked a hint of concern. "What of Sir John?"

Kenworth sank back in the chair and drummed his fingers on the arm. "I have given the matter much thought. Hamelin wants me to believe he has fled, just as he wanted everyone to believe he had merely gone hunting. A wily ruse befitting a traitor. I will not be fooled, however. He is nearby, waiting to see what I do next." He leaned forward to grab hold of his goblet and took a healthy swallow. "On the morn we will again send out patrols. Among my men are two of the most skilled trackers in the kingdom. If Hamelin is in the area, we will find him."

Eloise thought back on her brief talk with her father. He'd said 'twas best she didn't know where he went. She'd only assumed he'd gone far and fast.

Kenworth speared a chunk of the odious eel. Her stomach roiled, again, worse now than before. 'Twas a breach of manners to leave the table before the person of highest rank finished his meal. But if she didn't leave, she'd commit a worse offense.

"My lord, the day has been long and trying. If you will permit, I should like to retire."

He regarded her with disapproval, then waved a dismissing hand. "You do look rather . . . worn. You are permitted the use of your bedchamber upon your oath you will stay within until morn."

She wanted nothing more than a measure of privacy and the comfort of her bed. "You have my oath."

"Be aware a guard will be posted in the upper hall to ensure you keep it."

A guard at her door. Not to protect her from harm but to imprison her within. How many more insults must she endure, without recourse, before the loathsome earl left?

"Then I bid thee good eve."

Eloise rose. On the edge of her vision she saw Isolde rise from her place at the lower tables to make her way to the stairs. With her stomach in complete rebellion, Eloise didn't wait for her maid but bolted for her bedchamber.

Once there she made straight for the narrow window and threw open the shutters. After several deep breaths of cool, misty night air, she thought she might avoid being sick.

Sweet mercy, but she hated eel. And the earl of Kenworth. And Roland St. Marten. And this whole nasty mess her father expected her to deal with.

Not until she eased down on the bed did she notice the scroll resting beside the bolsters.

Confused, she unrolled the parchment, the writing easily recognizable as her father's.

Continue to follow my orders and all will be well. Take heart. I am watching and will return when Kenworth leaves.

Her hands shook.

How had her father managed to send her a message? But more important, how could she inform him that coming home wasn't wise?

As the earl suspected, her father watched events at Lelleford. Perhaps he could continue to avoid capture as he had today. All well and good if that were the only problem.

Unfortunately, while the earl might leave soon, Roland St. Marten would not. He was to remain at Lelleford along with his squire and a small company of men-at-arms. The moment her father came home, Roland would feel it his duty to make the arrest.

From out in the hallway she heard Isolde's awkward shuffle. The maid surely realized by now that her brother might well be in dire trouble for aiding Sir John. Now both lord and squire might return, thinking themselves safe, only to be arrested.

Eloise laid the parchment aside and stood, wondering

how she should impart the bad news. When the door opened, all thoughts of preparing her maid fled.

Directly behind Isolde stood the one man whose presence, and duty, blocked her father's safe return home.

Roland St. Marten.

Chapter Four

ELOISE'S APPREHENSION vanished so swiftly Roland almost doubted his eyesight and instincts. Before he could further contemplate her reaction, she looked away and busied her hands, casually picking up a parchment scroll from near the edge of her bed, then tucking it into the gold-link girdle belting her trim waist.

Her composure now under command, with tilted head and delicately raised brows, Eloise looked askance at his presence in the doorway.

He eased around the maid who blocked his path and entered the bedchamber, a richly appointed and pleasantly scented room appropriate for the woman who inhabited it.

'Twas a cozy chamber. Woven rush mats were scattered about the polished plank floor. Large, colorful tapestries of floral design hung on the whitewashed walls. A deep blue velvet coverlet matched the draperies—tied back with gold cord—adorning her bed. Isolde's pallet occupied a corner, not far from two high-backed, ornately carved chairs flanking a claw-footed brass brazier.

He caught a glimpse of white porcelain under the bed—a chamber pot, likely—that matched the washbasin on a table strewn with feminine possessions. A silvered glass competed for space with ribbons, combs, and tiny colorful bottles.

A flash of lightning momentarily brightened the room, heralding an approaching storm. A whisper of cool breeze played with the crimson and gold ribbons woven into Eloise's braid. He smothered the urge to capture them, unwind them until her tresses hung loose and flowing.

Roland knew Hugh had spent time in this bedchamber with his betrothed, insisting the two of them get to know each other better before they wed. He couldn't help wonder if the couple had done more than talk. To his mortification he envisioned besotted Hugh and his willful bride-to-be, Eloise's ribbons undone, bodies entwined on the blue velvet coverlet.

Whatever the relationship between Hugh and Eloise, it had ended with Hugh's death. Still, the erotic vision of Eloise pressed against the mattress beneath Hugh wasn't easily put aside.

"I wish a word with you, Lady Eloise. You and I must come to an understanding."

Her expression turned mocking. "An understanding, Sir Roland? You have invaded my home. In return for that offense, you expect me to feed and board you and your minions in grand style. Play the meek maid while you play lord of the castle. Pray tell, good sir, just what is it you believe I do not understand?"

He crossed his arms and summoned his patience, which he hoped would hold out over the next weeks. Dealing with Eloise Hamelin sorely taxed his usually amiable nature.

Keeping his attention on Eloise, he told the maid,

"Isolde, you will wait in the passageway. Close the door behind you."

Eloise's eyes hardened. "My maid may stay."

"You forget who is in charge, my lady. 'Twould be a mistake to condone your servant's disobedience of my orders."

"A ridiculous order."

"But an order nonetheless. Isolde?"

With pursed lips Eloise nodded at the maid, and soon he heard Isolde's distinctive shuffle and the door snicker closed.

Only the flicked tip of her pink tongue over her full bottom lip betrayed her nervousness. "Have your say and be done."

He wanted nothing more than to quit the room, have no more to do with Eloise than he must.

"Both Sir Simon and I warned you of Kenworth's volatile nature, yet you risked his wrath by leaving the hall before 'twas proper. I come only to caution you to do nothing more to displease him while he is here."

She arched an eyebrow. "Tell me. Would I have displeased him less had I become violently ill while seated next to him? I should think him gratified I left."

He saw no sign she suffered. Truth to tell, she appeared the very bloom of good health. "You are ill?"

"No longer. My stomach rebels at the smell of eel, so I thought it wise to leave before my affliction became apparent."

"Then why serve eel?"

"Simon told me the earl is partial to it."

So she'd served a dish she couldn't tolerate as a

placating gesture toward Kenworth, who Roland knew considered the grand meal no more than his due.

"A wasted gesture, I fear. The only thing that will appease the earl is Sir John's capture. Unless you can serve your father up on a platter, no amount of eel, no matter how well prepared, will improve Kenworth's humor."

"So I am beginning to understand." She glanced down at her clasped hands, where one thumb brushed restlessly over the other. "What will happen to my father should he be captured?"

Roland took a fortifying breath. She'd heard all this before. Nothing had changed.

"He will be taken to Westminster for trial."

"Will he? Or will Kenworth decide to administer immediate justice?" The last word came out harshly, echoing his own reservations about Kenworth's intentions. "Simon tells me my father is accused of conspiring with the Scots. I refuse to believe it. Father approves of the king. He thought Edward's handling of the latest uprising most admirable. This charge of treason defies sense. Whoever accuses my father is gravely mistaken."

Spoken like a loyal daughter, and Roland grudgingly gave her credit for her constancy.

"Truly, I know not who brought the matter to the king's attention. I know only that Edward is in possession of a missive which indicates Sir John's guilt."

"Have you seen this missive?"

"Nay, only told of its existence. By the king. If it is any comfort"—and he had no idea why he thought offering comfort was necessary, nor did he have reason to think she'd accept it from him—"Edward is hard-pressed to believe Sir John a traitor. 'Twould be best if your father states his defense directly to the king as quickly as possible."

She mulled that over for a moment. "Then if you were asked, you would advise my father to hie to the king?"

"I would." Something in the tone and way of her question pricked at him. "Eloise, do you know where your father is? Can you send him that advice?"

She gave a disgruntled laugh. "I wish I had such knowledge and could pass along your counsel." She tossed a hand in the air. "Verily, I suspect Kenworth will not allow my father the chance to give his defense."

"You cannot know that for sure."

"Nay, I do not. There is so much I do not know, except that my father is gone, Kenworth is bent on his capture, and *you* are now in charge of Lelleford. All three are beyond reason and understanding."

Her bottom lip trembled. Her eyes misted, and damn if he didn't feel a responding tremor in his innards, which he quickly squelched. She indulged in self-pity, 'twas all, an emotion he couldn't abide.

"Perhaps you become overset because you remind yourself of your plight so forcefully."

"I am *not* overset!"

With that she spun around and strode over to close the window shutters. One stuck open, and after she struggled with it to no avail, he reluctantly went to her aid.

A mistake. He'd forgotten how he'd battled throughout supper to ignore the tang of Eloise's scent. How much willpower he expended to keep from drifting toward her in an effort to identify what spice or pungent flower emitted so keen yet pleasing a fragrance.

With a sharp, effective rap the shutter closed.

He should move away, except his feet refused to move.

Eloise looked up at him with moist eyes, reflecting her own befuddlement. She didn't move either, simply stood still and silent in his shadow, too close and far too vibrant and tempting.

Eloise's appeal drew male reaction as if iron to lodestone, and Roland cursed the part of his body that swelled in perfectly understandable male response to an enticing female. The response might be natural, but succumbing wasn't permissible. Not when he had to make her understand she must submit to his authority. Not when the vision of Eloise entwined with Hugh remained too fresh in his vivid imagination.

He stepped back. "Perhaps you will find the situation more easily tolerated on the morn."

"Will you still be here? And the earl?"

"Aye."

"Then the situation will still be intolerable. Pray send Isolde in when you leave."

A regal dismissal. He should take umbrage, but couldn't think of a good reason to argue, and hated that she was probably right about tomorrow, especially if Sir John continued to elude capture.

"Do you think they found a dry place in which to shelter, milady?"

From her cross-legged position in the middle of her bed, Eloise glanced over at where Isolde was tucked into her pallet. The only light in the room came from glowing coals in the elegant brass brazier they'd lit against the chill of a stormy night.

"Likely." The weak assurance didn't ease her worry over her father and undoubtedly wouldn't satisfy Isolde's concern for her brother.

"Sir John did right to take Edgar with him," Isolde stated. "My brother knows these lands and the castle nigh as well as his lordship."

Eloise heard both fear and pride. Whatever fate awaited Sir John, Edgar would share in it. When this was over, the squire would either be rewarded handsomely or hang beside the lord he served.

She shivered, blaming the thinness of her white linen nightrail, and glanced down at the parchment in her lap. Somehow, she'd concluded, Edgar must have snuck into Lelleford and placed the message on her bed. How, she didn't know, but 'twas the only reasonable explanation.

"Both Father and Edgar are resourceful. I just wish I knew how to alert them to what goes on here."

Especially to Roland St. Marten's role in the affair. Even if, as her father seemed to believe, Kenworth would leave soon, Father shouldn't return only to be caught unaware of Roland's presence.

She'd certainly been caught unaware earlier.

After managing to ignore him all through supper, she'd been forced to deal with Roland in her chamber, a place she never dreamed to encounter him. She might have successfully hidden the message from him, but not her unruly emotions.

Eloise couldn't remember when she'd last allowed her tears to surface in anyone's presence. Always, if tears threatened too hard, she sought privacy. Too, crying inevitably left her weak and drained, and she so detested losing control she'd learned how to ruthlessly maintain her composure.

She had *not* been overset. The tears had surfaced, but not flowed. But it had been damn hard to withhold them when Roland's deeply timbered voice rumbled through her with a surprising offer of comfort.

Damn the man. She neither wanted nor appreciated his attempt at courtesy. He was the enemy, the invader. The despicable toad who'd tried to convince his half brother not to marry her.

One brief and oddly tender encounter didn't absolve him of his sins against her. Nor did the few happier moments they'd shared before he'd proved false count in his favor.

She'd been so sure of his good opinion. On one occasion in particular. Roland had come into the stable while she was there, and at the time she fancied he'd sought her out apurpose. They'd spent a long time companionably admiring each other's horses.

He'd appreciated the grace and heart of her elderly mare; she'd admired the elegance and power of his stallion. He'd impressed her with his charm and wit, and she'd basked in his gallantry. 'Twas a shame, she'd thought then, that Roland was the youngest of his bevy of siblings, still a squire with hardly a copper to his name, and not the immediate heir to his father's barony.

Her disloyalty to Hugh had caused her a twinge of guilt, which worsened when she overheard how little Roland thought of her, then nearly became unbearable with Hugh's death.

In her head she knew her unwise preference for

Roland hadn't brought on Hugh's death, but her heart whispered of divine punishment.

Isolde sat up on her pallet. "Milady, ye do not think to try to warn them, do ye? 'Twould be foolhardy and dangerous."

Jarred out of her musings, Eloise glanced down at her father's note. Since finding it, several plans had presented themselves, each as daring as the next, and probably as doomed to failure. Even if she could find a way to sneak out of Lelleford, she doubted she'd locate her father easily, then be able to sneak back in.

As she saw it, her duty was here, with Lelleford's people, and her father wouldn't appreciate her putting the holding at further risk.

Roland believed himself in charge of her home. He needed to be watched closely, prevented from abusing his power. Besides, the better time to warn her father might be after Kenworth and his forces left, when the gates were no longer guarded so heavily and her father might be easier to find.

"Nay, I doubt I could leave the castle without anyone noticing. And if the patrols are not able to find him, I doubt I would have better luck. Best I trust my father to do what he feels right."

As she must do what she felt right. Which was why she'd allowed Isolde to see the message, knowing the maid would keep the secret because of her brother's involvement. On the morn she would tell Simon about her father's plan and seek his counsel on what course of action to take, if any.

No one else must be allowed to see or hear of the

message. Already she'd been careless with it, almost allowed it to fall into enemy hands.

Eloise slid out of bed and padded across the room. She picked up the pair of tongs from the circular brass plate on which the brazier's lion-paw feet stood. With the thick parchment firmly clasped in the tongs, she touched a corner to red-hot coals. The edge browned and curled, smoldered and smoked, but didn't flare.

Isolde coughed and waved a hand before her face. " 'Tis a most wicked stench, milady."

That it was, and would get worse as the substantial sheet made from animal hide burned.

"Open the shutters."

Thunder yet rumbled in the distance, but the worst of the storm had passed, the heavy rain of earlier diminishing to a light shower. A gentle breeze blew a few raindrops into the chamber, and would carry both smoke and stench back out with it.

Determined to hurriedly destroy the message, Eloise again touched parchment to coals. Again the edge browned and curled. Then the breeze fanned the edge and a tiny flame sparked.

Fascinated, Eloise watched the fire creep ever closer to her father's written words, waving smoke away from her face, hearing Isolde's cough.

From the passageway came the bellow of "Fire!" The door crashed open, startling her into spinning around. Roland stood in the doorway, his eyes wide with panic.

Isolde screeched. "Milady, the rush mat!"

Eloise jerked her attention back to the burning parchment. A piece had broken off, landing on the mat at her bare feet. Before she could collect her thoughts, Roland sped across the room, grabbing the washbasin on his way.

She backed up and gasped as water hit her chest and arm. The dregs he tossed at her feet.

One would think an army pounded up the stairway from the noise in the passageway. Simon rounded the doorway. He carried a bucket, as did several others.

Eloise felt her embarrassment rise clear from her toes. She'd meant to reduce one piece of parchment to ashes. Roland's intensely disapproving expression accused her of trying to burn down the entire castle.

Isolde's hands covered her face. Simon pursed his lips and shook his head. As Eloise wished she could fly out the window to escape, from down the passageway came a roar.

"What the devil goes on here?"

The earl. Ye gods.

Roland's chest heaved, then he blew out a long breath and tossed the basin onto the bed. "Simon, waylay Kenworth if you can. The danger is past. Everyone can return to their pallets or duties."

With a nod, Simon herded her would-be rescuers from the room. Eloise hoped Roland would simply follow the others, a futile wish. The door closed with too loud a bang.

He tilted his head, his brows arching—a demand for an explanation.

Eloise raised her chin. "You should be ashamed of yourself. There was no call to raise an alarm."

Roland couldn't believe her temerity. From the moment he'd smelled smoke his heart thudded hard against his ribs. He'd envisioned horrors. The room in flames.

The women trapped, or worse. He'd seen and smelled charred flesh during the war with the Scots, and didn't care to repeat the experience. He could still smell the stench, made worse by the pungent smoke that would linger into the night, perhaps for days.

He flung a hand toward the door. "Had you been standing guard without and smelled biting smoke, would you not have raised the alarm?"

She frowned. "You guard my door?"

"My cursed luck to lose the toss of the dice."

"To whom did you lose?"

"Simon, whose sleep we just interrupted. He takes on the duty later."

"Oh. Well, then, perhaps you should have taken a moment to fully assess the danger first so as not to disturb Simon."

"One does not take chances with fire." He glanced at the now wet parchment still clamped in the tongs, assumed it the same parchment she'd picked up off the bed earlier.

He'd dismissed it as unimportant, too busy noticing the coziness of the chamber, envisioning Hugh curled up with Eloise on the bed.

"What is that you tried to burn?"

She eased the tongs behind her. "'Tis none of your concern."

"Everything that happens at Lelleford is now my concern. Give over."

Eloise's stubborn, beautifully carved chin rose higher. "'Tis private. 'Tis also unseemly for you to remain in my bedchamber, where you intrude without my leave."

"Perhaps you should have bolted your door!"

"I have never had the need! No one has ever before dared enter without being invited!"

He had no intention of begging her pardon. He took an intentionally menacing step toward her, casting her a scowl that had been known to set soldiers to quivering. "Either hand the scroll over or I shall take it from you."

"Cur!"

Was a cur better or worse than a despicable toad? He decided not to ask, just held out his hand and wiggled his fingers. "Now, Eloise."

"You have no right!"

He wasn't about to wrestle her for it before a witness. To salvage some of his pride and spare Eloise shame, he issued an order. "Isolde, out."

"Again?" the maid mumbled.

The maid must have caught her cursed insolence from her mistress. "'Twill not be for long, I assure you."

Eloise's brow scrunched at that. Perhaps she finally realized he was serious. Surely she didn't believe he'd issue an order, whether to a maid or a knight's daughter, and not demand obedience.

Isolde shuffled toward the door. "Ye mark her, milord, and there'll be the devil to pay."

"Any marks she may suffer will be of her own doing." Blast, why was he assuring a maid of her mistress's safety? He didn't have to explain himself to anyone!

With the door closed, he found himself alone with an obstinate, glorious female whose wetted nightrail merely veiled her finely shaped, beautifully hued attributes. Dark, hardened nipples poked at gauzy linen, an erotic invitation to a man's hands. His palm fairly itched to answer.

Could he seduce her to his will? A tempting thought, and one he dismissed immediately. His mission to protect Lelleford included its inhabitants, most especially the lord's daughter.

He truly didn't want to do battle with her, either mentally or physically. Unfortunately, Eloise utterly refused to accept his authority.

His hand extended, he walked toward her. For each of his steps forward, she took one back until she bumped into the wall.

"You have no more room to retreat, my lady. Give over."

She gracefully slid down the wall, her white nightrail puddling around her like a cloud. She sat on the parchment, crossed her arms under her pert breasts. "Begone, villain, or I swear, you shall regret this night's devilry."

Roland inwardly sighed, giving in to the inevitable, already regretting what he must do. "You give me no choice, my lady."

"You would not dare touch me. A proper, chivalrous knight would—"

The challenge proved all the provocation he could stand. He grasped her arms and hauled her up, her attempt to protest lost in a grunt and whoosh of breath when she landed stomach down on his shoulder.

He placed a steadying hand on the sweetly rounded buttocks pressed against his cheek. His nostrils flared at her scent, his body stirred at the feel of firm flesh beneath his fingers.

Her fist struck the small of his back, ending an exquisite fantasy of turning his head enough to nuzzle her softness.

"Put me down, beast!"

He patted her rump, firmly enough to serve as warning but not hard enough to sting. "You would do well to court my favor right now. I could leave a mark here where no one could see."

She went very quiet, very still.

Roland glanced at the parchment and tongs on the floor. First he'd rid himself of the termagant, then fetch the partially burned parchment.

Almost reluctant to give up the blessed peace—and to his chagrin, the warmth of her body pressed close even in this untoward position—he turned toward the bed.

"I am not your enemy, Eloise. Believe me or nay, I will ensure no harm comes to you or your people or the holding in your father's absence. Your cooperation is not vital, but would go far to make my task easier."

She huffed. "Why would I wish to?"

"Because our goals are the same. We both wish justice done and the holding to prosper."

"Except you believe my father is guilty."

"Guilty or not, our situation is the same. If you continue to fight me, Eloise, I shall have to take harsh measures with you, and I should hate to do so. Do not force my hand."

His hand, he noticed, had moved. Was still moving. Circling her rump, her thigh. Eloise seemed to gentle to the petting, much like a kitten he'd once owned that nipped and scratched until deciding she could trust him not to hurt her. Except Eloise wasn't a kitten, but a regal lioness with sharper claws and less reason to trust.

What would she do if he slipped his hand beneath her nightrail, caressed her properly? Could she be tamed to his touch, induced to purr? Another intriguing notion he dared not act upon.

"Pray, put me down."

A request, not a demand.

"If I do, will you stay put? If I must race you across the room for possession of the parchment, I swear I will not be so gentle with you next time."

He felt her sigh. Resignation?

"I concede this skirmish to you, Sir Roland. All I ask is you grant me a boon once you read the message."

Roland went cold. A message? From whom? Sir John? By what right did she ask a boon?

"What might that be?"

"I truly dislike this awkward position. My head begins to spin."

Would she be off balance enough to prevent her from bolting? Perhaps. Besides, he couldn't stand here all night with Eloise draped over his shoulder, arse end up and completely subject to his whims.

Whims, he admitted, he had no right to entertain.

He glanced over to where he'd tossed the washbasin, then eased Eloise down onto the velvet coverlet. She lay before him in all her feminine glory, her eyes wide and slightly glazed, aware of her vulnerability. Sweet mercy, Eloise might as well be naked for all her wetted nightrail hid.

She took too deep a breath for his comfort, the rise and fall of her breasts mesmerizing, kicking up his pulse.

If he leaned forward, he might taste the tips of her ripe breasts, indulge in a sumptuous feast—and likely suffer an ache in his loins for the remainder of the night.

"What boon?"

"That you carefully consider the consequences before you act on what you learn."

"I am a careful man, Eloise."

"Are you? Your brother Hugh was. Of you I am not sure."

Once more the vision of Hugh and Eloise tumbling on the deep blue velvet plagued him. Had Hugh gentled the lioness with his caresses, kisses, lovemaking?

Roland tore his attention back to where it belonged. Without making further assurances, he crossed the room and snatched up the parchment. From the few words not burned away by her fire or smeared by his water, he caught the meaning of the message, knew who must have sent it.

If Sir John had given his daughter orders before fleeing, then Eloise had known of her father's whereabouts all along.

He crumpled the parchment. "You saw your father before he fled. You knew Sir John was not out hunting."

"I knew."

Her voice came from too close for her to have stayed on the bed. He turned to find her right behind him.

"Where does he hide?"

She shook her head. "He ordered me to allow the earl in the gates, do whatever I must to ensure Kenworth did not feel the need to take Lelleford by force of arms. Then he left." She waved a hand at the parchment. "Beyond that, I know only that he watches for an opportunity to return. Roland, I beseech thee to keep this knowledge from Kenworth."

Eloise asked him to join in her conspiracy. What gall!

But then, 'twas to be expected of a willful woman, was it not?

"In God's name why should I?"

Her fingers landed lightly on his arm. "Because if the earl knows my father watches, no one at Lelleford is safe, which you claim is your responsibility. Think on it. What might you do if the earl decides to torch the keep or use me as bait to draw my father out? Could you stop him, keep your oath to the king?"

Damned if the woman didn't have a point.

Irritated, he held up the parchment. "How did you come by this?"

"I found it on my bed. I know not how it came to be there."

Dare he believe her?

"Obviously someone delivered it."

She nodded, but volunteered no information. 'Twasn't truly necessary. If Sir John hadn't done so himself, then his squire must have, which meant there was another way in and out of the castle than through either the main or postern gates.

"Who else knows of this message?"

"Isolde."

"No one else? Simon? One of the other knights?"

She shook her head, and he wondered again whether or not to believe her. Eloise might look sincere, but she'd tricked him, fooled everyone.

'Twas several hours before dawn, time enough to decide what to do with the information. As he'd told Eloise, he tended to be a careful man, and he walked a thin line here between aiding a fugitive from justice and keeping faith with the king's direct order.

"I will give you my answer on the morn."

Eloise removed her hand from his sleeve. "I will pray you decide rightly."

Roland doubted he'd trust his decision to prayer. 'Twould take very careful consideration over what to tell, or not tell, the perverse earl.

Chapter Five

ELOISE WARILY eased down the stairway. 'Struth, she'd been tempted to hide out in her bedchamber, but resisted the urge as unacceptable cowardice.

She needed to learn what had transpired during her restless night spent curious as to how someone had delivered her father's message, and frightened over what Roland would decide to do with the information. The uncertainty had her stomach in knots.

All the while she'd also wrestled with her annoying reaction to Roland's manhandling.

Mercy, the man was strong. He'd hefted her up off the floor and tossed her over his shoulder as if she weighed no more than a sack of grain, in a display of both power and frustration with what she had to admit was her callow behavior.

Instead of childishly sitting on the half-burned scroll, she should have tried to strike a bargain for his cooperation.

Worse, after he eased her down onto the bed, she'd sensed his lust. Fully prepared for him to lower down atop her, she'd felt no fear, only strange, tingling sensations thrumming through her entire being.

'Twas most bothersome to admit she'd not uttered one word in protest or raised a finger in defense. Inexcusable.

To Roland's credit, he'd won his struggle for control by remembering his role as her protector. This morn she was counting on that same strong sense of duty, on his honor as a knight, to render her indiscretion harmless. She never should have told him of her concerns about Kenworth's intentions toward her father.

Eloise glanced around the hall, noting the unusual lack of people gathered at the trestle tables to break their fast. Of Lelleford's knights, only Simon was present. She cringed at the sight of two guards garbed in the earl's livery standing near the door, but neither Kenworth nor Roland was about.

Relieved, but confused, she slid onto the bench next to Simon. He looked tired, likely from having his sleep disturbed before taking his turn guarding her door last night, which didn't make sense to her. Shouldn't Kenworth's knights act as her guards? Befuddling.

"Where is everyone?"

Simon swallowed a mouthful of pottage. "Kenworth paced the hall until the first ray of dawn. He is so sure of his trackers he wanted to be with the patrol when they find Sir John. Some of our knights are with him, others are out with St. Marten, hunting for Brother Walter."

Another mystery. Where the devil could the monk have gone off to, and why did he hide? She silently wished Roland good fortune, hoped he met with success before Kenworth returned. She had a few questions for the monk.

"I am surprised Kenworth allowed our knights to leave the hall."

"Kenworth fears we will conspire if left alone together too long. We are all held hostage to the others' good behavior." He raised an eyebrow. "Yours, too. I beg you, milady, to restrain yourself."

As she hadn't last eve, he meant.

Since Kenworth hadn't burst into her bedchamber, she assumed Simon had given the earl some explanation of why several people tramped around in the passageway lugging buckets of water. Another point she must concede to Roland—had she stood outside the chamber and smelled smoke, she'd have raised an alarm just as he had done.

Given the results of her impetuous actions, she should have waited until this morning to destroy the scroll, tossed it into the flames of the hearth. Then Roland wouldn't know her father was in the area, couldn't betray him to Kenworth.

"Have you spoken with Roland this morn?"

Simon tossed his pewter spoon in the now empty wooden bowl and shoved it aside. Just above a whisper, he answered, "He told me of the message, which he destroyed. 'Tis fortunate for us he felt no compulsion to give it to the earl."

The knots in her stomach eased somewhat. Roland's stance on the matter brought no sense of triumph, only a bit of relief.

"'Twould seem he is not as interested in my father's capture as in fulfilling his duty to the king."

Simon nodded. "His duty lies with us."

'Twas reassuring, but that didn't mean the situation had changed. Roland was still the invader, and she still inwardly railed against his royally granted authority over her home.

Knowing she could do nothing for the nonce, she moved on to her next concern. "Simon, is there a way to enter the castle except through the main or postern gates?"

Simon rubbed at his chin. "I thought not, but am beginning to believe there must be. Roland says you found the message on your bed when you went up to your chamber after evening meal, long after Kenworth ordered the gates closed and heavily guarded."

"I assume Edgar snuck in somehow and placed it in my bedchamber, but cannot discern how he did so."

"'Tis a puzzle." Simon shifted beside her, revealing his discomfort over how someone could get in and out of the castle in some secret way. "Perhaps there is a passage through the storage rooms or undercroft dating back to ancient days, fallen into disuse but known of by his lordship."

Simon didn't have to say that if her father knew of such a passage, he should have informed his steward. Eloise thought he should have informed his daughter, too.

She stifled a yawn and stretched her limbs. If she didn't get up and move she'd fall asleep at the table. Now that she knew Roland wouldn't use last night's events against her or her father, she could relax some.

For now, she'd leave in Simon's hands the matter of the secret passageway. He'd investigate and inform her if he discovered anything.

She dare not mention the last disturbing incident that interfered with her sleep. If she allowed herself to sit here and mull over her near escape from a kiss, or more, she'd go witless.

"Are you confined to the hall?" she asked Simon.

"Aye. You are not, but do not be alarmed if one of the guards follows you. Should he show you the least discourtesy, inform me immediately and I will set the man aright."

She had to smile at Simon's confidence. "I gather you feel you have some authority over the earl's men."

"I am a knight, Lelleford's steward, and therefore possess authority. Besides, the men who guard us now are among those who will remain here with St. Marten. Best they know their place and limits from the beginning."

"And St. Marten?"

"Best tread carefully there, milady. He rules us with the king's blessing. How tight a noose we suffer will depend greatly on how well we deal together."

Her smile became strained at the mention of a noose. "So you say I should be pleasant to him?"

"'Twould not be amiss."

She rose from the bench, hearing echoes of her father's orders to placate Kenworth. 'Twas still galling. Now Simon suggested she not annoy Roland, either.

So how did one deal with thorns one couldn't pluck out? Ignore them as much as possible, she supposed.

First she'd eat. Then talk with the cook about nooning and evening meal. Then a word with the laundress—aye, she'd occupy her time and mind so fully she'd not have time to fret over Kenworth and his trackers or over her father's or Brother Walter's whereabouts.

Or wonder if she might have enjoyed Roland's kiss. Where Hugh's lips had been thin and dry, his half brother's were full and lush. A tempting mouth.

Damn. She had to stop comparing the half brothers. 'Twasn't fair to either and only reminded her of her disloyalty to Hugh.

One of the earl's guards followed her into the kitchen and then on to the laundry. He hovered at a respectful distance and kept mum. Though he didn't intrude, she chafed at his presence.

Just before nooning, about the time she realized that no amount of busy work could hold her fretting at bay, Roland and Marcus strode through the hall's doors with a bedraggled Brother Walter in tow. The monk provided ample distraction from the too handsome man who'd haunted her night and snared too many of her thoughts this morn.

Brother Walter's robes were mud-caked and torn. He'd lost a sandal. Eloise caught a whiff of him and nearly gagged on the stench. 'Twasn't mud coating his robe.

Behind her, Simon uttered an appropriate curse.

Appalled, she pointed at the door. "He does not enter the hall until he no longer stinks. I shall have buckets of water taken out to the bailey."

Roland seemed about to object, then apparently changed his mind. "See if you can find Brother Walter less odorous garb," he told Marcus, then roughly ushered the monk out the door.

Marcus's amusement lit his face.

Eloise wasn't the least amused. "What possessed you to bring the monk into the hall? Sweet mercy, where did you find him?"

His smile widened. "Running across the bailey toward the stables. We gave chase. Somehow he landed in the dung heap. I think Roland brought him straight in here because he did not know what else to do with him. By your leave, milady, I shall see if our monk owns a spare robe and sandals."

Eloise had to admit the vision a bit humorous, and considered Brother Walter's current plight only what he deserved.

The cleansing of Brother Walter took several buckets of water, the first few used to dislodge most of the muck from his robe. He stood stoic through the dousing, and turned red at the order to disrobe. Roland firmly cut short a meek attempt to object.

Eloise averted her gaze when the monk obeyed, catching a mere glimpse of his wet small clothes. Not so for the others in the crowd who gathered around to witness the unusual bath. More than one of the servant girls giggled. Eloise supposed she should have ordered the girls away, but the monk had brought this on himself.

"Have a sniff, Lady Eloise. Does he still offend?"

Roland's command brought forth more giggles and snickers from the crowd. Thank the Fates Marcus had found the monk's spare robe.

Eloise took pity on the monk and resisted the urge to actually sniff. "He no longer reeks. He may enter the hall."

"My lady," Brother Walter said softly. "I would prefer the solitude of the chapel that I might pray—"

Roland grabbed him by the hood of his robe. "Into the hall with you, good monk. Now that I have you I am loathe to let you out of my sight. Besides, I am eager to hear your reasons for hiding."

So was Eloise, even though she feared she wasn't going to like whatever the monk had to say.

With his meal consumed and a fresh ale in hand, Roland plopped down on the bench across the trestle table from Marcus and Simon. He couldn't think of a more pleasant way to wile away the time before Kenworth returned than in the company of the knights.

Besides, they provided a diversion from the lady who proved far too distracting.

All the while he searched for Brother Walter, he'd mused over his encounter with Eloise last eve.

Tossing the water at her had seemed an efficient way of dousing the flames on both the parchment in her hand and the rush mat beneath her feet. Unfortunately it also wetted her nightrail, turning the thin white linen into a sheer veil over her breasts. That her nipples were a dusky rose was more than he needed to know.

He wasn't particularly proud of himself for picking her up and tossing her over his shoulder. It was a barbaric display of manners for a knight. Still, he'd known of no other way to swiftly separate Eloise from the parchment she sat on.

The memory of her warm, supple weight draped over him in such intimate fashion kept him awake most of the night. The scent of her lingered in his nostrils. Worse, neither would the memory fade of Eloise sprawled on the bed, expectant of a kiss, or more.

He'd come far too close to fulfilling her expectation.

She'd been as aware of him as he of her. She'd gone very still, perhaps also confused by the inexplicable attraction between a man and woman who couldn't abide each other.

Eloise fascinated him.

As she did now. She was vexed, and the blame lay clearly at Brother Walter's sandal-less feet. The monk wasn't talking. He'd told her he couldn't tell anyone anything until after speaking with Sir John.

Roland didn't much care. He'd completed his assigned task by finding the monk for Kenworth, who seemed to think the cleric could provide information regarding Sir John's treason. The monk's refusal to answer any of Eloise's questions, however, irritated the lady to within a gnat's breath of a fit of pique.

Eloise on the verge of eruption was a glorious sight to behold. She moved about the hall seeing to the cleaning up after the noon meal with the efficiency of a commander of troops. No commander of troops, however, moved with such a beguiling sway of hips.

And every time she passed the stool near the hearth where the hapless monk sulked, she shot him a glare that consigned him to Hades.

Marcus leaned forward, the gleam in his eyes hinting of mischief. "How long do you think the good monk will remain silent when Kenworth gets hold of him?"

Simon huffed. "Not long at all. The earl will not hesitate to use harsher measures than Lady Eloise to pry him open."

Roland silently agreed, and truly didn't want to think about what tortures Kenworth might devise for the reticent monk should Sir John remain missing.

Indeed, he wished he could close the gates to keep the earl outside of Lelleford. Kenworth was going to be unbearable whether he succeeded in his search for Sir John or not, either gloating or glowering.

And, damn, as Roland saw his duty, he'd have to protect the monk from Kenworth, just as he'd drawn a sword to stand beside Simon, and just as he'd guarded Eloise's door to ensure the lady's safety.

For a man used to being responsible for only himself, he'd certainly taken several others under his wing of late. Timothy. Eloise. The monk. The entire populace of Lelleford.

A daunting thought.

A smile eased across Marcus's mouth. "Brother Walter will be sorry he left the safety of the dung heap. I still do not understand why he thought he could hide from us in the stable." His elbow nudged Simon. "Even you would have laughed at the sight of him when we dragged him out of the heap."

While Roland and Marcus both chuckled, Simon allowed only the corner of his mouth to twitch.

On his first visit to Lelleford, Roland had dubbed these two Marcus the Jester and Simon the Serious. For many years both had loyally served Sir John Hamelin, a lesser baron who held enough land to support several knights in fine style.

This charge of treason affected the knights as much as it did John. If judged guilty, John would hang and the king would grant possession of Lelleford to a favorite. Whether a knight was allowed to remain at Lelleford depended upon the new holder's whim, and the knight's personal feeling on swearing fealty to the new lord.

Roland took a sip of ale and tried not to covet what Sir

John Hamelin might lose. "What bothers me is why the monk felt compelled to hide to begin with. He is most adamant about speaking to John."

Simon rubbed his chin. "As he was yesterday. For a usually quiet man, he has done a lot of wailing and thrashing about of late."

"Perhaps we should try to find out what he knows before Kenworth gets back."

Simon rose off the bench. "Just what I was thinking," he muttered, then headed for the hearth, with Roland and Marcus close behind.

Simon crossed his arms and hovered above the seated monk, an intimidating stance the monk could not ignore.

"'Tis most probable Kenworth will not find Sir John," Simon stated, "and will return in a foul mood. For all of our sakes, I believe you should reveal to us what you know."

The monk looked up at Simon with sad eyes. "Nay. Sir John must decide what he wishes you to know of his affairs. I will not break trust with him for either you or the earl."

Roland heard the rustle of Eloise's silk skirts as she came to stand beside him.

"You have already broken my father's trust." Eloise's accusation caused Brother Walter to blink. "'Tis my opinion the wound to your head resulted from an argument between you and my father, not an unfortunate mishap."

The monk quietly answered, "'Tis true, milady, that your father and I exchanged harsh words, but you may be assured my wound is not of his doing. Had I not suffered, as you put it, an unfortunate mishap, his lordship might not . . ." He shook his head. "I can say no more."

The hall's doors opened and Kenworth strode in, followed by several of Lelleford's knights. His mighty scowl revealed the result of his search for Sir John. Roland wasn't sure the tracker's failure to locate their prey was good or not.

In some ways 'twould be best for all, except perhaps for Sir John, if Kenworth captured John and left Lelleford with his prisoner in tow. On the other hand, Roland harbored some doubts over Sir John's guilt, doubts planted by Eloise's and the knights' absolute, steadfast surety over his innocence.

Kenworth's eyes lit up when he spotted Brother Walter.

"Well, well. One of our fugitives is found. Where the hell have you been, Walter?"

Brother Walter rose with a visible effort, steeling himself against the earl's displeasure. "Praying for guidance, my lord earl."

A niggling sense of something not quite right pricked at Roland, though he couldn't say why. Perhaps the monk's suddenly straight spine, or his use of 'my lord earl' in a tone of familiarity.

"Why ever would you need guidance?" Kenworth asked. "Your duty is clear enough to me." He waved a hand at Eloise. "Have food brought up to the accounting room. The monk and I have papers to sort through. By all that is holy, if I cannot find the traitor, I will find the proof of his treason!"

Eloise bristled, but possessed the good sense to nod an acknowledgment of the order.

The earl spun on his heel, the monk reluctantly trailed in his wake. Duty bound, Roland did, too.

Near the stairway, the earl turned his head, and spotting Roland, came to a halt. "Your presence is not required, St. Marten."

"I believe it is, my lord. Should anything untoward happen to Brother Walter, the king will hold me responsible."

"Not so," Kenworth said, a sly smile appearing. "Walter does not serve Lelleford, but me, and so is no concern of yours."

Stunned, Roland looked to the monk, whose expression remained stoic. And who didn't dispute the earl's claim.

Now Roland knew why Kenworth had been so sure of Sir John Hamelin's presence at Lelleford and the lack of concern over his capture. The monk was Kenworth's spy, must have informed the earl beforehand of Sir John's plans. Had the monk also supplied the earl with evidence of treason?

Roland did the only thing he could under the circumstances. With a slight bow to the earl, he backed away. "I shall leave the two of you to your task, then."

Without further comment, the earl and monk disappeared up the stairway. Roland didn't have to decide whether or not to tell the others. They'd heard.

Eloise sank down on the stool the monk had vacated, her disbelief warring for dominance with her outrage.

"The fiend!" she spat out. "How dare he spout nonsense about not breaking faith with my father when all the while he was in league with the earl?"

The urge to comfort Eloise nearly overcame Roland's

good sense. He couldn't take her in his arms and . . . what? Tell her everything would be well? A falsehood. Besides, she neither appeared close to tears nor in need of anyone's comfort, least of all his.

So he turned his attention to Sir Peter, one of Lelleford's household knights. "The trackers failed?"

"Not entirely. If Sir John is still in the area, he is well hidden."

"Are the patrols yet out?"

"Aye, they are instructed to remain out until nightfall if need be."

"Why did Kenworth return?"

Peter gave a small smile. "Kenworth is not a patient man."

"And the rest of you?"

The big knight shrugged. "Either Kenworth did not wish us to witness his trackers' final failure, or he feared we might break away from the patrol and somehow aid Sir John. All I know is that when yet another promising trail proved fruitless, he told his men to continue and ordered us to return with him."

Eloise elegantly rose from the short stool. "So what do we do now?"

"We wait," Roland answered, aware the knights were likely wondering the same thing and probably chafing to take some kind of action. "Much depends upon the success of the patrols, and on whatever Kenworth finds in your father's accounting room."

Eloise glanced at the stairs, then gave each knight a pointed look. "I hate doing nothing," she stated, then flounced off in the direction of the kitchen.

Chapter Six

ROLAND LEFT the keep, his thoughts in turmoil.

Like Eloise, he hated doing nothing, allowing events to happen as they would without having much influence or control.

Not that he'd exerted any influence over the good things that happened to him recently. A twist of fate had brought him to King Edward's attention. A mere happenstance led to an opportunity to better his lot in life.

But all could be lost in the blink of an earl's eyelash.

Hands clasped behind his back, he wandered toward the inner gate. The guards, Kenworth's men-at-arms, nodded a greeting as he passed through the arch and under the iron gate.

Both the inner and outer baileys were too quiet. Where one might expect to find castle folk attending their daily errands, or tenant farmers visiting the various tradesmen's shops lining the outer curtain wall, today few souls wandered about.

The blacksmith's hammer was quiet; the cobbler's door was closed. Women visited the common well but didn't linger to gossip. No children played with sticks and hoops. The only activity was near the stables, where squires and stable boys worked to put away the recently arrived horses.

Disquieting. As if everyone held their breath in anticipation of their lord's capture, or the earl's wrath if their lord escaped.

Kenworth and the monk would likely be occupied in the accounting room for some time, searching for evidence of Hamelin's guilt. 'Twas stunning to think the earl had placed a spy in Hamelin's service, that Sir John hadn't realized he harbored an informant.

That sword swung both ways, however. Just as the monk had informed on John, he must also have been the one to give warning, perhaps unintentionally, of the earl's imminent arrival, allowing John to escape Lelleford before he could be arrested. Roland shuddered to think of what the earl was going to do to his informant for letting that information slip.

None of his concern. The monk must have realized he placed himself in danger when accepting the position of spy. Now he'd pay the price of failure.

Instinctively, Roland scanned the wall walk set high and sturdy along the thick stone wall of the fortress. Archers clad in the earl's livery patrolled the walk, searching for signs of trouble or for the rest of Kenworth's men returning.

If the trackers didn't find Hamelin, there would be the devil to pay tonight. And if Hamelin was captured—that would be best for all concerned. Except, perhaps, for John, or his daughter.

Roland shook his head. Best not to allow his thoughts to linger on Eloise. Already too many times he'd been affected by a whiff of her scent or the memory of how he'd tossed her down on her bed and damn near kissed her. Too vividly he remembered how she'd gazed up at him with wide sapphire eyes, waiting, wondering, anticipating.

The increased force of the pull between them had caught him unaware, and he couldn't afford to make the grave mistake of becoming physically involved with a woman he was supposed to protect. The king would have his head for the breech of duty—if the knights of Lelleford didn't slice it off first for violating their lady.

'Twouldn't happen. Not with Eloise. Not with the woman who'd come so close to being his brother's wife. Not with the lady over whom he and Hugh had exchanged harsh words, the last they'd spoken before Hugh's death.

An angry shout rang out from near the stables.

The squires of the knights of Kenworth stood aligned against their counterparts of Lelleford. Arms crossed over chests, the squires hurled taunts at each other.

The loudest of them was the earl's squire, Gregory. A tall, stout lad and a nephew of Kenworth's, he took the position of leader. The lad grated on Roland's nerves. Gregory often used his gravelly voice and menacing stance to ensure his fellow squires knew him superior in wealth and rank. Within two months he would be knighted, and Roland felt pity for the as-yet-unknown lad who Gregory might choose for his squire.

He quickened his pace when Gregory waved an upraised fist.

"He will hang, as he deserves!" the squire declared, eliciting agreeing cheers on one side and protesting snarls from the other.

Roland quickly scanned the crowd for Timothy. The lad stood apart, near Lelleford's squires but not quite among them, as if ready to take their side if required but not yet committed.

Just as Roland had stood apart until required to aid Simon against Kenworth.

The lad learned quickly and well.

"Your almighty earl has to *find* him before he can hang him! Not having much luck in that endeavor, is he?" came the answering insult.

Roland didn't know which Lelleford squire dared. Not that it made any difference, he'd simply stated the feelings of all his fellows.

Without hesitation Roland strode into the small space separating the two factions. Almost immediately the fierce looks eased, arms lowered, and quiet ruled. The squires might have at each other without qualm, but they respected Roland's rank and authority, which spoke well for their training if naught else.

'Twas also in his favor that most of the squires were mere lads, only a few of them older and nearing their own knighthood. On those faces fierce scowls lingered, and from them would come trouble later if their knights didn't take them in hand and impress upon them the need for peace, reinforce the tenets of chivalry that demanded honorable behavior toward their peers.

Unfortunately, Roland couldn't imagine Kenworth giving any such instruction to Gregory.

"I give you all warning," Roland stated, his voice soft and low so they needed to strain to hear. "Any squire who strikes one of his peers will find himself pitching dung as the penalty for ignoble behavior. I suggest you find tasks to perform more fitting to your stations than shouting at each other like common rabble."

Feet shuffled. Eyes shifted. All but two seemed ready to give ground. Gregory, naturally, and Alan, who Roland now recognized as Sir Marcus's squire. Wonderful. The squire of the earl and the squire of the captain of Lelleford's guards. They had glares only for each other.

"Gregory, Alan, as the most senior squires I expect the two of you to set an example of chivalrous behavior for the others." Both turned to him then, their glares changing to appalled surprise. "Should any of the younger lads succumb to the temptation to exchange blows, you will not only make them cease but will suffer the penalty with them."

In Alan's eyes Roland saw ire, though the squire bit his bottom lip to withhold comment. Not so Gregory, who puffed up with offense.

"You overstep, Sir Roland. Kenworth shall hear of this."

Roland leaned forward, damn tired of having his authority questioned. "You threaten me with Kenworth. He threatens me with the king. On my oath, I tremble in my boots at what the king will do to me when he hears I halted a fight between the squires, then dared to compel them to take responsibility for their part in keeping the peace at Lelleford."

He backed up and glanced about at both groups of squires. " 'Tis not for any of us to judge, convict or acquit. Mind your duties. If you lads have not enough to occupy your minds and hands, I vow I can find more!"

He didn't need to tell them to disperse. None of them were pleased with his interference, but they obeyed; the last two to break eye contact were Gregory and Alan. There would be trouble between the two again if this situation didn't end soon. Best for all if Kenworth left Lelleford—with or without John Hamelin—taking his knights and their squires with him.

He'd lost count of how often in the past two days he'd wished Kenworth gone. How many more times had Eloise wished the entire lot of them to leave Lelleford? Especially since she'd found her father's message on her bed.

"Nicely done, milord."

Timothy's praise probably wasn't deserved. Roland truly didn't know if he should have let Gregory and Alan come to blows and rid themselves of their anger. Unfortunately, no matter the outcome, 'twould have done little to settle the hostility between the squires.

The only squire to remain, Timothy looked up with what Roland perceived as admiration. That unabashed esteem could lift his spirits as nothing else could, not that he'd done anything special to earn the lad's respect and loyalty.

"Perhaps. Until Kenworth leaves and the two factions are no longer within taunting distance of each other, these skirmishes are likely to continue. The lads loyal to Sir John are wont to defend his honesty and honor as hard as his daughter and knights do."

Timothy's brow scrunched. "'Twas not about Sir John, but his squire. Gregory claims Edgar will hang beside his lord for aiding his attempt to escape. Is that so?"

Gregory had hit lower than Roland guessed.

"That depends upon the king's whim, I fear. One could

argue that Edgar had no choice but to obey his lord's command, and is therefore faultless."

"Or the king could decide the squire aided a traitor, and so is guilty of treason, too." Timothy's countenance softened. "Should that happen, 'twould leave Edgar's sister in a bad way. He is her protector against insult, and worse."

Because of her disfigurement, Isolde likely suffered both physical and mental pain. People, particularly young males, could be crude and cruel to a peasant maid who had no one to defend her against either insult or assault.

"I doubt Lady Eloise would allow anyone to harm her maid."

Timothy gave a derisive snort. "Highborn ladies tend not to notice injury to anyone beneath them, if they notice at all."

Roland guessed there must be a personal tale behind his squire's declaration. Timothy came from peasant stock. By his own forward ways and hard work he'd managed to secure a position on the king's household staff. He'd worked in the stables before the king presented him, with four others, to Roland as candidates for his squire.

Why he'd chosen Timothy he couldn't say precisely. Perhaps because of the lad's wit, or because in his eagerness to please he sometimes tripped over his feet. More likely because Roland doubted few knights would consider a lowborn lad as their squire. But it didn't matter. They got along well, and the lad often anticipated a need before Roland voiced an order. Timothy suited him fine.

"Not fond of highborn ladies, are you?"

"Not much."

A shadow passed over Timothy's normally bright features, and Roland knew he'd get no more of the tale voluntarily. The lad could be closemouthed, which Roland considered a good trait. He'd never have to worry about his squire spreading gossip about his knight.

Timothy's head tilted. "I doubt Lady Eloise is different from the others I met in the king's court. Only see how she ignores everyone while she takes her stroll."

Roland looked over his shoulder. Indeed, Eloise strode through the outer bailey, her spine strait and eyes forward, as if arrowed in on a target.

She walked with purpose, yet with a grace that declared her not only a highborn but willowy female. Commanding, with the ability to bend under violent wind and withstand the strongest storm.

Eloise might not notice anyone, but everyone noticed her, judging by the turn of heads as she passed. Roland envied the guard several paces behind her, treated to the lithe sway of Eloise's hips, all in the name of duty.

"Perhaps Lady Eloise is merely intent on her destination."

"Must be important then."

Which made him wonder what her destination might be.

Suspicion needling him, Roland took leave of Timothy, waved off Eloise's guard, and fell into step beside her. She gave him a sidelong glance, acknowledging his presence but giving no sign of how she felt about his joining her.

"Taking the air?" he asked.

"Seeking a moment of solitude, which I now have lost."

Whether she wanted his company or no, now that he'd dismissed her guard, she had no choice but to suffer him. Besides, his curiosity pleaded for satisfaction.

"I beg pardon for the intrusion, but since I have already broken your peace, you might tell me why you are really out here."

"You find it difficult to believe I wish to sort my thoughts and stretch my legs at the same time?"

A reasonable pursuit for any other woman but this one. From what he'd observed, Eloise did nothing without a reason. Still, he didn't want to exchange harsh words, or have her deem him beneath her regal notice and ignore him totally.

"How goes the sorting of your thoughts?"

Eloise knew she dare not tell Roland St. Marten about any of her thoughts. Some, those of him, were too personal and annoying. Others, of her father and Lelleford, could lead to trouble. Those concerning the disloyal monk and the man's treachery left her speechless.

Nay, confiding her worries to Roland wasn't smart.

Nor could she tell him she was inspecting the outer wall as closely as she dared without being too obvious. There must be a way out of Lelleford besides the main or postern gates, either through a secret door along the wall or through a passage running beneath the keep.

She wouldn't use the secret way herself. Her absence would be noticed too quickly, and the knights held hostage to her cooperation would be punished. However, someone else might be trusted to sneak out of the keep. Who, and when, depended upon how urgent the need became—and whether or not the passage could be located.

She'd begun her search for it out here because the day

was bright and warm for the weeks after harvest, and she needed space to breathe deeply to stave off panic. If Roland was bent on walking with her, then it was best to change the direction of this conversation.

"I saw you over by the stables, speaking with the squires. A problem there?"

His smile said he recognized her ploy, and was gallant enough to accept it. "Everyone feels the tension, and some are prone to make use of it to their own ends."

Eloise risked another glance at Roland, and caught a hint of Hugh in his profile. Sweet, gentle Hugh, who'd died at her feet. She barely withheld a shudder.

He returned her gaze, and the soft resemblance to his half brother disappeared. "Kenworth's squires taunt Lelleford's over your father's guilt, and the possible penalty Edgar might suffer for aiding his lord. The longer the squires are within each other's company, well . . . 'twould be best for all concerned if the situation were resolved soon."

Except the situation wouldn't ease until after Kenworth left, wouldn't resolve until her father was found innocent of treason and Roland St. Marten left Lelleford.

"How much longer do you expect Kenworth to stay at Lelleford?"

"Until he decides your father has left the area, or is captured."

Eloise bit her bottom lip. She and Roland both knew Sir John Hamelin might not budge from his hiding place anytime soon, especially when it proved so effective.

She came to a halt, hating that she was beholden to Roland for his silence about her father's message. But she knew she must thank him for withholding the contents from Kenworth.

Eloise clasped her hands tightly to keep them still.

"You did not tell Kenworth you know my father hides nearby. Why?"

He crossed his arms, disturbed by indecision. She kept silent, hoping his hesitation would fade, though she knew he trusted her nearly as much as she trusted him, which wasn't much at all.

"Many reasons, among them my wish for the earl's absence. On that, I believe, you and I are in accord."

He had the right of it. Except the earl leaving solved only a portion of the problem. The other portion stood before her. Too sure of himself. Too appealing. Threatening her father's return home and her peace of mind.

"'Tis among my many wishes to have you *all* leave."

The upward quirk of his mouth also sparked something deep and dangerous in his exquisite hazel eyes, and her traitorous heart skipped a beat.

"I fear, my lady, I cannot grant all of your wishes," he said softly, the rumble of his voice low and thrilling, as if he'd read her mind and ferreted out every desire of her heart. As if Roland were aware some of those desires had naught to do with her father, or the earl, or hidden passages.

Impossible. Roland was a mere man, couldn't possibly divine her innermost, foolish thoughts.

"You are right. We are in accord where the earl is concerned. So how do we rid ourselves of him?"

His smile widened. "Now I wish I had an answer for you." He shrugged. "Unfortunately, we must wait him out."

Eloise crossed her arms, kicked at the dirt, her brow scrunched. "Waiting out Kenworth may drive us all witless."

"We will survive. Come, my lady, the shadows grow longer. You should return to the hall."

She couldn't continue to search for a hidden passage with Roland acting as her guard. Besides, sometime during her walk she'd begun to wonder if a passage existed at all. Surely, if there was one, either Simon or Marcus would know of it, and neither did.

But how else had Edgar entered the keep to deliver the message? Puzzling.

They walked slowly toward the inner gate.

"Do you expect further trouble from the squires?" she asked.

"Possibly. Especially from Gregory, Kenworth's squire."

"How so?"

"Gregory is as arrogant as his master, as bent on seeing Edgar hang as Kenworth is of your father." Now Roland came to a halt. "Timothy expressed concern for Edgar's sister's safety. 'Twould not be amiss to keep a close watch on Isolde."

Eloise's anger flashed bright and hot. "Should anyone lay a hand on her, he will lose not only the offending hand but his worthless head! Just because her brother is not here to protect her does *not* mean she is vulnerable! Why, the very idea of taking advantage of one so innocent—"

Roland's hand landed on her shoulder. "I hear you, Eloise, and I agree. The squires have been warned to keep the peace and mind their manners. If need be, I will set a guard on her, too. Just tell her to have a care."

The warmth of his hand and calm tone didn't banish her upset, but went a long way to reassure her. If anything untoward happened to Isolde—but it wouldn't. Because Roland wouldn't allow it—and she believed him and trusted his word, on this anyway.

Naturally, she'd do her part to keep her maid safe from insult, but it was Roland's absolute determination to do his duty that allowed Eloise's fear to ease.

He realized at the same moment she did that he still touched her. So large, his hands. The fingers long, the palm wide. She felt strength, and warmth, and the oddest sensation that if she leaned forward and sought succor in his arms, she'd find him willing and welcoming.

Always she'd been the one to give comfort, not seek it.

'Twas part of her duty as her father's chatelaine to give alms to the poor and administer medicinals to the sick. A duty she'd never shunned because she enjoyed the tasks. Eloise knew that betimes a mere smile from her could brighten a villager's day, her touch could halt a wailing child's tears.

Few dared touch her without her express permission or invitation. And then 'twas with the respect due her rank.

That Roland dared . . . how strange she felt no urge to shake him off, demand he cease.

Except one didn't seek succor in the arms of the enemy. For all the accord they found in their attitude toward the earl, they were yet on opposite sides. She for her father and Lelleford, he for the king and himself.

Nor dare she forget Roland St. Marten didn't like her, had declared her brazen, an unfit mate for his brother.

She slipped out from under his hand.

"I will see to Isolde," she managed to say, then silently, alone, made her way to the keep.

On a thickly wooded hill nigh on half a league away, Sir John Hamelin sat atop his gray palfrey and studied the stronghold he considered the jewel of his holdings.

Lelleford. So close and yet so far.

Damn, but he wanted to sleep in his own bed this night instead of on the hard ground. Not possible. And if he thought too much on to whom Eloise had given over the use of his bed, with its thick feather mattress and warm wool coverlet, he'd become angry. A luxury he couldn't afford right now.

If he didn't keep his wits calm and keen to avoid Kenworth's trackers, he'd be sleeping in his own damp, dark dungeon soon enough. Edgar with him.

Damn Kenworth. The man should have given up the search after that first day. But nay. The wily old fox hadn't fallen for the ruse of a false trail. Instead, he'd settled in to enjoy fine wine and crackling fires—and a soft bed—sending out patrols to scour the countryside.

John smiled and admitted a bit of admiration for his foe. The two had tangled hard and often, knew each other well. The next time they met face-to-face, he'd have to compliment William, one knight to another, on a campaign smartly executed.

Edgar finally came out of the thicket, adjusting his scabbard over his tunic. All of six and ten, on the verge of manhood, the squire had taken to this competition of hide-and-seek like a fish to the stream.

John had dismissed the twinges of guilt over bringing the lad with him. Edgar had proved his worth several times over, was both loyal and good company. He'd earned his spurs, and when the time came for the actual knighting, John intended to gift the lad with the finest arraignment, armor, and horse he could find.

First they had to get out of this mire of a legal mess. And he wasn't about to think too hard on that matter, either, or he'd become furious.

Edgar swung onto his horse, adjusted the reins in his gloved hands, and shot John a smile that lightened his heart.

"Where to now, milord? Shall it be the mill tonight?"

"Nay. 'Twould probably be safe enough, but we should not spend the night in the same place twice."

Edgar glanced up through the canopy of treetops swaying overhead. "'Twill rain tonight. We will need shelter. I know you hesitate to involve innocents, but not one of the villagers would turn you away."

"I will not risk it."

"The caves, then?"

A possibility, but John had another destination in mind. He disliked the necessity, but the situation being what it was, it seemed the only reasonable course of action.

"Think you we could make The Fox and Dove by nightfall?"

Edgar's smile faded. "You have decided to leave Lelleford lands."

Not an easy decision.

John disliked leaving his daughter, though most capable, to get by as best she may. She had Simon and Marcus to aid her, and perhaps Julius would soon return from Italy and relieve Eloise of the enormous responsibility for overseeing the whole of the family holdings while their father fought the charge of treason.

He yearned to get his hands around clumsy Brother Walter's neck until the wretch turned blue and revealed all that he knew.

Most of all he hated Kenworth's knowing he'd won this opening skirmish. Giving ground to the earl tore at John's innards, but damn, he saw little choice if he intended to win the war. And he would.

Besides, only in London could he enlist the aid he needed to fight the charges. Who to approach? He knew several men who might be willing, but hadn't yet decided who to trust.

He had time yet, but not much.

"Aye. Leaving seems the only way to draw Kenworth out of my castle. I want that bastard out of my bed."

Edgar's head turned to take in the hilltop view, and John saw the lad's yearning for home. Then worry, likely for Isolde, followed by the decision to attend his lord no matter where John led him.

"We can reach Cambridge with ease if we take the road," Edgar said. "Might be best if we first lay a few misleading tracks, though."

"Nay, I want Kenworth to believe we are well and truly gone, and worry over whether or not we are out of his reach."

A spark of mischief lit the squire's eyes. "We could lay tracks heading north, toward Scotland. Would that not turn the earl's bowels to water?"

John threw his head back and laughed for the first time in days.

Chapter Seven

ONE OF Kenworth's prized trackers scrunched low and, with the point of a stick, sketched a rough map in the dirt.

"We found fresh horse droppings on the ridge. They spent some time up there." He looked up at Kenworth. "Watching us, I imagine. He could see inside this bailey if his eyes are good."

Roland noticed the downward bent of Kenworth's mouth, but kept his own face expressionless, enforcing his neutrality.

That neutrality had slipped in recent days.

In the beginning, he'd believed John Hamelin guilty, mostly because the king had railed his displeasure over the contents of the missive in his possession. Now, Roland wasn't so sure. Not after spending several days with the people who knew and loved Sir John. Despite the grievous charge of treason, Hamelin's retainers and men-at-arms, not to mention his adamant daughter, stood steadfastly loyal to their lord.

Such devotion was to be commended, and Roland began to believe their support of their lord not misplaced.

He just wished Sir John had handled this affair differently.

However, no matter what he believed about Sir John's guilt, his duty remained the same, to hold Lelleford in the king's name to ensure its well-being. Roland thought his duty best carried out without Kenworth hanging about.

The tracker again bent over his map and wielded his stick. "From the ridge the tracks lead to the mill, then go nigh on straight north. Near as we can tell, milord, they keep goin'."

Kenworth rubbed his chin. "How far?"

The tracker stood. "We followed 'em all the way to the river. Could see where they forded and climbed the opposite bank. Looks like Sir John has finally made his move."

Ignoring his knight's disgruntled murmurs, the earl commented, "Could be a ruse."

"Perhaps, milord, but 'twould be my guess he ran out of places to hide," the tracker answered. "We were closing in on him and I think he decided 'twas time to go farther afield."

The tracker sounded so sure of himself Roland wanted to believe him.

"Why now? And why north?" the earl muttered nearly to himself, then glanced around at the group gathered in the bailey. "What is Hamelin about?"

"Perhaps he seeks aid from an ally," one knight offered. "I think it unwise of him to involve others in his troubles, but perhaps he grows desperate."

Desperate? Roland didn't think so. More likely, Sir John had simply realized the earl wasn't about to leave Lelleford and so formed another plan to dislodge his enemy. A good plan, but in Roland's opinion, John had gone the wrong direction. He should be heading for London, and the king, not making tracks all over the north land.

Again Kenworth rubbed his chin. "I mistrust these tracks. Our prey spends several days successfully eluding our patrols, then suddenly leaves. Saints help us, I wish I knew what the man was truly thinking, what his reasons are."

Roland doubted the earl would appreciate his unasked-for opinion, but at this point he'd do most anything to hurry the earl along.

"Sir John had to either surrender or flee. 'Tis possible he hoped that when you arrived and found him gone, you would leave immediately. But when you guessed his game and stayed, he had to come up with another plan. What that plan is I cannot guess, but I believe your tracker is correct in believing Sir John has left Lelleford. If so, then you must follow wherever he leads you, or risk losing him."

"What bothers me is that the trail is so clear. Aye, he wants me to follow, I will give you that. I sense a trap, and would I not be foolish to ride into it?"

Another of the knights cleared his throat. "If I may say, my lord, 'tis also possible the trail is clear because of Sir John's need for haste. He may take no time to cover his tracks because he wishes to reach Scotland's border—"

Kenworth went sickly pale. "Scotland!"

Roland kept mum the uncharitable thought that it would serve the earl right if he had to chase Hamelin all the way to the Scottish border and beyond if he dared.

The knight continued. "Does it not make sense for the traitor to seek shelter and aid from a laird? Perhaps the very one with whom he plots against the king?"

The tracker turned toward the earl. "If that is so, milord, then Sir John has several hours' lead and we will have the devil's own time catching him before he reaches the border."

The earl recovered his composure and some of his color. "Not even Hamelin could be so foolish. Heading for Scotland is nigh on an admission of guilt for which there is no defense."

"Be that as it may, my lord, 'tis our duty to capture him," the knight persisted. "The farther his lead, the less our chance for success, no matter his intentions."

The knights seemed in agreement. Only Kenworth balked, and Roland could think of only one reason why he hesitated.

"My lord, if you worry over Hamelin gaining sway over Lelleford, I pledge you he shall not. Should he try, I vow we will capture him and send word to you. All you need do is keep me informed of your whereabouts."

Kenworth sighed. "I am not convinced we do not follow a false trail, but it seems the only sure trail we have. Ready the men. We depart within the hour."

The knights scrambled, shouting for squires and horses, ordering carts and men made ready.

Though eager to tell Eloise one of her wishes was about to come true, Roland stood at the earl's side and watched the initial preparations.

'Twas the day he'd been waiting for since he arrived. Relief gave way to anticipation, then flirted with dread.

Each emotion flitted through him swiftly, kicking at his insecurities over ruling Lelleford.

Oh, he knew how to oversee a holding. One mostly let the events of long habit run their course. He anticipated no resistance from Simon and Marcus, and most of Lelleford's folk would follow their lead.

'Twas Eloise he wasn't sure of, though she'd seemed to make a begrudged peace with the situation. Perhaps, if he were very fortunate, she'd accept his rule without overt rebellion.

He wasn't counting on it, however.

"Come along, St. Marten," the earl ordered, already taking a stride toward the keep. "We need to ensure an understanding."

Roland fell into step, quite willing to go along with nigh on anything the earl wanted at the moment.

"What might that be, my lord?"

"Hamelin is up to some trickery. I feel it in my bones. And you stated my worst fear, that after I am gone he may try to enter Lelleford and close the gates against me. Should he succeed, he could stand for a very long time." The earl proceeded up the outer stairs to the keep's great doors. "I leave you a small force. Do you think it enough to deny Hamelin entry, capture him if he gives you opportunity?"

"I do, my lord."

"You are given a grave responsibility here."

"And I shall do my utmost to live up to the king's expectations."

Kenworth glanced sideways at him at the mention of the king, as if he'd forgotten who'd placed Roland in charge from the beginning.

"Well, then. Pray keep the gates closed for at least two more days, so none of Lelleford's knights can get ahead of me and possibly warn Hamelin that I am on his tail."

"As you say."

Roland entered the hall behind Kenworth, who bellowed for Gregory even as he reached the circular stairway to the upper floor.

Eloise wasn't to be seen, but Simon sat in his accustomed place at the trestle table, so long confined to the hall he must be more than ready to escape by now.

As soon as the earl disappeared up the stairs, Roland eased down onto the bench across the trestle table from Simon.

"You are about to be set free, Sir Simon," he began with a grin, then briefly told the steward about the trackers' report and Kenworth's decision to leave.

Simon took a long drag of his ale, then set the mug down with a flourish. "Praise be the saints. Within the hour, you say? Good tidings, indeed!"

So where was Eloise so he could watch her face light up with joy, too?

"Aye, good tidings, though we shall not be able to fling the gates wide for some days. The earl is concerned over someone giving Sir John warning. Still, our situation here improves and for that I praise both the Lord and Fates."

"So shall we all."

A commotion on the stairs interrupted their celebration. Kenworth burst into the hall, followed by Gregory, bearing the earl's clothing chest, and Brother Walter, burdened with a large sack Roland assumed held the cleric's possessions.

While Gregory headed out the doorway, the monk lagged behind with the earl.

"I wish only a moment of her time," Brother Walter grumbled.

"Nonsense," the earl answered. "I doubt Lady Eloise has any interest in whatever you might wish to say. Follow Gregory. He will find you a seat in a cart."

The monk cast an entreating glance Simon's way. Simon pointedly turned his back on the cleric, shunning the monk who'd spied on John Hamelin.

Though curious over the monk's request, Roland didn't interfere. 'Twas best the cleric left without upsetting Eloise.

Kenworth approached the trestle table, and Simon and Roland both stood.

"After we capture Sir John, I may find it necessary to return. I trust I will find all in order."

Roland gave the earl his due—a parting bow—but didn't dip too low. "I trust you will. You will keep me informed of your whereabouts in the event there is need."

Kenworth shrugged, settling the charcoal gray woolen cloak on his shoulders. "Let us both hope there is no need."

The earl strode out of the hall, ignoring everyone he passed, including Timothy, who gave the man a courtly bow in which Roland sensed little reverence.

"Where *is* Lady Eloise?" Roland asked Simon. "She should be told of the earl's leaving."

"I am unsure, but she cannot be far."

Which meant she could be roaming about anywhere.

Roland beckoned to Timothy, who traversed the hall

swiftly. "Find her ladyship. She does not yet know that Kenworth departs."

The squire smiled. "So it is true then? Kenworth goes to chase after Sir John?"

At Roland's affirming nod, the lad's smile widened and he made a dash for the kitchen.

Roland's mood lightened further, until he turned to look at Simon, who thoughtfully took another swig of his ale.

The steward might be pleased about the earl leaving, but he wasn't happy about why. Neither, Roland suspected, would Eloise.

Her heart beating too fast, her breath shallow, Eloise lifted the torch higher, spreading the circle of light far enough to startle yet another rat. The vermin scurried to hide behind a pile of smelly refuse in the dungeon's corner, sending a shiver along her spine.

She'd already searched every storage room and the undercroft, every dark, musty corner of the keep, but found no sign of a hidden passage, no door she hadn't been through at some time in her life. She held little hope of finding a passage down here, either, but she had to look.

The guard behind her grunted his disgust. "What are we doin' down here, milady?"

'Twas the first time he'd spoken to her. Usually he simply followed her around, not questioning her activities, merely observing. Clearly, he thought her touched in the head for coming down into the otherwise unoccupied dungeon.

"'Tis my father's habit to inspect all areas of the

castle once a sennight. In his absence, I intend to do the same."

"Would not spend much time down here, if I was you. Sure 'tain't no place for a lady."

She had to agree, running a quick glance over the manacles bolted to the stone walls, and the huge, menacing rack in the middle of the floor. Not a nice place for anyone to spend time, but then, wasn't that the whole idea behind a dungeon?

Get it done.

Eloise moved forward, searching along the walls, avoiding all thoughts of rats and other lurking vermin. Something cracked beneath her foot. Something round and white. A bone.

She cried out her horror, put a hand to her throat, her imagination taking flight over the ill fate of some poor fellow left to rot—nay, not possible. At least she didn't think so, didn't want to believe her father could be so cruel.

An animal's bone then. The remains of a meal.

The guard smirked, and embarrassment burned on her cheeks. Sweet mercy, she'd scared herself witless for no good reason.

From the head of the stairway she heard her name being called and recognized the voice of Timothy, Roland's squire.

"Down here!"

His footsteps thudded down the stairs. He landed with a bounce and grin. A raucous lad at heart, she thought, with an adorable face that hadn't lost its boyish softness. A likable lad, if only for his particular attitude toward Isolde.

Where outsiders tended either to ignore or pointedly shun the disfigured maid, Timothy made himself both available and agreeable, a tribute to whomever had a hand in shaping his deportment. Roland? Not likely. Probably a woman.

The always mannerly squire sketched her a bow. "You must come up, my lady, bid his lordship Godspeed."

She absorbed his words, but not quite his meaning. "His lordship?"

"William, earl of Kenworth, is readying to depart. 'Twould be a sight worth seeing, methinks."

"Now?"

"If you do not hurry you will miss it."

Eloise shoved the torch into her guard's hands and took the stairs as fast as her legs would carry her. She sped through the hallways until she reached the great hall. Deserted, except for Isolde, who shuffled toward her.

"Did ye hear, milady? The earl departs."

"So Timothy told me. Has he gone already?"

"Might be. All I know is everyone headed for the gates. Ye had best hurry if you wish to watch him go."

Hurry Eloise did, making her way downhill through the inner bailey until she passed into the outer. From the high vantage point she saw the crowd surrounding the earl, his knights, their squires and horses, the carts loaded down with belongings.

She caught a glimpse of Brother Walter, seated on one of the carts already headed toward the rising portcullis. How lovely that the earl took his spy with him.

Oh, glorious day!

But as she rushed forward, gained ground on her

destination, she wondered why everyone didn't share her joy. The crowd was eerily quiet, the only noise that of the departing retinue.

Simon and Marcus scowled. Even Roland looked grim.

She'd allowed her elation to overshadow her common sense, so happy Kenworth was leaving she hadn't given a thought to why.

Had her father been captured?

Dread clutched her innards. Slowing her pace, she looked for signs of her father's presence, or Edgar's. Seeing neither, her dread eased, until she realized that, perhaps, the earl held both in the field beyond the gate.

She eased into the small space between Marcus and Simon, neither man so much as acknowledging her presence, both too intent on Kenworth as he swung up into the saddle. From that great height the earl peered down at Roland.

" 'Tis my fondest wish my first message to you is of our success. If our prey eludes us, then 'twill inform you of my whereabouts should the traitor be so foolish as to return here."

Eloise's knees went weak. Her father hadn't yet been captured.

"Godspeed, my lord," Roland uttered.

Without further comment, Kenworth wheeled his horse and made for the gate, his knights following suit, raising a cloud of dust as the company picked up speed.

Eloise tugged on Marcus's sleeve. "What happened?"

"The trackers found what they believe is Sir John's trail. The earl has decided to follow it."

"Are the trackers right?"

Marcus sighed. "Likely."

Eloise fought the urge to call to the earl, invite him back into the keep, and lavish him with whatever attention he required to keep him contentedly lounging by the hearth. A foolish thought. He'd laugh in her face.

Simon huffed. "If the trail is so clear, then Sir John wanted Kenworth to follow. I would not despair of his lordship's fate yet, my lady."

"Nor should she hold false hope for his freedom," Roland said. "Sir John will eventually have to answer to the charge of treason, whether he is taken prisoner by the earl or whether he turns himself in on his own terms."

Heart heavy, Eloise left the men behind and made her way to the tower stairs and up to the wall walk.

A crisp wind tugged at her garments and blew her veil around, impeding her view of the fields surrounding the castle. She wrapped the sheer white silk around her neck, leaned against the cold, thick stone, and watched the last of Kenworth's knights cross the drawbridge.

Good riddance to them all.

Yet, 'twas such a helpless feeling, knowing her father was out there somewhere and naught she could do might help him. She'd felt a shadow of despair from the moment he'd left her alone and frightened in his accounting room. She'd fought it as best she knew how, tried to banish it with anger.

Now the shadow loomed as an insurmountable wall she could neither batter down nor go around. Tears welled up. She didn't stop them from falling, couldn't have if she tried.

"Godspeed, Father," she whispered, wishing beyond reason he could somehow hear.

He couldn't, of course. Too far away. Too involved in his problems to hear a daughter's voice or heed her worries.

Heavy boots pounding on stone steps alerted her to an intruder. With the heel of her hand she wiped the wetness from her cheeks.

To her dismay, Roland appeared at the top of the stairs.

What did the man want of her now? She wanted to rail at him, send him away with the earl. Except she couldn't trust her voice not to break or her tears not to flow again. Besides, he rarely listened to her anyway.

He might not listen well, but he always seemed to be near during her worst emotional upheavals. Did he sense she'd come up here to be alone until she could control her heartache? Could he know that with the slightest invitation she'd curl into him, cling and cry like a babe? She dared not. 'Twould give him too much advantage, especially now that he had sole rule over Lelleford.

One did not give ground to the enemy.

Unfortunately, thinking of Roland as the enemy became harder each day. She hated his control over her home, but the man, the knight whose power didn't diminish a whit when he chose to be gentle, intrigued her.

He gave her a slight, beguiling smile before he leaned on the wall beside her, their shoulders nearly touching, and bent forward to observe the men-at-arms break camp.

Roland's sheer bulk blocked the bite of the wind, easing the chill, performing a service she doubted he meant to perform. As long as he'd ruined her solitude, she felt no guilt over taking advantage of the bit of shelter he provided.

Below, men scurried to stow their belongings and

tents, take up their arms, and form into marching order. So many men were required to accompany one earl, to capture one man, and they hadn't yet succeeded. Praise be the crops had all been harvested. The field used for the small army's camping ground was now a quagmire.

With the earl at the head, the front of the column began to move like a long, dark snake slithering through the fields—in the opposite direction than she'd expected.

"They go north?"

"Sir John's tracks lead north, to the river and beyond. One of Kenworth's knights suggested he may be headed for Scotland."

Eloise tamped down a twinge of panic. "That is absurd."

He took a long breath, as if summoning patience. "I did not say he does, only that some believe he seeks the protection of a laird. Eloise, no matter what your father's intentions, there is naught we can do to either help or hinder."

So she'd already surmised.

The last of the line rumbled forward, a dozen or more carts loaded down with baggage and provisions. In one of the carts sat Brother Walter, his hooded brown cloak wrapped tightly around him against the chill. She'd never seen a more forlorn figure, but she couldn't deny she was happy to see him go.

"I suppose I should be upset that the earl takes his spy with him. Now we shall never know his secrets. Had I known the full measure of his treachery that first morn, I swear, I would have allowed Marcus to hold a sword to his throat to force him to speak."

"I heard you found him wounded on the accounting-room floor, bleeding and confused."

She was sure her father and the monk had exchanged harsh words, that perhaps during the argument her father had shoved the monk into the desk, even though the cleric assured her his own clumsiness was at fault.

"He refused to tell me how he was injured, refused to reveal what he knew of my father's disappearance. I should have insisted." But she hadn't, and then Kenworth arrived, and between the monk making a dolt of himself and then being ensconced with the earl, she'd barely seen him since.

"He wanted to speak with you before he left. The earl would not allow it. I wonder what changed the monk's mind."

She had no notion. "Did the two of them find anything of import in the accounting room?"

"I have my doubts. 'Twouldn't be like the earl not to gloat if they had."

A small comfort.

"Perhaps there was nothing to find."

Kenworth entered the northern woodlands, and the thick forest soon swallowed him up. Gone. Finally gone. At the edge of her awareness, she heard the squeal of the drawbridge being raised, the portcullis lowered.

Roland backed up half a step, allowing the wind to bite her while he turned to face her. He leaned his hip against the wall, his expression thoughtful. Then he grasped her hand and ran his thumb across the knuckles to brush away a smudge of dirt. The tenderness of the gesture plucked a sweet chord that sang to her soul.

"Timothy tells me he found you in the dungeon. A

wretched place for a high born lady to roam. To what purpose?"

She couldn't tell him what she searched for. "Merely an inspection."

He smiled at that. "So said your guard. I do not think he believed you either. You searched for a hidden passage, did you not?"

How irritating that he guessed her purpose. Reminded of her embarrassment and fright in that horrible place, she answered with silence.

"So I thought." His grip on her hand tightened. "Eloise, you are not the only one who wondered how your father's message was delivered. I know what you were looking for because Marcus and I have searched the keep and walls stone by stone, even the dungeon, and found nothing."

Damn.

"If there is no secret passage, then how?"

"I know not. 'Tis yet a puzzle. Perhaps if we all put our minds to it we can solve it. None of us likes the idea of someone being able to secretly gain entrance."

He again grazed her knuckles with his thumb, an absent, possessive gesture, as if he had the right with no one to gainsay him. She should pull away, put some space between them, for with Kenworth gone Roland was now completely in charge.

Would he prove fair and honorable in carrying out his responsibility? Or would he choose to wield his power forcefully, holding a giant hammer over their heads?

Everyone at Lelleford seemed willing to accept Roland's rule over the holding. Simon and Marcus considered him fair and just. She might balk at the breadth of his authority, but she wanted more of the man.

This attraction to Roland was inexcusable. Yet she reveled in the sensation of her hand cradled in his, yearned to explore the depths of the allure further.

The longer he stayed, the more opportunity to make a fool of herself, or worse. If she followed her impulses, she betrayed her father's trust.

She pulled her hand from his, the warmth immediately giving way to the cold. The shadow threatened to swamp her again. With a will her father would be proud of, she turned her thoughts outward.

"The villagers will be glad to see the gates open again. As soon as they realize the earl has fled, they will flock to the bailey to learn all the news."

"Their curiosity must wait. The gates remain closed for at least two days. 'Twould not do to have one of the knights ride out to overtake and warn your father."

Eloise gritted her teeth. With the earl's leaving, she'd expected a taste of freedom. So quickly Roland had snatched the morsel away.

"So we are still prisoners."

"Two days, Eloise. Surely you can endure for two days."

Chapter Eight

ROLAND THOUGHT it a mean twist of fate that on this third morning after Kenworth's departure, the day dawned with the threat of a downpour. Eloise paced in front of the hearth, her cloak at the ready, eager for release.

She hadn't endured the extended confinement well, not even when he'd given her full freedom of the castle with no guard on her heels.

If only it was the weather that forced him to postpone Eloise's ride to the village. Perhaps then she might not be hurling bolts of lightning his way.

Roland tossed back a chunk of bread and tried to concentrate on his morning meal, not watching Eloise stew.

Impossible. The woman was magnificent in her pique—mouth pinched, hands clasped behind her back, her impatient strides long and graceful.

She shot him another scathing bolt, singeing him clear through. 'Twas all he could do to not squirm in his seat.

"This is absurd, Roland. I assure you there is not a band of ruffians anywhere near Lelleford. No scoundrel would dare intrude on my father's lands."

Judging by what he knew of Sir John Hamelin's fervor

in protecting his holding, she was probably right. The area was regularly patrolled and villains dealt with in swift, harsh fashion. Roland intended to carry on in the same mien.

"The patrols should return soon, and the moment Simon and Marcus assure me no bandits lurk on the road, you can go."

"How much longer might that be?"

"However long it takes."

She aimed for a stool near the hearth and sat down with a huff. "If they do not hurry, I shall have to worry more about being drenched than attacked."

"Then perhaps you should delay your trip to the village until after the rain has ended."

The suggestion earned him a baleful look.

Roland gathered his patience. "The village will be there this noon as well."

"Aye, it will. But the villagers have been denied entry to the keep for several days. That has never happened before, and I am sure some of them suffered hardships, or are frightened. They depend upon us for protection and in some cases for their livelihood. 'Tis best I show myself as soon as is possible, reassure them their well-being will not be adversely affected by my father's troubles."

Roland knew Marcus intended to ride through the village, a sign to all that despite their lord's troubles, life would return to near normalcy. He also knew that a visit from their lord's daughter would do wonders to calm the peasants' unease.

Still, he knew better than to think her haste completely due to her concern for the villagers.

"You also itch to get back on a horse."

"Certes. I like to ride as much as you do."

They'd discovered the common delight in the days before Hugh's death. Roland remembered seeing Eloise go into the stable, and thinking it a good time to get to know his brother's bride better, he'd followed her inside.

They'd traded tales of enjoyable hunts, of near misses when jumping logs and long rides on peaceful paths. He went in curious and came out enchanted—and absolutely sure Eloise Hamelin an unsuitable wife for his meek half brother.

He now wished, for several reasons, he'd kept his curiosity to himself, never come to know the woman nor decided to make his observation known to Hugh.

"Do you still ride the chestnut mare?"

Her expression softened slightly. "Aye. Despite her age she is yet eager for a brisk ride, though of necessity not as fast and shorter than of old. And you, the black stallion?"

"Not the same one. He fell in Scotland."

"Oh, how sad. In battle?"

"Aye. Valiant to the end."

Roland had mourned the loss of a wondrous horse, but admitted the loss softened by the steed's replacement. A magnificent young black with impeccable bloodlines and impressive stamina. A gift from a grateful king.

Timothy leaned over Roland's shoulder to pour more ale into the goblet. "More bread or cheese, milord?"

"Nay, nothing more."

"If you have no further need of me, I am off to the practice yard."

As far as Roland knew, most of the knights and squires

were out roaming the countryside, ensuring Lelleford's security.

"Against whom do you practice?"

"Until the others return, I will content myself with quintain and lance."

Roland thought it odd his squire would take to the yard alone to challenge the quintain, but wouldn't question the lad's diligence in honing a skill at which he was becoming quite proficient.

"Go then. Keep the point up."

A smile spread across the squire's face. "I shall strive to keep my seat, too. By your leave, milord."

Timothy left, and Roland noted that the hall was beginning to empty. Most of the castle folk had finished with their meal and were setting about their daily tasks.

Roland wished he had set tasks to perform.

As he'd hoped everyone fell back into their daily habits with little fuss and no direction needed on his part. That was good.

Except their self-reliance also spawned boredom, which made him restless. Not overly, but there were times he hunted up tasks to keep himself busy—so he wouldn't be tempted to happen across Eloise's path, just to see where she was and what she was doing. So he wouldn't ask her some inane question just to hear the sound of her voice.

Perhaps he should join Timothy in the tiltyard.

The opening door spared him the decision. Simon walked in, removing his mist-sheened cloak.

Eloise immediately rose. "What news?"

The steward bowed slightly. "We seem to have weathered the upheaval in good order, my lady. We found nothing out of the ordinary. I expect Marcus will report the same."

She spun to face Roland. "Now may I go?"

He shook his head. "Marcus searches the area around the village. We await his report."

Flinging her hands in the air, she rolled her eyes and plopped back down on the stool, her exasperation acute.

He tried not to smile, noticed Simon doing the same.

'Twasn't odd, he supposed, that on occasion Simon and Marcus reacted to some comment or action of Eloise's like tolerant uncles. They adored her, would protect her with their lives without any order or hesitation. Eloise returned their devotion, turning to them for advice, seeking their company of an eve.

He often joined them, knowing he was accepted, but still felt the outsider.

Probably best that way. He might have temporary control over Lelleford, but someday either Sir John would return to his holding or the king would give it to another lord. Either way, Roland would have to relinquish control.

How soon that day arrived depended upon the outcome of John's capture and trial. Since Roland hadn't yet received word from either the earl or the king, he had no idea how events progressed.

Eloise sat with her arms crossed, her toe tapping on the stone floor set before the massive hearth.

Simon joined him at the trestle table, looking happier for his escape from the keep.

The steward leaned forward and whispered, "Truly, Roland, I do not believe there is any danger this morn.

Besides, you intend to send an escort with her, do you not?"

Tap. Tap. Tap.

Roland answered in kind. "Aye. We cannot allow her outside the walls unprotected. Any unscrupulous lout who might think to seize Sir John's lands would have too much of an advantage should he capture and force a marriage upon Hamelin's daughter. Will she balk at an escort?"

"Not if she realizes the necessity, I think."

Tap. Tap. Tap.

Roland tossed back the last of his ale and got up.

"Come along, Eloise, before you dent that stone."

Her eyes narrowed. "Where do we go?"

"To the village. That is what you wanted, is it not?"

She shot off the stool. "Aye, but . . . I see no reason for you to accompany me."

"Your father has enemies. Should one of them seize you we would have the devil's own time getting you back. You must give me your word not to go outside the gate without escort."

She bit her bottom lip, the implications of her possible seizure and the sense of his order taking hold.

"You have my word."

He believed her. Eloise was an intelligent as well as beautiful woman who recognized the danger to her as well as to her father's holding. He didn't want to worry her, but he didn't want her taking unnecessary risks, either.

"Let us go, then," he said with a smile, eager to escape the walls himself. "You can admire my new stallion."

She flung on her cloak as they hurried out of the hall. Amusement lit her eyes.

"Is he so grand?"

A grander horse than he'd ever hoped for, a warhorse bred for the king's stables. "Judge for yourself."

They entered the outer bailey, and Roland glanced toward the tiltyard. Timothy no longer had the field to himself.

One by one the squires who'd returned with Simon gripped lances tight against their sides and charged the quintain. Most of them hit the target square and true, making the pass without getting knocked from their saddles—to the delight of the group of females who'd gathered to watch and cheer.

Roland's steps slowed as Timothy set his lance. The lad usually gave a good account of himself, and this time proved no different. With a flourish, he made his pass, wheeling his horse at the end of the run to accept the accolades of the maids.

Roland couldn't help a burst of laughter. "No wonder Timothy could hardly wait to leave the hall."

"And Isolde said she had errands to attend. I wonder which task led her to the tiltyard." Eloise sighed. "'Tis grand to hear joyful sounds in the bailey again."

Roland agreed. In silence they stood and watched the young people, the males showing off their talent and prowess to the delight of giddy, appreciative females. It soon became apparent to which female Timothy made his lowest bow, and for whom Isolde cheered the loudest.

The unease Roland exchanged with Eloise didn't need verbal expression. His squire, her maid. Both young but of an age to know their own minds—and bodies.

"Isolde is but ten and four. Should I be concerned for her?" Eloise asked.

At ten and six, Timothy was a good lad, but doubtless suffered the raging urges of young males everywhere. Normally, Roland wouldn't give a thought to whether or not his squire was tupping a willing maid. However, Isolde's maimed foot prevented her from fleeing unwanted advances, thus leaving her more vulnerable than most.

Nor was her brother, Edgar, here to defend her honor if warranted. Had Timothy taken on that duty? He may have, given the lad's concerns for her the other day.

"If they enjoy each other's company, I see no reason to interfere. However, if you sense a need for concern, tell me and I will speak with Timothy."

She regarded him with a mixture of gratitude and an emotion he couldn't quite define. Surprise, perhaps? But before he could study the depths of her sapphire eyes further, she moved off toward the stable, eager to complete her errand.

Along the way, Roland hailed two men-at-arms—one of Kenworth's men assigned to him and one a soldier of Lelleford. With the aid of the stable boys the four of them readied horses and were soon on their way.

Eloise sat a horse with the ease of a highborn woman trained from early youth and handled the reins with the skill of a man. Roland led the party over the drawbridge, too aware of what a fine figure Eloise presented on horseback, even when covered up with a fur-lined cloak.

"A faster pace, if you please," she called out. "Your fine stallion looks quite capable of speed."

Not a complaint, merely a cheerfully given request.

Roland glanced up at the darkening, thickening clouds, and decided to grant it.

"You lead, then, so I will not have to worry whether you keep pace."

With a most unladylike snort, Eloise gave her mare a sharp kick and bolted past him. He caught up easily, noted her smug expression, and rode at her side until she slowed when they neared the village.

Cotter's huts, built of timber and roofed with thatch, circled the village green and common well. The gardens, which not two months ago flourished with vegetables and flowers, had been stripped. Cattle and fowl were now allowed to nibble at what little greenery remained.

With the harvest in, the tenants tended to chores suited to the season. They added thatch to roofs, mended latches and fences, chopped firewood gathered from the nearby forest.

They labored to ready for the hardships of a long, cold winter.

Noticing Eloise, the children scampered into the road and gleefully called out her name. With so many little ones descending on them, the company came to a halt.

"Have a care, there! I should hate to have you squashed like a bug!" Eloise's laughter mingled with the sharp command, belying any harshness.

He'd never heard her laugh before, not like this, without restraint. Her happiness wove a spell around him and for a moment he forgot where he was and why he accompanied Eloise, just enjoyed the sight of a beautiful woman whose deep-throated, merry laughter rang through the green.

Eloise dismounted and greeted each child by name.

Some she blessed with a quick tousle of hair, others received a brief hug. One particular little urchin pulled on her skirts until she picked him up and held him close for several long moments.

'Twas a side of her he'd not seen before, warm and loving, and the sight tugged at his innards.

She poured affection on the children, yet she retained all the dignity of her rank, that regal bearing that set her apart and above the peasants.

The children's squeals of glee alerted their parents, who left their work to attend their lady. Naturally, Eloise again knew every name, asked after those she'd known were ill, inquired into the state of affairs in the village. Even as she exchanged pleasantries and information, she smiled brightly, bestowing her sincere interest upon those she cared for.

Inevitably, a man stepped forward, his brow scrunched. "Is it true, milady? His lordship is accused of treason?"

Her wide smile diminished only slightly.

"Can you imagine a more ridiculous notion? Of all the men in this kingdom, no one serves Edward better than my father. Have you not all heard him expound on the king's many virtues?" She paused, waiting until here and there men nodded before continuing. "Does Sir John Hamelin not serve his forty days' knight's service himself instead of paying scutage as so many lords do these days?"

This time the agreement came more readily.

"That he does, milady."

"Takes his duty serious, does Sir John."

"I should say he does," she declared. "Whoever makes

this absurd charge shall soon realize his mistake, I assure you. Have no fear. My father will be proved innocent." With the aid of the village green's mounting block, she swung back up on her horse, then waved a hand his way. "This is Sir Roland St. Marten. Many of you will remember him."

Again the nods, and Roland felt the weight of their stares. He didn't recognize a single villager's face, but they'd obviously observed and remembered him from his previous visit.

"Sir Roland and his men augment our guard in my father's absence. So you see, we are well prepared for any untoward event. You need not fear for your lives or livelihood. All will be well."

It took him a moment to realize she'd minimized his position as Lelleford's overseer, giving the villagers the impression he was no more than an extra sword in case of trouble.

How dare she?

He rode up beside her, leaning over so only she could hear. "I do more than augment the guard, milady. Should you not tell them the truth?"

She arched an eyebrow. "Do not your soldiers perform the same service as Lelleford's guards?"

"Aye, but—"

"And are you not their commander?"

"You know I am."

"Well then, I told no lies, did I? Come, let us get out of the rain."

Before he could answer, Eloise flipped up the hood of her cloak against the increasing drizzle, shutting him out of her line of sight.

An effective battle maneuver, a swift strike and hasty retreat, meant to throw an enemy off balance.

The minx! So, that was how she intended to carry on, was it? Fine with him. She'd soon learn he didn't unbalance easily.

For the next few moments, Eloise bid the villagers fare-thee-well, releasing them to seek shelter from the rain. When she finally turned back to him, 'twas with a look of such innocence he had to wonder if he'd imagined it all.

"Ready to return?" she asked, and Roland had to shake off his momentary confusion.

If they made a quick dash back to the castle, Roland reasoned, they might escape a wetting.

As they'd ridden into the village, he'd deliberately avoided looking at the neat stone church, but the site of Hugh's death refused denial.

Grief hit him hard, memories of that day unfolding in vivid color and minute detail.

He could see Hugh standing on the steps, resplendent in wedding garb, happy and proud, facing Eloise, clasping her hands.

The day had been warm, the sunshine bright, and the groom unaware of all except his beautiful bride, whose honor and suitability he'd defended to a meddlesome half brother not an hour before.

Hugh had neither spoken to nor looked at Roland since. He'd died angry at the half brother who'd dared voice concern over the wisdom of the marriage.

As if sensing his painful thoughts, Eloise said softly, "I still cannot pass the church without remembering."

Roland again experienced the shock of watching Hugh

grasp his chest, his face twist in agony, his body crumple onto the stone stair.

"I thought I left my grief behind at his tomb." He heard the strain in his voice, and cleared his throat to banish the tension and threat of tears.

She looked at him with soulful eyes. "That must have been awful for you, laying to rest a sibling you cared for so deeply. Both of my brothers are alive and well as far as I know. I would be desolate if I lost either of them, or my sister."

She hadn't experienced desolation at Hugh's death, hadn't even been sad enough to shed a single tear that he knew of.

"You did not love Hugh as he deserved."

She blinked at the harshly delivered accusation. "I admit I did not love Hugh. We were allowed but two days to become acquainted, and mere hours to speak alone. All in all, I thought him a kind and gentle man. Honorable."

An apt description of Hugh. Many people had loved him, but respect was another matter.

Hugh might have been lovable, but he wasn't a strong leader. He'd tried to please everyone and ended up satisfying few. As a result, people took advantage of him.

Without a doubt, Hugh would have become lost in Eloise's shadow, giving in to her every whim.

"Hugh loved you from the moment he first saw you."

She smiled sadly. "So he said. I did not believe his chivalric declarations, of course. No one gives another their heart so quickly. He uttered sweet words to impress his betrothed, no more."

Didn't Eloise know Hugh had fallen deep and hard, become fully enamored? Roland could yet see his half brother's eyes glaze in besotted wonder while he expounded on his bride's beauty and charm. Men had fought for, even died for, the attentions of such a woman.

"You are a beautiful woman, Eloise. I have no doubt most men find you attractive and alluring upon first glance. Why do you doubt Hugh admired and desired you above all others?"

Eloise went very still, and though her cloak's hood shadowed her face, he would swear she blushed. Because he'd called her beautiful? Surely, she'd been told so before. She must realize her face and form placed her among the most desirable women in the kingdom.

"If a comely face is all that is required to engage a man's affection, then you are all fools," she fervently declared.

He admitted he'd seen men make utter fools of themselves over a woman, but so was the reverse true. He'd witnessed members of the fair sex, from lusty kitchen maids to ardent noblewomen, go to wanton lengths to attract the attention of a handsome male. When attraction sparked desire, people's good sense could run amok.

"Are women so different? Are you not first attracted to the cut of a man's face, the breadth of his shoulders?"

In that brazen manner he'd warned Hugh against, she blatantly assessed his face, skimmed over his shoulders, her inspection finally ending where his thighs tightened more snugly on his mount. A shameless perusal that heated his loins.

"I do not deny that one finds a handsome male enjoyable to look upon. You have a fine-featured face, a well-honed form. I do not doubt many women have been drawn to you because of your looks. That does not mean any one of them gifted you with her heart." She tugged on the reins, and her mare immediately backed up. "Love runs deeper than the desire to possess an appealing bauble. Or at least it should."

She set her mare to the path just as the rain began to fall in earnest. Roland tipped his face upward, grateful for the cold and wet. Perhaps, by the time they returned to the castle he'd have his natural male response to a female's appreciation back under control.

An appealing bauble, was he?

He couldn't deny his physical attraction to Eloise Hamelin. He'd once tried to keep his reaction to her firmly under control, knowing she was to be Hugh's wife. He still couldn't allow himself to pursue her, no matter how much the thought appealed.

She'd come within words of being his sister-by-marriage. She was the daughter of a man accused of treason, and so poison to a man hoping to better his position. And if the charges resolved in Sir John's favor, she'd again be destined to marry a man of higher rank and wealth than Roland St. Marten.

A lost cause. Untouchable.

A woman whose delectable body his hands fair itched to touch and arouse. Whose long delicate fingers he yearned to have pressed against his own arousal. Into whose depths, under other circumstances, he might eagerly plummet if given a sliver of encouragement.

After a last glance at the church, Roland nudged his stallion forward, the ache in his private parts acute, the pain in his heart worse, his guilt nearly overwhelming.

He craved a woman he couldn't have, shouldn't want—and may have badly misjudged. Perhaps Eloise was right. Maybe all men were fools when it came to women.

Eloise stepped into the accounting room where Simon sat at the large oak desk, making notations in a narrow ledger—sheaves of vellum bound with leather.

He looked up when he heard her. "My lady?"

She heard the greeting, but couldn't stop staring at the blood staining the planks at the side of the desk. Brother Walter's blood. 'Twould take a strong potion and many scrubbings to bleach it out.

She could still see the cleric lying there, motionless, hear her father's angry voice fill the room.

And now both men were gone and she still didn't know what had happened between them.

Feeling more deserted than she knew was warranted, she focused on the present and why she'd sought out Simon.

"Have you found anything amiss in here?"

Simon waved the feather quill. "Nay, everything seems in order. The ledgers, your father's deeds and documents, all are here. If the earl found something of value to his cause, he took it with him."

"Roland thinks the earl would have gloated had he come across anything to aid his cause."

Simon gave a slight nod. "A good assumption, though we cannot be sure."

Eloise debated whether or not to tell Simon of the scrolls her father had taken with him. How much did she yet need to keep secret, and from whom?

Her father's knights were loyal to their lord, but could

that loyalty be shaken if told Sir John might have taken damaging evidence with him?

"Simon, you have served my father since before I was born, been his trusted steward for many years. Of us all, you may know him best. I ask you, can there be any truth at all to the charges?"

His expression turned stormy. She held up a hand to stave off a quick denial.

"Think a moment. His position puts him in contact with many people of many beliefs. Perhaps while at court or during his travels to his other estates, could someone have led him into a situation which could be misunderstood? Or, more to my father's nature, could he have become involved in a scheme to make a profit or further his position in court and the plan went astray?"

She didn't like the expression on Simon's face. Both of them knew that when there was profit to be made, her father could disregard a law as a minor inconvenience if he thought he could get around it.

"'Tis a difficult question to answer, my lady." He waved a hand around the room. "Nothing here gives the least hint one way or the other, and I swear to you, I knew of no schemes. His lordship may nudge the illegal, but to commit treason . . . I am at a loss."

So until she talked to her father—whenever that might be—she still could neither acquit nor condemn him.

Eloise took a mind-clearing breath and turned her thoughts to the other, more urgent matter on which she needed Simon's advice.

"Have you seen the proof of Roland's authority over Lelleford?"

He looked taken aback. "To what purpose?"

That's what she'd thought. Simon and Marcus had taken Roland at his word.

"Roland claims to possess a royal writ granting his authority, which he was to present to my father. In my father's absence, should not we demand Roland produce it?"

After a moment's thought, Simon set aside his quill. "I trust St. Marten's word. He would not make a false claim."

Simon's unconditional faith set her teeth on edge.

"Merely because he is a knight?"

"Because I know him to be an honorable man." He tilted his head. "As I believe you do, too. Why is it, my lady, that you set yourself against him?"

Because I want him gone.

Because she feared what might happen if he was allowed to stay. She saw the flashes of desire in his eyes and responded too readily.

And, damn, she was beginning to like the man. 'Twas becoming nigh impossible to hold herself against him when by action and deed he proved himself other than what she wanted him to be. She didn't question his honor, not after he'd offered to speak to Timothy if she thought it necessary . . . what other knight would be concerned over a maid's well-being at the hands of his squire? Especially a disfigured maid whose only male relative was in the company of a man suspected of treason.

And at the church, she'd wanted to throw her arms around him, comfort him. Some of his words may have been harsh, but she understood the grief that prompted them, and was far too willing to forgive him the lapse of courtesy.

If she could send him away, she wouldn't have to deal with him anymore. He battered at her defenses, and she grasped at what might be her last chance to raise a shield. "If my father were here he would demand to see the king's writ. I simply believe we should do the same."

Simon studied her intently for a moment, then gave her a soft smile, one she recognized as lovingly tolerant. "Then you should make your demand, my lady, and pay no heed to my foolish concern."

So she intended, just as soon as she saw Roland again.

Chapter Nine

ROLAND HESITATED to enter the great hall, which Eloise had transformed into a grand sewing room.

Lengths of fabric in a variety of colors draped across numerous trestle tables, each table attended by females with scissors in hand.

Eloise glided through the organized chaos, a general among the troops, completely comfortable with her command. She moved from table to table and inspected each piece of fabric. Her brow furrowed as she considered her decisions, then eased when, satisfied, she told the maids in precise detail how she expected the cloth cut.

Though he couldn't catch her every word, he heard enough to learn most of the fabric would soon be tunics for Sir John, the rest made into gowns for Eloise.

Roland eased up to Isolde, who oversaw the table used to sort the finer threads for sewing and various yarns used to embroider decorative hems and necklines.

"What goes on here?"

She cocked an eyebrow, as if she thought him daft for not recognizing the obvious. "My lord?"

"'Tis obvious you make garments, but so many at once?"

"Ah," she said, his confusion now clear. "Lady Eloise wishes the garments finished well ahead of Christmas court, so we do them now."

Garments that might never be worn if Sir John spent the season in a judicial court instead of in the king's lavish court. Still Eloise strove to carry on as if nothing untoward stood in the way of the original plan to spend the holiday in the gracious surroundings of the nobles and the palace.

Eloise now stood at the head of a nearby table, peering down at a length of sapphire blue so bright and true it rivaled the color of her eyes.

He envisioned her draped in it, the soft wool wrapped in luxurious folds over her ample curves, tucked and snugged in all the right places.

But then, there wasn't a wrong place on the woman's perfect form. And damn, he could also see himself tugging at laces, unfolding her, revealing what soft loveliness lay beneath the as-yet-unmade gown.

Her expression wistful, she picked up a corner of the cloth and sampled the texture between her thumb and forefinger, the simple action so sensual he could hardly breathe.

She put the fabric down and turned to the maid with the scissors. "A tunic for his lordship. The hem should be trimmed in gold braid—"

"A waste."

Her surprise at his interruption matched his shock that he'd spoken his reaction aloud. Without words she made it quite clear she expected him to explain his unusual outburst. He should walk away, not interfere with what was none of his business.

"The color matches your eyes. 'Twould be a waste to make that fabric up into anything but a gown for you."

The slight quirk of her mouth told him he'd pleased or at least amused her. Once again she looked down at the fabric, her longing for it still apparent. She lightly stroked the wool, her fingertips causing nary a ripple in the fabric, causing a slow melt in his innards, imagining those same fingertips stroking his skin.

"'Tis the most costly and beautiful of the lot, so should therefore go to the one who pays for it."

He gathered his unraveling composure. "Your father did not strike me as a vain man. Besides, think of the pride he would feel when presenting his lovely, richly garbed daughter to the court."

She peeked up at him through dark, lush lashes. "Think you?"

She couldn't possibly be questioning her loveliness, so he assumed she questioned the matter of pride. Not that Sir John would likely be in a position to present her to court this Christmas. Still, he could envision Eloise on her father's arm, floating into Westminster Palace's grand hall and making her curtsy to the king. She'd turn the head and heat the loins of every man present.

A flash of unwarranted possessiveness, bordering on jealousy, almost made him retreat. He had no right to her, never would. 'Twas inevitable some other man would someday possess Eloise Hamelin, no matter how much that bothered him.

"I do."

"Sir Roland is right, milady." Isolde came up beside him. "If styled as is your crimson velvet, 'twould be most becoming."

'Twould be utterly stunning.

Eloise apparently thought so, too, for her sapphire eyes widened and sparkled. "Oh, my, Isolde. What a wonderful idea." With a flip of her hand, she relented. "So be it then. For me, in the style of the crimson velvet. Oversee the cutting, Isolde, so it is done correctly."

Isolde moved closer to the table, and Eloise came toward him, her smile widening with each step. His pulse picked up as it did every time she got too near, and for the life of him, he couldn't move away, give himself a chance to break her maddening spell over him.

She stopped but a few feet before him, close enough to reach out and touch. He crossed his arms and made sure his feet were planted firmly on the rushes.

"I suppose I should give you thanks," she said, just above a whisper. With a conspiratorial wink, she added, "I must admit, I sought the merest excuse to have the blue made into a gown. 'Tis a wondrous color, and so soft to the touch."

Courtly manners came to his rescue. "Delighted to be of service, my lady. Now, if you will beg pardon, I must—"

Her fingertips landed on his arm, stopping him cold.

"A word first, if you please?"

His plan for retreat thwarted, he nodded his agreement.

She withdrew her hand and glanced about the hall. "Over there, where we will not be overheard."

Curiosity pricked, he followed her to an alcove not far from the stairs. Her smile had faded, and he mourned the loss.

"Is aught amiss?"

She rubbed her hands together, a small action he'd noticed every time she appeared nervous or upset. "I believe not, but Simon and I agree that we should be sure." She glanced away briefly, the merest flicker of uncertainty that she quickly overcame. "When you arrived, you said you carried a writ from the king to present to my father, giving you authority over Lelleford in his absence. We have been lax in not asking to see it."

A perfectly reasonable request. So why did it feel as if this was just one more attempt on her part to discredit him?

"You talked this over with Simon?"

"He agreed that in my father's absence, one of us should see the writ."

"And that someone should be you."

She tilted her head. "Or Simon, if you prefer."

Perhaps he was taking offense for no reason. He'd been ordered to give the writ to Sir John. Except Sir John wasn't here. Eloise was only looking out for her father's interests, and he couldn't truly fault her for it.

"Can you read the writ?"

"I am not unlettered. I have a fair command of both French and Latin."

"Then come along."

Surprised that he gave her no further argument, Eloise followed Roland up the winding stairs, with nowhere to look but at the sway of his backside, the play of muscles in his lower legs.

Right after their confrontation at the church, she'd vowed she would never again notice his handsome face and powerful shoulders. Heat bloomed on her cheeks at the realization of which part of his body she admired now. Parts of the male body she'd never dreamed of admiring on any man.

Roland was a sight to behold, from front or back, and 'twas impossible not to appreciate the quality of his form.

At the top of the stairs he turned right, leading the way to the chamber he occupied. It had belonged to her brothers, neither of whom had seen fit to occupy it for many a month.

She glanced around at the familiar furnishings. Two beds, Julius's draped in blue, Geoffrey's in green. An oak table flanked by two chairs, a chessboard in the center, the pieces arranged for a game.

Only Julius's clothing trunk sat beneath the shuttered window, awaiting his return from Italy, whenever that might be. Not long ago she'd packed all of Geoffrey's belongings into his trunk and taken it with her to Cornwall when attending his marriage to Leah. Well, almost all of his belongings.

While Roland pulled a large sack from beneath the bed, Eloise crossed to the mantel and picked up her favorite of the winsome carvings she hadn't been able to part with. The fat toad sat back on his hind legs, the look on his face one of immense satisfaction, as if he'd just swallowed the biggest, juiciest bug in the pond for his supper.

Geoffrey had carved it to make her smile, and its magic took hold of her now. She closed her hand around the smooth wood, wishing its carver were here to bear part of the burden of dealing with her father's troubles. Why her father hadn't wanted Geoffrey, with his knowledge of the law, to come to his aid, Eloise couldn't fathom.

"I am told Geoffrey carved those," Roland said. "A useful talent for a man to have."

"Selling his carvings kept Geoffrey from starving while he was in Paris." She put the toad back on the mantel, knowing that if her brother hadn't been able to sell his carvings to pay for his schooling, food, and shelter, he might have come home years sooner, and so saved them both worry and grief. But those bad times were over now, and not worth thinking about. "These are but a sample of his talent. The horses in my father's chamber are magnificent."

"You will have to show them to me sometime."

He sounded sincere, so perhaps she would.

Roland held out a scroll, bright red wax sealing it shut. "The writ."

She took it, but didn't break it open. The king's seal was imprinted in the wax, proof enough for her that Roland had told the truth, that she'd lost. Roland St. Marten had been granted authority over Lelleford, and he'd be staying for however long it took for her father's fate to be decided. And there wasn't anything she could do to send him away.

A pox on the king for sending Roland her way! Why the one man who set her insides aflutter with no effort on his part? Why the knight with a warrior's build and courtly manners that she couldn't avoid admiring? Why Roland St. Marten, who'd warned his brother that she was too brazen and strong-willed to make a good wife?

What he wanted for his brother, Roland likely wanted for himself, a woman meek and gentle, which Eloise knew was beyond her.

Oh, Roland wanted her. Sometimes when he looked at

her, she could see the embers smolder, feel his lust. They could easily become lovers the pull was so strong. Too strong.

"How did you come to be in royal service?"

He tilted his head and his eyes narrowed, making her realize she'd taken him off guard again. As always, he recovered swiftly.

"I was in the wrong place at the right time. Sometimes a battle takes a turn no one expects. I found myself guarding Edward's back, and for the service gained a reward I am not sure I deserved."

"He took you into his service."

"Took me to court, gave me new armor, horses, and a squire."

Eloise knew how royal favor worked. For good service a knight in royal service could rise high and amass a fortune quickly.

"No land?"

"Not as yet."

She looked down at the king's seal, then back at Roland, a shiver slithering down her spine.

"Is that what you hope to gain here? Land? Lelleford?"

He gave her a wry smile. "Nay, my lady, nothing so grand as Lelleford. I hope for no more than a small manor with enough income to support my knighthood. My service here warrants no more."

That eased her mind, somewhat. There were other ways kings tended to reward those who'd proved their loyalty.

"Perhaps Edward will grant you an heiress."

He shrugged a shoulder. "One never knows what form the king's generosity will take."

He would take whatever favor Edward granted, be grateful for it, then strive to add to his wealth.

And wasn't that the way of the world? Some men were born to inherit, others had to earn their way or marry well.

Roland had chosen to earn what came his way, and she couldn't fault him for his ambition, a trait that ran strong in the males in her family. She just wished he'd been given some other task to perform to prove his worthiness.

"Do you intend to read the writ?"

His question brought her back to her purpose.

"Nay. There is no need. I recognize the king's seal. I trust the document gives you authority over Lelleford, as you said it does." She put the scroll down next to the chess pieces. "I will put it with my father's documents, of course. He will want to see it . . . someday."

"Well, well. The lady relents. I had thought I would not live to see the day."

"I am sure I do not know what you mean."

"Yes, you do. You had hoped I could not produce the writ, thus giving you an excuse to demand I leave. Admit it, Eloise. You must now finally accept what you cannot change."

She took a long breath. Admittance came hard, not liking that he'd seen through her scheme. Not only was he braw and nicely mannered, but intelligent as well. A lethal combination.

"Had the earl marched into your home to arrest your father and put a stranger in charge of all of the St. Marten's holdings, how would you have felt?"

"No doubt the same as you." He ran a hand through his raven hair, a flash of ire lit his hazel eyes. "I would be livid, disbelieving, and rebellious, defending my father with my last breath and with my sword if need be."

"Would that I could wield a sword!"

He smiled at her heartfelt wish. Unfortunately, not only couldn't she heft a blade, she'd been ordered to allow the earl to breech the gates without a fight.

"You would make a fierce opponent, Eloise Hamelin."

"A compliment, Sir Roland?"

He held out his hand in the style men used to seal bargains.

"A truce, my lady?"

She stared at his hand. "You ask much."

"I do not ask for your surrender, only that you no longer fight me at every turn. Truly, Eloise, I mean you and yours no harm."

Except he'd already wrought havoc. With her nicely patterned life. With her beliefs about duty. With her senses.

Mostly with her senses. She hadn't touched him yet and already she felt tingly all over from the prospect.

Unable to resist, she placed her hand in his firm grasp, and withstood the heat that shimmered through her whole being.

"Mon Dieu."

Several heartbeats later, he admitted in a low whisper, "I know, I feel it, too."

She looked up into hazel eyes darkened with desire. Did he truly feel the same sensations, as if her blood turned hot and sluggish?

"This should not be."

"The attraction between us is there, whether we will it so or not."

"But you do not like me."

He looked genuinely confused. "I never said so."

"You told Hugh I was too brazen, unfit for . . ."

What she couldn't utter aloud, he did.

"Unfit as Hugh's wife. Though I regret the way I told him, and that you were hurt by my words, I still believe so. You may have been a poor match for Hugh, but for another man . . ." He took a step forward, narrowing the space between them, and gently brushed a finger along her chin. "For another, less meek man, you might be . . . perfect."

She closed her eyes and swallowed hard, gripping his hand tighter in a vain attempt to keep her mind balanced—and it wasn't working.

"A man like you?"

"I would never presume."

One of them should pull away, end this most improper encounter. So her common sense told her. Her body, however, leaned toward his, remembering the last time she'd been sure he wanted to kiss her and found the will to withdraw.

"But you want to presume."

"What I want is of no import. I was sent here to ensure the well-being of Lelleford and its people, including you."

His duty be damned!

"I am not fragile, Roland. I assure you I am most capable of taking care of myself."

For that she earned another stroke under her chin, a light touch that nearly melted her knees.

"Not fragile, but vulnerable. 'Twould be knavish of me to take advantage."

"Then what do we do, Roland? You said yourself the attraction is there. Do we pretend it does not exist? Seems to me we have tried and failed."

His hand cupped her cheek, a battle playing out on his rugged features. "You tempt me beyond reason, woman."

"No more than you tempt me."

His wry smile returned before his forehead pressed against hers, his breath warm on her face. "Have you ever been kissed, Eloise?"

"A time or two."

"By Hugh?"

"Nay."

Then his mouth slid over hers, gentle and moist, making her head go light and her nether regions burn. With eyes closed, she rushed headlong into unfamiliar territory and reveled in the sensations that both frightened and thrilled her.

She'd lied to him. She'd never been *kissed,* not like this.

He tasted of ale, smelled of wool and hearth smoke, and the scent that was uniquely Roland's.

She felt him pull back, ending the too-short but stunning kiss.

"Ah, Eloise, what have I done?"

His remorse was almost more than she could bear. Hadn't he been swept into a dreamland, too? Perhaps she needed more practice at the art. Another kiss, maybe two, and she could take him with her.

"You did very well, by my measure. Apparently I did not. Shall we try it again?"

"Nay." He took a long breath, glanced up at the overhead beams. "Oh, my lady, nay."

"Why ever not? I know I lack skill, but I can learn."

He shook his head, as if he couldn't believe what she asked of him. "Is that what you think, that you lack skill? Sweet mercy, Eloise. One more kiss like the last and I would forget who we are and . . ."

Abruptly, he stepped back, kissed the back of her hand that he'd held all the while, then released it. "I have to go."

"But, Roland—"

"*One* of us has to be sensible."

He backed up without looking, bumped into the partially open door and sent it crashing fully open. With a vile curse he spun on his heel and fled.

Shaken, Eloise lowered onto one of the nearby chairs, her hands trembling and her heart fluttering. After a moment, her muddled thoughts cleared, envisioning those last few moments in a new light.

Roland hadn't left because she displeased him, but because he'd liked the kiss as much if not more than she. He'd been so rattled that the graceful, surefooted warrior had actually bumped into a door.

She put her fingertips to her lips, felt the soft smile on her still warm mouth.

By the saints, she shouldn't feel smug about his imbalance. 'Twas a loathsome thing to take pleasure in his misery.

She glanced at her brothers' beds, wondering which one Roland slept in. Probably Julius's, under which he kept his belongings.

Roland's thoughts must have wandered far beyond a

simple kiss, to what seemed to come naturally after—if the talk she'd heard among the female servants was to be believed.

To coupling. Joining bodies. Becoming lovers.

What kind of lover would Roland be?

According to gossip, some lovers were tender and slow, others rough and quick. Some women declared the act messy, others thought it wondrous.

'Twas utterly wicked of her that she desperately wanted Roland to return, throw the latch on the door, and take her to even more unfamiliar territories.

She waited, willing her thoughts to stop dwelling on the forbidden. Chagrined that she truly waited for Roland to come back through the door, she picked up the scroll and rose, her legs still unsteady.

When she reached the door, her steps froze at the sound of voices, low and urgent, from near the servants' stairway.

"We should not have come up here. We were nearly seen," a young male voice complained, distraught.

"But we were not."

Isolde?

"I will not have you suffer shame. Perhaps we should—"

Timothy?

Isolde laughed lightly. "You worry overmuch. Come. I know where we can go where no one will find us."

"Are you sure, sweetling?"

"I am."

The rustle of fabric. A shift of boots.

"You need not carry me, Tim. I can walk down the stairs."

Silence. Two heartbeats' worth.

"Do you truly want me to put you down? I swear I will not drop you."

A long sigh. A kiss?

"Aye, and are you not a big, strong lad who wields a lance with such ease? I have no fears."

"I will not hurt you, Isolde. Not ever."

"I know, Tim. I know."

Eloise closed her eyes and bowed her head, hearing Tim's boots echo off the stairs. Should she chase after the pair or let them be?

Sweet Jesu, they were so young, and Isolde so vulnerable.

Or perhaps not. Eloise remembered being ten and four, moonstruck over a knight who didn't dare approach her because she was the lord's daughter. Chagrined, she'd envied the other maids their secret liaisons and stolen kisses.

Neither would thank her for interfering, just as she would have been irate had anyone dared to interrupt Roland's kiss.

Except Tim and Isolde were about to do more than kiss. And even knowing that, did she have the right to try to protect Isolde from what the maid obviously desired from Tim?

From what Eloise desired from Roland?

She closed the chamber door behind her, very aware she envied Isolde for the ease with which she took a lover, for the obvious care Tim intended to bestow.

With the king's writ in hand, she couldn't help thinking all the way to her father's accounting room that Tim was indeed his knight's squire. She was utterly sure his master would also take great pains to please his lover.

Could it be so simple, so straightforward for master and mistress? Could she take Roland by the hand and lead him off to a private place where no one would find them, where no one would know but the two of them?

Roland thought he'd made it to the battlements without anyone noticing his befuddlement or arousal. But then, he was in no shape to have done much noticing on his own. Everyone in the place might have marked his progress, noted his agitation and the bulge in his breeches, and guessed why he sought privacy.

He pressed up against the cold stone wall and turned his face to the chill of the wind.

Ye, gods.

He'd been seduced into a kiss, by Eloise, and for the life of him he couldn't understand why he'd lowered his guard so far to allow it to happen.

Oh, Eloise was truly brazen!

He'd resisted. God knew he'd tried. But her willingness had been too apparent, the temptation too strong.

The moment she confessed that Hugh hadn't kissed her, releasing him from the horrible feeling she might be comparing them, he'd given in.

He should have gone up to the chamber, fetched the writ, and delivered it to her down in the hall. Then he wouldn't now know how her lips tasted, wouldn't be suffering the demons of hell he suspected would torment him well into the night.

He'd been entrusted with Lelleford, and that meant protecting its residents, especially the lord's daughter.

Who would have thought he'd have to protect her from himself?

Wasn't Eloise the same woman he'd warned his half brother against, who he'd thought coldhearted for her lack of tears at Hugh's death?

No, she wasn't, and that was part of his hell. Willful, yes, but warm and giving, too. A regal lioness, who could be made to purr.

Sweet mercy, he wanted her. How he'd managed to leave Eloise, in a chamber with a stout lock on the door and two soft beds readily available, he didn't know.

But he had, and that was for the best, no matter how much he suffered.

She wasn't for him, would never be.

"Then what do we do, Roland? You said yourself the attraction is there. Do we pretend it does not exist? Seems to me we have tried and failed."

Aye, he'd failed. Miserably. Dishonorably.

And if she tempted him again, entrapped him in her sapphire gaze, tilted her chin up to an angle that showed her lips to perfection, he'd probably give in again. And again.

She wasn't the first woman he'd kissed, far from it. But not one of his former lovers, from an endearing dairymaid on his father's estate to a noblewoman in the king's court, had reduced him to soft pudding, singed his soul with a mere kiss.

If he didn't have Eloise, he'd go mad.

But he'd be mad to have Eloise.

Roland shoved away from the wall. As he saw it, he had only two choices. Leave Lelleford, which he couldn't do, or take Eloise as his lover.

He laughed at his arrogance. As if it were his decision alone. He'd never taken a female by force, and wasn't about to start now, especially with a woman who had no qualms about making her wishes very clear to all and sundry.

Perhaps he'd read too much in her kiss. Perhaps his own yearnings led him astray. Just perhaps, she'd bargained for no more than a simple kiss.

Except his instincts, which hadn't failed him yet, told him he could have led Eloise over to one of the beds and she'd have let him, lain with him.

Verily, as she'd said, she wasn't fragile. No woman he knew could speak her mind as well as Eloise. None other had her force of will. And if it was her will that they should be lovers, he'd be daft to deny her.

They would need to be discreet. Both her reputation and his position as overseer of Lelleford could be jeopardized if they were discovered. But if they were careful—

So be it. He'd not resist, but neither would he be the one to initiate an affair. If she wanted him, she'd let him know. He would let Eloise be the one to lure him into her bed so he couldn't be accused of taking advantage of her.

Lord knew, she wouldn't need to use much bait at all.

Chapter Ten

WITH THE fabric cut and stored away—stacked in the order in which she wished the garments completed—Eloise began to worry about Isolde's whereabouts.

When the girl wasn't to be found in either hall or bedchamber, she tossed on her cloak against the day's chill and headed out-of-doors. She found Isolde where the maid had been the other day—seated on a bench along the near wall of the practice yard while watching Timothy wield a lance.

At the moment only Roland and Timothy engaged in a lesson in swordplay. They used wooden practice swords, wore no chain mail or even a padded gambeson for protection. In snug, short-sleeved brown tunics, they slowly thrust and parried in a mock fight.

Eloise tried not to notice Roland's eloquent form, the grace and power with which he moved. Now was the perfect time to have a private, heartfelt talk with Isolde about Timothy, and she'd not let the man's surefooted, well-timed movements distract her.

As Eloise slid onto the bench, Isolde greeted her with a slight frown. "Did ye have need of me, milady?"

"Nay. I merely wondered what kept you from the hall so long. Now I see."

Isolde's frown reversed into a soft smile. "He is wonderful to watch."

Eloise glanced toward the object of Isolde's attraction, thinking the lad's master wonderful to watch, too. "Is he?"

"Aye, milady." She sighed. "He will make an excellent knight someday, just like Sir Roland."

The men had lowered their swords, Roland speaking to his squire in too low a voice for Eloise to make out the words. Then Timothy nodded, put a determined look on his face, and again crossed swords with Roland. The pace picked up, wood striking wood in quicker and louder fashion.

Indeed, the lad kept up with his master, whose skill was unparalleled, even at this meager practice pace.

"He well may," she acknowledged, which boded ill for Isolde, an orphaned peasant. The higher Timothy rose, the less likely he would be to choose Isolde's company.

But then, if Edgar gained his knighthood, his sister would benefit with a rise in station, too. Unfortunately, Edgar's prospects didn't look good at the moment, not if John Hamelin's fortunes fell to ruin.

Eloise steeled her courage and dove headlong into giving counsel she wasn't sure was necessary or wanted, hoping she didn't make a mess of the whole thing.

"Isolde, I know you have been with Timothy for most of the afternoon. Do you wish to tell me about it?"

Isolde tilted her head, the question there easily discernible.

"I was upstairs and overheard the two of you talking.

I did not mean to listen, but neither did I wish to interrupt."

The maid looked neither angry nor embarrassed at having been found out, merely thoughtful. "Do ye disapprove of him?"

"Not necessarily." 'Struth, she'd thought Timothy both caring and gallant. "I just want to ensure you are not harmed."

"Ye mean ye do not want me to get with child."

Eloise hadn't thought that far ahead, merely worried over Isolde's feelings when Timothy left Lelleford, as he would someday. As would Roland.

"'Twould not be a good thing, you being so young."

"Truly, ye need not be concerned. I know how to prevent such a thing from happening."

This was news, both that a way existed and that Isolde was worldly enough to know.

"Is this prevention you speak of . . . effective?"

"Most times." Isolde's smile went sly. "Why, milady? Are ye thinking of taking a lover?"

Eloise didn't want to think of what had shown on her face or come through in her tone to make Isolde think so. Unfortunately, the maid had hit the mark, not that Eloise would ever confirm it.

"There is likely to come a day when such knowledge might be useful."

"Like with Sir Roland?"

"Isolde! Such insolence!"

The maid shrugged a shoulder. "'Twould come as no surprise if ye did. We have all seen the long gazes, how the two of you dance around each other. 'Tis the talk of the hall."

Eloise closed her eyes, slumped against the stone wall, and groaned. She'd often been the subject of the servants' gossip. It was unavoidable for the mistress of the household—who apparently should have guarded her actions more closely when dealing with Roland.

Why was it those sharp eyes never missed a thing, and those tongues wagged faster than bees' wings?

And if the household servants talked, then the guards were privy to the speculation, and by now even the villagers had heard somewhat of the mistress's admiration for Sir Roland.

Damnation.

"Is nothing sacred or even private?"

"Not much, milady. If it eases yer mind, everyone thinks it's grand. In fact, Cook thinks yer overdue for a lusty, rousing affair. Do ye good, she says."

Eloise's eyes snapped open. "She does, does she?"

"Aye. And why not? Sir Roland is a fine figure of a man, and an honorable knight to boot. Ain't a soul in Lelleford who would blame ye for takin' him to yer bed. Includin' me."

Her cheeks flushed with heat, Eloise thought this was probably the most unseemly conversation she'd ever shared with Isolde. They'd always been blunt with each other, but never to this degree, or on so delicate a subject.

But with whom else could she do so? Certainly not her father or brothers. Her mother had died long before this talk would have been necessary, and her sister had married young and moved away. Still, to discuss these things with a maid, a *younger* maid, who seemed to know more about life and the goings-on in the keep than her mistress wasn't seemly!

"I do not recall asking for anyone's permission, including yours."

"Ye do not need our permission, milady. I just thought ye might like to know."

They sat in silence for a while, watching the males go through their paces. Sweat gleamed on Timothy's brow while Roland seemed to hold himself back for his squire's sake.

Damn, but the man looked good. He appealed to her so much that sometimes her heart beat dangerously fast and her knees went appallingly weak. She could sit and watch Roland for hours, admiring the play of muscle in his arms and the grace of his long legs.

'Twasn't fair he was also gallant when the occasion called for a mannerly mien, and considerate of her feelings when she needed him to be. Oh, he could be forthright, even rude when his own emotions got the better of him, like when they'd exchanged words at the village church.

But then he could be gentle, even tender, as this morning when they'd kissed. When she'd begun to have the most sinful, delicious thoughts about where another kiss or two might lead. To her bed or his. To acts she'd only heard meager hints about and not yet experienced for herself.

All her life she'd believed the first man she would ever bed would be her husband, been told she must protect her maidenhead and virtue at all costs. But she knew not every noble bride went to the marriage bed a virgin, that betrothal contracts between families were more concerned with the transfer of property and coin than the state of a woman's virginity. So long as the woman didn't carry another man's child at the time of the marriage, such things might be overlooked, depending on the groom's pride.

Could she truly take a lover and not suffer the worst of consequences? But more, would it not be wonderful if her first experience with coupling was with a man she knew would be gentle with her, a man she'd come to care for more than she ought?

A man she desired.

Eloise nudged Isolde. "Tell me."

Isolde didn't mistake the meaning. "If ye do the deed with the female atop, then the male's seed mostly runs out on its own."

Eloise wrinkled her nose. "Sounds messy."

"And some men do not like having the woman above. So if the man is on top, then he has to jerk his rod out before he spills his seed."

She was beginning to wonder if she wanted to do this at all. "Messier still."

Isolde giggled. "Aye. Everything gets all sticky if the male is not mindful of what he is about." She paused, then added, "I have also heard you can wash yer insides out real good right after with lemon water. 'Tis said to kill the seed before it can plant."

"Lemon water?"

"With lots of lemon."

"Lemons are costly."

"Which is why we mostly use the other two ways."

Eloise decided she didn't want to know which method Isolde and Timothy had used.

With a hearty laugh, Roland clapped Timothy on the arm and handed the squire his practice sword. The lad sprinted off toward the nearby armory and Roland turned toward the inner gate, likely planning to go up to the keep.

Then he spied her, and shifted his direction.

Isolde rose off the bench. "If ye ask me, milady, 'twould be good to have a lemon or two on hand before All Hallows."

All Hallows. A mere two days hence. A holiday marked by bonfires and feasting, dressing up in disguises to perform good-natured trickery. Some of the superstitious still practiced pagan rituals to ward off ghosts, witches, devils, and assorted demons, and the village priest turned a blind eye because he could do nothing to stop them.

A day on which a good deal of ale and wine flowed and much debauchery occurred.

Isolde gave Roland a courteous bow of her head as she passed him in the yard. His smile for the maid was gracious, though he didn't speak to her or even slow his steps.

Eloise started to rise, but a wave of his hand commanded that she remain seated. She obeyed, the tingling sensation he evoked affecting her innards and weakening her knees. Considering the subject of her talk with Isolde, her fast heartbeat didn't surprise her.

He took the seat Isolde vacated. He leaned forward with his hands clasped between his knees, then let out a long breath, steeling himself for whatever he had to say.

"Timothy and Isolde. They did it."

They certainly had, and Eloise still wasn't sure how she felt about it. On the one hand, Isolde seemed to know what she was about, but on the other, sweet mercy, the girl was only ten and four. Her lover was not much older.

"I know. Timothy told you?"

"He was late coming to the practice yard, and there was a certain swagger to his walk that gave much away. When I called him on it, he admitted what he'd been about. Isolde confided in you?"

Eloise crossed her arms and slumped against the wall behind her. "I overheard a conversation not meant for my ears. When you left after we . . . talked, had you turned toward the servants' stairs instead of the main stairs, so might you have come across them." She sighed. "I could have interfered then, but did not."

"Do you wish now you had?"

"I am undecided."

Roland nodded, understanding. "Shall I order Timothy away from her?"

"Would he if you did?"

"I should like to think so."

"Then the question is, would we be doing them a service, or merely interfering with what is truly none of our affair?"

He glanced sideways at her. "Timothy is my squire and Isolde your maid. Who better has the right to interfere for their own good?"

"Then you think we should?"

Now Roland crossed his arms and leaned back, their shoulders nearly touching. To her amazement, given her previous reactions to his nearness, she felt comfortable. She merely wanted to lean her head against his shoulder and bask in his shadow for a while.

"Is Isolde upset?"

"Far from it. She seems . . . content, happy, which is rather rare for her. Timothy?"

He gave a short sharp laugh. "Strutting like a cock. When I asked if he knew how to protect Isolde from . . . consequences, he looked at me as if I had gone daft. He said he knew what he was about. 'Twas such a strange conversation to have with the lad. Made me feel old."

Eloise knew exactly how he felt. Not only had she felt old, but ignorant. But thanks to her maid, ignorant no longer.

"Isolde knows, too." She sighed. "Which means, I suppose, we should leave them be."

After a moment's silence, he said, "They are young, but not children. I know of marriages that have occurred between younger parties. And they seem to care for each other."

She had to smile at a sudden realization. "So we are talking each other into doing nothing about the situation, which sits hard for both of us."

He turned his head toward her then, and Eloise didn't try to tamp down the tingles his intense gaze evoked. Sweet mercy, Roland possessed the most gorgeous eyes, and up this close she could see gold flecks amid the brownish green.

"Betimes 'tis best to allow events to run their natural course."

His voice had gone lower, softer, and she had the distinct feeling they were no longer discussing their maid and squire.

"Betimes," she whispered, willing him to catch her meaning.

His gaze lowered to her mouth. "You truly think so?"

"Aye."

The bang of the armory door jolted her, made her remember they sat in a very public place. Timothy had come out, and was now strolling across the yard, doing his best to ignore the two people who sat on the bench.

The spell broken, Roland rose from the bench and held out his hand. Too formally for her taste, he said, "Come, milady, I will escort you back to the hall. I desperately need a wash."

Eloise took his hand to rise and willed her knees to obedience. He dropped her hand almost immediately, making her wonder if she'd imagined more than he'd intended.

All the way back to the keep, he kept silent and distant and Eloise wondered if she'd truly have need of the lemons she knew were in the storage room.

Except for meals, Roland had seen little of Eloise during the past two days. Between overseeing the sewing and making preparations for the All Hallows' celebration, she'd flitted between upstairs and down, the kitchen and the village.

Roland stood beside Marcus and watched her, torch in hand, bend to light the first of the bonfires that would burn all afternoon and well into the night. A cheer went up from the crowd as the flame caught hold, the wood hissing and crackling and spitting sparks.

Her smile was wide and joyful, as brilliant as the flames meant to welcome kindly spirits and keep the evil ones from coming near.

Two days of pondering, and he still didn't know if he'd understood her correctly or misunderstood her completely. After their talk on the bench, she'd given him no sign one way or the other, and it was frustrating the hell out of him.

Marcus nudged him and pointed to a group of boys who'd donned animal furs and masks, now sneaking up on a group of girls, who naturally went running—shrieking as only little girls can—as soon as the boys growled and roared.

With a chuckle he noticed disguises other than animal skins, on both children and adults. Devils and demons mingled with the occasional saint, mixing the earthy pagan celebration of Samhain and the Christian holy day of All Saints.

Eloise had apparently decided to spend the day as herself, as did Roland and most of the knights and men-at-arms. Someone had to look after the security of the keep while others spent the day in revelry.

Barrels of ale had been brought out and set along the inner wall of the outer bailey. Tables were laden with platters of dark bread and yellow cheese, large bowls of nuts and baskets of bright red apples.

"I need to light two more bonfires between the keep and the village," Marcus said. "Care to come along?"

Roland considered for a moment, then caught sight of Eloise making her way to the food tables. Suddenly he was in the mood for an apple.

"Nay, go have your fun. I will keep an eye on things here."

Before Marcus could take a step, two blond-haired little girls came running at him, their eyes wide with fear, which he would have thought real if not for the huge smiles on their bright faces.

"Save us, Papa! Save us!"

Marcus a father? Roland hadn't thought any of the household knights married, and didn't remember seeing the girls about the keep, nor being introduced to a wife.

A masked lad bore down on the girls, draped in a piece of bear's fur, growling his loudest and meanest.

With a laugh, Marcus scooped up the girls. Roland captured the bear, picking him up and tossing him over a shoulder.

"Not fair," grumbled the lad, his voice muffled behind the mask. "You always save them, Papa."

Marcus gave the girls a squeeze. "That I do, as I expect of you when you are not bent on terrorizing them."

"'Tis only in fun."

Marcus chuckled. "Fun for you, mayhap. Your mother tells me a different tale." He set down the girls. "Run along, now. Try to stay out of trouble, will you?"

With assurances no clear-thinking grown-up would believe, the girls scurried off. The boy gave out an aggrieved sigh.

Roland bounced the lad, guessing him no more than seven. "So what do we do with this bear, Marcus? Such a fierce predator should not be allowed to harry the countryside."

The boy stiffened, just now realizing he'd been caught up by someone he didn't know.

"What say you, Otto? Shall I let Sir Roland deal with you as I dealt with the bear whose hide you wear?"

"Nay!" Otto rose up and flipped off his mask, revealing a face undeniably similar to Marcus's. "You would not let him skin me, Papa, would you?"

Marcus rubbed his chin. "Well, now, 'tis a puzzle.

Mean bears cannot be allowed to roam at will. Perhaps, if you were a tamed bear . . ."

"Or at least better-tempered," Roland said. "Perhaps if Lady Eloise can find him a sweet or two to satisfy his hunger, Otto will be less inclined to growl at his sisters."

Otto's surrender to the bribe came as no surprise, though Roland, remembering his own childhood, realized the solution likely wouldn't last long. The boy's sisters would need saving several times over before the day was through.

Roland handed Otto into his father's outstretched arms. After a brief hug and affectionate swat on the hindquarters, Marcus put the boy on his feet and left to light the bonfires.

Otto stared up at Roland, wary.

With hands on hips, Roland stared back at the tyke. "So, what sweet do you like best?"

"Tarts."

"Any tart in particular?"

Otto shook his head.

"Not fussy, hmmm? Let us see what her ladyship has to offer."

They strode across the bailey in companionable silence, dodging other scrambling children, greeting people along the way. Otto put his mask back in place as they neared the table.

Eloise spotted them, her hand going to her chest as she inspected Otto. "Sweet mercy, Sir Roland. A fierce bear has breeched the gate! Whatever are we to do?"

The boy giggled through a growl.

"The bear is in search of a tart. He promises not to maul or eat anyone if we can pay his price."

"A hard bargain, but I do believe I saw . . ." Eloise glanced back toward the table. "Will apricot do?"

Otto nodded vigorously.

The tart presented with a flourish, Eloise sent the boy off with another warning to not torment his sisters. She turned to him then, her smile softening.

"Now that the bear is vanquished, perhaps his captor should enjoy a reward, too. A tart?"

A kiss.

Roland reached for an apple. "This will do," he said, then took a bite to keep his mouth busy, to keep from blurting out what he considered a suitable reward.

He took too big a bite. A drop of juice escaped through the corner of his mouth. Before he could bring his hand up to wipe it away, Eloise dispatched it with a fingertip.

He froze, carefully swallowing so he wouldn't choke.

"How did you come to be with Otto?" she asked quietly.

The last chunk of apple slid down his throat. "I was with Marcus when his girls rushed him, begging to be saved. He picked up the girls, I caught the lad."

"A good strategy."

"So it seemed. I did not realize Marcus married."

"He is not. His mistress lives in the village with their children." She sighed. "Marcus would marry Claire if she would have him, but she has already buried two husbands and refuses to take a third. She claims she enjoys the freedoms of a widow. 'Tis my opinion she fears if she marries Marcus something untoward will happen to him."

As had happened to Eloise. With Hugh.

Enough. The last thing he wanted was to remind Eloise of his half brother.

"So, what other festivities are planned for the day?"

"Games for the children. Bobbing for apples. Tonight there will be music and dancing. I know of one group of girls who intend to go down to the stream this eve and wash their gowns."

To his arched eyebrow, she explained, "'Tis said that if one washes a gown in a cold stream on All Hallows' eve, one can see the face of one's true love in the wet skirt."

"Sounds highly doubtful to me."

"Possibly, but a woman takes assurances where she can get them."

She said it so seriously he feared they were once again talking about Hugh. But Hugh was gone. His face couldn't possibly appear in the skirt of her wet gown.

"Going to the stream with them?"

Her sapphire eyes glittered with something akin to mischief. Feminine mischief. "Nay. I have . . . other plans for the eve."

She flirted with him. Ye gods.

"Such as?"

Eloise blushed, a rosy bloom highlighting her cheekbones. Enchanting. As seductive as a siren's song.

"Oh, we shall think of something. Perhaps a dance."

The confirmation that her plans included him set his mind reeling and blood boiling. He could dance, all night long if it meant he could hold and touch Eloise.

"I like to dance."

"Wonderful." She glanced at his hand. "Finish your apple, Sir Roland. They are best eaten before they turn brown."

He'd forgotten about the damn apple, but took another

bite as he watched her walk away. Did her hips sway more than usual? Did the brief glance over her shoulder beckon him to follow?

He might have whooped for joy if not in the midst of so large a crowd. A crowd that would become more boisterous as the ale flowed, some of the revelers likely passing out before the dancing began.

Aye, he would dance around the bonfire with Eloise, and when assured few would notice, whirl her off into some dark, secluded bower and steal a kiss, mayhap two. Mayhap more.

Eloise nearly stamped her foot in frustration.

'Twas finally evening. The music had started and she saw no sign of Roland in the yard. Surely he knew she would be waiting here for him.

Sweet mercy, she'd been so forward this morn her cheeks burned whenever she thought of how blatantly she touched the corner of his mouth. How she nearly commanded him to dance with her around the bonfire.

Never before had she courted a man's amorous attention, and now she began to wonder if she'd done it badly.

For the past two days she'd watched the maids, noted the telling glances and how they moved their bodies when among the men. She'd learned much in her observations and endeavored to practice the more subtle ways of seduction.

Perhaps she'd been too subtle. Maybe he didn't truly know she had plans for a dance, and then more intimate contact. Well, there was still time to correct any error she might have made. The night was yet young, and everything was ready.

She'd found and secreted away two precious lemons, their juice now mixed with water and hidden in her bed-chamber. Isolde had casually informed her mistress not to expect her in the chamber tonight.

All she needed now was the man she intended to make her lover, a prospect that thrilled and terrified her all at once.

She saw him then, on the other side of the fire, prowling around the edge of the light, searching the crowd. She barely refrained from jumping up and waving to give him her location.

Her stomach fluttered when he saw her at last. It seemed an eternity before he stood before her and made a courtly bow.

"Will you honor me, milady?"

She found her voice. "How could I refuse so gallant an invitation, kind sir?"

He held out his hand, and as she slipped hers into his, all trepidation and doubt fled. This felt so right, so inevitable, that she should be twirling about the fire with Roland St. Marten. Into his arms and out, slides and bows. She heard the music, felt the warmth of the flames, but heeded nothing else than the glow in his eyes.

Then the music dimmed and the light faded. Alone in the dark—she knew not where and didn't care—he pulled her against him so hard and fully she could feel his arousal.

His lips whispered across hers, "Will you be missed?"

"No more than you."

Another kiss, harder this time, setting loose the tingling sensation she'd come to expect when near him.

"Are you sure, Eloise?"

Echoes of Timothy. *"Are you sure, sweetling?"* Like squire, like master. She had no fears either.

"I am."

"Where?"

"My chamber. All is ready."

He smiled at that. "I certainly am."

Hands entwined, he led her across the bailey, keeping to the deepest shadows. They'd nearly made it to the inner gate when Simon appeared in their path.

He glanced down at their clasped hands and heaved a sigh. Eloise gave the barest thought to being embarrassed when he said, "I beg pardon, milady, Roland. A messenger from the earl of Lancaster has arrived. He brings news of Sir John."

Chapter Eleven

S HE REVEALED no emotion as she read the missive in the dim torchlight of the great hall.

Was this the same bright-smiled woman he'd observed all day? The same warm, blatantly sensual woman he'd kissed in the dark, who'd been leading him up to her bedchamber? Roland could hardly believe how instantly she'd changed from wanton to regal, from sheer woman to mistress of the keep.

And yet, Roland had to admire Eloise's dignity in the face of adversity. If there was a battle to be fought, he'd want her on his side. Look how long it had taken them to come to a wary truce, longer yet to reach an accord. Physical attraction sped the process, or they might yet be snapping at each other.

She rolled up the scroll before she addressed the messenger. "You will find food and drink aplenty in the outer bailey. Pray partake of our hospitality."

The messenger bowed. "My thanks, my lady. I must be on my way at first light, and would be pleased to carry a reply, if you so wish."

The messenger dismissed, she handed the missive over to Simon. "'Tis not good news."

She began to pace, rubbing her hands together, palm sliding over palm, a sure sign of her agitation.

He wanted to go after her, hold her, tell her all would be well, but held his ground. First he had to find out how bad was the news. Nor did he think she'd welcome an embrace just now, in front of Simon. She'd been taken aback enough when the steward caught them holding hands.

Eloise might intend to allow him liberties she allowed no other man—but in her own time, privately. 'Twas his intention, too, to keep them both from derision.

Simon sat at a trestle table and unrolled the scroll. Roland tore his attention from Eloise to read over the steward's shoulder.

With the earl of Kenworth hot on his trail, Sir John had made for London and turned himself over to the protection of Henry, earl of Lancaster, who Roland knew to be a staunch supporter of King Edward. Instead of giving sanctuary, Lancaster had sent Sir John—and Roland imagined Edgar, too—to the Tower of London to await the king's pleasure.

That had happened two days ago.

No wonder Roland hadn't heard from Kenworth. The earl must have picked up John Hamelin's trail and forced the man's hand.

"Why did he go to Lancaster?" Eloise asked.

Simon pondered a moment. "Lancaster is a reasonable man. He and your father often agree on the issues brought before a parliament. They are not fast friends, but I suppose Sir John considered the man his best ally."

"A misjudgment."

Roland didn't think so. Henry of Grosmont was not

only the earl of Lancaster, but also of Leicester, Debry, and Lincoln. A powerful ally. Nor was the Tower of London merely a prison, but a fortress that boasted the royal armory and mint, a menagerie, and a very secure royal residence.

"Beg pardon, my lady, but your father may have made a good choice."

She took exception. "Lancaster locked him in the Tower! How can that possibly be good?"

"The Tower is not so bad a place." To her incredulous look, he explained. "True, your father is locked in a chamber, but his rank affords him some comforts. He will have a decent bed and meals and be allowed, under guard, of course, to stretch his legs in the yard. Too, he is in the heart of London. From there he can contact those he believes might aid his cause, and have access to the latest gossip. Most importantly, he is no longer in any danger from Kenworth."

She rubbed at her forehead, as though she tried to ease an ache. "So what do we do to help him?"

Just like Eloise. Wanting to do something when there was nothing to be done.

Simon answered. "Your father asks us to bide our time. We will send him the coin he needs and await further instructions."

She gave a little huff. "Again he asks me to do nothing."

"Again?"

Eloise bit her bottom lip and cast a chagrined glance between him and Simon.

A shiver slithered down Roland's spine. When he'd caught Eloise trying to burn her father's missive, he'd thought she'd revealed everything she knew before John Hamelin took flight from Lelleford. Apparently not. She yet kept a secret.

He couldn't keep his disappointment from his voice. "Eloise, is there something important we should know?"

She eased down on the bench next to Simon. "On the morning he left, my father summoned me to his accounting room. Brother Walter lay on the floor, bleeding, not moving." She paused, no doubt reliving the experience. "Father was furious with the monk, called him untrustworthy. Then he told me the earl of Kenworth would arrive within hours, and why. He instructed me to allow the earl in the gate, wine and dine him, do nothing to prod the earl into taking Lelleford by force."

Simon frowned in disapproval. "All along you knew the earl's true intentions, knew your father had not gone out hunting. Yet you gave neither me nor Marcus a warning?"

"My father did not *suggest* I do nothing, Simon. 'Twas an order I could not disobey! Had it been you he called to his accounting room, would you not have done the same, said not a word to me?"

Simon squirmed. "Then why tell me now?"

"Because I can no longer sit back and watch my father be punished for a crime I do not believe he committed. Father also said I was not to contact my siblings to enlist their aid. I think the time has come to send for Geoffrey."

After a moment, Simon nodded. "Sir John may not be pleased to see him, but 'twould seem sensible."

Roland couldn't help ask, "Why Geoffrey?"

"My brother studied law in Paris."

He realized how little he knew of Eloise's siblings.

Her sister, Jeanne, had married very young, and he'd heard gossip about a falling out between Sir John and Jeanne's husband, which had prevented her from attending the ill-fated wedding. Nor had her eldest brother, Julius, attended, being off on pilgrimage to Italy. Nothing had been said about Geoffrey's whereabouts.

One would think a man in trouble would seek help from a son who read law.

"Why did your father not want Geoffrey to know?"

Eloise's spine stiffened. "The two do not get along well."

Roland guessed there was a long, hurtful tale here, one Eloise hadn't told him about the other day while in her brothers' bedchamber and didn't seem willing to relate now. And now was not the time to push for answers to satisfy his curiosity.

"Will your brother answer the summons?"

"I believe he will. I just hope he can get to my father in time to do some good. 'Twill take days for my message to reach Cornwall, then several more for Geoffrey to travel to London. By then . . ."

She closed her eyes and took a deep breath. Roland could well imagine the horrors she must be contemplating. A fast hearing. A hastily carried out sentence.

"Geoffrey has time," Roland said. "From what I have observed, these things can take weeks, even months. I know of one man who has been in the Tower since spring awaiting the king's decision on his fate."

When she opened her eyes he saw hope, and wondered if he made a mistake in giving it to her. He also knew of a man who'd been dispatched within days of capture. But that man had murdered a king's squire, his guilt attested to by several witnesses.

Roland hoped the case against John wasn't so quickly and damningly provable. He'd been told of evidence— the missive in the king's possession—but not of its contents.

Eloise rose from the bench. "Simon, choose a reliable man to carry a missive to Geoffrey. Also inform Lancaster's messenger that I will make up a packet to send back with him."

"I know just the man to send," Simon informed her, and left to fetch him, leaving Roland and Eloise alone in the hall.

She picked up the missive, rolled it up. "You will excuse me, Sir Roland. I have much to accomplish tonight."

A regal dismissal if he'd ever heard one. How could she be so cold and distant when only minutes ago they'd been about to become lovers?

He put his hands on her shoulders, so stiff and unyielding he almost pulled away. Then she looked up at him, sapphire eyes snapping with ire, as if he were merely an obstacle in her way. Still he held on, willing her to soften and allow whatever comfort he could give her.

Nay, there would be no bed play tonight. The coupling he'd looked forward to with eager anticipation must wait. But he and Eloise would become lovers, if not tonight then another. The attraction between them was too strong to resist for long. He'd give her time to get over this latest upheaval in her life, be patient and available.

Then he'd coax her from her regal throne to a soft bed, make her purr like the kitten he knew she could be.

When her stiff tension finally eased, 'twas like a reward, a precious gift.

"I beg pardon, Roland. I had wished the night . . .
different."

He placed a gentle kiss on her forehead. "Do what you
must do. I will still be here. Can I help?"

She shook her head. "I need to write letters to both
Geoffrey and my father, then pack up several tunics and
some coins for my father. 'Tis best I do it alone."

There must be something he could do. "What about
Edgar? He might appreciate a change of garments."

Eloise groaned and lowered her head to his chest, her
hair tickling his chin, the smell of the bonfire and some
spicy scent he couldn't identify teasing his senses.

"Isolde. She must be told. 'Struth, I have no notion
where she might be found."

"I will find her. Go write your letters."

He meant to kiss her again, but she slipped away too
fast, leaving his arms empty and heart heavy.

Eloise sanded the letter to Geoffrey, an easy message
to write. Now, if she could only decide what to say to her
father.

She'd begun twice and not finished either letter—one
too angry, one too cold—making her wonder if she
should write at all. Perhaps she should merely send him
the coin he'd requested and the tunics he hadn't and be
done.

Was he as comfortably settled into a chamber as
Roland seemed to think? Or had they tossed him in a dungeon with the rats and foul refuse? She shuddered, remembering her visit to Lelleford's dungeon, imagining

the Tower's much worse. Her father had given no hint either way in his missive, just a short, terse telling of how he'd come to be in the Tower and that he required coin. He hadn't mentioned Edgar. Heaven knew where the squire might be.

And what could she tell her father anyway? That life at Lelleford went on, that they'd lit the bonfires for All Hallows as if he were here to enjoy the festivities? That she'd allowed herself to push aside his horrendous problems while she planned to make Roland her lover?

Guilt and self-loathing nearly overwhelmed her. She could almost hear her father's booming voice, in a grand rant, telling her what he thought of her scheme, of her wasteful use of lemons.

How could she think, for one moment, she could blithely take a lover and not suffer any consequences? Especially with the man who'd been sent to oversee Lelleford. A king's man. Connected to those who wished to see her father brought low, convicted of treason.

The enemy. The invader.

Except he was also a gallant knight, a man whose kisses and gentle touches thrilled her as no other man's had ever done.

'Twas folly to recall how vigorously he'd kissed her in the dark, setting her head to spinning and yet conveying she had nothing to fear. And later, how he'd grasped hold of her shoulders and not let go. Forced her to realize he intended to be there for her whether she wanted him or no.

Eloise pushed the letter to Geoffrey aside and fetched a large leather pouch. Into it she stuffed as many coins as it would hold and still draw the strings tight. 'Twas a hefty sum to entrust to a messenger, a stranger who might not be trustworthy. But what else could she do?

She wrapped the pouch in a long-sleeved, heavy wool tunic that would ward off any chill, then stuffed it into the sack that already contained two others. One of lighter weight linen, the other of midnight blue velvet she deemed appropriate for an audience with the king.

Father must look his best for the trial. Appearances, she knew, counted for much. A clean, richly decorated tunic would remind all of Sir John Hamelin's rank and wealth, of whatever power he might have left to wield.

Surely he had allies to lend aid, perhaps even Lancaster despite what seemed to her now as treachery. Roland judged the Tower a good place for her father to be. She wished she knew more of how these things worked so she could judge with better clarity.

Then again, soon her father would have Geoffrey to give him aid—of that she had little doubt—and that calmed her some. At least one family member in whom Father could place complete trust would be in London. And perhaps Geoffrey's willingness to help might give rise to a healing of old wounds, bring father and son closer together.

She wished she could be there to see it.

Her hand stilled on the bundle.

She could go to London with the messenger.

Eloise scoffed at the notion. Wouldn't everyone have a grand fit if she announced such a plan? Simon and Marcus would flatly refuse to consider allowing her to travel so far. Her father would shout the beams down at her arrival.

Roland would likely object, too.

In the face of all the opposition, dare she even think about doing what she yearned to do, go to London and be with her father and brother?

Geoffrey might be the only one who approved, or at least understood her reasoning. Did she truly need more?

From the hallway she heard Isolde's shuffle.

'Twould also be nice if someone could check on Edgar, report back to his sister. Her father wasn't the only one in deep trouble.

Dare she act on the impulse?

Isolde entered, two of her brother's tunics folded over her arm, a tear in her eye.

"Is it true, milady? Are they in the Tower of London?"

"So 'twould seem. Here. Put Edgar's garments in with my father's."

The sack wasn't yet full. There was room for a gown if carefully folded.

It could be done, not without raising a few eyebrows between the stable lads and the guards at the gate, but 'twas possible she could leave with the messenger and be well on her way to London before most of the keep was aware.

Before Simon, Marcus, and Roland could tell her once again to do nothing.

Marcus tossed his gloves on the trestle table, his ire overflowing. "Her ladyship left just before dawn, with the messenger from her father."

Simon nearly choked on his cheese.

Roland's heart sank clear to his toes, shocked to his core.

Marcus continued. "She told the guards she was going

to the village church, to ensure all in readiness for All Souls. When the guards objected to her going alone, she said the messenger was all the protection she needed. They assumed that as long as someone was with her, all would be well."

Roland pushed aside his trencher, no longer hungry. "I take it she is not at the church."

"Nay. I prayed all the way out to the village that she was, but she is not. I believe we all know where she goes."

London. To see her father in the Tower.

Simon groaned. "Sir John will be furious when he finds out. Damn! I thought her content with sending a packet to him and a letter to her brother. I should have known better."

Marcus dropped onto the bench opposite Roland, next to Simon. "Aye, we should have. So, what do we do now?"

Roland didn't have any doubt. "Go after her and bring her back."

Both knights looked at him as if he'd proposed to contain a flood without a dam.

"You have not yet tried to talk Eloise out of something on which she has her mind set," Marcus commented. "'Tis nigh impossible."

"A waste of breath," Simon agreed.

Roland disagreed. "Eloise can be reasonable."

"When she wants to be. Unfortunately, in this instance, I very much fear she will not listen to reason."

He rose from the bench, not happy with either man. "If neither of you believes you can sway her, then I will go. I do not intend to give her a choice."

Eloise had about two hours' head start. If he was fortunate, he could catch up with her by early noon and have
her back by nightfall to sleep in her own bed, where she
belonged. If he weren't blessed with good fortune—nay,
he'd not contemplate failure before he even set out.

"Did she take her mare?"

"Nay. One of her father's swifter palfreys."

Damn. Then he'd need to take bedrolls and food, just
in case they must spend the night on the road.

That idiot of a messenger was going to pay dearly for
his folly, either way.

Roland shot up the stairs, shouting for Timothy.

All the while the two of them readied for the ride,
Roland debated the wisdom of his actions. He shouldn't
be leaving Lelleford, abandoning his duty, too. He briefly
considered sending Simon or Marcus, but they were too
susceptible to her whims.

Besides, Eloise was a part of his duty, too. She was
under his protection, and he'd allowed her to slip away.
Without warning. Without fully considering the consequences of her actions.

He understood why Eloise yearned to go to London.
She loved her father, and wanted to be available to aid
him if the need arose. Apparently sending for her brother
hadn't been enough to ease her mind over her father's
fate.

Duty he understood. Loyalty to and love of a parent he
comprehended. Were his father in the same position,
Roland wouldn't have hesitated to do all he could to help.

'Twas different for a man. A woman had to be more
careful, the dangers to her person on the road a greater
risk. She could also become a pawn in the political

maneuvering—*Mon Dieu,* if Kenworth somehow got hold of her, the results could be disastrous for not only her father's cause but for Eloise as well.

'Twouldn't happen. He'd find Eloise and bring her back to Lelleford where she belonged. And she'd stay here, by God, if he had to place her under guard again, day and night, a duty he might take upon himself.

Roland slipped into his chain mail, sat down on the stool to allow Timothy to latch the shoulder fastenings.

"I think we have all we need," the lad said. "All but food, that is. Need we more than for a day?"

Roland glanced at the bed where a second bedroll rested next to his own. Lost in his thoughts he hadn't realized Timothy prepared to go along. Probably a good idea. With his squire in attendance, he might not surrender to the temptation to strangle the messenger for allowing Eloise to put herself in harm's way.

He wasn't taking anyone else, however. He wanted nothing to do with any of the guards who'd neither stopped her from leaving the keep nor provided escort. Timothy could keep up with the pace he intended to set. Fast. At least for the first few hours.

"Bring enough to get us through the night and part of the morrow, if need be."

Timothy snapped the last latch. "I am off to the kitchen, then, and will meet you in the stable."

The lad grabbed both rope-bound blankets on his way out, leaving Roland to strap on his sword and don a woolen cloak. At the bottom of the stairway, Marcus and Simon awaited him, both frowning deeply.

Roland tugged on his gauntlets. "I hope to be back before nightfall. I trust that the two of you can oversee Lelleford in my absence."

Simon rolled his shoulders. "You need not worry over us. 'Tis Eloise for whom we are concerned." He glanced at Marcus. "We ask you not to be overly hard on her."

Roland wanted to shake them. Had someone taken a hard line with Eloise early in her life, tamped down her strong will, she might still be here, safe, instead of out on the treacherous road to London. Under the protection of one damn messenger.

"If she does not cooperate, I will bind her up and toss her over the rear of my horse if I must. You two take care of Lelleford. I will take care of Lady Eloise."

Intent on his mission, he didn't see the men's frowns turn into smiles as soon as he was out the door.

Marcus chuckled. "I do believe Lady Eloise has met her match."

Simon crossed his arms. "Perhaps, but I am willing to wager she talks Roland into taking her to London."

"I am not so big a fool as to part with my coin so easily."

Isolde handed Tim the food packet. "I had Cook gather enough for three days, plus a bit extra. Ye will take care."

Tim brushed the tear from the corner of her eye, loath to let it fall. No one had ever cared enough for him to cry over him before, and he wasn't sure how to deal with it.

"Have no fears on my account."

"I wish ye did not have to go, too."

"Where Sir Roland goes, I go. 'Tis the life of a squire."

"I know, but still . . ."

"Come now, do not be sad. I will not be gone long."

She heaved a great sigh, her pert, ripe breasts rising and lowering, distracting him from his purpose. He gave himself a mental shake. Roland was waiting in the stable. He couldn't tarry.

Wineskin and food packet in one arm, Tim gathered the bedrolls in the other. "Come walk with me a way, tell me what you will do while I am gone."

She smiled then, that endearing curve of mouth he would miss greatly. "Perhaps I shall make progress on Lady Eloise's gown. She particularly wants the blue one finished before Christmas."

Tim wondered where he'd be at Christmas. Still here at Lelleford? Or off with Sir Roland somewhere else? Perhaps at the king's court, or maybe at the St. Marten's estate. Either way, 'twas unlikely he'd spend the holiday with Isolde.

Or any other holiday for that matter. He was but a squire, with nothing to his name, with nothing to offer her, and they both knew and accepted it. 'Twas foolhardy to wish for more.

"You like to sew?"

"I am good at it, and it gives me pleasure to see people wear something I have made." She stopped then. They hadn't quite reached the inner gate. "Would ye do me a great favor?"

Didn't she know he'd go to great lengths to please her?

"Whatever you require, sweetling."

Her smile widened briefly at the endearment, then faded. "If you see Edgar, will ye give him my love, tell him not to worry over me? I am sure it sits hard with him."

Isolde worried over her brother, who all assumed languished in the Tower with Sir John. She asked a favor Timothy doubted he would get a chance to grant.

"We are not traveling so far as London. Sir Roland hopes to find Lady Eloise soon after nooning and return by nightfall."

"So Sir Roland intends. If his plan goes awry, and I assure ye Lady Eloise will do all in her power to see that it does, will ye speak to Edgar for me?"

"Sir Roland is not easily swayed."

Isolde simply tilted her head, and in that small motion he caught an admonishment for not immediately agreeing to do her will. She'd learned that from Lady Eloise, Tim was sure. What could he do but comply?

"All right. Should I happen to see Edgar, I will give him your regards and assure him you are well. Satisfied?"

Her bright smile was all the reward he required, the brief kiss she planted on his cheek an added boon. With a sad smile, she returned to the keep.

Timothy trundled on to the stables.

God's wounds, he was like butter in the lass's hands, too easily shaped and molded, too ready to melt. She wasn't his first lass, but none affected him so deeply as Isolde.

Lady Eloise, now there was a fine lady, and a strong one. And from what he'd observed, Sir Roland was smitten. Roland, however, was more experienced with the fairer sex, didn't seem to give into Eloise's whims as easily as Tim gave in to Isolde.

Roland would bring her ladyship back, as he said he would, even though the lady objected.

Tim smiled to himself. Perhaps he should watch more closely how a knight handled a lady, see how it was done.

How to be firm and yet gallant. How to win a stubborn woman over to his way of thinking while remaining, at all times, chivalrous.

Verily, a squire could learn more skills from his knight than merely how to wield a sword.

Chapter Twelve

ELOISE SWORE every muscle in her body ached, except those that had gone numb. She'd managed to get off the horse and wasn't looking forward to getting back on. Pacing along the wide path that served as a road helped work out the worst of the knots, but her legs and back would never be the same.

Not once during last night's planning and growing excitement over going to London had she considered it might *hurt*. But then in all of her years she'd never ridden for several hours at a stretch over uncountable leagues.

"Are you ready, my lady?"

Eloise noted the apology in the messenger's voice. When Daniel agreed to allow her to accompany him, he warned her—hoping to dissuade her from her folly, she was sure—that he must return to London with all haste, that he wouldn't halt often to rest. 'Twas now nigh on noon, and they'd stopped to water the horses in a convenient stream and partake of a light meal.

Eloise answered his question by tossing the apple core to the side of the road and pulling her palfrey to a log high enough to help her mount. "Will we make Windsor by nightfall?"

He smiled shyly, enforcing her impression that Daniel was both young and a bit wary of her, quite unaccustomed to dealing with headstrong women.

"In plenty of time to enjoy a hot, hearty meal and allow a full night's rest. The Boar's Head is a decent inn. I hope you find it comfortable."

Eloise shifted in the saddle, firmly believing she'd find anything short of a plank floor more comfortable than hard leather.

Not an hour later, her legs again screamed for mercy. But there was nothing to do but hang on and try not to think about the pain. She'd talked Daniel into letting her accompany him, agreeing to all his terms. She couldn't very well forswear the bargain now, no matter how deep her misery.

At least the weather held in her favor. A few clouds passed over, casting the road into deeper shadow at times, but no rain threatened. A small thing to be grateful for, but then, she looked for the good things to take her mind off the bad.

She'd spent all morning wondering about how to explain her rash action to her father, or worrying about the uproar she'd likely caused at Lelleford.

Would her father be furious and arrange to send her home?

How quickly had her absence from Lelleford been discovered, and had anyone been sent to fetch her back?

Was Roland so furious he'd not look at her tenderly again?

She really had to stop thinking about Roland St. Marten and banish these wayward longings for what might have been sweet and loving between them.

Such a fool she'd been to allow a woman's yearnings to push aside her duty as a daughter. Her father's situation must come first, to the exclusion of all else. She owed her loyalty and devotion to him, not to a man who might prove a diverting lover, a duty driven home forcefully last eve upon Daniel's arrival.

So why, then, did she occasionally glance over her shoulder, looking for Roland? 'Struth, if anyone did come after her, 'twould likely be Simon or Marcus, not Roland.

The afternoon wore on, and just about the time she was sure she'd fall out of the saddle because her legs couldn't hold tight anymore, Daniel—blessedly—pulled to the side of the road for another rest.

Unlike last time, Daniel wordlessly offered to help her dismount. Swinging her leg over the saddle nearly killed her, but she pushed through the pain, and was rather proud of herself for not collapsing onto the road.

She noted, however, that the young man held on to her elbows until *he* was sure she stood upright on her own power.

"You look about done in, my lady."

She could hardly deny his observation, absolutely sure she looked as bad as she felt.

"I thank you for your concern, but I will survive."

Eloise ignored the furrowing of his brow that revealed his doubts in her ability. She *would* survive. She'd ride as far and as fast as she must if she had to tie herself to the saddle to accomplish such a feat.

With each carefully placed step alongside the road, she felt stronger. With each bite of apple, she felt renewed— or so she told herself. As soon as her bottom hit the log she'd decided to rest on, she wondered if she'd be able to get up with any grace at all.

'Twas then she heard the sound of hoofbeats, heavy and fast, coming up the road they'd just traveled.

Daniel placed himself—feet spread and short sword in hand—directly between her and her view of the road. Images of bandits and ruffians, stories she'd heard of travelers accosted on the road, flitted through her and settled in a lump in her stomach. The accompanying rush of fear set her heart thumping, and guided her hand to her boot and the dagger hidden within.

Perhaps the other travelers would simply pass them by. She prayed so, but would be ready if they didn't. She wasn't helpless and could defend herself if need be. Growing up in a household of mainly men and watching them train with weapons now stood her in good stead. What she lacked in skill could be made up with enthusiasm.

All the while her hand trembled on the dagger's handle.

Then the hoofbeats slowed, and Daniel's heretofore tight shoulders slumped slightly as he lowered his sword. Eloise forced herself to rise and peek around the messenger.

Roland. Timothy right behind him. She'd been caught.

Even as she noted the stark look on Roland's face, knew without doubt he was about to unleash his anger, she thrilled at the sight of him galloping up the road.

She bent over to put her dagger back in her boot, and had to place a hand on Daniel's back to keep from tumbling over.

"My lady?"

"I am fine, merely unsteady."

Roland's stallion barely came to a stop when he dismounted in one graceful, powerful move. He waved a threatening finger at Daniel.

"*You* I will deal with later!"

No fool, the messenger stepped aside, leaving her vulnerable to Roland's glare and whims.

With long, steady strides he came toward her, menacing in his ire. She couldn't tamp down the chagrin that even though he'd ridden the same distance at what must have been a punishing pace, he showed no sign of weariness or weakness.

The closer he came, the more she knew she should be worried and prepared to argue against his insistence that she return home. But sweet mercy, the stirring surrounding her heart refused to acknowledge anything else but that he'd come for her. 'Twas all she could do to keep from tossing her arms around his neck and shouting for joy.

He stopped within a breath in front of her and crossed his arms. "Do you have any notion . . . any idea . . . what the devil possessed you?" and then he gave up trying to speak. He rolled his eyes heavenward, beseeching guidance, then closed them with a heavy sigh.

Her heart sang a joyful melody. He wasn't so much angry as worried.

She laid tentative fingertips on his arm. "I have come to no harm, Roland."

"So I see. Just give me a moment."

Roland brought his turmoil under control, not easy with her fingers rubbing small circles on his arm, providing a threadlike connection between him and the woman he'd too often envisioned lying in a bloody heap alongside the road.

He didn't dare touch her yet, undecided between shaking her fiercely for her temerity and for dragging him through hell, or crushing her against his chest, holding her tight so she'd not get away from him again.

"How did you find us?" she asked softly.

Somewhat calmed, he opened his eyes to find her smiling up at him, as if they were in some private place back at the keep and not in the middle of the road. His heart skipped a beat, and he tightened his arms to keep them in place.

"A nail came out of one of your palfrey's shoes, the impression easy enough to track."

"Oh." The soft puff of air nearly stole his breath away. "Such a small thing. Perhaps when we stop at the inn tonight we can have the nail replaced."

Simon and Marcus had warned him she wouldn't give in easily to returning home, nothing he hadn't known himself. He'd just found her and was having trouble not wrapping his arms around her. He certainly didn't want to argue. With his insides all churned up, how was he supposed to present clear arguments to . . . except that was the wrong way to go about winning.

Orders, not cajoling, would win the day.

"You are not going any farther south than this spot. I am taking you home."

She raised an eyebrow. Her fingers stilled but didn't leave his arm.

"But I must go on. Roland, my father is in dire need of aid and I cannot forsake him."

"You sent for Geoffrey and fulfilled the requests in

your father's message. Eloise, there is naught more you can do for him."

"There *must* be."

"Such as what?"

"I will not know until I speak with my father."

He was getting nowhere. He should just pick her up, put her back on her horse, and lead her north, toward home, where she'd be safe. The thought tempted mightily, but the plea in her eyes stopped him cold.

Still, giving into her whim, no matter how strongly felt, wasn't acceptable.

"If you will not listen to reason for your own sake, then think of your father. He believes you home, protected from the worst of what is to come. If you go to London, then he must not only be concerned for his own situation, but will worry over you. Sir John does not need the distraction of having his daughter running loose in the city and at risk."

She bit her bottom lip. "Geoffrey will be there soon."

"Not for several days, too much time for Kenworth to learn you are in the area and take advantage. The risk to you, to your father's cause, is too great, Eloise. 'Tis best you return to Lelleford. Now."

"Beg pardon, my lord."

Roland glanced over his shoulder at the approaching messenger, who he hadn't yet strangled for his part in Eloise's escape. "Why for?"

To Daniel's credit, he didn't cower. "It may be best for you to continue to the inn for the night. 'Tis but an hour away and her ladyship needs the rest. She is in pain and—"

Roland spun back to Eloise. "You are in pain?"

She shot Daniel an irritated glance. "Not so much that I cannot ride."

"But not far," the messenger stated. "Truly, Sir Roland, I only stopped here because every time I looked back I saw her strain become worse. I began to worry if she could keep her seat. Even now she is not steady."

Her hand tightened on his arm. "That will be enough, Daniel! My legs still hold me up."

"Barely," the messenger murmured, then backed away toward his mount.

Roland could have kicked himself for not seeing the obvious before, for not realizing she held on to his arm not because she wanted to touch him, but for balance. His own legs felt the abuse of a punishing ride, and he was used to it. Eloise wasn't.

The time for both orders and arguments had come to a halt.

He picked her up. Ignoring her feeble protests, he strode toward the stallion that could easily carry them both. And now that he had Eloise in his arms, snug against his chest, right where he wanted her, he loathed letting her go.

"Which inn, Daniel?"

"The Boar's Head in Windsor."

"Lead on. Timothy, lead Eloise's palfrey."

"I can ride, Roland," the minx in his arms grumbled.

"If you ride with me, I do not have to worry about you falling off your horse."

"You have no cause to worry about me at all."

She was wrong, but that argument was for another time.

Once mounted, he settled a stiffly irate Eloise across

his thighs, arranged her cloak over her legs, and nudged the stallion forward. The messenger set a swift but not harsh pace.

They rode in silence. Roland did his best to concentrate on the road and not the woman who began to reluctantly relax, eventually snuggling against him, her head pressing against his shoulder.

He smelled the threat of rain. Heard the hoofbeats that assured him Timothy rode close behind, and the steady jingle of his stallion's tack that seemed to echo his own breathing.

But mostly he felt Eloise's solid but not unduly heavy weight press against his thighs, her warmth seeping through layer upon layer of garments and chain mail. His loins heated, and the thought of a soft bed at the inn rose up to taunt him.

Perhaps tonight. . .

"Roland, I need to go to London."

The fantasy faded.

"You need to go home."

"But we are so close, only a half day's ride away."

"Eloise, I cannot in good conscience allow you—"

"Then silence your conscience by coming with me."

Another foolhardy notion.

"I cannot. My duty to the king demands I return to Lelleford."

She squirmed, and his loins flared to full flame. Her hand came up to his chest to cover his heart. "Your damned duty. Can it not be set aside for a few days?"

"Nay, and you know it."

"I expected either Simon or Marcus to chase after me, not you. Have you not already abandoned your duty?"

A valid point, but of no consequence.

"Your protection is part of my duty. Now that I have you we must return with all haste."

She was silent for a few moments. "I have a proposition for you."

"Eloise, give over. I am not listening."

"Take me to London. Let me see my father. If he then orders me home, I will return with you without argument."

"Eloise—"

"I beg you, Roland. I need to see him, ensure he is not in a filthy dungeon, has food and drink. See for myself that he is well and unharmed. Please, Roland. A day or two is all I ask."

His heart melted at the bleakness in her voice. Nor had he ever dreamed to hear this strong-willed, confident woman beg. Either it was a measure of her upset or she was playing him for a fool. He pushed back her hood, tilted her chin upward.

The moisture glittering in her sapphire eyes tore at his soul.

"No argument?"

"Not a word of protest, I give you my oath."

A raindrop hit her high cheekbone. She never flinched nor did she brush it away. The drop hovered for a moment before sliding away on its own.

Unable to hold back, he kissed her—the sealing of a bargain borne out of his own needs—and was rewarded with a satisfied sigh. Because she liked the kiss or because she'd won?

He'd probably regret his weakness later, especially when he had to explain his actions to the king. But for now he had Eloise securely in his arms, their mouths melded in the sweetest kiss he'd ever known, and the rest of the world could go hang.

Though he considered the danger low, Roland slept fitfully—eyes closed and ears open—seated outside Eloise's room, his back against her door.

At dawn, he opened the door a crack, heard no noise but her soft, steady breathing, then crept away before his lust overcame his better sense.

One of the problems with sleeping were the accompanying dreams, fed by yesterday's ride and kiss. Of Eloise, of her warmth and sparkling eyes, of her soft smiles and how well she fit against him. He'd wanted more of her and suffered for it.

She needed her sleep, had damned near fallen face first in her supper last night, and required her strength for the ride today. Only a villainous lout would deprive her of her needs simply to assuage his own.

Ye gods, but he'd gone ridiculously soft. He'd yielded, agreed to take Eloise to London, and 'twas too late now to go back on his word.

He eased down the stairs and through the inn's homey and now abandoned common room, his destination the stable, his intention to talk to Daniel, who should now be preparing for the last leg of his journey.

Nay, he hadn't strangled the man yet, and wouldn't. Roland could hardly berate Daniel for allowing Eloise to talk him into this foolish journey, not after Roland allowed her to talk him into continuing it.

Roland brushed aside the nagging guilt for abandoning his duty at Lelleford and pushed away his utter foolishness for allowing Eloise to have her way. What was done was done, and the quicker over the better.

Daniel greeted him with a smile that conveyed understanding of Roland's turmoil, and pleasure at having been relieved of the burden of Eloise.

"A good morn to you, my lord. Is Lady Eloise yet sleeping?"

"Soundly. I imagine she will be out awhile longer, and will be unhappy about not taking leave of you."

"She is gracious. Perhaps we will meet up again in London."

Roland had his doubts. Daniel served Lancaster, an earl Roland didn't plan to allow within shouting distance of Eloise. The earl might be her father's ally, but of late Roland had developed a healthy distrust of earls.

"If we do not, pray give Lancaster our thanks for sending you to Lelleford. 'Tis well her ladyship learned of her father's whereabouts, even if it did lead to this."

Daniel shook his head, chagrined. "I tried to talk her out of making the journey, but . . ."

Roland laughed lightly, imagining the poor lad trying to stand firm against Eloise's pleas. "Do not be too hard on yourself. She is hard to resist."

"Nigh on impossible." Daniel swung up into the saddle. "To do the lady credit, she is also hardy. Not only did she keep up, she never complained. I swear she would have fallen off her horse before she deigned to ask me to slow down or take an added rest. Most women are not so sturdy or steadfast."

Or headstrong, or single-minded, or so accustomed to getting their way.

"She is . . . uncommon."

"An apt description." Daniel looked up the road. "Is there any other message you wish me to deliver? To Sir John, mayhap?"

Roland had given thought to warning Sir John about Eloise's visit, then decided not. Best to let father and daughter meet on equal footing, not give the father time to dream up possible punishments for her actions.

Roland intended to secure lodging for tonight, take her to see her father, and on the morn head back to Lelleford. Not for one moment did he doubt Sir John would vehemently order his wayward daughter to go home.

"Nay, no message. Take care on the road."

"You also, Sir Roland. My regards to the lady."

Roland watched the messenger raise a cloud of dust in his wake, then entered the stable. Timothy still slept, wrapped up in a blanket in his horse's stall. Roland let the lad be. No sense waking the squire until Eloise stirred. Time enough then to prepare for the day ahead.

Quietly he slipped into the palfrey's stall and checked the shoe that had thrown a nail, thankful the horse hadn't also thrown the shoe, and possibly stumbled, and thrown the rider, and . . . he shook off the morbid thoughts that had plagued him during most of yesterday. The new nail seemed solid enough to hold the shoe in place until turned over to Lelleford's smithy.

He'd not set a fast pace into London, allowing Eloise several rests. If they made the city by midafternoon, 'twould give him plenty of time to secure lodgings and for Eloise to see Sir John.

They'd be in and out of the city within a day.

She'd sworn him an oath, and he intended to hold her to it.

* * *

"Have you ever been to London?"

Eloise feasted on the sight of the western gate, the huge stone arch allowing passage through the thick walls that surrounded the city.

"Twice. Once when I was a little girl, barely old enough to have memory of it. Then again about seven years ago. That I remember quite clearly."

"What was the occasion?"

She glanced at Roland, who'd been making conversation all morning, mostly, she suspected, to keep her mind off her numb bottom. He'd set a leisurely pace, stopped several times. She found the consideration endearing, but at times had wanted him to pick up speed just to have the journey over with.

Was he truly interested? And how much should she tell him?

"Father was to attend a parliament, one where most of the bishops would also attend. He had his sights set on a church appointment for Geoffrey, so he brought my brother to talk to several of the bishops to see what could be accomplished."

Roland frowned slightly. "That would not leave your father much time to look after you. I am surprised he took you with him."

Eloise sighed inwardly. She should really keep her mouth shut, but Roland already knew her a willful female, so might as well hear the tale.

"He did not take me. I abhorred the thought of being left alone—again—at home while the two of them were about to embark on what I thought was a grand adventure. I snuck into a tarp-covered baggage cart. By the time Father caught me, 'twas too late for him to do aught about it."

Did she detect an effort to withhold a smile?

"When were you caught?"

"As they were unloading the cart to haul the baggage into the rooms Father had let."

"So you spent two days bouncing in the back of a cart."

"Three."

He shook his head in disbelief. "How did you manage without someone seeing you? I mean, you had to crawl out sometime. To eat. For relief."

She'd been rather proud of her accomplishment, even though her father turned her bare backside a bright red afterward. Still, he'd not sent her home, just as he wouldn't send her home now, she hoped.

"I slept the day away and climbed out at night for . . . necessities. One can get along for several days on dried fruit and nuts."

"You planned ahead, took food along."

"Well, nay. Sacks of them were in the cart."

He was still shaking his head when he pulled ahead of her to speak to the guard at the city's gate. Given permission to enter, he signaled her to follow.

The lanes were as narrow as she remembered. The upper stories of the buildings—filled with shops on the bottom and residences above—had been built out over the street to create a canopy, casting the streets and people below into shadow.

Eloise endured the foul smell of bodily refuse in the gutters, of the stench created by too many people crowded into too small an area. 'Twas not easy to hold one's breath until they turned onto a wider lane. Roland slowed his horse, signaled her to again come alongside.

"If Geoffrey went to the Church, then why is he now married to . . . Leah, is it?"

"Geoffrey did not believe he had a calling, could not bear the thought of a tonsure. The best he and Father could agree upon was the advantage of an education. Geoffrey spent two years as a student at Westminster Abbey before he came home for a visit." And such a row that had caused! Eloise guided her horse around a merchant's fruit cart before she continued. "Father pressed him, then, to take vows. Geoffrey decided to escape. He went to Paris to continue his studies."

"He married in Paris, then?"

If only he had stayed in Paris, then he wouldn't have been on a ship when it sank, nearly killing him, harming his mind—all because of her.

"Nay. He was coming home to attend my . . . wedding when he met Leah. She nursed him through a very bad time and they grew close. I am so glad he found her, for now he is truly happy."

"But not yet reconciled with your father, I take it. Yet you expect Geoffrey to come to London?"

She hadn't a doubt. "He will come. They may not get along well, but they are father and son. Family. Geoffrey will come."

Roland pulled up before an apothecary, a small sign bearing a mortar and pestle hung over the door. Without a word he dismounted and went inside.

Was he ill? He'd said not a word, and she'd seen no sign of sickness.

She turned around to Timothy. "Is aught amiss with Sir Roland?"

He smiled and shook his head. "Nay, milady, he merely inquires about rooms to let. We have stayed here before. The rooms are clean and the price fair. 'Tis also not far from the Tower. 'Twould be convenient if the room is unoccupied."

Eloise righted herself, aware of just how ill-prepared she'd been to make this trip. She had no idea of where she might have found lodging, or what was a fair price. But then, Daniel could have supplied the information, she was sure.

Roland came out the door and reached up to untie the bedroll behind his saddle. "You know where to take the horses, Timothy?"

Timothy dismounted and grabbed hold of the stallion's reins. "Aye, milord. To Master Victor."

Roland tossed his bedroll to the ground. "Have him look at the nail in the palfrey's shoe. If he is not satisfied that it will hold for a full day's hard ride, have him make whatever repair he deems necessary." He approached her horse and untied the sack of garments behind her saddle. "When you return, Mistress Green has an errand or two she would like you to run for her."

Tim frowned. "Beg pardon, Sir Roland, but I had hoped to go with you and Lady Eloise to the Tower."

Roland put the sack down next to his bedroll. "Why so?"

"To meet Edgar, if he is there. Isolde . . . entrusted me with a message for him."

Eloise could imagine what that message might be, one to assure Edgar of her well-being. 'Twas a measure of the maid's trust in Timothy to entrust such a message to her brother.

"The errands can probably wait. Mistress Green did not say they were urgent."

Eloise assumed Mistress Green to be the wife of the apothecary, but she didn't have time to ponder further. Roland stood by her side, his arms outstretched, waiting to help her dismount.

They'd been through this process several times today when he'd stopped to allow her to rest. Now, as before, she placed her hands on his wide shoulders and noticed how securely he held her about the waist. Only once, the first time, did she lean too far forward too fast, making him catch her.

Not that his holding her close to his chest was unpleasant, far from it. But that had been in the wilds, with only Timothy to observe, not an entire city.

Her dismount this time was a more dignified affair, even though the same tingles shot through her body, the same stiffness afflicted her legs.

Timothy left with the horses; Roland picked up their belongings and led her to the back of the shop. After a brief introduction to the rotund, sweet-faced Mistress Green, they headed up the stairway.

The squire had the right of it. The room facing the street seemed clean, the bed appeared sturdy. A brass brazier filled with charcoal would adequately heat the room. She noted a stack of pallets in one corner, a small table with a pitcher and bowl and single candle in another.

But what drew her across the room was the view out the window.

The glass wasn't of the best quality. Small bubbles marred the surface, and a wavy texture fogged the clarity. Neither mattered, for off in the distance, over the rooftops of London, she could see the tops of the four stark-white turrets of White Tower, which she knew stood in the center of the fortress that was the Tower of London.

Soon, she'd see her father. Perhaps sooner than she liked, she'd learn the truth about how he'd come to be suspected of treason.

Her hand trembled as she touched the cold, hard glass, wondering if, just maybe, she'd made a mistake in coming.

Chapter Thirteen

HER SHOULDERS slumped at the view of the Tower of London, as if the weight of the world rested on those slender shoulders.

Roland tossed his bedroll and her sack on the bed, knowing she must be having second thoughts about her ill-advised journey. He also knew what she'd say if he suggested they simply turn around and go back to Lelleford, so he didn't bother.

Right or wrong, whatever course of action Eloise set, she carried through, and since he'd gone along with her scheme, he'd help her however he could.

So instead of chiding her about her folly, he eased up behind Eloise and put his hands on her shoulders. Immediately they squared.

"Imposing sight, is it not?" he asked.

"White Tower really is white."

From the center of the Tower grounds, the square corner turrets rose above the stone walls surrounding the fortress, their dark, pyramidal roofs pointing skyward.

"Your father may not be held in White Tower. There are other, smaller towers on the grounds."

"Do they all have dungeons?"

He had to admire her calm, given the foreboding nature of her question. She envisioned her father languishing in a dark, dank cell, manacles on his wrists, rats scurrying across the floor.

'Twas possible, but Roland had his doubts.

"Not all. Verily, several of them are nicely furnished, with fireplaces and handy garderobes. Even when kept prisoner, those of high rank are furnished their comforts."

She turned around. He dropped his hands to his sides.

"But we do not know for sure, do we?"

Deciding nothing would convince her until she saw for herself, Roland turned his thoughts to the practical.

"With the money I assume you brought along he can buy himself comforts he might not already have."

She frowned. "I hope I brought enough then."

"Where is the pouch?"

"In the sack, wrapped in one of his tunics."

"Best carry it on your person. The guards may search the sack. Better they do not know how large a purse your father has available."

Eloise untied the rope securing the sack and pulled out what Roland recognized as her crimson gown and two tunics he deemed too small for Sir John. Edgar's? The next tunic, of heavy brown wool, she unrolled on the bed, revealing a huge leather pouch stuffed so full of coins the seams strained.

"*Mon Dieu,* Eloise. I doubt your father wanted you to empty his entire coffin."

She picked up the pouch. "I did not. My father is a wealthy man. This is but a portion of . . . well. I also brought a small pouch of my own, and I have several coins sewn into the hem of my cloak." She looked up at him then. "We do not lack for funds. Whatever expenses we have, I can pay for. This room, stabling the horses, our meals. You need not bear any of the costs for accompanying me."

The amount of money she carried made him sweat. She'd come overly prepared, to the point of being extremely dangerous. Not for any reason would he walk the city streets with her bearing that much money, certainly not take it into the Tower. Not on the first visit anyway.

"We need to hide some of that."

"Why for?"

"We dare not take that much coin into the Tower until we know where your father is held, how secure his chamber. No sense taking it in only to have the guards confiscate it."

Her eyes widened as understanding took hold. "Ah. Well, then . . ." She glanced around the room. "Where?"

A half memory from the last time he'd let these rooms drew him to the corner and the stack of pallets. He pulled them into the middle of the room. With slow, heavy steps, he tested the floor, and smiled when a loose board groaned.

"Under here." He pulled his dagger from his boot to pry up the nails.

"Wait, use mine."

Eloise brushed aside her cloak and pulled a heavy silver dagger from her right boot. Stunned, he stared at the bulky weapon in her outstretched hand.

"'Tis an old one of Julius's," she explained. "He will not miss it if it becomes ruined. No sense in marring yours."

Roland briefly wondered how many more surprises he

might suffer today. He took the offered dagger and soon had the floor plank pried up to where he thought he could slip the large pouch beneath to rest between the joists.

"How large is your purse?"

Eloise removed her cloak and tossed it on the bed. She faced him, hands clasped in front of her, a regal expression on her face. "You will divert your eyes, if you please."

Realizing she needed to partially undress in order to retrieve her purse, Roland's baser self reared up and couldn't be silenced.

"Do you need assistance? A lace untied, a fastening undone? I humbly offer—"

"Roland, turn around."

The order was blunt, but he detected a faint hint of humor.

As much as he would love to divest Eloise of whichever garments she must rearrange, there wasn't now time for sport, not if she wanted to visit her father today. Nor did he think her in any mood to be diverted.

For now, he'd settle for bringing a smile to her face, a lightening of her burden.

"I am told I am very nimble-fingered."

"Ro-land!" came out on a chuckle.

Satisfied, he gave an aggrieved sigh and turned to face the opposite wall. "Very well, if you insist. I merely strove to be helpful."

"Hmmm." To the rustling of skirts, she added, "You have already been of great help. I do not wish to overtax you."

"Believe me, my lady, 'twould be no great burden."

More rustling of fabric, the jingle of the gold-link

girdle she wore about her waist. If he turned around he would likely see her skirts hiked up, revealing her chemise. Long or short? Thick or thin? White or—

"You may turn around now."

He spun quickly. Fully covered, she tossed him a small doeskin purse containing only a few coins.

Brought back to his purpose, he tugged open the strings and inspected the contents. She hadn't stuffed it.

" 'Tis a decent size. We will add a few more coins and give it to your father this afternoon."

She brought him the large pouch. "Take whatever you need for our expenses thus far."

He wasn't above allowing Sir John to pay the costs, but was willing to trust Eloise for reimbursement.

"We can settle accounts later, after we know more. Best take out another handful, for the guards."

"The guards?"

"They are the ones who let us in, who unlock your father's chamber door, and more importantly, they let us out again. They will expect appreciation."

Eloise nodded and shook more coins into her hand.

Roland secured the hoard, eased the board into place, and pressed the nails down with his boot heel. With the pallets dragged back into place, one would never know a small fortune lay under the flooring.

Eloise sat down on the bed, her former humor no longer in evidence. "What next?"

Roland unstrapped his scabbard, leaned it against the wall. "Have you any more weapons?"

"Nay. Are you not taking your sword?"

He'd feel naked without it, but 'twas best to leave it.

"'Tis not allowed to take weapons near a prisoner. Your dagger stays here, too."

"And yours?"

"Stays in my boot. I will entrust it to whichever guard demands it, and give him an extra coin to ensure he remembers he has it. I refuse to walk the streets of London without a weapon, especially if we are out after nightfall."

Eloise rose off the bed, came toward him, took a deep breath before speaking. "I owe you many thanks. I might have been able to find lodging for me and my horse, but the rest . . . " She glanced at her dagger. "I might have blundered badly with the money. The weapons. Dealing with the guards. I thought all I had to do was walk up to the gate and ask to see my father." With a disparaging laugh she admitted, "I do not even know where the gate is."

Guessing at how much the entire admission cost her, he put a finger under her chin, turned her head so he could see her eyes. Those gorgeous sapphire eyes.

"The only land entrance is on the western face, over a drawbridge. You could not have missed it if you tried."

With a sad smile she put her hand on his chest. "Perhaps not, but I thank you for coming with me all the same."

His insides stirred, as always, when this close to Eloise. So many times since catching up with her he'd wanted to kiss her senseless, make her forget herself and her family's problems for a time. Lose himself in her.

He would have now if not for Timothy's footsteps on the stairway.

*   *   *

Eloise carried the purse through the city's streets, but as they crossed the first drawbridge and she caught a glimpse of the guards at the barbican, she handed it over to Roland.

"'Tis best you deal with the guards. I might not show them enough appreciation, or worse, too much."

If he saw her nervousness, he didn't comment, or chide her for her uncharacteristic admission of insecurity. 'Twas easy enough to hide any self-doubts when at Lelleford, a place where she could put a name to every face, where she felt comfortable in her own skin.

Walking the city's streets, she'd felt most uncomfortable, unused to the jostle of strange people accompanied by the assault of loud sounds and stinging smells. The mere sight of the Tower of London's high walls alone frightened her witless.

Were she by herself, she'd brazen it out, do whatever she must to see her father. Perhaps she took the coward's way out by taking advantage of Roland's willingness to help, but sweet mercy, she didn't want to do anything wrong to raise a guard's suspicions and thus deny them entry. Getting in to see her father quickly and without trouble was worth swallowing her pride.

Roland approached one of the barbican's several guards. "We request entry to see a prisoner, Sir John Hamelin. I am Sir Roland St. Marten. With me are my squire, Timothy, and Lady Eloise, Sir John's daughter."

The sentry looked them over, his keen eyes alert and wary, judging their worthiness. They must have passed his inspection because he led them into the barbican.

"Weapons must be left here. You can collect them on your way out," he stated.

Roland and Timothy both handed over daggers, which were placed on a table with others. If a coin changed hands with the daggers, Eloise didn't see it happen.

The guard waved at another guard. "Visitors for Sir John Hamelin."

And so they were given escort over to a gatehouse, its twin towers bragging a double portcullis and several arrow loops. Again Roland explained their presence and made introductions, only to be passed to another guard who escorted them over the second drawbridge to the first curtain wall and another twin-towered gatehouse, augmented with murder holes chiseled through the arch above.

The heavy defenses and number of guards brought into sharp focus that the Tower wasn't merely a place to house highborn prisoners, but a fortress designed to protect the royal families of England. In times of unrest, in a residence within these walls, they could shelter and be assured of safety. Still, as Roland made his third explanation of their presence to a grizzled, narrow-eyed guard, Eloise fought the suffocating feeling of being trapped.

The guard scratched his chin. "Hamelin, eh? Seems to me I heard the name, but cannot quite recollect which tower—" This time Roland wasn't subtle about passing a coin. "Ah, yes, the gent over in Baliol's. I will take ye over to meet the warder myself."

Eloise breathed a sigh of relief that they weren't following the guard to the White Tower and down into its dungeon.

Keeping pace, she leaned toward Roland. "Baliol sounds familiar. Why?"

"I assume you have heard of John Baliol, a Scottish

king who tried to defy English rule. He was housed here for a time after his surrender." Roland smiled slightly. "Apparently they gave his name to the tower where he stayed. One does not house a king, even a deposed king, in less than a comfortable chamber."

Good news, except she didn't like the implication.

"So they house my father in Baliol's Tower because they believe him in league with the Scots."

"Or someone paid well to have him put in the finest chamber available."

"Lancaster?"

Roland merely shrugged a shoulder.

Baliol's Tower turned out to be a round tower set into the far southeast corner of the inner curtain wall. The warder must have appreciated whatever Roland gave him because he bowed courteously after Roland, again, gave him their names and requested to see Sir John. Eloise wryly thought that by now everyone in the place must know who they were and why they were there—and had to admit that made sense given the nature of their visit.

The warder led them up the narrow, winding stairs, his ring of large keys jingling with each step. "I would wager his lordship will be pleased for the company. Ain't had any other visitors as yet. He and his squire been playing a lot o' chess to pass the time. Mind ye, curfew is at sunset. Ye'll hear the bell."

Eloise said a silent prayer of thanks. She'd worried about her father, of course, but also about Edgar. 'Struth, her father truly *could* have let her know of the squire's whereabouts.

"We thank you for the warning," Roland answered the warder for them both.

The warder pounded on the heavy door on the first landing. "Sir John! Ye got visitors! Yer lovely daughter is here."

"What?" came a roar from inside. "Eloise?"

The warder looked apologetic, and probably didn't understand her smile. For the first time since leaving Lelleford she was on solid footing. She well knew the difference between her father's irritated bluster and his furious anger. Mere bluster she could deal with easily.

"Aye, 'tis me, Father. May I come in?"

"You had best let her in, Oswald, so the minx can explain what the devil brings her here!"

The warder set the key in the lock, gave it a twist, and pushed the squealing door open. Eloise charged in, barely noticing the opulence of the room. She made straight for her father, who was garbed in the same clothes in which she'd last seen him, his face set in stern lines.

Behind her she heard the snick of the latch, the heavy key locking the door.

Eloise knew shows of affection discomfited her father, but she wrapped her arms solidly around him anyway and buried her face in his shoulder. The embrace wasn't so much for him as for her, and he'd put her through so much hell he would simply have to put up with her whim.

She damn near cried when his arms finally came around her, but knew better than to push her luck too far. Tears would only serve to make him angry.

"St. Marten. Have I you to thank for allowing my daughter out of Lelleford?"

"Nay, milord. She left on her own. I merely followed to ensure she did not get herself murdered on the road."

Eloise ignored them both, easing away far enough to

inspect her father. "You feel solid enough. Are you getting enough to eat?"

"I take it you did not hide away in a baggage cart."

"Not this time. I stole your fastest palfrey. Are they treating you well here?"

"Ye gods, Eloise, that horse is barely broken to saddle. Have you no sense at all?"

He avoided answering every one of her questions, but she could see for herself he didn't suffer overly so she let it pass.

"This tunic reeks. I brought you several, along with the money you asked for. Have you engaged legal help as yet?"

"Nay. That is part of the reason I needed coin."

"Good. 'Tis an unnecessary expense. I also sent for Geoffrey. He should be here—"

"Eloise, I specifically told you—"

"I know what you said." She tried to strike a balance between contrite and irritated. "I beg pardon, but I could no longer bear to do nothing after learning you had been put in the Tower. 'Struth, Father, your message could have been more revealing. I envisioned you in a loathsome dungeon, not in a grand chamber." For the first time, Eloise looked around the room. With a large, velvet-draped bed and a hooded fireplace, the chamber was truly grand. Silver goblets and a gracefully carved chess set graced the table. She also saw Edgar in the corner of the room with Timothy. "And you said not a word about Edgar."

Her father slumped into an ornate chair. "I had little time to write the message. No matter, you should not have come."

"I was supposed to trust a messenger with a large sack of coin? I think not. 'Twas best to bring it myself."

"I should thrash your backside for your disobedience."

His bluster was giving out, and in its fading revealed his weariness.

"The warder says we do not have much time until curfew, so there isn't enough time for a proper thrashing. Besides, you are not all that unhappy to see me."

He reached out and took her hand, bringing a lump to her throat.

"I am most displeased you left Lelleford, make no mistake. 'Twas a rash thing to do. Perhaps I should be grateful you did not do something worse, like raise an army and storm the gates to effect my release."

She had to smile at his exaggeration, tilted her head coyly. "Do you want me to?"

He laughed lightly. "Let us hope it does not come to that." He released her hand. "Sit down before I change my mind about that thrashing."

As she eased down into the other chair, he turned to Roland.

"I was told you were placed in charge of Lelleford. Why are you playing escort to my daughter instead of ensuring my holding is secure?"

Roland revealed his discomfort by rubbing the back of his neck. "Simon and Marcus are quite capable of securing Lelleford for the time I intended to be gone. I decided Eloise's safety was the more urgent matter."

Father glanced at her before he again spoke to Roland. "Could not convince her to go home, could you?"

"Father, you must not blame Roland. He thought it best—"

"Oh, but I do hold him at fault. And he can correct his error by seeing you safely home. Where is the coin I asked for?"

Damn. Well, she'd been prepared for him to order her home.

Roland handed over the pouch. "This is but a portion of what Eloise brought. A pouch three times this size is well hidden in the room we let."

Incredulous, Father shook his head. "Three times?"

Eloise tossed a dismissive hand in the air. "You were not specific about the amount, and I did not know what you needed the money for. We will bring the rest on the morrow. You can keep what you believe you need and I will take the rest back with me."

Except, if she had her way, she wasn't going home for several days. True, she'd promised Roland she wouldn't argue if her father pointed to the door and ordered her to leave immediately. That hadn't happened, thank the Lord, and her father had unwittingly bought her some time. At least tomorrow. Maybe more. With luck, she would still be here to see Geoffrey.

Her father leaned back in his chair. "So, what happened after I left?"

Eloise launched into what Roland considered a very detailed account of tending Brother Walter and Kenworth's eventual arrival, some of which he hadn't heard from her side before.

Roland noticed she glazed over her ire at seeing *him* again, how pointedly she'd objected to his duty.

He could envision Eloise as she'd appeared that morning, gliding across the floor of the great hall, cool and serene, to greet an earl she already knew intended to arrest her father for treason. She'd given away not a hint of her upset over her father's hasty escape from Lelleford. Even now only small traces of her fears underscored her tale.

She'd done much the same this morning, worn that regal expression through the city streets. Only he knew she'd lost a portion of her courage on the first drawbridge, revealed in the slightest tremble of her hand when she handed over the pouch.

He'd expected her to forge ahead on her own, deal with the guards. She could have done it, too, if she'd given herself a chance. What prompted her to give him the pouch he wasn't sure, but he had to admit he was touched by the show of trust, not only then but when they hid the money under the floor.

Eloise could be reasonable, when she wanted to be, or when circumstances dictated that she must.

To Roland's way of thinking, he'd done right to bring Eloise to London, for her sake as well as her father's. The weariness in Sir John's eyes boded ill for the older man. To face the days ahead he must be strong, healthy, and confident. Perhaps this visit from Eloise would bolster his will.

Roland also couldn't miss the affection the two held for each other, despite the small skirmish of earlier. Today, and tomorrow, might be the last time she saw him alive if his trial went badly.

Inevitably, the curfew bell tolled. Eloise again hugged Sir John, who accepted it with more grace this time.

"We will be back tomorrow with the clothing and coin, and then you can tell me how you ended up here."

"'Tis not a long tale."

She shrugged. "All the same."

The warder's key sounded in the lock, and Eloise turned to Edgar to wrap a hug around the squire. "You look to be all right, too. Are you?"

"Right as rain, milady. You need not have worried over me."

The door opened and the warder poked his head in. "Curfew. Ye'd best hurry before they close the gates."

Roland ushered Eloise and Timothy out ahead of him.

"St. Marten." Roland paused at Sir John's soft call. "My thanks for looking after my daughter. Guard her close. London is not a safe place for her."

With Sir John's caution echoing in his head, Roland hurried them along the emptying streets, wanting to be back in the room well before full dark. He wished he'd brought his sword. Though he'd known all along London wasn't a safe place for a woman alone, Sir John's warning suggested a specific threat. From whom?

Roland's thoughts arrowed in on Kenworth, the only formidable enemy of John Hamelin's that he knew of.

They paused only twice along the way, once at the barbican to fetch the daggers—both of which were right where the guard had put them—and at a vendor to buy hot, fragrant meat pies for their supper.

Eloise was quiet, her cool expression firmly in place. Timothy, however, filled the void, describing to Eloise the significance of a few of the sights along the way. The lad loved London, its crowded lanes and bargaining with vendors, his vibrant pleasure making Eloise smile a time or two.

'Twas after one of those smiles, she said, "I take it you and Edgar had a nice talk."

Timothy nodded. "I gave him Isolde's message, told him what transpired at Lelleford. He was glad for the news. He also told me he has not been charged with any crime so he is free to come and go as he pleases, with the guard's permission."

That brought Eloise's spirits up. "Truly?"

"Aye, milady. He chooses to stay with Sir John because that is where he feels his duty lies."

She reached out and ruffled Timothy's hair. "My thanks. The news does my heart good."

When they reached the apothecary, Timothy took his meat pie and announced his intention to check on the horses, and possibly play dice with the stable lads after. Roland led the way up to the room, opening the door for Eloise to enter.

She slowly untied her cloak and tossed it on the bed, removed her boots. In hose-covered feet she padded over to the window.

'Twas light enough to make out the turrets of White Tower, but wouldn't be for long.

Roland tossed his own cloak on the bed, placed the paper-wrapped meat pies on the small table, and lit the candle. When he turned back, she yet stared out the window, arms crossed over her middle, one hand pressed to her lips.

"Come eat before the pies get cold."

"I cannot . . . yet."

The hitch in her voice disturbed him.

"What is amiss?"

"Everything. Damn."

She bowed her head, her hand covering her eyes. She

took a very deep breath, fighting so hard not to cry and not quite succeeding.

Well, sometimes tears did a body good. Roland eased up behind her, turned her around, and gathered her into his arms. She melded against him so easily, so thoroughly, he momentarily wondered if he held the right woman.

"Not everything, Eloise. You saw for yourself that Sir John is comfortable."

"But they still . . . lock the door."

"Which means he is hard to get at in secret. Keep that in mind. He may be a prisoner, but he is also protected."

She sniffed. "Why would anyone bother? Give the guards enough coin and they will let anyone in."

Point taken. And they'd probably not question anyone of very high rank, like an earl, unless they were under orders not to admit certain personages. He'd have to talk to the warder—Oswald?—tomorrow to see if any such orders existed.

He couldn't become deeply involved in Sir John's problems with the king, and he wouldn't, at least not any deeper than necessary to ease Eloise's mind so she could go home in peace.

He brushed a stray strand of hair back from her forehead. So soft, her skin. So silky, her hair.

"Roland?"

"Hmmm?"

"When we go back to . . . the Tower tomorrow, I want to bribe the guards."

"Tokens of appreciation."

"Call it what you wish, I still want to hand over the

coins. You will have to show me how to do so with discretion."

Roland heard the firmness return to her voice, and once again marveled at the force of her will. Other women would have sobbed all over him in their upset. Not Eloise. She simply dug deep within for the strength to go on, do what must be done.

"On the morrow. Come eat."

She unfolded her arms and coiled her fingers around fistfuls of his tunic. "Not yet. A moment more."

Then Eloise looked up at him, her bright eyes moist and tinged with red, and what he read in their depths banished all thought of meat pies. Her tongue flicked out to wet her lips, and Roland forgot to think at all.

He bent his head and kissed her, tenderly at first, igniting fires probably best left unlit but too enticing to resist. Desire hit him hard, a heavy fist enclosed in a velvet glove.

Then *she* deepened the kiss, pulling his weakened will under to drown in her sweet allure.

She wanted him. He wanted her. 'Twas more than enough knowledge to ease them both over to the bed. If she showed the merest hesitancy he'd stop. If not, he'd show her how nimble his fingers could be on her laces.

Chapter Fourteen

A NIGGLING VOICE in the far reaches of Eloise's conscience whispered dire warnings. She swiftly hushed it, too overwhelmed by the tingling sensations coursing through her body to listen closely anyway.

She was right where she wanted to be, within the circle of Roland's arms, on the verge of a grand adventure. Nothing, not even her aching muscles, could prevent her from taking full advantage.

She'd fantasized about this moment for what seemed an eternity, but had allowed solid, practical reasons to dissuade her. No longer. Not when being pressed against him felt so right, not when his mouth melded warmly, persuasively against hers.

Never before did she so desperately want to be persuaded, to experience the intimate joy she knew within her grasp with Roland. Never before did her heart beat so hard or so fast or rule so completely over her common sense.

And it felt good, and right, and inevitable.

Her legs bumped against the bed. The whispers again tried to intrude.

Eloise wrapped her arms firmly around Roland and pulled him down atop her.

He twisted and landed beside her, a gallant gesture to save her from the press of his full weight. Except she wanted to feel his weight. 'Twould come later, she knew, when they joined. Given the burn in her nether regions she hoped the moment came soon.

He propped up on an elbow, his look of wonder endearing.

"This is where I am supposed to whisper sweet words, praise your beauty, tell you how long and hard I have dreamed to have you beside me." His hand gently cupped her cheek. "My tongue fails me, Eloise. No words I might utter would do you justice. No turn of phrase could describe the depth of my yearning."

She ran a hand along his square, chiseled jaw, marveling at his sense of the poetic. "I must say your tongue works very well. Are your hands as skilled? My laces need undoing."

He backed away slightly, frowned. "I am supposed to calm your maidenly fears. 'Tis generally how it is done."

So she'd done something wrong. Not surprising, because she didn't know what she was doing.

"I beg pardon, then. Do I do the same? Tell you I delight in your kisses, believe you are the most handsome, honorable, and considerate knight in the kingdom? You are beyond my experience, Roland. Exotically foreign and yet someone I might have known all of my life."

He smiled. "You learn quickly."

"That is to my advantage, because there is much I wish you to teach me. I am not fragile, nor have I ever been very good at being demure, so might we skip that part in preference for where we remove our garments? I have heard coupling is best done naked."

She'd stunned him again, turning his smile into a frown. But since he didn't leap off the bed in indignation, she mustn't have blundered too badly.

"Have you no fears at all?"

"A concern or two, but owe them to mine own ignorance. Be assured I do not fear you, Roland, nor does the thought of coupling with you scare me. Does that quell *your* fears?"

His smile returned, a wry twist of his mouth. "Not a bit. You scare me witless. But I will move beyond it, I swear."

"Brave man. Now do we undo my laces?"

"The last time I offered to undo your laces you refused me."

"With good reason. If I recall correctly we were expecting Timothy at any moment." Which led her to ask, "He will be gone a good long while tonight, will he not?"

"Likely." He kissed the tip of her nose. "But just in case I misjudge the time, I shall lock the door. Stay right where you are. Do not even fiddle with a lace."

She'd never been good at obeying orders she thought senseless, either. She left her laces alone, but flipped over on her stomach to watch Roland secure the latch.

What a fine specimen of male grace and beauty he was. He had most likely turned the head and undone the laces of many a woman. She was suddenly unwarrantedly jealous of every one of them, but took comfort that he was with her now, and she was about to benefit from his experience.

The door secure, he sat down on the other edge of the

bed, his back to her, and removed his boots. Then his belt. When he reached for his throat she could stay still no longer.

She rose up to her knees and scooted toward him. "Wait. Let me do that."

He glanced back at her but said nothing. Eloise pressed snug against his back, reached over those wide shoulders, and untied his tunic's lacing. She spread the fabric wide, and with an economy of motion, also undid his shirte.

Beneath she found warm, taut skin. Her fingertips itched to roam, but she got no farther in her exploration than just below the ridge of his collarbone when he shivered and grabbed hold of her hands.

"Cold?" she asked.

"Nay. You? Shall I light the brazier?"

She didn't want him to get that far away from her again, nor did she feel any chill. Truth to tell, she was overly warm.

"Not necessary for me."

He squeezed her hands, spread her arms, and slipped away.

She would have protested if she could have spoken, but her mouth and throat went dry when he pulled off his tunic and sherte in one fluid motion, revealing a wide, muscled back. He tossed his garments to the floor and turned around.

Sweet mercy. She knew Roland to be a strong, powerfully built man, but hadn't realized how magnificently sculpted his chest would be, each muscle defined. From just beneath his collarbone to the waist of his breeches, from sloped shoulder to shoulder, a sprinkling of dark, shining hair enticed her to touch.

He tugged at the end of one of the strings holding up his breeches. More laces.

"Want to undo these, too?"

She might, if she weren't frozen in place, if she could do more than stare at where his fingers pulled slowly at strings.

"Perhaps another time."

Her voice sounded thready, as if spoken by someone else. She blamed her dry throat.

Down went his breeches, up went the heat in her cheeks and along with it the degree of her fascination. He didn't give her long to inspect the enthralling part of him that made him male before he knelt before her on the bed.

"Now your laces."

About time. He kissed her all the while his hands loosened the ties along her sides. She paid utterly no attention to how her gown, chemise, and hose disappeared, of how they ended up prone and pressed together on the bed. She only felt the shock and delight of being skin to skin at last.

His hands weren't still, his petting gentle but so arousing. He was particularly attentive to her breasts, cupping them, kneading them, then driving her wild when his thumb grazed the tips. And his mouth, sweet mercy, his mouth caressed those now swollen, yearning tips with nips and licks until she thought she'd lose her mind completely.

But something wasn't right. He was doing all these marvelous things to her body. Shouldn't she be doing something likewise to his? Oh, she'd touched him, too—

along his side, over his back. Threaded her fingers through the hair on his chest, and now knew it short and silky. She even dared several strokes along his buttocks.

But 'struth, there were other parts of him she wanted to touch, to explore and learn more of. Except every time her fingers wandered anywhere near his male parts, he grasped hold of her hand and placed it somewhere else, like up on his shoulder or on his chest.

The pressure boiling up inside her was both pleasant and irksome. She wanted the fondling to go on forever, and yet she wanted it over. Was that natural? She wished she knew.

"Roland, I feel so strange."

He lifted his head, removing his mouth from her breast, but immediately made up for the loss with his palm.

"How so?"

"I cannot help but feel I should be learning something more."

"Oh, you will. All in good time. We are far from finished."

"I know we have yet to couple, but should I not be doing something to you? I am just lying here, doing nothing—"

He kissed her into silence, a long, hardy kiss that almost made her forget her resolve.

"Allow me to have my way this time, Eloise. Relax. Enjoy. Next time you can take an active part, but this first time I do not want to risk your disappointment."

Well, that was sweet of him, but—

"And you? If there is something I should do, I want to know. I would hate to have you disappointed."

He laughed lightly. "No chance of that, believe me." Then he reached down, ran his hand from her knee up her inner thigh to where she ached so badly. Her hips rose up off the bed when he slid a finger inside. "Once joined to you, I will know the greatest bliss a man can know with a woman. I need to be sure you will feel it, too, before I come inside."

She heard what he said, and it all made sense through the foglike haze muddling her head. This first time he wanted her surrender. She so rarely felt vulnerable that she nearly didn't recognize it. And yet, her trust in Roland diminished the emotion. He wouldn't harm her, this warrior turned lover. In the end, surrender came appallingly quickly, easily.

"You will come inside soon?"

"Just a few more moments." He accompanied his promise with several strokes through the juices between her spread legs. "Very soon now."

"I certainly hope so."

And with that, Eloise closed her eyes.

Roland shook his head. He should have known making love with Eloise would be different from encounters he'd shared with other women.

Though a virgin, she was as bold and brash as an experienced paramour. He'd only managed to hold a tight rein on his body's urges because he knew the first time might bring her pain, and he could only ease it by being gentle. If he allowed her to touch him as she'd tried, several times, he might lose control and plow too hard into her depths.

He was so damn hard he should be glad Eloise was neither shy nor afraid, because he wasn't sure how much longer his control could last. Keeping himself from entering her was painfully difficult.

He'd never taken this much care with a woman. Coupling had always been a physical act, an enjoyment of mutual pleasure, nothing more. With Eloise 'twas more, much more, and he feared he knew why. Because his heart was involved, his emotions entangled with the beautiful, brazen woman whose hips again rose off the bed, a soft hiss parting her lush lips.

She opened her eyes when he moved atop her, covering her, the call to mate an urgent cry for release. He knew the moment when she felt the tip press against her sensitive nub, and her eyes went wider when he slid inside, just an inch.

"Roland?"

He didn't truly know what she asked, but guessed. "There may be a bit of pain. Do not fret. 'Twill pass."

She licked her lips, and her woman's sheath tightened around him like a velvet glove, as though she feared if she didn't hold him tighter he might pull away.

He couldn't stop now if he'd applied every ounce of will to the task. So he glided home, past the barrier that broke so easily she never flinched, until buried to the hilt. Again she tightened around him, driving him to the brink of madness.

"Oh, my. Oh, yes." Her sapphire eyes glittered with wonder and desire. "I did not know. Sweet mercy that feels good."

Stroke followed stroke, deeper, harder, until Eloise tossed back her head and cried out. With both relief and triumph, he gave himself over to his own quest for release, thrusting in rhythm to her soft pulses.

At the very last moment he withdrew, and with the aid of a towel from the bedside table, allowed his pleasure to flow. He'd withdrawn from other women, the only way he knew to protect them from getting with child. Even while his penis yet pounded and the ache in his loins eased, he knew he'd done right by Eloise. So why did his heart protest, his mind scream that this was wrong?

In time, he rolled to his side, bringing her with him to snuggle into a cocoon of warm bodies and soft blankets. She eased a leg over his thigh, and an arm across his chest to lay her hand on his shoulder.

In the mellow voice of a woman well loved, she said, "I did not know one could be so invigorated one moment and so replete the next. Are the feelings the same every time?"

He nearly told her the truth, but he experienced the most ridiculous confidence that with Eloise the peaks would be the norm, the valleys few.

"Most every time."

"'Tis hard to believe."

"Give me an hour and I will prove it to you."

She rose up, a small frown on her face. "Were you . . . disappointed?"

Only in mind, not body. He gently pushed her head back to his shoulder, where it belonged.

"Nay. I feel as replete as you."

'Struth, he couldn't remember a time when the physical act had felt so good. Nor did he need an hour to recover, but within a few minutes, Eloise slept, and from the sound of her breathing went deeply under.

Probably a good thing. Timothy would be back soon.

As easily as he could fall asleep holding Eloise, spend

the night cuddled against her, he didn't dare. Timothy might not care, or gossip, but Roland didn't want to take the risk of damaging her reputation. That Eloise had given herself to him was dangerous enough. To have others know was unacceptable.

After a kiss to her forehead, he eased away from her warmth and got out of bed. The chilly night air went far to banish his languor.

A brief search of the floor turned up his breeches, which he put on. His tunic and shirte he tossed on the end of the bed along with Eloise's gown and chemise. From the corner he dragged out two pallets, leaving the third to cover the loose board and the treasure beneath.

With the door unlocked to allow Timothy entrance, Roland bent to light the brazier. 'Twas then he heard the scrape of boots on stairs and the murmur of voices.

Neither voice Timothy's.

The hair on the back of Roland's neck itched, and he'd learned long ago to heed his instincts. Whoever came up the stairs didn't belong here—and meant no good.

He crept back to the corner and silently slipped his sword from its scabbard—then put it back. His dagger was a better choice for close quarters in the dark. Damn, where were his boots? On the other side of the bed.

Roland briefly considered waking Eloise, order her to wrap up in a blanket and curl up in the far corner. But just as he retrieved his dagger, the scraping sounds stopped. He stilled, listening hard in the stillness of the night air, where voices tended to carry.

"This it?" a man whispered.

"Aye. Hush now," the other answered.

Were these common footpads bent on robbery? Or worse villains, perhaps after Eloise?

Sir John's words of warning about her danger came back to haunt him.

Wishing for more light than the faint moonbeams allowed in through the window, he took two steps toward the door. The latch snicked open, the door moved the merest crack. Then all went still as the intruders listened for sound.

Smiling, Roland decided to give them something to hear.

He drew a long breath, and with his best battlefield roar, he charged the door.

Startled out of sleep, heart thudding, Eloise sat straight up in what took her a moment to remember was a bed in a room above an apothecary. Completely disoriented, she strove to make sense out of what seemed senseless.

For some reason the door was open, and what appeared to be three men struggled on the landing. The tallest must be Roland. Grunts and groans followed kicks and punches. Then one man fell backward and tumbled down the stairs. Roland grabbed hold of the other and pushed him up against the wall.

"What are you doing here?" he growled. "What are you after?"

"Did not mean no harm."

She knew she should be frightened witless, but mercy, Roland had ended the scuffle before she'd fully understood what was going on.

Roland pulled the hapless fellow forward, shoved him back into the wall again. "Answers, man, and I want them now!"

Unable to stay put any longer, Eloise slid from the bed and wrapped a blanket around her. She eased toward the door, knowing better than to show herself but she needed to hear clearly.

"Don't know nothing, I swear."

Eloise caught the glint of metal as Roland brought his dagger to the lout's throat.

"If you do not loosen your tongue, you will lose it."

She winced at the threat, which broke the man's resistance within the space of two heartbeats.

"A man paid my partner to bring him the lady."

"What man?"

"Never saw him. He dealt with my partner."

"Where were you to take the lady?"

"Southwark. The docks. That's all I know, I swear."

From the bottom of the stairs came a female's gasp. Roland never moved a muscle.

"Mistress Green, summon a watchman. Our friends here are up to mischief."

The tinkle of the bell above the door. Mistress Green's panicked shouts. Eloise heard them as far-off sounds through the sudden pounding in her head, brought on by the horror of what the villains had planned. They'd come to kidnap her, haul her off to the docks for who knew what foul purpose.

Why?

She didn't realize she breeched the threshold and spoke aloud until Roland jerked, his head coming around. The distraction allowed the villain to give Roland a shove and slip out of his captor's grasp. By the time Roland recovered his balance, the lout had already pounded down the stairs.

Roland cursed and went after him, leaping over the man who lay still and silent at the bottom of the stairs.

Eloise trembled along the entire length of her.

Why?

John Hamelin only had to look at his daughter's face to know something was horribly wrong. Very little shook Eloise to the point of paleness, dimmed the spark in her blue eyes. He'd not seen her in such a state since her mother's death, and she'd been a little girl at the time.

He gathered her in his arms and addressed Roland, who handed a large sack over to Edgar. The knight looked like he hadn't slept much either.

"What happened?"

"We had visitors last eve."

"Who?"

"Two men. One broke his neck from a fall down the stairs, the other got away."

"My fault," Eloise whispered. "I . . . interfered."

"My fault," Roland countered. "I should have put my boots on before I gave chase."

My fault. Eloise wouldn't be in London if not for love of and concern for him. He should have been much more forthcoming in his message home.

By God, he'd made too many blunders of late, and not only with his daughter.

"So you do not know their identities?"

Roland shook his head. "Nay, but we do know they were after Eloise. The one who got away told me they were hired by someone to take her to Southwark."

Southwark! A nasty area where villains roamed at will,

where brothels lined the streets. Did Eloise fully realize what might have happened to her? He dearly hoped not.

Kenworth—and he was as sure as he stood in Baliol's Tower that Kenworth was ultimately behind this atrocity—had gone too far.

John led Eloise over to a chair, poured her a goblet of wine. "Tell me all."

Eloise took a sip, then looked up at him, a slight trace of ire giving him hope. "Near as we know, the men somehow knew where our horses were stabled. They . . . they . . ."

The crack in her voice broke his heart.

Roland cleared his throat. "When Timothy went to check on the horses last eve, the men joined in a dice game with Timothy and some of the stable lads. Timothy did not like the looks of them, nor some of the questions they asked, so he left. They waylaid him on a nearby street." Roland's pause didn't bode well for the lad. "They took their fists to him, and when he would not tell them of Eloise's whereabouts, they tied his hands and bound his mouth. While one hid Timothy, the other went back to tell the stable master that the lad had been injured, and they'd be happy to take him to his lodgings if given direction. Victor knew, of course."

"And your squire?"

"The watchmen found him. He is bruised, two cracked ribs. He is sore hurt but he will recover. Mistress Green is looking after him now."

John knew from Roland's stance, from the undertone running beneath the flatly delivered tale, the knight wanted revenge for his squire. That could prove useful. Except he would rather St. Marten take Eloise back to

Lelleford, where stone walls and a full garrison stood between her and Kenworth.

"When do you return to Lelleford?"

"As soon as Timothy is able to ride. Mistress Green feels that will not be for another day or two." Roland's expression changed, and John braced for what he saw coming. "You told me yesterday that Eloise was not safe in London. Last eve proved you right. What are we up against, Hamelin?"

Someday this youngest St. Marten son was going to be a powerful man. He may not yet have property or wealth, but he possessed the presence and forthright attitude of a man on the rise. Roland reminded John of himself at a younger age.

"I believe the earl of Kenworth is responsible, but I cannot offer proof."

Eloise perked up. "What does Kenworth want with me?"

"To hold you hostage against my cooperation. He wants my confession for treason, and will do whatever he must to obtain it." John tried to tamp down his ire and failed. "There is a piece of land I set aside for your dowry he craves. He offered to purchase it and I refused. Then he offered a marriage bargain between you and his second son, which I also refused—adamantly and, unfortunately, before several witnesses. He took the refusal as a grave insult, and thus he pursues this ridiculous treason charge so ruthlessly."

"You said nothing of this betrothal offer," Eloise complained.

"Since nothing came of it, I saw no reason for you to know."

Roland crossed his arms. "Was this before or after you betrothed Eloise to Hugh?"

"Kenworth knew your father and I were negotiating the betrothal to Hugh when he made his offer, which made the insult worse, knowing I would prefer to ally myself to your family than to him."

"Was it Kenworth who brought charges against you, gave the king the missive which is rumored to point to your guilt?"

John liked the knight's intelligence. "That he did."

"Father, what is contained in those scrolls you took with you?"

"What scrolls?" Roland asked.

John wished she hadn't mentioned them, but he could undo part of the damage.

"Documents I need to prove my innocence. They are now safely in the possession of the earl of Lancaster."

"Can you trust him with them?"

"I had no choice."

At least not much of a choice, and the longer Lancaster cautioned patience, the more John wondered if going to the powerful earl had been his biggest mistake.

Roland was pacing, and John could well imagine the path of his thoughts. He also noticed how Eloise watched Roland, as if she expected him to solve all of her problems, tilt her world right side up again. The amount of trust she placed in the knight she'd once professed a particular dislike for surprised him.

But there was more here. He knew his daughter. There was trust, and respect, but also . . . affection? John sighed inwardly. If so, then he could add one more problem to an already long list.

Roland stopped pacing. "Sir John, do you believe Kenworth faked the missive to frame you for treason?"

This game went far deeper than Roland surmised. And as in a good chess game, all the pieces must be in perfect position in order to win. They weren't as yet, might never be. He could very well hang for a crime he didn't commit.

"I put nothing beyond Kenworth."

"Sweet mercy, Father, why not just sell Kenworth the land if that is what he wants?"

"Months ago that might have worked, but no longer. Now he not only wants the land but revenge for the insult, too."

Roland looked puzzled. "Then why did he not take Eloise from Lelleford when he went to capture you, marry her off to his son? He had the perfect opportunity then."

"Because he sees the opportunity to have more. If I am convicted of treason, my lands are forfeit to the king, and Kenworth is confident he can talk Edward into giving him a portion, not only the land he craves but more as well."

Again Eloise complained, "Is not your life a rather high price to ask for an insult?"

Not to an earl, especially not to Kenworth. Whatever royalty wanted, royalty usually obtained, no matter who they must plow under or trample over to get it.

"One does not insult an earl and get off lightly. But come, this is my coil to unwind." He held a hand out to Eloise. "Show me what you brought for me."

She got up reluctantly. She wanted more answers, and he couldn't give them to her. Not yet.

From the sack she pulled two tunics and gave them to Edgar. "Isolde chose these for you. I assume Timothy told you she sends her love."

The squire blushed. "Timothy also said I was not to worry over her, but I do. This must be hard for her."

"As it is for all of us. Perhaps a letter from you might ease her mind."

Edgar nodded, and John felt sorry for the lad, but not too sorry. Loyalty to one's lord was expected of a squire, and 'struth, without Edgar's company he might have gone mad. There would be a reward for that loyalty at the end—if fate allowed.

Then Eloise pulled out the biggest of his leather pouches, near bursting at the seams with coin. "Is it safe for you to keep all this here?"

John hefted the burgeoning pouch. "Safe enough. Have you coin to see you through your stay and to get home?"

"I sewed coin into the hem of my cloak, as you ordered me to. If you give me back my purse, I should have plenty."

The exchange made, she emptied the sack of three more tunics, one of them his best midnight blue velvet trimmed in gold. She ran a soothing hand over the velvet.

"I thought you might need this for . . . court."

He just might. He'd raised a wise daughter.

"You do me proud, Eloise."

She rewarded him with a small smile. "I do my best. What would you have me do now?"

"Get some rest. You look awful. See to it, St. Marten."

They took their leave, Eloise insisting on another hug, Roland vowing he would look after her. When they were gone, John eased down into the chair he'd become accustomed to occupying, stared down at the pieces on the chessboard.

"You did not tell them everything," Edgar said.

"Nay. I know Roland St. Marten is from a fine family and I have heard of his prowess in Scotland. He is a man on the rise in the king's service. All points in the man's favor. What I do not know is if I can trust him."

"Lady Eloise seems to."

John picked up the white knight, a beautifully carved depiction of a horse's head, reminding him of Geoffrey's carvings. His son could do such fine work, already had, as witnessed by the two statues that John kept on the mantel of his bedchamber at Lelleford. Two horses, one a destrier, one a palfrey. Gifts from his talented son.

Was Geoffrey as gifted with his knowledge of law?

Eloise had sent for Geoffrey. He'd be here soon, which meant two of his children would be in harm's way. Most troubling, indeed.

John twirled the white knight between his fingers. "I fear she does trust St. Marten. Only time will tell if her trust is misplaced."

Chapter Fifteen

E LOISE FELT as much a prisoner as her father, trapped in the room above the apothecary with Roland as her warder—who was currently downstairs checking on Mistress Green.

'Twas now the third day of enforced confinement. Except for their daily visits to her father, who grew more reluctant to discuss his situation, she had little to do but pace the floor and keep Timothy company.

He slept now, on the pallet he'd occupied since being injured. With each day he grew stronger and his bruises faded. Timothy declared himself able to endure the two-day ride to Lelleford; Roland disagreed and ordered the lad to rest. And Eloise couldn't decide if Roland's protectiveness was a boon or curse.

She could do nothing for her father. He wasn't telling her the whole of his entanglements, she knew, probably because he feared she might try to become further involved. Still, she was able to spend time with him each day, which he seemed to appreciate even though he urged Roland to take her home.

Roland might be overprotective of Timothy, but Eloise

suspected there was more to his willingness to linger in London than the health of his squire.

What, she didn't know, for Roland wasn't forthcoming either.

She could understand why he asked no further questions of her father. 'Twas not in his best interest to become too involved with a man accused of treason. Nor were his best interests served by becoming overly involved with her, Hamelin's daughter. If convicted, the taint of the father would rub off on the daughter, and no man of any ambition should link his name to hers.

Roland might have chased after her to take her back home—but he'd done so out of a sense of duty. He might have bedded her—but the physical intimacy could be attributed to lust. He liked her, she knew, but he held back what she craved, his love.

Which further depressed her because she'd fallen in love with Roland. Completely. Heart over head. A foolhardy thing to do, but there it was.

She saw no sense in telling him, fearing a reaction of horror. If Father was convicted, she'd be shunned by most men of rank, Roland among them, if he was wise. Nor was there a future for them even if Father was exonerated, for he'd never allow her marriage to a landless knight, no matter how honorable or lovable that knight might be.

Nay, no sense in revealing her deepest, most heartfelt feelings when the man she loved wasn't free to return them. Not, she thought wryly, that he did. The fantasy of being loved in return was hers, not his.

Nor could she express her love physically. Not when Timothy lay on his pallet, healing. Not when Mistress

Green, who Eloise now knew was a widow, slept on a pallet in the chamber at Roland's insistence, while he slept in the hallway outside the door with his sword at his side.

They were never alone, and the lack of privacy gnawed at her temperament.

She almost wished she'd not surrendered, not tasted the heady joy of lovemaking with Roland. Then, ignorance intact, she'd not know what she missed. Unfortunately, she also knew that if given the same offer of ecstasy, she'd succumb again in a heartbeat. If Roland beckoned, she'd answer.

What a coil she'd wound for herself, allowing her heart to reach out to another, allowing her body to know its mate.

All for naught.

At least no more villains had come prowling in the night. No one had accosted them on the streets. If Kenworth were truly behind her attempted abduction, he seemed to have given up on the plan at the first attempt's failure.

She heard footsteps on the stairs. Voices. Two men. One Roland, the other . . . sweet mercy, could it be? She was already halfway to the door when it opened, revealing the answer to several earnest prayers.

Eloise threw herself into her brother's arms. "Geoffrey! Sweet Lord, you came. You came!"

He chuckled. "Did you doubt?"

"Only in my night terrors."

She stepped back and basked in the sight of him. A few years her senior, taller by more than a hand span, she and Geoffrey shared the coloring of their mother—dark brown hair and deep blue eyes. They might be separated by years and distance, but not by affection. Even while Geoffrey resided in Paris he'd not forgotten her, sending her several letters.

Then he'd nearly died on his way home, answering her plea to attend her wedding, a request for which she might never forgive herself. But that was past. He was here now, and apparently none the worse for his journey.

"How did you get here so quickly?"

"The messenger from Lelleford nearly killed a horse to deliver your message, and I left for London within an hour of receiving it." He tilted his head. "Imagine my surprise to learn you were here, too."

Eloise ignored the faint admonition. "You have already been to see Father, then? Of course, you must have. That's how you knew how to find me."

Geoffrey sighed and dropped his hands from her waist, her signal to let go, too. She did so reluctantly.

"He is not pleased with either of us I fear," he said.

"Oh, now _there_ is news."

"Make that three of us," Roland commented as he finally entered the room, closing the door behind him. She'd been half aware he stood in the doorway, leaning against the jam, observing her reunion with Geoffrey. "Sir John is displeased that I have not yet taken Eloise back to Lelleford."

"So Father told me." Geoffrey glanced over to the pallet where Timothy lay, who'd awakened and propped up on an elbow. "How do you, Timothy?"

"Better, my lord. My thanks for troubling to inquire."

"So far you have born the worst effects of this affair. 'Tis only right that I inquire." He turned back to her, and she didn't like his expression. "'Tis you, however, Father worries over most. Nor does he want me in London. He suggested, rather forcefully, that I leave for Cornwall with due haste—and take you with me."

Eloise's heart sank. "Nay, Geoffrey."

"Eloise, Father fears Kenworth will get hold of one or the other of us and he prefers us both out of harm's way. After listening to his tale"—Geoffrey glanced briefly at Roland—"and from what Sir Roland told me downstairs, I cannot say I think it a bad idea. I can protect you at Pecham better than I can here, and Leah would be delighted for the company."

Well, she'd like to see her sister-by-marriage, too, but not now. Eloise crossed her arms. "Roland has done a fine job of keeping me safe. I see no sense in traveling clear across the kingdom—"

"Hold, Eloise. Your brother makes sense."

Roland's agreement to this nefarious scheme hit her in her already sore heart. He wanted to send her away, far away. If she went, she might never see him again. It hurt deeply, but her personal misery wasn't at issue here.

Against all common sense she wanted to stamp her feet, cry, scream at all three males for being so obstinate, for believing they always knew what was best for her. Except her father wasn't here to witness, and tossing a fit had never been her way.

"I prefer to go back to Lelleford if I must go anywhere. And I am not going anywhere until assured Father has the best legal counsel to be found." She put a hand on Geoffrey's arm. "When you talked to him, did you get the impression he did not reveal all, that he withheld something vital to his case?"

"We barely spoke of his case. I spent most of the time listening to his tirade about having his orders disobeyed by his children. He does not want my help. He wants you safely tucked behind thick stone walls. He is adamant that Sir Roland return to Lelleford to carry out his duty there."

"I understand all that. Now, how do we make him accept that we will not desert him when he needs us the most? Especially you. He needs you now more than ever before."

Geoffrey closed his eyes and bowed his head. "Father has never needed me, does not now."

"But he does! And because he does, he pushes both of us away. We cannot allow him his way this time. The stakes are too great. We speak of his very life, Geoffrey. How do we make him see sense?"

When he opened his eyes, Eloise saw the pain of years of being at odds with their father. The arguments. Geoffrey's self-imposed exile in Paris. Years of strife, a relationship never repaired. If the two were ever to come to terms with each other, the time was now.

"Perhaps he would listen to Julius—"

"But our brother is in Italy. No help there. Nor will our sister's husband become involved, so no help there either. He has only us, Geoffrey. We cannot desert him."

"He has Henry of Grosmont. What can I do for Father that the earl of Leicester, Lancaster, Derby, and Lincoln cannot?"

Eloise sensed defeat. Perhaps Geoffrey was right. With an ally who possessed the power of four earldoms behind him, what did Father need with his children? Except, perhaps, their support and love, which he seemed very willing to do without. She was almost ready to give in when Roland spoke.

"Perhaps more than you think, Geoffrey. Lancaster *did* have your father confined to the Tower, under the guise of both imprisoning a wanted man and partly to protect him from his accusers." He shot her a glance—a guilty glance? "I also happen to know he intended to isolate Sir John. Lancaster left orders that your father was to have no visitors."

This *was* news.

"When did you learn this?"

"Two days ago," he admitted. "When you played chess with your father, Edgar and I took a walk."

More secrets. How many more . . . later. She'd deal with them later.

"If Father is not allowed visitors, then why are we allowed to see him?"

"Edgar's doing. He took it upon himself to petition Lancaster to allow either you or Geoffrey to see Sir John, as an act of compassion. The earl must believe you of no danger to John, so he agreed. I am only allowed in because I go with you." Roland waved a hand in the air. "My point being, Lancaster might possibly have your father's best interests at heart, but be assured, the earl has his own reasons for becoming involved, too. What those reasons are?" He shrugged a shoulder.

She wasn't terribly happy with Roland for keeping secrets, but Eloise could have kissed him—right there in front of the squire and her brother—for aiding her cause.

"We have to find out what Father is hiding from us, Geoffrey."

"You expect Father to tell me?"

"By God, I do." Eloise grabbed her cloak. "I expect him to tell both of us. Coming?"

"Even if he is not, I am," Roland announced, strapping on his sword. Ever since the attack he'd carried his sword whenever outside, even to the Tower, where he'd become very friendly with the guard who held the weapons. "In your present mood, the people of London are not safe."

She smiled at the quip and tossed her cloak over her shoulders. "You come because you fear I might lose my way."

"That, too." He waved a hand at Timothy, who'd started to rise. "You stay. I will send Mistress Green up to tend you."

The squire groaned, but obeyed.

Eloise put her hand on the latch. "Are we ready?"

She might as well have announced she intended to run naked through the streets for all Geoffrey and Roland paid her heed.

The two blatantly stared at each other, measuring, evaluating. Each seeming to issue a challenge, both accepting.

Then Geoffrey smiled softly, as if during that mystical male ritual the two came to an understanding. "In the face of such solidarity, how can I refuse?"

Roland wasn't surprised Eloise sailed through the streets like a princess gracing the rabble with her presence. Nor did her regal handling of bribing the guards give him pause.

What held him in thrall was her smile. With it she blessed her brother, the rabble, the guards, and even Edgar. She'd cast but a small ray of it in his direction while in the room, then let it beam for everyone else, her happiness at Geoffrey's arrival overflowing.

He was going to miss the woman.

The moment Geoffrey put forth the suggestion she return with him to Pecham, which Roland guessed must be his holding in Cornwall, he'd realized how hard it would be to let Eloise go.

He hadn't envisioned an imminent parting, thinking they would have weeks together yet—the days here in London, the trip back to Lelleford, and then awaiting the outcome of Sir John's judgment.

The realization that she could be gone from his life within hours churned his gut, battered his heart.

He'd never see her smile again. There would be a hole in his soul that could never be filled by anyone but Eloise.

Nothing permanent could come from loving her— which he could no longer deny. He'd tried. Telling himself his concern for her was born of duty. Convincing himself the attraction between them amounted to no more than a healthy male's appreciation for a beautiful woman. What drivel. But even conceding he loved Eloise did him no good.

He well knew the way of the world. He had nothing of value to offer her father for her hand. He might be of good blood and he might have attained the rank of knight, but he stood to inherit only a small sum from his father—

no land, no riches. While he might someday rise high enough to make an acceptable offer for a lady of Eloise's station, that day loomed far into the future.

Even if Sir John's trial went badly, if he were stripped of lands and wealth, Eloise wouldn't be left destitute. Her brothers would care for her, see to her future. Geoffrey was certainly willing, Julius might be, too.

Useless conjecture—unless he tried to claim rights to her by revealing their one-night affair, and oh, wouldn't Eloise just love him for that? She'd be horrified at the breech of trust, a trust she'd given him completely only a few nights before.

While he lay with Eloise, Timothy suffered a severe beating.

In one fateful night he managed to both ravage Eloise's virginity and fail to protect his squire. He'd badly misjudged the danger in both instances, and now both people he loved might suffer permanent harm— Eloise to her reputation, Timothy from his injuries.

Guilt nagged at him from every corner. For leaving Lelleford for so much longer than he'd planned, and for not yet presenting himself to King Edward to explain why. For not being nearby when Timothy had needed him most.

For thoroughly losing himself in Eloise, the woman his brother had been enamored of at the time of his death. He could envision Hugh's reaction to the liaison—appalled.

Perhaps it was best if Eloise went home with Geoffrey now, before he did something else outrageously stupid to harm her.

Then why had he opened his big mouth to convince

Geoffrey to try one more confrontation with Sir John? There was only one answer—because 'twas what Eloise passionately wanted, what she felt was right.

He couldn't deny her.

Fool.

True, Roland wanted a few answers from Sir John, too, but those answers could have waited until after Eloise was safely out of London. But no, he again guided her to the Tower of London, to Baliol's Tower and her father's chamber on the upper floor.

Eloise had shucked her cloak, now stood before her father with hands on hips—leaving Roland, Geoffrey, and Edgar to brace themselves as best they could.

"'Tis time to give over, Father. Geoffrey and I both know you have not told us the entire tale."

"You accuse me of lying?"

"Never."

Geoffrey stepped to Eloise's side. "She accuses you of bending the truth to suit your purposes. You are very good at that, you know."

"So are you."

"I learned from the master."

"As did I," Eloise added. "Which is why we know evasion when we hear it. Father, we may be your children, but we are your *grown* children. We are both reasonably intelligent and sufficiently capable of dealing with whatever it is you strive to spare us."

"So now I am being unreasonable."

"Nay, just your usual stubborn self. Be warned, we can be stubborn, too. Neither Geoffrey nor I intend to leave London until we have the whole truth. If we have to share your imprisonment, hound you day and night, so be it."

Roland remembered no such pact between the siblings, but since Geoffrey didn't contradict her, he let it pass.

"Is it so wrong of me to want my children out of harm's way?"

Geoffrey reached out, put a hand on John's shoulder. "Not wrong, but in this case misguided. We cannot sit by and see you hang for a crime neither of us believe you committed. Am I right in that?"

"Aye."

"Then Kenworth is either framing or blackmailing you. From what I gather, you are also not getting the support you would like from Lancaster. You need us, Father, if for no other reason than our support, for our belief in your innocence."

John looked from Eloise to Geoffrey and back again. "Perhaps you give your support too lightly."

Eloise tossed a dismissive hand in the air. "Rubbish. You may bend the truth, even hedge a law or two, but treason? You can swear on St. Peter's bones that you have conspired with the Scots and I will not believe you."

John huffed, and after a long, thoughtful pause, relented. "All right, then. I—"

Roland felt the sudden weight of John's narrow-eyed stare, could almost taste the mistrust.

"You should not worry overmuch about Sir Roland," Geoffrey said. "His loyalty is to Eloise, which means he will do or say nothing to bring her harm. 'Struth, anyone who dares lay a finger on her will find himself skewered on the tip of a double-edged sword."

Eloise blushed slightly. Silence reigned while Roland inwardly admitted Geoffrey's assertion.

There had been a moment, back in the room, when he thought Geoffrey might protest his insistence on escorting Eloise. They didn't know each other, and Roland was well aware he was too deeply involved in what should be a family affair. Geoffrey not only relented but now gave his support, and while Roland wasn't sure why, he also wasn't about to let it go to waste.

"My thanks, Sir Geoffrey. In your father's position I might be distrustful of outsiders, too. If I may put your mind at rest, Sir John, I wish you to know I have a stake in this affair as well. If Kenworth, indeed, was behind the attack on Timothy, I want a piece of the man."

"Revenge for your squire?"

Revenge for the beating, revenge for scaring Eloise witless.

Absolution for allowing both.

But there was more. Despite attempts to stay clear of Sir John's problems, he believed the man innocent. Perhaps Simon and Marcus's adamant support of their lord first swayed him, but Eloise's defense of her father, so staunch and resolute, had caused him to pay further heed.

Sir John might be no saint, but no devil either. If innocent, he deserved justice.

"Aye, I want revenge for Timothy. The lad did not deserve his bruises. The beating and the attempt to kidnap Eloise convinced me you have a powerful enemy who is not above abusing innocents. Whether or not you are guilty, I find Kenworth's methods abhorrent. The man deserves comeuppance."

John tilted his head, his expression thoughtful. "All in the name of chivalry, then?"

"I am no model of knighthood. I have faults aplenty. Perhaps I simply have an aversion to tyrants."

Geoffrey rubbed his hands together. "We have much to do in little time. Talk, Father. Ramble. I want every detail. One never knows what small piece of information may hold significance when put together with others."

And so they began, the father and his children, to put the puzzle together. John told Geoffrey of his insults to Kenworth and the results. Then of taking Brother Walter into his service, not realizing the cleric a spy for Kenworth. Of fleeing the keep for the woodland, keeping one step ahead of the patrols.

Eloise held up a staying hand. "Father, I have wondered how you managed to sneak your message to me into my bedchamber."

"With our men-at-arms who brought my falcon back. When they found us at the mill, I gave one man the falcon and another the message." His eyes narrowed. "He was not discovered with it, was he? I told him to have a care."

Eloise bit her bottom lip, and Roland guessed she felt as foolish as he did, remembering the hours they'd spent looking for a secret passageway.

"Nay, he snuck it up into my bedchamber where I found it on my bed, nor did any of the men of the patrol ever admit they saw you. I merely wondered how it got there. Proceed with your tale."

"But first, go back to Brother Walter," Geoffrey requested. "What made you realize he was a spy?"

"I found several scrolls in my accounting room, all of them written in the same hand. No names are mentioned, but they were obviously written by a Highlander to a sympathizer in England. I questioned Brother Walter about how they came to be among my papers. At first he denied any knowledge of them, then had a change of heart. He confessed to putting them there."

"Then those documents are fake, placed in your possession to frame you."

"Oh, no, Geoffrey. I believe those missives are quite genuine communications between a Scotsman and Englishman."

Geoffrey softly asked, "Who?"

John firmly answered, "The Scot? I know not. The Englishman? Kenworth."

Roland could hardly believe what he heard. "Kenworth used missives sent to him to frame you?"

John nodded. "As I said, there are no names mentioned, a precaution to protect both parties, I assume. I have no notion of who the Scot is, but I do know they were sent to Kenworth."

"How?"

"Brother Walter. When he confessed and warned me of Kenworth's plan to arrest me in my own home, he did a thorough job of that, too."

Eloise put her face in her hands. "I had the monk right there. All I had to do was hide him away until . . ."

"Nay, Eloise, 'twas best you did not," John said. "If the monk were not available to greet Kenworth, he would have known immediately that more was amiss than my absence."

"Well, he was not there to greet the earl. The monk took himself off to hide for two days. Roland finally found him and turned him over to Kenworth."

"How did he explain himself?"

"Whatever he said, he said to Kenworth alone. Brother Walter refused to talk to me, vowing he would say nothing of the whole affair without your permission. Drove me witless."

John smiled at that. "I imagine it did. Roland, did he speak to you at all?"

"Nay, not a word. Nor did Kenworth comment on it." Roland couldn't withhold a chuckle. "It just occurred to me. On the way to Lelleford, Kenworth was so sure he could simply ride through the gate and apprehend you. Now I know why. He knew you to be at home because the monk likely confirmed your schedule. No wonder Kenworth went into a fury when you weren't there. By all that is holy, I should like to have heard what went through his mind when he could not find the scrolls either."

John smiled. "The vision of that moment has crossed my mind many times. It still amuses me."

"Father, this is no time for amusement."

"Nay, Daughter, probably not. But I am still amused, and I will not be denied what little joy I can find in this mess."

She sighed. "I beg pardon. What I should like to know is why you went to Lancaster. Roland once said he thought you should have gone to the king."

"I almost did, but perhaps 'tis a good thing I did not.

Edward may have hung me on the spot when I showed up with those scrolls. Lancaster gave me sanctuary"—he glanced about the comfortable chamber with the locked door—"such as it is. And for that he earned Edward's ire. Lancaster has tried to obtain an audience with Edward, but the king refuses to see him. So Lancaster advises patience, until either Edward lets go his pique, or Kenworth makes a bold move."

Eloise huffed. "'Tis easy for an earl to advise patience. *He* is not sitting in Baliol's Tower."

Geoffrey leaned back in his chair. "Lancaster will try to convince the king of Kenworth's involvement?"

John shook his head. "Not immediately. First he wants to see what is contained in the missive in Edward's possession."

Roland tried to ignore the itch at the back of his neck, but it refused to go away even when he rubbed at it.

"What disturbs you, Roland?" Geoffrey asked.

Perceptive man, which likely made him a good lawyer.

"Edward told me of that missive, but not what it contained, only that on the strength of it he was sending Kenworth to capture John, and me to oversee your holdings. I fear that missive may be more damaging than those you have seen, Sir John."

"That is what Lancaster wants to know before we take further steps."

He should keep his mouth shut. He shouldn't make any offer that might land him in more trouble than he might already be with King Edward over abandoning his duty at Lelleford to chase after Eloise. What he'd originally planned as no more than an overnight absence had stretched out for several days. That he left with good intentions, leaving the holding under Simon and Marcus's capable supervision, or that he'd delayed returning to give his squire more time to heal from his beating, might not appease royal ire.

Except Eloise looked so forlorn he could barely stand to look at her without wanting to wrap her in his arms and soothe the worry away. If he didn't help give her father back to her, he'd never be able to live with himself.

Perhaps, when she someday looked back at this horrible time in her life, she would remember him fondly for this one deed alone.

"King Edward will see me."

Four pairs of eyes stared at him. Edgar excited, Geoffrey and John wary, Eloise . . . worshipful. As if he'd just handed her a dream come true. Roland hoped he could deliver what she hoped for—her father's freedom. The best he could do was let John and Geoffrey know what they faced—if Edward allowed him to see the missive.

"I truly should have gone to see the king when I first arrived in London, let him know the circumstances under which I left Lelleford. Then we suffered the attack, and I could not leave Eloise alone, nor did I dare take her with me into the king's presence."

"Why ever not?" Eloise asked, all innocence.

"Because if you think an earl can be a danger, you do not wish to know what a king is capable of when crossed."

"Oh." She glanced down at her hands in her lap, then peered up at him through her long lashes. "You propose to place yourself in a precarious position. If Edward takes exception to your meddling, you jeopardize your future in royal service."

"I did that several days ago when I left Lelleford. Whether or not Edward allows me to see the missive, I should still go and explain myself to him."

John rose from his chair, stood before him. "My children are convinced I should trust you, and so I shall. If you truly mean to do this, be very careful, Roland. A king's wrath can be heinous."

"I am well aware of that, Sir John."

"Then Godspeed, lad."

Geoffrey rose. "Then there is no more we can do until after Roland talks to the king. I do not know about the rest of you, but I have missed several meals in the past few days and am *starving*. Eloise, Roland, might I treat you to a bite to eat?"

'Twas just enough to break the heavy tension in the room, and Roland silently thanked Geoffrey for getting them out of the Tower. His head spun with the ramifications of what he'd done, but how could he have done otherwise?

Once down at the barbican, Roland collected his weapons, then handed over his scabbard and sword to Geoffrey, who toted only a dagger.

Geoffrey stared at the scabbard now in his hand. "Why give me this?"

"You know how to use it, I assume."

"Aye."

"Take Eloise back to the room. She can show you from which vendor to purchase the tastiest meat pies in London."

For the first time since their lovemaking, Eloise

touched him, her fingers to his arm. "Where are you going?"

"Westminster Palace."

"So soon?"

"May as well get it done."

And then she was in his arms, holding tight, as if they had every right in the world to embrace on a public street. Roland buried his face in her hair, lost himself in the exotically sweet scent of her he'd never been able to identify.

She felt of heaven, smelled of forever, neither of which were his to grab hold of.

"You will be careful," she whispered.

"On my honor."

"I—" She swallowed. "We will buy you a pie for your supper. Hurry back."

Chapter Sixteen

ELOISE TUCKED her hand into the crook of her brother's arm, grateful for the support. She needed to feel close to someone right now and her brother was the perfect choice.

She could hardly believe Roland made the offer to speak with the king, then left to get it done so soon. He put himself in a precarious position, yet he seemed confident . . . but then, didn't he always? And so far wasn't that confidence warranted?

Perhaps she worried overmuch.

Certes, she shouldn't have hugged him, but how else could she show her appreciation for involving himself in this most crucial plan to prove her father's innocence? 'Struth, hadn't she truly hugged him in a vain effort to hold him back, keep him from possible dangers?

Ye gods, if the king took exception to Roland's meddling, he could end up in a chamber in the Tower of London, too. Then she'd have two men she loved locked away.

"He will be fine, Eloise."

"Can you read minds now?"

"You think loudly, and your hold on my arm reveals your upset."

And her unconventional hug for Roland gave Geoffrey a clear indication of who she presently worried over. Eloise loosened her grip enough to prevent nail marks in her brother's arm.

Geoffrey patted her hand. "He surprised me with his offer."

Roland stunned them all, Father the most.

"Surprised me, too. I knew he was upset by Timothy's beating. He blames himself for not looking after the lad."

Roland had been in bed with her, a place he shouldn't have been, making love, which they shouldn't have done. Now Roland suffered pangs of conscience for both.

Geoffrey stopped walking and looked down at her as if she were an exasperating child. "He involves himself because of you, Eloise, only in part for Timothy."

"I believe you are mistaken."

Geoffrey shook his head and began walking again. "The last time we spoke of Roland St. Marten, you described him as a disgusting toad. You have apparently changed your opinion."

Eloise remembered that short conversation with Geoffrey in the hallway at Lelleford. "I was angry with Roland. He had told Hugh he thought me too brazen to make a suitable wife. All I could hear was his disapproval of me, and so . . ."

"He became a disgusting toad. I understand. What changed your mind?"

Eloise took a long breath. "Roland. He loved Hugh. Had I truly been listening I would have realized he was only concerned for his brother. I might have been too hasty to take offense."

She shouldn't have been listening at all, and had judged Roland too quickly on snippets of their conversation.

"So Roland has proved himself worthy of your regard."

"Many times over. He can be gallant or firm, as the situation calls for it. He is honorable, loyal to the king. Did you know he was knighted for bravery on the battlefield?"

"Was he?"

"Guarded the king's back, so I understand. And he has an easy way with children, and both Simon and Marcus trusted him right away. And—"

"I get your message. A true paragon of knighthood. Ah, I smell meat pies."

She let go of Geoffrey's arm so he could make the purchase. Four pies. Theirs, one for Roland, the last for Timothy.

Geoffrey wore a disturbed expression, and Eloise realized she rambled on more than she ought. Especially after Geoffrey had seen her embrace Roland. She offered to carry the pies as she did when Roland wore his sword. A man couldn't properly draw one, if the need arose, with his hands full.

They walked on, the apothecary mere blocks away.

Geoffrey clasped his hands behind his back. "So, this paragon of yours—"

"Roland is not mine. I only enumerated his qualities to convince you our trust in him is not misplaced."

"Truly?"

"Aye."

"Then your admiration for him is due to his gallantry and honor."

"In part. He has also been my protector and advisor. I left Lelleford with little more planned than getting to London and going to see Father. Roland knew where to stable the horses, let a room. He guided me to the Tower, showed me the way of keeping on the guards' good side. Without him, I might not have gotten in. I owe him a debt. And given his actions this afternoon, the debt becomes larger."

"You need not pay him with your heart, Eloise."

"Gratitude has nothing to do with why I love—" Damn Geoffrey. He'd led her right into the admission and she hadn't seen it coming. "Not fair, Geoffrey. You tricked me into that admission."

"'Tis the only way to deal with you at times. So you love Roland St. Marten?"

"I would deny it if I thought you might believe me."

"Too late." He laughed lightly. "'Twas too late the moment I saw the way you looked at him. Your affection for him shines in your eyes. I imagine Father has noticed, too. Perhaps that is part of why he wants me to take you to Cornwall and send Roland back to Lelleford."

"To part us."

"I fear so. Does Roland know you love him?"

She shook her head, her heart hurting. "Nay, I have not told him, nor will I. There is no future for us, no matter the outcome of Father's trial. Roland is as aware of his station and duty as I am of mine. 'Tis hopeless to wish otherwise."

"Is it? I thought my situation with Leah hopeless, too,

and look how that worked out. We are now married, have a child on the way—"

Eloise's spirits soared. "You do! How wonderful! Did I not tell you Leah would make you happy? When is the babe due? I am to be godmother to your firstborn, remember? Oh, this is grand!"

"The babe should be born late winter, and aye, you shall be godmother—no matter that you never gave me a choice." Then he sighed. "I wish the same happiness for you, marriage to a man who loves you as I love Leah, who can give you a home and children and cherish his blessings."

"Perhaps Roland could, but I am not sure he wants those things with me. Besides, could you see me trying to convince Father to allow me to marry a landless knight?"

"Hmmm. There is that."

"There most certainly is."

Geoffrey grabbed hold of the door latch and jerked, only to find the apothecary's door locked.

At his puzzled look, Eloise explained. "Roland insists that when he is not about, Mistress Green is to close her shop and lock all the doors, including the one to the room where she stays with Timothy. When she hears the bell, she looks out the window to see who rings and only admits those people she knows and trusts. I am sure she will be down any moment now."

"Roland fears another attack?"

Eloise shivered at the thought of the last one. "Perhaps, but more likely he simply strives to keep safe all of those he considers his charges."

"An impossible thing to do."

"Try telling that to Roland."

*   *   *

Roland poured wine from a gold flagon and handed the goblet to Edward, then continued his explanation for requesting this audience.

"So I chased after the Lady Eloise. By the time I caught up to her I decided I might as well bring her into the city to see her father, otherwise I would have to worry about her taking it into her head to try for London on her own."

"A headstrong woman, then. Like her father."

The king didn't have any notion of how strong-willed and persistent Eloise could be, and Roland wasn't about to tell him, at least not yet.

"I am confident Lelleford is in good hands in my absence. Both Simon and Marcus are capable commanders. Their belief in Sir John's innocence will ensure they do their utmost to hold the castle safe. I am convinced that if Sir John is guilty of the charges, neither of his most trusted knights knew of their lord's activities."

"And the Lady Eloise?"

"The same, my liege. All were genuinely shocked and dismayed to hear the charges, and will swear no Scot has ever passed through Lelleford's gates."

Edward walked toward the brocade chair in his sitting room, and Roland again marveled at the man. They were but a year apart in age, and yet Edward ruled a kingdom, had done so for several years now. Every day he dealt with heavy issues of state, endured a bevy of advisors who pulled him every which way. Earls, knights—his own wife.

The queen, Philippa, could be headstrong, too, but in a

gentler manner than Eloise. And Edward loved his young wife even though the marriage had been arranged.

Edward eased into his chair. "Has the lady visited the Tower as yet?"

"Several times, actually."

Edward tilted his head. "You have been in the city long?"

"Unfortunately." Roland swirled the wine in a jewel-encrusted gold goblet. "My original plan was to stay but one night, allow Lady Eloise to see her father, and then begin the journey back to Lelleford the next day. Events intervened. Do you remember Timothy, my squire?"

"A lad from the stables, as I recall. A problem there? Shall I find you another squire?"

"Nay, Timothy suits me fine. But there is a problem. He currently recovers from an unwarranted, loathsome beating he endured the other night at the hands of knaves. He will heal, but does so slowly. Thus my continued presence in London."

Edward pinched the bridge of his hawklike nose between thumb and forefinger. "The streets of London overflow with vermin, particularly after nightfall. Seems no matter how many watchmen the city's aldermen hire, the worse the problem."

"Aye, well, these two vermin were after more than a bit of sport with Timothy. I will not bore you with all the details, but the villains had set out to kidnap Lady Eloise. I scuffled with both. One fell down a flight of stairs and died, the other managed to escape me—in a moment of my distraction I very much regret—but not before I learned they were hired to whisk Eloise off to Southwark."

Edward's eyes narrowed. "An unholy place. I assume you informed the watchmen?"

"Naturally. I did not get a good look at the man who escaped, but Timothy did. The watchmen hold little hope for catching the culprit, however."

"Truly, I should have a word with the bishop of Winchester about the brothels in his domain. Innocent women should not be forced into such a life. 'Tis odd, and disturbing, the villains thought to sell a nobly born woman into prostitution. They usually choose peasant girls who no one will miss overmuch."

Disturbing, indeed, how any woman of any station could come to such a pass. He didn't want to think of what horrors Eloise might have faced.

"I do not believe London's noblewomen have much to worry over in this case, my liege. These ruffians were after one particular noblewoman. Lady Eloise. Whoever hired these men paid them to snare Eloise, no one else. I fear the reason has to do with her father's situation."

Edward rose, his expression fathomless, and walked over to the high, arched window that overlooked the palace garden. "Perhaps the daughter of a traitor deserves such a fate."

The king's sentiment shocked him. Roland strove for a balance between admonishment and respect.

"My liege, you above all should be grateful that the child must not suffer for the sins of the father."

Edward's head spun around. "You dare?"

"Only because I firmly believe Lady Eloise should not suffer harm because her father committed a crime, which I understand is yet to be proven, just as your reign thus far is so successful because you are compared to your grandfather and not your father. My liege, if the people blamed you for your father's ineptitude, would you now enjoy their respect and love?"

"One has naught to do with the other! My . . . father's intentions were always good. Granted, he made errors in judgment, but he never purposely harmed his kingdom. Sir John has deliberately harmed England by selling weapons to Highlanders! By harming England, he harms me, the person to whom he has sworn his loyalty. The offense is unforgivable."

Edward's tone might be sharp, but not unbridled. The king did have a grand temper, but so far, showed no sign of letting it loose.

"Any disloyalty to you is worthy of punishment. What eats at my craw is that whoever hired these ruffians— and I would dearly love to know who that scoundrel might be—sought to punish a woman whose only crime is concern and love for her father. She means you no harm, my liege. Lady Eloise merely seeks a fair hearing on the charges."

The king huffed. "I have all the proof I need of Sir John's culpability in the contents of one missive."

Edward tossed back his wine, set the goblet on an ornate, highly polished table, the legs of which were footed in the shape of lion's paws. A table worthy of a king, as were the rest of the sitting room's furnishings. No matter how wealthy and powerful the king, however, Edward was still a young man, his heart and head swimming with hopes and dreams and fears of failure, like every young man, like Roland himself.

Unlike Roland, Edward possessed the royal power to force his hopes and dreams into reality, and to sweep his failures under a concealing rug. Edward hadn't ordered Sir John's immediate execution, and Roland found himself wondering why.

"If the proof is so solid, then why not just hang the man and be done?"

"Believe me, Roland, I wanted to. Kenworth urged me to, and I was on the verge of carrying the rope over to the Tower and wrapping it around Sir John's neck myself. Then that damned fool Lancaster began his rounds of my advisors, urging caution, claiming that perhaps not all was as it seemed." Edward waved a hand in the air. "They stayed my hand. Insisted I wait. For what? The man is guilty. So now he sits in a comfortable chamber in the Tower instead of lying in his grave, a most unfortunate twist of fate, I say."

"You are that sure of Sir John's guilt?"

"Look for yourself."

Roland put his goblet down, strove to keep his hands from trembling, giddy with delight for what he'd accomplished, yet dreading what he might see.

Edward opened a drawer in his desk, withdrew a scroll, then waved it in the air. "Here. Read. Then tell me if I am not justified in my anger."

Roland unrolled the scroll, and his heart fell. He couldn't read the language of the Highlanders, but saw why the king's anger was justified. Here were names — Sir John Hamelin, and MacLeod, chief of a mighty clan.

"My skills at language do not include Scottish, my liege."

"MacLeod thanks Hamelin for pikes and swords to use against our army. Apparently Hamelin also provided delicacies for the chief's table and flour for his storerooms."

Roland rolled up the parchment and gave it back to Edward. "Rather damning. Might I ask how Kenworth came by it?"

Edward tossed the scroll back in the desk drawer and slammed it shut. "Caught a Scot messenger riding through his holdings in the north and this was in his packs. Without that bit of luck we might never have known."

Bit of luck? Roland's head whirled with other possibilities, but he pushed them aside. He'd come to learn the missive's contents, and that done, shouldn't push his own luck any further.

"My liege, if I may, I should also advise caution."

"Oh, Roland, not you, too!"

Roland smiled at the aggrieved tone. "I fear so. Granted, the missive is damning, and if Sir John is guilty you should, quite righteously, hang him. But that missive . . . 'tis so blatant. I understand there are more missives, in Lancaster's possession. Have you seen them as yet?"

Edward's spine grew rigid. "Not as yet."

Roland wasn't about to comment on the king's obstinacy in refusing to grant Lancaster an audience out of pique.

"'Twould be interesting to compare the documents, would it not?"

"Perhaps."

Roland saw an opportunity to not only further his cause but be of service to Edward—to help bridge the crevice between the king and Lancaster.

"Would you like me to look at the documents for you?"

Edward tilted his head. "I have to ask myself why you are so willing to involve yourself in this affair."

"For justice's sake. To be of service to you where I can. Choose whichever reason you like."

Edward glanced toward the window, stood still and silent for more moments than Roland liked. Then he smiled softly.

"What if I choose Lady Eloise?"

Hellfire.

The reaction must have shown on his face. Edward chuckled.

"Come now, Roland. Your willingness to do her bidding is rather telling. You wish to know whether or not I am going to hang the lady's father, do you not?"

Roland took a deep breath and decided that diplomacy wasn't within his realm of skills. "For her sake, I would rather you did not. However, if he is guilty, then I would help you haul the rope to the Tower."

"I know, and for that I thank you. I also think you have your suspicions about who hired the ruffians who roughly handled your squire and tried to kidnap Eloise."

"Sir John seems to think Kenworth—"

"Ah, yes. His old enemy, the one who gave me this missive." Edward shook his head. "Always the struggle for power. Always one lord against another. Kenworth urges a swift trial and hanging; Lancaster urges caution despite the evidence. 'Tis mind-numbing, betimes."

"My liege, I know both Kenworth and Lancaster are related to you, so you strive to keep on good terms with both. My question is how much trust do you place in either?"

Edward never hesitated. "Only as much as I dare, nor

can I afford to show preference. So long as they pick at each other they do not harry me."

"Might I have your leave to carry on? See what I can discover?"

"You have my leave, but you have not much time. I must bring this situation to conclusion with a few days. God's wounds, I would welcome some small piece of evidence to sway the tide either way. And be careful of both earls, Roland. Be *most* careful."

So Eloise had told him. And being careful had landed him in deeper water yet.

The meat pie was cold, but Roland didn't seem to mind. He ate while standing. Between bites he'd related the outcome of his audience with the king. Neither she nor Geoffrey interrupted, except once, when she let out a groan at mention of names in the missive the king allowed him to read.

Roland wiped his hands on a linen towel. "Edward is not averse to my doing some prying. He never said so, but I think he has some doubt about the missive's validity. The missive angers him, and aye, if your father had gone to Edward he might have found himself at the end of a rope immediately. By enlisting Lancaster's aid, he gained some time. Problem is, now that we have time, what do we do with it? Confront Kenworth? Question Lancaster?"

She had no immediate suggestion to give. Nor did Geoffrey.

Her brother stood at the end of the bed, lost in thought. As much as she appreciated his company over the past few hours, she hadn't been able to relax until she heard

Roland's footsteps on the stairs. She had barely been able to contain her relief to have him back in the room where she could see him. Now Geoffrey's presence, and Timothy's, prevented her from doing what she longed to do—throw herself in Roland's arms and sob her joy that he'd not been sent to the Tower.

Forced to rein in her emotions and deal with the issue at hand, Eloise vented her frustration. "What I would dearly love to know is if the missives are real or fake."

"Father believes the ones he saw are real," Geoffrey commented.

"Only because Brother Walter told him so. I am not sure I trust the word of the monk."

Geoffrey rubbed at his forehead. "As Roland said, having both Father's and the MacLeod's names given in the king's missive seems blatant when the other missives are written differently. Could the missives Father saw be real and the one in the king's possession fake?"

"Possible," Roland said, "but 'twould seem to me they must be written by the same person. Kenworth intended to capture your father and bring him back to London along with the missives he would conveniently find in your father's accounting room. We must assume he intended to use those missives as further evidence against Sir John. If all the missives were purportedly sent from MacLeod to your father, then all must be written in the same hand or Kenworth's scheme would not work. So, they must all be fake or all be real."

Geoffrey shook his head. "Not necessarily. 'Tis quite possible the one with the names is a forgery. Done well enough, 'twould be most difficult to tell them apart."

Eloise put her hands to her temples, the ache beginning to throb. "So how do we find someone who can tell the difference?"

Geoffrey began pacing, the thud of his boots on the planks an ominous beat. Even the patter of rain on the window irritated her taut nerves. There must be some way to untangle this mess, but her mind refused to force order out of the muddle.

Roland put a hand on the back of her neck, massaged gently.

"Shall I ask Mistress Green for a potion for your head?"

She would rather lean against him, close her eyes, and allow his fingers to work their magic than swallow a potion. Just having the warmth of his hand on her neck, his fingers circling, felt like heaven.

"Mayhap later. 'Tis not unbearable."

Geoffrey stopped pacing. Eloise turned her head slightly to see him staring out the window.

"I spent many months with monks," he said, his voice soft. "We students were expected to write in a legible manner, so toiled with chalk and slate, stylus and wax tablet, until we could form our letters to the teacher's satisfaction." He turned around then, his voice becoming stronger. "Those who had an interest in taking vows and being of service in a monastery's scriptorium were held to a higher standard. Over and over they practiced a single letter, on and on until each letter was a perfect copy of the other.

"Do either of you happen to know what Brother Walter did before Father took him into his service as a clerk?"

Roland's hand stilled.

Eloise could only stare at Geoffrey, stunned at the implication. "You think Brother Walter forged the missive?"

" 'Twould seem possible. If we assume the missive giving names is forged, then Kenworth must have given *someone* a real missive from which to copy the handwriting. Why not a cleric who might already have practiced the rudiments of making letters appear as exact as the next?"

A memory niggled at Eloise, of the monk lying on the floor, bleeding, her so angry at her father for deserting her. She'd taken the cleric down to tend his head, him becoming distressed because her father wasn't about.

"A good theory, Geoffrey," Roland said. "But your father said Brother Walter made a thorough confession about Kenworth's plan. Would the monk not mention having forged either one or possibly all of—"

"That is it!" Eloise jumped off the bed, her excitement too great to contain.

Both men looked at her as if she'd gone witless. But she hadn't. Not yet, anyway.

She put her hands up, palms outward, holding back the flood of impressions and memories, sorting through them, hoping her logic held firm. Eloise closed her eyes to help her concentrate.

"That morning, Father called me up to his accounting room. Brother Walter lay unconscious on the floor. Father told me what was happening, that he considered the monk untrustworthy. Then he stuffed the scrolls into a traveling pouch, gave me advice about how to deal with the earl, and left.

"Naturally, I was stunned. I also assumed Father and the monk had scuffled—though the monk told me later that his own clumsiness was at fault, that he'd tripped and hit his head against the desk. Anyway, when I finally took the monk down to have his gash tended, he began asking about Father's whereabouts, became very agitated when I could not answer him."

Eloise opened her eyes, sure of her conjecture now. "He ran about the keep and grounds searching for Father, insisting he must speak with him immediately, and issuing dire warnings of the doom to befall us if he did not."

She looked from Roland to Geoffrey and back again. "What if Brother Walter hit his head before he finished confessing his part in Kenworth's plot? Could he have been on the verge of admitting that he forged the missive in the king's possession?"

Geoffrey rubbed at his chin. "Perhaps. But if the sin sat so heavy on his mind, then why not tell you later?"

"He was adamant that he speak with Father. I should have pressed him, but I was so angry with him I could hardly bear to look at him. And I had to prepare for the earl's arrival. In hindsight, I should have allowed Marcus to press him for information." She flopped down on the bed in disgust. "Damn."

"He may not have, anyway, Eloise," Roland said. "If you will remember, Simon, Marcus, and I tried to get him to talk after we found him. He would not then either. If I had allowed him to remain in hiding—"

"You had no choice. Kenworth wanted him found. Sweet mercy, I wanted him found so I could show him the gate."

Geoffrey softly commented, "'Tis possible he did the forgery, and even if not, he may know who did. One of his fellow clerics, perhaps. Where is Brother Walter now?"

Knowing full well, Eloise groaned and put her face in her hands, allowing Roland to answer.

"Kenworth has him." Roland shook his head. "If the monk made a similar confession to Kenworth, I fear for the monk's life."

"Then let us hope the man showed some sense," Geoffrey commented. "Assuming he lives, where would he be?"

"Likely at Kenworth's residence."

"Do you know where it is?"

"Aye. We began our journey to Lelleford there."

Hearing the rising excitement in the men's voices, Eloise looked up at Roland and Geoffrey. "I beg pardon, but you cannot walk up to the door and demand Kenworth hand over Brother Walter."

"Perhaps not," Roland admitted. "However, there may be a way to reach the monk without Kenworth knowing. I could go over, watch the place, see what I can learn."

"I can go along," Geoffrey offered with a grin. "I do have some experience in skulking around in the dark, moving quietly."

Roland immediately took exception. "One of us has to stay here to guard Eloise and the others."

"I can go."

Eloise glanced over her shoulder at Timothy, who'd sat cross-legged on his pallet and said nary a word until now.

"Nay," Roland said firmly.

Timothy sighed. "You must allow me out of this room sometime, my lord. I know where the residence is located. I also know how to get in through the servants' entrance. 'Twould be rather simple for me to find out if the monk is there." He rubbed at his ribs. "Besides, Kenworth owes me. If the lout who attacked me lurks about the place, I should like to know."

Eloise didn't like the softening of Roland's eyes, but this wasn't her decision. It was a matter between knight and squire.

"Can you accomplish the task during day's light?"

"Aye, my lord."

"Without causing yourself further hurt or getting caught?"

Timothy unfolded his legs and got to his feet. "I shall do my best to avoid either."

Roland was quiet a moment, then shook a finger at Timothy. "You are to take no chances, and if you are not back within the hour, I am coming after you."

Timothy smiled, then left the room.

Eloise closed her eyes and prayed.

Chapter Seventeen

WITH TIMOTHY gone and Eloise asleep upstairs, Roland paced the narrow space in front of the stairway. Geoffrey sat on the stairs, his hands dangling between his knees.

Geoffrey cleared his throat. "I must thank you for what you have done for Eloise. Without your guidance she might—" He shivered. "I do not want to think of what might have happened if you had not saved her from the kidnappers. Southwark is no place for a lady."

London was no place for this particular lady. How many times had Roland berated himself for bringing her into the city? How much suffering, both hers and Timothy's, could have been avoided if he had just taken her home?

Even now her head ached, relieved a bit by Mistress Green's potion and, 'twas to be hoped, banished by quiet and sleep.

"Give me no praise. Had I forced Eloise to go home, she would not have been in London for the villains to try to snatch."

"But you did not, and they did, and she came to no harm."

"Timothy did."

Geoffrey waved a dismissive hand. "Eloise said you blamed yourself on that score. A useless endeavor. You cannot be everywhere at once, nor did you suspect your presence here noted. 'Twould be interesting to find out how Kenworth knew you and Eloise were in the city."

Roland had wondered about that, too, and could come up with only one answer. "I imagine Kenworth took an interest in anyone who wished to visit Sir John. A coin or two to the right guard and he would have the information quickly. A search of the stables for three horses recently placed, one a blooded stallion—easily accomplished."

"You have a fine sense of the logical."

Roland nearly laughed, knowing some of his thoughts lately leaned to the fantastical. Those of Eloise.

"So do you. I assume one needs a sense of logic to practice law."

"'Tis the first time that knowledge has proved useful, though it certainly has not proved successful as yet. I have little use for it at Pecham beyond the usual estate business."

Roland welcomed the new direction of conversation. Not only did it take his mind off Timothy and Eloise, but he liked Geoffrey and wanted to know him better.

"Seems a waste of a fine talent."

"Suits me fine. Pecham is high on a cliff on Cornwall's northern coast. Between the calls of the seabirds, the rush of an ever-present wind, and the crash of waves, one can hardly hear oneself talk at times. From the farms and the tin mine we earn enough to feed and clothe everyone with a bit to spare." He put an elbow on his knee, his chin in his upraised palm. "Then, of course, there is that other business which brings in an added pound or two."

Roland tilted his head in inquiry.

Geoffrey raised an eyebrow. "Eloise did not tell you?"

"Nay. Should she have?"

"No particular reason, I suppose. I merely noted how much she trusts you so I assumed she had confided my little secret."

Roland remembered how long Eloise had taken to tell him everything about the morning of her father's flight from Lelleford. "'Tis rather hard to pry confidences from Eloise."

"She does not trust easily, which is why I feel I can trust you, too."

Perhaps the family had placed too much trust in him already. "You need not confide your secrets."

Geoffrey glanced around the shop. Mistress Green puttered in her backyard garden, tending the herbs she used in her potions. The last patron had left several minutes ago.

He leaned forward. "If ever you need an ell or two of the finest silk to be had in the kingdom, or the smoothest Burgundy wine to pass your lips, all for a portion of the usual price, I am your man."

Roland opened his mouth to ask how, but then he knew. Cornwall. Luxury items at low cost. The confession shocked him.

He lowered his voice to just above a whisper. "You are a smuggler?"

"Aye. Leah and I are trying to wean our people off the heady profits and encouraging everyone to live on what can be earned legally. But they have had a taste of an easy life and 'tis hard for them to give it up."

Since Geoffrey didn't seem averse to discussing the illegal trade, Roland asked, "How did you, a man who studied law, get involved with smuggling?"

"Not my idea, I assure you. 'Twas part of the life I accepted when I married Leah. Her family had been involved for many years. When we married, her life became mine, and though there are times I wish to knock my head against a wall, I would do nothing to change my circumstance."

"Pecham is Leah's birthright, I take it."

"Every cliff cave and a goodly portion of tin ore. And the keep and the demesne lands, of course." He was quiet for a moment, then went on. "The death of both her father and only brother were hard on Leah. The future looks brighter now with our first child on the way. 'Twill be hard enough explaining to our children that one grandfather was a notorious smuggler without adding that the other was hanged as a traitor."

"Perhaps 'twill not come to that."

"I dearly hope not. Unfortunately, all this conjecture about Brother Walter is merely that—conjecture. We could be wasting our time chasing down a false trail."

"Then we will have to find another trail."

Problem was, at the moment he saw no other path to explore. He highly doubted Kenworth could be forced to confess to framing John. If the handwriting in all the missives compared favorably, then the king would be forced to take the evidence as presented and John would hang.

"Do you believe in my father's innocence?"

Roland remembered his inability to evade the king's questions.

"Whether your father is guilty or not, he is entitled to a fair hearing. For your sister's sake, I mean to help him get it. Besides, I have a score to settle with Kenworth."

Geoffrey nodded his understanding. "Eloise is grateful, too. Unfortunately, if my father is convicted, Eloise stands to lose much. True, my father loses his life, and my brother loses his inheritance. But my father will be beyond caring, and Julius can petition to have his inheritance restored. That can take years, but other sons have been successful so the fight is worth the effort. 'Tis Eloise who suffers the immediate loss of her dowry. Without it, I fear she will be forced to marry far below her station, if she marries at all. A crime, that. She has much to offer a man."

All of this had occurred to Roland. Geoffrey's statement of the effects on Eloise merely confirmed his own conclusions, except one.

"You and Julius would see to her future."

"Aye, as much as we are able. 'Tis a shame your brother died before speaking his marriage vows. Then Eloise's dowry would not be endangered, nor her reputation damaged by association with my father. Since she is the only one of us children still living at Lelleford, people will think she must have known of Father's activities and condemn her right along with him."

"Not fair."

"Most unfair, but people are quick to judge harshly, and those of rank are quicker to distance themselves from anyone deemed unworthy."

Roland agreed, and with a flash of insight, finally

caught the drift of where Geoffrey's comments led. Speechless, he stared at Eloise's brother, barely able to contain the joy of being offered her hand in marriage, but resentful of being used in a scheme to save her dowry.

Or did he completely misread Geoffrey's intentions? Did his own desire to make Eloise his own, forever, taint what he heard in Geoffrey's words?

"You are suggesting I offer for Eloise?"

Geoffrey grinned. "I gather you do not find the idea abhorrent."

"I find your method abhorrent."

"I am pressed for time. I worry for my sister. Having her settled gives me the freedom to concentrate on more complicated matters."

"How convenient for you."

"And how utterly right for Eloise." Geoffrey rose, faced him squarely. "Let me be direct. She does not come to you barefoot in her shift. If I remember correctly, she brings you two manors, one not far from Lelleford, the other in Durham, which is the property I believe Kenworth lusts after for its proximity to Scotland. There are also her movables—furniture, linens, plates, and the like. I do not know precisely what sum of money my father has also gifted her with, but knowing him it is considerable."

Roland's temper almost got the better of him. He understood what Geoffrey sought to do: sell his sister off fast before her worth plummeted. He was trying to make the best bargain he could with the nearest candidate possible. 'Twas galling . . . and damned tempting.

"Perhaps you should speak with both your father and

Eloise before you attempt a betrothal bargain. Both may have objections."

"My father is hardly in a position to take exception. As for Eloise . . . I doubt she would." Geoffrey's grin returned. "We talked a bit. Imagine my surprise to learn she no longer considers you a disgusting toad."

Roland felt his ears warm. "Told you that story did she?"

"Not the whole of it, but enough. Her opinion of you has changed considerably. Quite an accomplishment on your part. 'Tis rare my sister admits she might be in error."

Eloise might be fond of him, had even gone to bed with him once — a single night of exploration and ecstasy. Given a chance, could they make a good marriage? Would she willingly bind herself to him for good or ill, forever?

Could she come to love him as much as he loved her, or would she come to view their marriage as a reminder of the worst days of her life?

Eloise's feelings aside, there were also Sir John's, who'd taken great care to select her last betrothed. Hugh. The heir to vast estates and considerable wealth. Worthy of Hamelin's daughter.

"I have nothing to offer her in return, Geoffrey. I may be of good blood, but I have only a knight's rank with no means to support it. And aye, while I know marrying an heiress is a time-honored, acceptable way of gaining both power and wealth, I find the idea foul. I believe your father will be of the same opinion."

Geoffrey shrugged. "Possibly. However, my father has already learned that not all plans for his children come to fulfillment. He can be practical when he must, and in this instance, I believe he will see things our way."

Our way, as if Roland had already agreed. As if Eloise would have him.

"There is also the king to consider. I need his consent, and under the circumstances, he might well refuse."

Geoffrey rubbed at his chin. "He may. And if you inform him afterward, he could dismiss you from his service. You must decide if what Eloise brings you is enough to compensate for any royal reward you have yet to gain."

Roland wanted to grasp the dream within his reach, and yet he hesitated. He glanced up the stairs where the woman he loved lay sleeping.

"She may not want me. You may sentence her to a marriage she only agrees to because she thinks you believe it best for her. What then, Geoffrey? She may end up hating us both."

The man was quiet for a moment before he answered. "I would not have made the suggestion if I thought Eloise might object. Nor would I allow her to marry a man I did not think would make her happy, a man who would protect and cherish her all her days. I love the little minx more than I ought, I suppose. Her happiness matters to me."

Roland heard a brother's love, his sincerity, and it made him wonder how Hugh would react. Would Hugh tell him to keep away from Eloise, or to do what he must for her?

"We may be discussing this for naught. If your father's case can be won, there is no need for Eloise to marry.

What say we wait to see how things go with Brother Walter before we discuss this further?"

"Agreed." Geoffrey looked about the shop again. "Bargaining is thirsty work. Has Mistress Green a keg of ale about the place?"

She did, and Roland knew where it was. For the next little while they filled mugs and talked about how Roland earned his knighthood, of the shipwreck that nearly cost Geoffrey his life.

When next the bell over the shop's door jangled, Timothy entered. He looked no worse for his adventure, for which Roland thanked the Fates. Timothy crossed to the keg, ladled out a mug of ale, and drank most in a continuous swallow.

After a sweep of sleeve across his mouth, Timothy began his report. "Brother Walter is not there. He did not return to London with Kenworth, and the servants do not know what happened to him."

Roland bowed his head. He'd hoped for better news. Even if the monk had been kept hidden in Kenworth's residence, there might have been a way to get to him. But if he wasn't in the city, he was either dead or . . . only God knew where.

He put a hand on Timothy's shoulder. "Our thanks. You feel all right?"

"Ribs hurt a bit, but I will survive."

"I take it you had no trouble getting in and out?"

Timothy glanced between Geoffrey and Roland, then confessed, "I might have been seen by a guard. I thought it best to talk to the stable lads about the monk 'cause they know all the comings and goings in the place. I tried to keep hidden best I could, but there is an open area between the stable and the servants' entrance I had to cross. I do not think anyone of any import saw me, but . . ."

"Will the stable lads mention your visit?"

"Not unless someone asks them direct."

"You did a fine job, Timothy. Go get some rest. Quietly. Eloise sleeps, too."

To Roland's surprise, Timothy gave no argument. He just finished off his ale and walked, slowly, up the stairs.

Geoffrey sighed. "'Twould seem our trail ends. Any thoughts on another we can follow?"

He wished he did. "Nary a one."

Geoffrey pinned him with sapphire eyes that matched Eloise's. "Shall I speak to my father?"

To tell John Hamelin about the king and the monk. To approach the father about the betrothal of his daughter.

All the ramifications considered, there was only one choice. Odd how, in the end, perhaps the biggest decision he'd ever made was also the easiest.

"'Tis my place to approach Sir John." Roland's hand on the latch, he turned back. "I prefer you not say anything to Eloise about a betrothal until after."

"As you wish. Godspeed."

Roland walked the familiar route with his mind awhirl. Not until he crossed the first drawbridge did he think to question if Sir John's warder would allow his visit without either Eloise or Geoffrey in attendance.

Perhaps he should have let Geoffrey come as he'd offered.

Nay, this was his task to perform. He'd never let another man take over a duty for him in the past, and he wouldn't now. He was here. He'd carry on and see what happened.

As it happened, Oswald the Warder must have considered him part of the family by now. He simply gave him a greeting and led the way up the stairs.

Sweat formed on Roland's palms as the door opened. He had nothing to offer Sir John. Not a dram of hope for his freedom. Not an ounce of gold nor even a plate of silver for his daughter.

Only his good name and a promise to take care of her for good or ill, no matter what happened.

The odds weren't in his favor.

John and Edgar sat at the table, playing yet another game of chess, one of their only entertainments. Edgar rose as Roland entered; John nodded a greeting and then looked past him, expecting to see his son or daughter.

Roland put a hand up to keep Oswald from immediately closing and locking the door.

"Edgar, I beg your indulgence. Some of what I have to say to Sir John must be kept private for the nonce."

John's eyes narrowed at the request, but he waved his permission for Edgar to leave.

With the squire out the door and the lock turned, Roland clasped his hands behind his back and crossed the room.

"I take it you bring bad news," John said. "Has the king ordered the scaffold readied?"

Roland allowed a small smile. "Not so bad as that."

"Then why so dour?"

He eased into the chair across from John. First things first. Roland related the details of his audience with the king.

"The missive Edward holds must be forged," John insisted. "I have never dealt with MacLeod. And I certainly sent him no pikes!"

"So your children and I assumed. We also assumed that if the missive is to be used as evidence against you, the handwriting in the missives Lancaster now holds must match the other. If, as you say, the three missives you saw are genuine, written to Kenworth by MacLeod, the fourth must have been written by someone very skilled at copying another's hand. We concluded the best candidate to be Brother Walter."

John scratched at his chin. "'Tis possible I suppose. The man did have a neat hand, very precise."

"Unfortunately, even if he is our forger, we do not know where he is. We hoped to question him, get a confession or else find out if he knew who might have forged the missive. The monk left Lelleford with Kenworth, but did not return to London with him. I fear his absence limits our choices of how to proceed."

Roland expected resignation, and got a wagging finger and thoughtful look instead.

"'Tis not surprising Kenworth did not keep him. The monk lost his usefulness, so either Kenworth did away with him or returned him to his monastery."

Roland felt a glimmer of hope. "Nearby?"

"Evesham Abbey."

Two days' ride away. Was there time to fetch the monk and bring him back? Or did he waste his time? 'Twas very possible Kenworth had done away with his spy.

"I will tell Geoffrey." Now for the hardest part, dealing with John Hamelin the father. "Geoffrey and I also discussed another matter. Eloise."

John sat back in his chair, drummed his fingers on the table. "What has she done now?"

Roland bit back a smile. "Nothing intemperate."

"Then what of her?"

Roland explained Geoffrey's reasoning for wishing Eloise to marry with due haste, to ensure the land and other property of her dowry removed from what the king would confiscate if the worst happened.

All through the explanation, John's expression changed from irritated to haggard.

"My son prepares for my death."

Roland realized John had always been concerned over the outcome, but only now faced the fact that he could truly hang.

"Geoffrey yet searches for answers and directs most of his energy toward clearing you of the charges." It didn't seem of much comfort to John but it was all Roland could offer. "Your son not only thinks of his sister but his brother. Should the king confiscate all of your holdings, I am sure Geoffrey intends to immediately file a petition, on Julius's behalf, to reclaim the inheritance."

"What of Geoffrey's own inheritance? He is entitled to a good bit of coin."

"He never mentioned anything for himself."

John rubbed at his weary eyes. "Because there will be nothing for him if Julius cannot win back my holdings."

John made Geoffrey's planning sound selfish. Roland didn't believe it, but held his peace on the matter.

"Are you opposed to a marriage for Eloise?"

"Not opposed, but God's wounds, I can think of no man worthy of her who would marry her in such haste with this damnable charge hanging over my head. Does Geoffrey have a man in mind?"

The moment had arrived, and he could truthfully say nay because he wasn't worthy of Eloise.

"Aye, my lord. Me."

Roland prepared for battle. John's stunned look wouldn't last long. But instead of seething anger, the outburst finally came out in hysterical laughter.

"You? Absurd! A sixth son with no more than a horse or two to his name? Surely, we can do better for her!"

So Roland believed, but he wasn't about to give up after a single volley. As in every battle, sometimes one needed to try several strategies in order to win the day.

Striving for a tone of calm reasoning, he answered, "If you object to my suit, then pray give me a list of others who may consider the marriage. I would be happy to pass it along to Geoffrey."

John slowly sobered. "There must be someone."

"As you say. 'Twould help if the man you chose is here in London, so the marriage can be performed immediately, so there will be no legal entanglements over the transfer of her dowry. Who shall we ask who might be able to overlook the possibility that you will be branded a traitor?"

He saw the answer in John's face. No one.

"You reach damned high, lad!"

So Roland knew and had admitted as much to Geoffrey.

"I am well aware that under other circumstances I would not be considered."

John's eyes narrowed. "You were sent to Lelleford to oversee the holding, not court my daughter. Was that your plan all along, to seek Eloise as your reward from the king?"

He nearly laughed at the accusation.

"Nay, Sir John. I had no such intention. Verily, I wanted nothing to do with her at the time. If you will remember, we were on less than agreeable terms."

"Ah, yes. She thought you a disagreeable toad."

Roland thought he could very well go through the rest of his life without hearing that again.

"She did. And I thought her too brazen and strong-willed for my taste. I had no designs on her whatsoever."

"Eloise is still brazen and strong-willed, always will be, and yet you would take her to wife?"

In a heartbeat, and for good or ill, he allowed his mask of calm reasoning to slide away and expose his heart. Let the father take whatever shot he wished.

"I assure you, Sir John, if Eloise came into my reach, as Geoffrey put it, barefoot in her shift, I would still take her. The dowry is of no import, your daughter is."

John's disbelief came fast and hard. "You expect me to believe you have developed an affection for Eloise? Come now, Roland, admit you crave the land, the money. For what other reason would you place your future in royal service at risk?"

Roland shook his head. "I love your daughter, Sir John. For no other reason would I consider the marriage."

John bolted from his chair and turned his back. Roland drew steady breaths against the sour roil of his stomach, prepared for John's outright refusal. After several long moments, wondering if John meant his silence and refusal to face Roland as his answer, he rose from the chair. His heart heavy, he took a step toward the door.

"You will protect her with your life, Roland."

He nearly melted into the floor.

"I do most humbly swear."

"Then I will allow the marriage on one condition." John finally turned around. "The manor in Durham. Kenworth may try to take it by force if his trickery fails. You will spend whatever you must to man the manor to the rafters and not let Kenworth have it. On my oath, if that manor falls, I will return to haunt you."

"You have my vow."

"Then have Geoffrey draw up the betrothal contract. Eloise is aware of every last piece of pewter that comes to her."

He noticed Sir John said nothing about obtaining Eloise's agreement, but then, most fathers didn't consider the daughter's feelings in such matters.

Roland considered Eloise's opinion of vital importance, and given her nature, obtaining her agreement might be harder than wrestling it from Sir John.

Chapter Eighteen

S TUNNED, ELOISE listened as Geoffrey and Roland presented her with very good reasons why she should marry with all due haste.

They'd told her about the lack of success in finding Brother Walter and had given her no time to recover before they launched arguments for this ridiculous scheme. She'd be protected, they claimed, and her dowry safe from the king's hands and thus out of Kenworth's reach should her father not prevail.

The two had worked out the details while she slept, she realized, each backing the other—against her or for her, she hadn't yet decided.

'Twas the part they hadn't yet told her about that frightened her to her toes. They'd not yet named the man they intended to approach.

She couldn't bear to look at Roland, who seemed anxious for her to agree. So she stared at Geoffrey, whose intentions were good, his reasons strong—and right now she wanted to hate him for it.

She'd always known someday she would marry to further her father's ambitions or to seal an alliance. For that reason she'd not protested her betrothal to Hugh, doing her duty as a good daughter ought.

Foolishly, she'd hoped for more the next time. She'd even allowed herself to think she might have a say on the second betrothal. Useless dreams. Senseless wishes.

"You have been too quiet, Eloise," Geoffrey said. "What are you thinking?"

"That you have both let your imaginations run amok. What man with a stable mind would take me? Granted, my dowry is sizable, but sweet mercy, Father is charged with treason! What fool man would wish to link his good name to ours with that threat of taint. Geoffrey, you cannot foist me off onto an unsuspecting soul!"

"Eloise—"

Geoffrey held up a hand to stay whatever Roland was about to say. "Did you think I would pull some poor man off the street and hold him at dagger point to marry you?"

"Of course not, but you must admit the choices are limited, if there are any choices at all."

His eyes narrowed. "I have never known you to debase your worth. Your dowry aside, you have much to offer a man in your own right. God's wounds, Eloise. What makes you think I need to search under rocks to find you a husband?"

Eloise swallowed hard. He'd given her a grand compliment, even if in an offhanded manner. Geoffrey loved her, she didn't doubt it. He'd once crossed the Channel in an effort to assure her happiness, and suffered horribly for it. Her brother would never, ever, force her into something she found abhorrent.

She gave him a weak smile, all she could muster. "What is it you want of me, Geoffrey?"

"At the moment, a stronger smile. I know you can do better. I would rather you fight me on this than just give in."

"Do make up your mind. You and Roland have spent the better part of an hour battering at my defenses."

"Then I beg your pardon. I did not mean to weaken you, only to give you all the reasons why we propose a marriage. You may refuse if you are opposed."

Eloise looked down at her hands, the palms reddened from rubbing them together so hard. "I assume you have already gained Father's agreement."

Geoffrey merely nodded.

"And the man you have in mind is neither cruel nor teetering on the edge of his grave."

Geoffrey glanced at Roland. "Hardly a tyrant or too old to perform husbandly duties."

"Enough," Roland commanded, then pointed at the door. "Geoffrey, Timothy, out."

Both men obeyed so quickly she barely had time to realize the door closed behind them when Roland held out his hands. She took them and rose from the edge of the bed. He pressed their clasped hands to his chest. His heart beat very hard, the look on his face pained with uncertainty.

"Eloise, as Geoffrey said, you are allowed to refuse." Roland drew a deep breath, and Eloise felt her heart begin to keep rhythm with his. "Marriage is for life, your life. Neither of us intends to force an unwanted marriage on you. If you do not give your consent, we will find another way to shelter your dowry."

"There is no other way. Roland, are you saying you believe I should refuse?"

He shook his head. "Just the opposite. I am hoping you will agree, and perhaps find contentment, even happiness." His hands tightened around hers. "Eloise, would you do me the great honor of becoming my wife?"

Stunned, she stared into his beloved hazel eyes as a thrill washed over her. Her fondest wish had come true, and she would shout a joyful agreement if not for the set of Roland's mouth, if not for the flat delivery of the proposal.

Geoffrey had talked Roland into agreeing to this marriage, just as he'd presented his reasons to her, making everything sound so sensible.

She wasn't the only one who should have the right to refuse.

"You need not do this."

"I know, but I cannot say I find the prospect unpalatable. What of you? I know I am not the most worthy man in the kingdom. Do you think we can make a decent marriage?"

How terribly unromantic. But then, he didn't propose out of love. She was very aware of what he gained by marrying her, land and wealth.

Once more the men in her life had decided what was best for her—and perhaps this time they'd gotten it right.

Roland obtained the income he needed to support his knighthood, and she got the man she loved. Not a bad bargain. And perhaps, with time, he might learn to love her, too.

'Twas certain she had no fear of the marriage bed. Eloise felt the heat rise to her cheeks, remembering their tryst on the mattress behind her.

"I believe we can deal well enough together."

"Then you consent."

"Aye."

His relief was immediate—a blowing out of breath, slumping of shoulders, and light laughter.

"I should rather face a troop of Scottish pikemen than have to go through that again."

She squeezed his hands. "You were afraid?"

"You have no notion. Convincing your father was less trying on the nerves."

Her father. *Mon Dieu,* he'd agreed! She wouldn't have thought it possible. And knowing how her father's mind worked, Eloise realized his consent must have come with a price.

"In return for his agreement, what does he demand of you?"

"That if the worst comes to pass, I must arm the manor in Durham and defend it at all cost against Kenworth." He let go her hands and gathered her in his arms, hers naturally sliding around his waist as if they'd embraced hundreds of times, not so few. "You are not to worry over that however. We will deal with all as needs be. Right now I just want to hold you and allow my mind to become used to the notion that we are to wed."

"I will strive not to make you regret marrying me."

His kiss was warm, tender, arousing. And to think she would soon have wifely rights to his mouth, his body.

"No regrets," he said on a sigh. "Well, perhaps just one. We must allow Geoffrey back in to draw up the agreement."

She smiled at his disgruntlement, hearing a promise for later, to which she added her own vow. "Only for a bit, then we can toss him back out."

Eloise sat back down on the mattress while Roland opened the door. Geoffrey entered grinning, parchment, quill, ink bottle, and jar of sand in hand. His smug confidence deserved a swipe.

"I refused."

His grin froze, and he juggled the items in his hands.

"Have pity, Eloise," Roland admonished her, barely holding back a laugh.

"Must I?"

"Punish him later. He has work to do."

"Oh, very well." Eloise smiled sweetly. "He has much to answer for."

Geoffrey leaned toward Roland. "She did accept, did she not?"

Roland burst out laughing.

For the next little while, Geoffrey wrote furiously to complete the agreement that bound her to Roland. For life. As his wife. All through her telling of what came to him with this marriage, Roland either paced the floor or stared out the window.

The list was long, beginning with the two manors and their location and what knight's fees they owed and the income he could expect. Furniture, jewelry, plates and platters, flagons and knives, tablecloths and bedding.

He raised an eyebrow at the sum she named in gold coin.

Geoffrey never batted an eyelash or asked if she remembered correctly.

"I also want Mother's loom and two dozen sheep. And a milk cow and a maid. Isolde goes with me, if she so chooses."

Geoffrey stopped writing. "Those are not a part of your dowry."

"They are now. If Father expects Roland to defend the manor in Durham, we shall need those items."

"Sounds practical to me. Anything else?"

"Those should be enough."

Geoffrey added the items, sanded the parchment, then rolled it up. He handed it over to Roland.

"All that is required is your and my father's signatures. Be sure to have it witnessed by at least two people. Edgar and Oswald should do."

Roland tapped the scroll against his palm, but what disturbed him he didn't say. He rolled back his shoulders and addressed Geoffrey.

"Were you able to find a priest who is not fussy about having the bans read?"

Butterflies fluttered in her stomach.

Geoffrey nodded. "A cousin of Mistress Green's serves at Westminster Abbey. We have only to send for him, she says."

"Then do it."

They'd said she should marry with haste, but so fast?

"Should we not wait until morning? 'Tis getting late, and the priest may not be able to come immediately."

Roland bowed his head and slowly approached her. He cupped her cheek. "You deserve better, *much* better, but I fear we must wed tonight. On the morn I must leave for Evesham. Your father believes that if Brother Walter is still alive, we will find him at the monastery there."

She grabbed hold of his wrist, torn between excitement at this new development and sadness that they'd have only this one night before he must leave her.

"Oh, Roland." She wanted to say more, but words failed. How could she beg him to stay when her father's life might depend upon his success?

Roland bent over, kissed her cheek, and whispered, "You may still withdraw. Be sure, Eloise."

She looked into his hazel eyes, saw her future, her love, and his worry.

"I am content."

Eloise paced the small open space at the bottom of the stairs, waiting for Roland. 'Twas already getting dark. He should be back by now.

Trying not to worry, she adjusted the small wreath of greenery Mistress Green fashioned for her to wear as a circlet over her veil. Within the strands of ivy—commonly known as an amulet for marriage—the apothecary had woven marjoram for happiness and sage for wisdom. Lovely sentiments. 'Twas the saffron, which Mistress Green claimed a powerful love potion, that made Eloise blush.

The dear widow now stood with her cousin the priest, Geoffrey, and Timothy, discussing the latest affairs in the city, to which Eloise paid no heed.

She'd given thought to changing her gown, but the only other she'd brought along was her crimson velvet. Worn twice. Once on a wedding day gone horribly wrong, the other on the day Kenworth arrived at Lelleford. Bad omens, a little voice had whispered, so she left it hanging on the peg.

What takes him so long?

Had Roland been attacked? Had he changed his mind?

Or did her father refuse to sign the document because of the items she added?

She rubbed her hands together, worried that perhaps in a small show of spirit, she'd botched the bargain altogether.

When at last the bell over the door rang, Roland walked in, smiling and waving the scroll. "Sir John balked at the cow, but he relented and signed."

Then he reached for her hand, placed the scroll on Mistress Green's worktable, and guided her over to the priest. Eloise forgot the haste and all of her worries, and concentrated on repeating words of love, honor, and obedience to Roland.

Then the priest turned to Roland, and as her groom began to say the vows that bound them, he raised her hands to his chest. She felt his heartbeat, fast-paced but strong, beat after beat.

This time her groom would live through the ceremony, and she realized Roland sought to reassure her. When tears welled up, she blinked them away, though a couple escaped down her cheeks before she could stop them.

Sweet mercy, she was, most definitely, content.

She is truly mine, now.

The phrase repeated over and over in Roland's head. If he gave himself time, repeated the phrase enough, perhaps he would begin to believe.

His palms sweated. His stomach flipped. 'Twas all he could do to keep his knees from melting.

What had he done to deserve such a prize? 'Struth, he wasn't worthy of Eloise at all. Yet here she stood, smiling with tears in her eyes.

He would never, ever, understand the way of a

woman's tears, and could barely keep from brushing the glistening drops from her cheeks. But holding her hands where she could feel his heartbeat seemed more important.

Ah, Hugh. I am sorry you are gone, but do not ask me to feel remorse that Eloise is now mine. I cannot do it. Now I understand what you felt when you looked at her. I was wrong, Hugh. Forgive me.

And in his heart, Roland knew Hugh wouldn't ask, nor would he hesitate to forgive.

They would make a good marriage, he and his bride. He would settle for nothing less. He'd make her happy, he vowed silently, as aloud he pledged to love, honor, and protect.

Nor could he help a smile when ordered to be fruitful and multiply.

"Have you a ring?" the priest asked.

"Aye," he answered, and let go Eloise's hands to fetch a ring from his money pouch. He held up a ring of gold set with rubies, and watched her eyes go wide with recognition. "Your father could not be here, but wanted to be with you in spirit. He loans us this until we can get you a proper ring of your own."

This time Roland understood the tears. He'd damn near shed them himself when Sir John pressed the ring into his hand.

With the overlarge ring on Eloise's finger, the priest wound a strip of linen around their clasped hands, blessed them, and bade them share a kiss of peace.

Peace. Hah! His entire body went riot at the taste of his bride's lips.

"Go in peace and love, my children. May God light and bless your path all your days."

And it was done. Their lives irrevocably entwined.

Ale was passed. Hugs and handshakes exchanged.

Roland unrolled the scroll far enough to allow all to see the approving signatures, and for the witnesses to the marriage to add their names and marks to the end. Sanded and dry, he tucked the proof of his union to Eloise into his tunic, his to hold safe against anyone who might question the marriage's validity.

The wedding supper consisted of savory beef stew and brown bread, and Roland made a mental note to pay Mistress Green extra for all her kindnesses, especially in light of the trouble he'd brought to her doorstep.

The priest paid and on his way, Timothy and Geoffrey went up the stairs to bring down two of the pallets, uttering ribald comments about why they must vacate the upstairs room.

When at last Roland had Eloise all to himself, the night dark and fleeting, by the flickering of candlelight, he slowly, reverently, undid her laces.

She ran a fingertip over his lips, smiling softly. "Husband," she whispered, as if trying out the title to see if it fit.

"My wife has a request?"

"Not this time. Now I know what you are capable of, and you promised I might take an active part this time. Lead on, Husband. I am most anxious to learn more."

Her confidence and willingness, which boded very well for the success of this marriage as well as the next hour, shot straight to his head.

"We have a long night ahead of us."

"Oh, I do hope so!"

He took his time removing her garments, one piece at a time, from her herbal circlet to her hose, worshiping her body with strokes and kisses as he uncovered creamy soft skin.

She returned the favor. Eloise struggled with his boots, but had no problem with the lacing on his tunic. 'Twas endearing when she fumbled with the ties on his breeches, but she forged ahead and pushed them down far enough for him to step out of them.

She stared overlong at his arousal.

'Twas sensuous and appealing and nigh on mind-bending to have a naked woman undress him and stare at his male parts with a degree of admiration bordering on awe. To think the woman standing before him in all her womanly glory was Eloise, his love and lover and now his wife, humbled him.

Then she touched him, the tip of her finger to hood, and he responded with an involuntary jerk.

"Sensitive?" she asked.

He unclenched his teeth. "Aye."

"Here, too?"

The stroke along the backside of his penis sent shivers through his whole body and brought forth an intolerable ache.

"There most especially."

She wrapped her hand around him. "So when you place . . . this inside me, you feel me around you, and—"

Roland pulled away and picked her up. The minx learned too fast.

"Aye, I feel you around me as you feel me inside you." He landed none too gently on the mattress, rolled them both into the middle of the bed to lay on their sides facing each other. "You are like a velvet glove, a perfect fit. I can feel you pulse when you reach your bliss."

She pressed against him in blatant invitation. "Show me."

"I thought you wanted to take an active part."

"Later. I ache for you, Roland. Perform those husbandly duties I understand I must endure."

Endure. Hah! He'd show her endure—if he could endure.

He eased down far enough to bring her leg up over his hip, spreading her wide, and slipped inside. Not far. But enough to make her close her eyes, arch her back, and hiss—her woman's place clenched tight around him.

"Have mercy, Roland."

Mercy for whom? Him or her? Didn't matter.

So he stroked, giving her more each time, keeping tight rein on his body's screams for release.

Sweat beaded on his upper lip. His hand gripped her buttocks, holding her still and tight against him. Buried to the hilt, he gave her all he had to give. Pleasure. Carnal ecstasy. A man's mating gift to his woman.

Her breath came in pants. Her fingers dug into his shoulders. He took a nipple into his mouth and suckled hard until he heard a throaty moan, her unique passionate plea.

He answered with his body, his heart, driving into her until her moans turned into cries of completion.

Still he endured. Softly stroking, enjoying the pulse of her ecstasy. Finally he stilled, allowing her senses to return, her mind to function. When at last she opened her eyes and looked at him, she gifted him with a smile that bordered on veneration.

"You felt it, all of it," she said.

"I did." He kissed the swell of her breast. "Remember the other night, you asked me if I was disappointed?"

"You said you were not." Her eyes clouded. "Are you now?"

"Nay, not yet, nor will I be. I wanted to show you one thing more—how to know without doubt if you have pleased your husband."

Once more he set a rhythm, this time loosening his willpower and relinquishing control.

"What need I do?"

"Naught for now, simply allow me . . . mmmmm."

He came fast and hard, his seed spilling into her with each hardy pound of his magnificent release. This time he felt complete, whole, as he hadn't the last. This time they were truly one.

"Oh, my."

"Ah, yes."

She brushed a hank of hair back from his now wet forehead. "Does that . . . hurt?"

"As much as yours did."

She smiled. Sweet mercy how he loved her smile.

"That much, hmmm? Perhaps you should show me again just to ensure I understand the way of it correctly."

And so he did.

Roland dressed in the dark.

The candle had gutted out hours ago, and the coals in the brazier were but glowing embers. Light didn't yet filter in through the window.

He didn't want to go anywhere. Not out from underneath the coverlet and snuggled around Eloise. Not out into the chill of a November day. Certainly not to Evesham Abbey.

Duty had never been so hard to perform, nor had it called so urgently. Already dressed, he eased onto the edge of the mattress to put on his boots.

Eloise's hand landed on his lower back, then crept slowly up his spine.

"I tried not to wake you."

"I grew cold." Her voice was low and thick with sleep, the most seductive sound he'd ever heard, except for, perhaps, the little noises she made in her throat when—

"Go back to sleep. You did not get much rest last night."

Her light laughter preceded a rustling of the bedding. She knelt, pressed her naked front to his tunic-covered back, her heat seeping through the wool. Her arms came around him to cross his chest, her mouth taking a light nip at his neck.

"Nor did you rest long."

"Your fault."

"I accept all blame."

He kissed the forearm tucked just under his chin. "If you do not let go, woman, I shall not be held responsible for my actions."

He felt her sigh. "I wish you did not have to go."

"Nor I, but go I must."

She kissed his neck below the ear, the combination of moist mouth and hot breath giving a kick to his loins.

"You will hurry back."

A command, which he'd obey for several reasons.

"As fast as I am able. I am taking your palfrey, for the monk."

"Let us hope you have need of him and his speed." She backed away. "What happens if the monk is not at the abbey?"

Roland hurriedly slipped on his boots and turned sideways to see her dark silhouette against the predawn gray.

"Geoffrey has some ideas he is working on. Do not despair, Eloise."

She shifted, and he soon found himself with his arms full, his mouth engaged. Ye gods, he could become accustomed to these rapturous leave takings. But he could hardly wait to celebrate a homecoming.

"Take care, St. Marten. I have become accustomed to you sharing my bed."

"After only one night?"

"You must admit you were impressive."

Leaving her was the hardest thing he'd done in an age.

Geoffrey was waiting for him at the bottom of the stairs, clad only in breeches, a small candle illuminating his form. "How does she?"

He could hardly tell Eloise's brother exactly how magnificently she'd done most everything, for several hours.

"She did not sleep well last night."

"'Twas her wedding night. Had she slept well I would wonder what was wrong with you."

"According to her, not a thing." He gave Geoffrey a good-natured slap on the arm. "Take care of her. I should be back within four days. Just so you know, I am taking the palfrey. 'Twould also not be amiss to send a message to Lelleford to have them pack Eloise's belongings."

"Anxious for the plunder, are you?"

'Twas said with such humor Roland didn't take offense. "Naturally. Will you see Lancaster today?"

"Aye. Best to have another form of defense in mind. Perhaps Lancaster has already formed a plan."

Roland hoped so, because nothing was sure about this journey to Evesham.

Chapter Nineteen

ROLAND HAD been gone for two days. Eloise missed him terribly, and worried over him more than she fretted over the outcome of the task he'd taken on. 'Twas probably disloyal to her father, but as she said her marriage vows, so had the center of her life shifted.

Husband. The word still sounded strange, but magical.

"Feels odd?" her father asked.

Knowing her father couldn't possibly hear her thoughts, she tilted her head in question.

He pointed at her hands in her lap. "For the past two days you have played with the ring. Is it so ill a fit?"

Not in the least, neither the ring nor the marriage, nor her father's unexpected show of affection in lending it to her. If not for the circumstances, she'd be joyous.

"Nay." She gave the ring a last twirl and stilled her hands. "I imagine your hand feels odd without it."

He wiggled his fingers. "I am becoming accustomed."

Just as he'd become accustomed to his chamber in Baliol's Tower. From her chair near the table, Eloise glanced around the room. 'Twas a pleasant chamber in many ways, but to be locked in all the time, with only brief walks out on the grounds for exercise—'Twould drive her mad.

Of late, she spent much time locked up with her father while Geoffrey went about the task of gathering information and seeking opinions about her father's case. Toward the end of each day, when he came to report his findings and fetch her, she was most ready to leave.

At present, Geoffrey sought a second audience with Lancaster, who the king had finally consented to see earlier this morning.

"St. Marten should be able to buy you a splendid ring with the money he gains. We truly made him a wealthy man."

A disgruntled statement. Roland hadn't made any comment about his bargaining with her father, and she'd not asked, mostly because there hadn't been time.

So much happened so quickly. From the moment of Geoffrey's arrival to Roland's leaving, much seemed a blur.

Except for the wedding night. That she remembered in vibrant detail.

"You knew you made Roland wealthy when you signed the document. 'Tis rather mean-spirited to begrudge him any portion of my dowry now." She narrowed her eyes. "You did not take anything out, did you?"

He picked up a pawn and moved it one square, where she could take it with her bishop. An ill-advised move? Or a trap for her?

"Nay, though *you* certainly added items. The sheep and loom I understood, but a cow?"

"We need milk to make cheese, and I could not remember what cattle belong to the holding in Durham. Surely you do not begrudge me one cow."

"Better you have it, I suppose, than Kenworth."

Another thing she'd noticed recently—her father's unusual submission to an intolerable fate. As the days dragged on, he became more dour and despairing. She hoped Geoffrey delivered hopeful news today, if only to lift her father's spirits.

"Kenworth will not get anything of yours. How can you be so morose when both Geoffrey and Roland work so diligently on your behalf? Surely one of them—"

He waved a dismissive hand. "Geoffrey scurries about London, talking to all who will listen, but only the king's opinion truly matters and I fear he believes me guilty. As for Roland, the lad means well, but his journey to Evesham may well be for naught. Even if our elusive monk is in his abbey, who is to say he is willing to speak on my behalf? Brother Walter is, after all is said and done, Kenworth's spy."

He got up, his agitation leading him to the window.

Once more she failed to cheer him, and finally conceded only good news from either Geoffrey or Roland would.

If all went well, Roland should arrive at the abbey this afternoon and be back in London on the day after tomorrow. Until then, all she could do was wait.

Again, she did nothing. Again it wore on her nerves. Patience had never been one of her better virtues.

Eloise abandoned the chess game that no longer held her father's interest either. She joined him at the window.

Two ravens perched on the wall walk that connected several towers along the inner wall. Startled by a noise from below, the ravens spread glossy black wings and glided skyward.

The noise came again, a bang of wood on wood, and Eloise peered down to see Timothy and Edgar happily sparring with practice swords.

"Wherever did they get the weapons?"

"Oswald, most likely. Weapons are stored on the lower floor."

"Still, they are weapons in the hands of squires, one of them yours. I am surprised Oswald allows the squires their use."

Her father shrugged. "I imagine Oswald demanded some kind of an oath from them first. Good lads, both."

Eloise agreed. "Timothy yet favors his ribs. See how he feints?"

"Edgar takes the injury into account. The lads have grown close, have they not?"

Eloise guessed Timothy hadn't told Edgar of the affair with Isolde or Edgar mightn't be so accepting.

But then, her own brother hadn't run his sister's lover through. 'Struth, Geoffrey and Roland seemed to get along quite well, which pleased her.

"Timothy and Edgar have much in common," she answered.

"Do you think Roland might be willing to take Edgar on as a squire? The lad will make a fine knight someday with the proper training."

This acceptance of defeat bothered her immensely.

"So besides me, you now give Edgar to Roland, too. Is that the best plan you can conjure, give away whatever you are able before the executioner slips a noose around your neck?"

He raised a warning eyebrow. Eloise ignored the sign that she pricked his ire. Better he shout at her than wallow in despair.

She crossed to the garment pegs, took down one of his tunics. "Who should I give this to? Perhaps 'twill fit Simon." And then his midnight blue velvet trimmed with gold, the one she packed so he would have suitable garb for his appearance before the king. "Marcus has always admired this one. Or should I sell it and give away the coin as alms for the poor?"

"Eloise—"

"Your stallion. Do you have someone in mind for him, or should Geoffrey have him?"

"Enough."

"Oh, I think not! Since you are certain neither your son nor my husband can find a way to aid you, I want to know how you wish your personal belongings disposed of so Kenworth cannot claim them."

"You go too far, Daughter."

None too gently, Eloise hung the tunics back on the pegs.

"If I do, then I beg your pardon, Father. 'Tis simply disheartening to hear you speak as if you are already headed for the gallows."

"You must face that it may come to that."

"I will if needs be, but until then, there is yet hope."

He gave out a short burst of laughter. "Always the optimist. Fine. Have things your way. You usually do." He tilted his head. "Like your marriage. Roland and Geoffrey both assure me you are content. True?"

A startling question. On presenting her with the betrothal bargain to Hugh, he'd not bothered to worry about her contentment, merely sought her agreement. But then, the betrothal to Hugh had been her father's doing, not Geoffrey's.

They'd never said a word, but Eloise didn't doubt that Geoffrey concocted the plan and convinced Roland. She saw it as her duty, a pleasurable duty, to ensure Roland didn't come to regret yielding.

"I am content. Did you have reason to doubt?"

"You were raised to expect better in a husband, and I have never known you to be content with less than your due."

Eloise remembered her grand plan to accompany her father to Christmas court, to look over the possible contenders for her hand. She'd have considered their position first, then their looks and health—never giving Roland St. Marten a second glance. Now here she was married to a sixth son with no prospects or land to recommend him, and was pleased with the bargain, for reasons her father wouldn't understand.

"I have no regrets, Father."

She turned to the jangle of keys. Oswald opened the door to let Geoffrey in. The look on her brother's face didn't promise hopeful news. Spirits sinking, she once more took the chair near the table.

Geoffrey tossed his cloak on the bed and waited for the sound of the warder's key locking the door before he began.

"Lancaster went to see Edward this morn. 'Twas not a pleasant audience, I am told. Kenworth was there, too." Geoffrey paused, as if choosing his words or gathering his thoughts. "Lancaster did not tell me all that was said, but the outcome is not in our favor. Edward wants the issue resolved. He has ordered all parties to his chambers on the morn."

She jumped up. "But that does not give Roland enough time to return with Brother Walter!"

"I know. I asked Lancaster to request a delay. He agreed to do so, but given the king's present mood, he is not hopeful. Kenworth pressures the king for action, and Lancaster does not know how long Edward can resist without appearing weak-willed."

"Not long," her father commented. "Edward's father tended to put off decisions until events made the decision for him, and betimes the results were disastrous. 'Tis not a reputation the son wishes to court. You told Lancaster where Roland went and why?"

"I did. Given what I know of Roland's audience with Edward, I thought the king might be willing to give Roland a chance to return."

"Or he may not." Father again turned to the window, his head bowed. "'Tis as I feared, that all will depend upon whether Edward believes me or the earl of Kenworth. I caution you not to place any wagers on my success."

Roland paced Abbot Clement's sitting room, careful not to bump into any of the excessively ornate furniture. He felt too big for the room, too heavy for the chairs, more ill at ease than he wanted to admit even to himself.

Since arriving at Evesham and requesting to see Brother Walter, Roland had been passed from monk to monk until he'd finally ended up in the abbot's office. Something wasn't right. Such a simple thing as a visit to a monk shouldn't require the consent or presence of the abbey's ruler.

Still, Abbot Clement had sent an assistant to fetch Brother Walter, so perhaps nothing horrible was amiss. Roland smiled to himself, realizing he'd caught Eloise's optimism. The lady had affected him in more ways than he'd thought.

"Patience, my son. 'Twill take some time to locate Brother Walter. May I offer you wine or ale?"

Time. Every moment counted. The abbot didn't know that, however, because Roland hadn't said why he needed to speak with Brother Walter, only that the reason was of great import.

"I appreciate your hospitality, my lord abbot."

Abbot Clement poured a generous amount of wine into a costly gold goblet of simple design. A portly man of seeming good humor, the abbot waved a hand beset by three heavy rings toward a heavy, brocade-cushioned chair.

"Rest yourself, Sir Roland. Tell me of news from London."

Short of being horribly rude to a man of the Church, Roland saw no way out. So he dredged up tidbits of gossip to relate, hoping each bit would be the last before Brother Walter came through the door.

He refrained from mentioning the charges against Sir John. Not until he'd left London did Roland wonder how widespread the news, or how much influence Kenworth might have over Evesham Abbey and its abbot. Best to withhold comment in front of people he wasn't sure he could trust and keep his reasons for seeking out the monk between himself and Brother Walter.

The wine went down smoothly, and with every sip Roland counted the moments wasted. They needed to get on the road and set a quick pace. For Sir John's sake. For his own.

He missed Eloise damn near more than he could bear.

Was it only two mornings ago he'd slipped out of her arms to make this dash to Evesham? Seemed like a life-time ago.

All the way to the abbey he'd thought of her, wondering what she was doing and where she might be. Her brother would keep her safe, Roland knew. Geoffrey would guard her or ensure her safety if he couldn't be with her. But until he saw Eloise again, Roland knew he wouldn't rest easy.

Sweet mercy, but she'd brought him low. He risked much—all for the love of a woman. A chivalrous notion that had no place in real life. One might yearn for a woman from afar, write poetry to a lady's beauty, or vow to perform some brave deed in her name. However, no sensible knight put his good name in jeopardy or risked his future in royal service in the name of love.

Yet he did. By aiding her father. By marrying Eloise.

Sir John might yet be convicted of treason. The king might not be pleased by the marriage to Eloise. However, no power on heaven or earth could have stopped Roland from marrying her once she gave her consent.

He drained his goblet.

She seemed content with the marriage, but Eloise was a proud, strong woman. How long would it be until she fully realized how far beneath her she'd married, perhaps come to resent what she may have given up? Would she still be content if her husband failed to give her back her father?

Why did his normal self-confidence in his strengths and abilities falter when it came to Eloise?

Because he loved her. Because he loathed the idea of losing the contentment and joy he found in her arms. For the first time in his life he'd surrendered to the urging of his heart despite the warnings in his head. Brought low, indeed.

Roland rose as the door opened. The abbot's assistant returned—without Brother Walter.

The monk bowed to his prelate. "Brother Walter begs your indulgence and asks to be excused from this audience. He expresses his desire to not speak with Sir Roland."

Roland almost tossed the goblet across the room. He'd not expected this.

"Did he give a reason why?" the abbot asked.

"Nay, my lord abbot, he did not."

The abbot tossed a questioning glance Roland's way.

Roland could think of several reasons why the monk might wish to hide, none of them for the abbot's ears. Remembering dragging the monk out of the stable at Lelleford, the embarrassing bath in the bailey, then giving him over to Kenworth, Roland strove for a balance between truth and evasion.

"I understand his reluctance. I fear our last meeting was less than friendly, but I hoped he had found it in his heart to forgive me. I assure you, my lord abbot, Brother Walter has nothing to fear from me."

Not much to fear, anyway. Not if the man came out of hiding and got on the horse.

The assistant shook his head. "Brother Walter was most adamant. He told me to wish Sir Roland Godspeed."

With neither the time nor patience to placate or negotiate, Roland placed his hands flat on the abbot's dark, highly polished desk and leaned forward.

"With due respect for Brother Walter's reluctance, I must speak with him. Whether the good monk here brings Walter to me, or takes me to him, I care not. I will not, however, leave without at least a word with him."

Roland guessed a man didn't rise to the position of abbot without possessing some power of his own. The abbot glowered.

"I will not force one of my monks to an audience where he feels threatened. On what business do you come?"

"The king's business." Not quite a lie, and very effective, eliciting raised eyebrows and an impressive gasp from the assistant.

Not so the abbot.

"The king, you say. What does Edward want with our brother?"

Roland backed up. "I am allowed to inform Brother Walter. If he wishes to tell you, he may. However, please know that a man's life may depend on information the monk possesses. Would you have a man die because Brother Walter is hesitant?"

The abbot didn't take long to think it over. "We will take you to Brother Walter, but I insist on being present when you speak with him."

"Only if he agrees."

"Fair enough."

Roland strode beside the abbot through the

passageways. Never having been in a monastery before, he was impressed by how much the place resembled a castle. Thick stone walls. A large hall with trestle tables set up along the length. People bustled about to perform their given tasks, the slap of sandals replacing the clunk of boots.

Except all the people were men, and all were respectfully quiet. Not an ominous hush, but close. 'Twas hard to imagine a man as big and vital as Geoffrey in a setting such as this, and not at all hard to imagine how a man of Brother Walter's skittish nature might find solace.

The monk leading them slowed as they neared an archway.

"In the garden?" the abbot asked.

"Aye, my lord abbot. On the far bench."

The abbot waved off the monk and strode through the archway into a space open to the sky in the middle of the abbey. In the far corner, one brown-robed monk huddled in a small alcove.

Roland felt his heartbeat quicken as he recognized his quarry. Fearing Brother Walter might bolt if approached too quickly, he once more matched his stride to the abbot's, being careful to stay half a step behind.

As they neared him, the monk's head slowly rose, his eyes going wide with stark fear. The abbot put up his hands, palms forward, and quickened his pace. Roland stopped in his tracks.

"Peace, my son. We mean you no harm," the abbot said.

The monk didn't believe it, but neither did he move, except for the visible flinch when the abbot's hand landed on his shoulder.

While the abbot whispered assurances, Roland realized something dreadful must have happened to Brother Walter after he'd left Lelleford. The man had been skittish, but not like a rabbit within talon's reach of a hawk. Kenworth's doing? Roland remembered thinking the monk might suffer consequences for alerting Sir John to Kenworth's arrival. Kenworth hadn't done away with his spy, but had assuredly inflicted punishment.

After much cajoling by the abbot, Brother Walter finally rose from the bench and tucked his hands up his wide sleeves. He wasn't shaking, but Roland sensed continuing fear.

Although impatient, Roland waited for the abbot's slight hand motion before approaching.

"Brother Walter," Roland said gently. "I have given Abbot Clement my word that I will do you no harm. As a knight, as a man who prides himself on his honor, I give you the same oath now. You have naught to fear from me."

"You serve . . . Kenworth."

Roland didn't know how much influence Kenworth held over the abbey or its abbot, if any, but decided he must take a slight risk.

"I am in the king's service, not Kenworth's. I come to you at the behest of another, who very much needs your help. May I beg your indulgence for a private word?"

The abbot patted the monk's shoulder. "I will not be far, only on yon bench."

Brother Walter swallowed hard, then gave a slight nod. The abbot took himself off to a bench not far away, but far enough.

Hoping to appear less threatening, Roland clasped his

hands behind his back. He had no time to question the monk and coax out what he knew of the case. But he could be gentle in his directness.

"I fear Kenworth is on the verge of making good his case against Sir John, who resides in the Tower of London awaiting his hearing. Brother Walter, Sir John cannot disprove the charges against him without your help. Will you come?"

"Nay, I cannot leave," Walter said, his voice thin. "I cannot."

Roland strove to remain calm in the face of the man's quietly stated panic.

"Lady Eloise believes you wanted to tell her father something vital on the morning Sir John left Lelleford to avoid Kenworth. Is she correct?"

The monk's head bobbed. "How does . . . her ladyship?"

'Twas Roland's turn to take a steadying breath. "She is in London, doing all she can to bolster her father's spirits." And then he knew how to begin to gain the monk's confidence. "We are now married, Lady Eloise and I."

The fear receded slightly. "You are Sir John's son-by-marriage?"

"I am, and as such, wish to help him any way I am able. Is my wife correct in believing you wished to tell her father about the missive in the king's possession?"

The monk closed his eyes, but remained mum.

"Brother Walter, Sir John may hang if you do not finish your confession."

A visible shiver ran through the man's body, his closed eyes tightening. For a moment, Roland thought the monk would bolt. Then he calmed and opened his eyes. The flash of something akin to defiance lit his features.

"Sir John is a good man," he said, his voice stronger.

"I believe so. How good is a judgment of God. In any event, he is not guilty of treason."

"Nay, he is not."

At last, Roland began to feel hope. "Will you come?"

"Kenworth will . . . will . . ."

Roland waited for the monk to finish, but he never did, the words seemingly stuck in his throat. Having never been this fearful of a man, Roland struggled to understand the terror.

"Kenworth will not harm you. Either I or Sir John's son, Geoffrey, will be your guards. 'Tis quite possible you may never see Kenworth at all."

Brother Walter glanced toward where the abbot sat on the bench. Looking for guidance?

Moments slid away, time growing short.

Roland held out his right hand. "I give you my oath, whether by guile or by sword, I shall do all I am able to keep you safe from Kenworth."

Brother Walter stared at the extended hand, then slowly slid his own from beneath his robe's generous sleeve.

Maimed. Twisted fingers. Shattered thumb. Knuckles huge and prominent.

Roland finally understood the monk's fear and managed to remain steady as the damaged hand slid into his. Roland gripped the monk's hand as firmly as he dared, and soon felt an answering squeeze, not hard, but with definite pressure.

"I will come," the monk said.

Relief washed over him, and his thoughts turned to the journey ahead. While Roland hated to refer to the man's deformity, the question had to be asked.

"Can you ride a horse?"

"Aye. I will fetch my cloak."

The monk sped through the garden, passed under the arch.

The abbot's hand landed on Roland's shoulder. "You did well, son. I have not seen such spirit in Brother Walter's step since he returned to us."

"What happened to his hand?"

"Brother Walter told me he fell and a wagon wheel ran over it."

Roland didn't doubt the damage caused by a wagon wheel, but had to wonder how the monk's hand came to be in the wheel's path. True, the man was clumsy, but Roland doubted the injury was a horrible happenstance.

" 'Twould have been best for Brother Walter had he never left the abbey."

The abbot gave a shrug. "Perhaps. I never thought to question when he volunteered to fulfill Sir John Hamelin's request for a clerk. I should have, I suppose."

"Why is that?"

"Brother Walter is the earl of Kenworth's bastard son. I am entrusting you to keep my monk safe. Do not disappoint me, Sir Roland."

Bastard son?

Roland reeled. Even as he struggled to absorb the news, his understanding of the monk's previous actions and his current fright rose.

Brother Walter had served as spy to please his father. The monk's conscience must have bothered him to the degree that he informed Sir John, who he'd come to like and respect. As punishment for his betrayal, Kenworth allowed Walter to live, but only with the reminder of where his loyalty had fallen short.

And now Roland asked him to fully betray his father.

Ye gods. Could the monk find the strength to go through what was required of him? And if he did, could Roland truly protect Brother Walter against Kenworth's wrath?

Chapter Twenty

GARBED IN her crimson gown, hands clasped in her lap, Eloise perched on the edge of a brocade-cushioned chair at the far edge of the king's sumptuous chamber.

On one side of the king's desk stood William, earl of Kenworth, and on the other Geoffrey and their father. Seated in a thronelike chair, King Edward leaned forward on his desk, arms crossed, all four missives spread out before him.

Lancaster wouldn't attend. Fearing the audience might decline into a power struggle between the king and the two earls and confident he could present their father's case convincingly, Geoffrey had requested Lancaster refrain from appearing.

Roland wasn't here either, and his continued absence tightened the knot in her stomach.

He should have been back yesterday afternoon, and with each passing hour Eloise fretted less over whether he'd found Brother Walter and more over his safety.

'Struth, she wanted Roland to arrive with the monk in tow, but right now she'd settle for word that no mishap had befallen him. She kept glancing at the doorway even as she strove to heed the arguments being presented in respectful, almost too civilized fashion, to King Edward. The king listened without comment, showing nothing of his thoughts, as Kenworth exchanged opposing views with Geoffrey over the believability of the missives and the quality of her father's character.

While she found Edward's lack of reaction irritating, Eloise was struck favorably by his poise and commanding presence. Perhaps she was swayed by her father's tales of the king's prowess, or perhaps she felt the magnetism of his power and position. Either way, if asked, she'd willingly take an oath of fealty to the young king.

Kenworth tossed a hand in the air. "My liege, the missives speak for themselves. The question is not if John Hamelin conspired with the Scottish chief, but for how long."

"Never," her father said quietly, the first time he'd spoken.

Kenworth wagged a finger at him. "You are well and truly caught, Hamelin. To deny the deed only brings you further dishonor."

"Never," Father repeated more strongly. "'Twas your spy who sneaked those missives into my accounting room. One must wonder where he obtained them. From you, Kenworth?"

Geoffrey winced, and Eloise tightened her clasped hands. Father and Geoffrey had agreed not to mention their suspicions about the exact nature of Brother Walter's role. Partly because most of their beliefs were speculation, but mostly because they couldn't prove anything without the monk's cooperation.

"Preposterous!" Kenworth's voice thundered through the spacious chamber.

The king ignored the outburst and merely arched an eyebrow at her father. "What spy?"

"A monk I took into my service as my clerk. On the morning Kenworth was to arrive, Brother Walter confessed to secreting the missives into Lelleford and forewarned me of Kenworth's arrival to arrest me for treason."

Kenworth shook his head. "Lie upon lie. 'Tis true Brother Walter knew of the missives. He did us good service, my liege, by informing me of their existence."

Edward glanced at Kenworth. "You did not inform me of this monk's role before."

" 'Twas of little import. The monk's discovery of the other missives merely supported what we already knew from the one obtained from MacLeod's messenger. 'Tis the missives' existence which are of import, not how we obtained them." Kenworth waved a hand at the desk. "These are all the proof we need to send this traitor to the gallows, my liege. Say the word and I shall order it so."

Eloise fought to keep from begging King Edward not to believe what he saw, to realize the evidence laid before him was false. But how could he disregard them? When all was said, 'twas her father's name on the missive linking him to the MacLeod, not Kenworth's.

Edward looked to Kenworth. "Where is this monk?"

Kenworth opened his mouth but Geoffrey spoke first. "We believe he is at Evesham Abbey, my liege. Roland St. Marten went to fetch him."

Kenworth huffed. "St. Marten. An untrustworthy cur. He has betrayed your trust, my liege. Are you aware he disobeyed your orders? Instead of remaining to oversee Lelleford, he has brought the traitor's daughter to London." He tossed her a brief, sneering glance, sending a shiver down her spine. "Are you aware, Hamelin, that they have been sharing a room over an apothecary? St. Marten has been boffing your daughter."

Eloise stifled a gasp at the base description of her intimate relations with Roland. Even as her face warmed with embarrassment and indignation on Roland's behalf, she realized Kenworth had just confessed to knowing of their whereabouts in London. Perhaps he had sent those villains to kidnap her as her father believed.

Her father waved a dismissing hand. "What St. Marten does or does not do with Eloise is his choice. Did you know, Kenworth, that they are wed?"

Eloise winced at the king's upraised eyebrow. Roland hadn't informed the king of the marriage as yet. That could mean trouble for Roland later.

Still, Kenworth's sudden pallor at realizing the manor in Durham was yet another step beyond his reach proved satisfying. "Wed? To St. Marten?"

Her father's smile widened. "Several nights ago."

Kenworth's agitation sharpened. "Impossible. I would have been aware of such a ceremony."

"St. Marten is in possession of the signed and witnessed betrothal bargain. Several people were present when the two exchanged vows." Father tilted his head. "I gather you have had Roland watched. One must also wonder at the quality of the men you hire as your spies and thugs."

Kenworth's hands fisted and opened several times, the

itch to pummel her father apparent to all observers. Including the king.

"Is the matter of St. Marten's marriage of import in this case?" Edward asked.

The earl quickly reined in his ire. "Nay, my liege. Nor is the monk. 'Struth, should St. Marten bring forth Brother Walter, the monk will merely confirm what I have told you."

Either Kenworth was very sure of the tale the monk would tell, or Brother Walter wasn't at Evesham for Roland to fetch.

Or Kenworth had ensured Roland couldn't bring Brother Walter to appear before the king.

Her clasped hands trembled. Had Kenworth's thugs followed Roland out of London? When they realized he was headed for Evesham Abbey, had the villains either captured or killed him?

The arrow to her heart pierced her fury. She rose from the chair, fully prepared to claw Kenworth to shreds if he didn't divulge Roland's whereabouts.

The wretch was saved only by the opening of the chamber's huge oak doors—and Roland crossing the threshold.

Alive. Covered with road dust. His hair disheveled. Looking weary and worn, but *alive*.

She quickly crossed the distance between them, flung her arms around his neck, and reveled in the feel of Roland's steady heartbeat against her own. Eloise closed her eyes and clung to the husband she'd feared for, the man she loved beyond reason.

Sweet mercy, but he'd brought her low.

Against all sense, she'd been about to confront an earl

on the wisp of a chance he might have harmed Roland, giving no thought at all to anyone else in the chamber.

She'd come damn close to embarrassing herself in front of the *king*! Only now did it occur to her that she likely embarrassed everyone in the chamber with her impulsive show of affection.

Eloise took comfort that Roland didn't seem to mind. His arms wrapped as tightly around her waist as her arms clutched him about the neck.

"Praise God," she whispered. "What took you so long?"

"Brother Walter does not sit a horse well," he said, his tone giving her the impression there was more to the tale. "I beg pardon if the delay caused you distress."

"I . . . worried."

After a reassuring squeeze, his arms loosened. "'Twill be over soon."

She reluctantly eased away and glanced at the monk who could save her father. Brother Walter stared at the floor, his hands tucked up into his sleeves. Looking as disheveled and weary as Roland, the monk's mouth moved in silent prayer.

Roland gingerly touched the monk's forearm. "I did not count on Kenworth being here. Can you carry on?"

Those pale blue eyes opened, and Eloise saw panic so overwhelming she wanted to put her arms around him, too.

Brother Walter's slight nod wasn't reassuring.

Roland tucked her hand into the crook of his arm and led her across the floor. Behind her she could hear the flap of the monk's sandals, the swish of his robes. Within a few steps of the king Roland stopped, and Eloise dipped into a curtsy in accord with his bow.

"My liege." Roland turned slightly to wave the monk forward. "This is Brother Walter of Evesham Abbey, who served as Sir John's clerk for several months. He has agreed to tell us what he knows of this affair."

Kenworth huffed. "I have already told you what the monk knows, my liege. 'Tis a waste of time to allow him to speak. However, if everyone insists, Brother Walter, do tell us how you aided me in bringing the traitor low."

Eloise wondered if she was the only one who heard a threat in Kenworth's tone. She wasn't. Brother Walter's gaze darted between Kenworth and her father before at last coming to rest on the king.

"What do you know, monk?" Edward asked.

Brother Walter opened his mouth, then pursed his lips. 'Twas then Eloise noted how badly he shook, how sweat beaded on his brow. His fright was palpable. Afraid of the king? Nay, most likely of Kenworth.

Eloise felt a moment's panic that he'd turn tail and run. If he didn't speak, didn't confirm all they'd guessed at . . . the consequences were too unbearable to contemplate. Not when her father was so close to being liberated.

She slipped from Roland's side and placed her hand on Brother Walter's arm. After a moment, his trembling eased.

Eloise hoped her tone was soothing. "Brother Walter, on the morning my father left Lelleford, you wished to tell him something of such import you declared us doomed if you could not find him. Much has happened since, and the doom is at hand. Only you can save him. I beg you, Brother Walter, to complete your confession."

He stared at her for a moment, then replied in a thin voice, "I wrote . . . the missive."

Eloise felt the men close in around her even as her world brightened.

"Which missive?"

"The one which names Sir John and the MacLeod."

The words hung in the air for several moments until Kenworth finally realized he no longer controlled his spy. His fury burst forth bright and menacing, his darting reach for the monk stopped by Roland's hand cuffing his wrist.

Beneath Eloise's fingertips, Brother Walter's arm again trembled.

The earl glared at Roland. "You dare lay hands on me? Again you forget your place, St. Marten!"

Roland gave the earl a feral smile that sent shivers down her spine.

"For the nonce, my place is between you and Brother Walter, my lord earl."

Kenworth tried to jerk his arm from Roland's grip, and failed. A shoving match ensued with Roland giving no ground. Instead he kept his big body steadfastly positioned between Kenworth and the monk.

"Cease!" the king shouted. "St. Marten, release the earl."

Roland obeyed, but didn't move from his protective position.

Kenworth shook his dignity back into place, but his confidence suffered. Concern deepened the lines of his brow.

"What say you, Kenworth?" The king picked up the

most condemning missive. "Did you have your spy write this missive in order to implicate Hamelin?"

"The monk lies! St. Marten has either threatened Walter or promised him a rich reward. I swear, if given an hour I can produce the man who took the missive from the Scottish messenger."

"And I give you my oath, my liege, that I promised the monk nothing but my protection," Roland stated. "He came of his own will."

Brother Walter cleared his throat. "Sir Roland did not force me to leave Evesham. My reward is to make amends for the wrong done to Sir John. May God forgive us all for this atrocity."

Kenworth whirled to face the king. "I stand wrongly accused, my liege, and demand satisfaction." He flung a hand toward the monk. "I demand he prove his charge. He claims to have written the missive. If so, then he should be able to make an exact copy. I am willing to wager he cannot."

Roland's head swiveled, his odd look for the monk disconcerting. Eloise felt her innards tighten. Something was wrong. If the monk had written the missive, then he *should* be able to make a copy. And once done, her father would be free.

To the monk's credit, he never hesitated. "I shall need writing materials, my liege."

The king rose up and waved Brother Walter into the thronelike chair. From a drawer the king drew parchment, quill, and a bottle of ink.

Eloise stifled a gasp when Brother Walter slid his hands from his sleeves, revealing a badly deformed right hand. Her heart sank to her toes as he reached out and brushed the plume on the quill with bent and broken fingers.

Then with lips pursed and haunted look in his eyes, Brother Walter picked up the quill in his *left* hand, dipped it in the ink bottle, and began to write.

Kenworth gave Roland a mighty shove and bolted for the door.

Later, Eloise couldn't have said who reached the earl first, Geoffrey or her father, or which one wrestled him to face down on the marble floor. But in the end, 'twas her father who knelt on William, the earl of Kenworth's back, holding the traitor captive until the king's guards rushed into the room.

Through the entire scuffle she stood at Roland's side, her stomach clenched until the door closed, blocking out Kenworth's string of vile curses as the guards hauled him away.

King Edward took a deep breath. "St. Marten, I may need your assistance in hauling a rope to the Tower."

Roland smiled slightly. "As you say, my liege."

They celebrated with dinner at an inn, her father insisting on treating the large group of his supporters to roasted leg o' mutton and several accompaniments.

At the huge round table, they hailed their success with several raised tankards, Father effusive in his thanks to all, including Mistress Green and Oswald the Warder. In his largess, Father even offered the position as his clerk back to Brother Walter, who quietly declined, claiming he preferred to return to Evesham Abbey.

Earlier, Roland had privately told her of the monk's relationship to Kenworth, and of what he suspected happened to Brother Walter's hand. Kenworth had paid so little heed to his bastard son he didn't know Walter was left-handed.

How sad for the monk to have had to betray, in the name of justice, a father he'd only wished to please. How horrible for the monk who must feel both used and unloved.

Eloise thrilled to watch her own father and brother, sitting side by side, more companionable than they'd ever been. Perhaps they'd not found complete accord, but at least they could now bear each other's presence without rancor.

The two squires were deep in their cups. Edgar and Timothy had formed a fast friendship that Eloise hoped would endure after the squires were reunited with Isolde. 'Twas to be hoped Edgar would accept Timothy's relationship with Isolde as easily as Geoffrey accepted her relationship with Roland. Only time would tell, and Eloise chose not to dwell on future problems tonight.

No plans had yet been made for the journey back to Lelleford. At least that's where Eloise assumed she and Roland would go, to collect her belongings if naught else. Sweet mercy, she didn't care where they went so long as Roland took her with him.

And all would be bright and good in her world if only Roland seemed happier. He'd been rather quiet during supper, accepting her father's accolades with grace but not with triumph. Even now, with the food cleared away and the ale flowing, she had the disquieting feeling he didn't consider himself a hero for having brought Brother Walter to the audience in time to aid her father.

Such modesty might be commendable, but Roland

was *her* hero, and her husband, and she'd show him how much she appreciated and adored him later. In a room upstairs. Not only had her father treated everyone to supper, but rented several of the inn's rooms so no one need brave the streets of London after nightfall.

Sweet mercy, she could hardly wait for Roland to lead her to the chamber, strip off her clothes, and press her onto the mattress. Eloise vowed to bring a genuine smile to her husband's face if it took all night.

Her woman's places warming, she leaned toward him, brushing against his arm. He glanced over and gave her a slight smile.

Good, but not good enough. She slid over until they touched thigh to thigh.

He arched an eyebrow, his eyes softening with humor. Not exactly the reaction she wanted, but better than the thoughtful, almost morose look he'd worn most of the eve.

She whispered, "Must I crawl onto your lap to gain more of your attention?"

The corner of his mouth quirked. "Feeling neglected?"

"I have slept alone for four nights and not slept well at all."

He glanced around at the others at the table, none of the company as boisterous as earlier. Timothy was already asleep, his head down on his crossed arms, where he'd likely spend the night.

"If you wish to retire, my lady, then so be it."

Finally! After a round of good nights, Eloise led the way up the stairs. Once in the room, she crossed to the clothing pegs while removing her circlet and veil. When she turned, she saw Roland standing by the door, staring at her with an intensity that both scared and thrilled her.

She wanted to tear off his clothes, arouse him into a frenzy so complete he'd have trouble remembering his name. 'Twas obvious he wanted the same—but something held him back.

"What troubles you, Roland?"

"Circumstances have . . . changed."

"Indeed they have, for the better. Everyone enjoyed tonight's celebration except you. And possibly Brother Walter. Does his plight weigh on your mind?"

He ran a hand through his hair. "Nay, the monk will be fine once we get him back to Evesham Abbey."

The tone of his voice gave her pause and set her feet to crossing the floor. She looked up into his beloved face.

"My father is free. The king is not upset about our marriage." Thank all the saints. She'd worried over Edward's reaction, but he'd not scolded Roland. He had even indicated there would be more riches coming his way. After all, the king now had the properties of an earldom with which to reward those who'd brought Kenworth to justice. "All has turned out for the best, a cause for rejoicing. Why, my dear husband, are you not celebrating by ravishing your wife?"

With gentle fingertips he brushed back her hair. "We need to talk first."

Now? Eloise took a deep breath and reined in her impatience, trying to remember that a good wife should yield to her husband's wishes. Some of them, anyway.

"About what?"

"Our marriage."

Her heart sank. 'Twas as she'd feared, that Roland

would come to regret his hasty, rash agreement to Geoffrey's pressure, even though the marriage had seemed wise at the time.

She put a hand to his chest. "Did we not agree to make the best marriage we could? I know I am not perfect, Roland, but I do vow to try to be a good wife to you, less strong-willed." She sighed. "And I have broken that vow already tonight by suggesting we come upstairs, practically demanding you make love to me. I beg pardon. Do you wish to go back downstairs?"

He smiled at that. "There is nowhere I would rather be than in bed with you. Anytime you want me, you have only to crook a finger and I will come straightaway."

Completely confused, Eloise tightened her hold on his tunic. "Then you must make your meaning more clear."

"You agreed to this marriage to save your dowry, because if events had gone sour for your father, men of your station would have shied away. That is not true anymore. Verily, Eloise, you could now have most any man in the kingdom you desired. I fear you will come to regret settling for less than you deserve."

Silly man. Didn't he know she'd obtained exactly what she wanted? Nay, he did not, because she'd been too afraid to expose her heart.

Eloise wrapped her arms around Roland's neck and clung to the man who held her heart and happiness in his hands, who she trusted to keep safe her life and love.

"Dearest Roland, you are right. I did not receive what I deserved. Instead of a lord, I married a knight. A man of courage and honor who I will love and adore and admire until my last breath. I love you, Roland. I am *most* content with our marriage."

His embrace came fast and hard and encompassing.

"I scarce believe I hear you aright."

'Twasn't like Roland to seek reassurance, but whatever he needed she'd give. Now. Tonight. Forever.

"I love you, Roland St. Marten, with my whole heart, my entire being. I meant the words of our vows. I will love and honor and cherish and occasionally obey you all the days of our lives."

He chuckled at that. "Then there is something I want you to see, my dear."

My dear. Not the declaration of his undying love she yearned for, but a lovely endearment. A beginning.

Reluctantly, she let him go. He pulled a scroll from the folds of his tunic, which Eloise recognized as their betrothal bargain.

"I know what the bargain contains."

"Not all of it. Not the part where it states that I do not come to you barefoot in my short pants."

An enticing image. If he'd made the comment with humor, she'd comment, but Eloise knew he'd always felt awkward about obtaining a vast sum and giving nothing in return, so she refrained.

"I do not need to see a listing of your horses and armor and equipage. Sweet mercy, Roland, I care nothing for—"

"I know, but I did." He tapped the scroll on his palm. "As I walked to the Tower to request your father's approval, I agonized over the disparity. I obtained wealth beyond my wildest dreams, and had nothing to give you as a bride price. That sat ill."

Wounded pride she understood. "Does it still?"

"A bit, but not as much." He untied the ribbon binding the scroll. "I rectified the situation as best I knew how, by giving you the only thing I possessed which seemed fitting."

"I need nothing but you."

He cupped the side of her face, his palm warm, speeding up her heartbeat. His eyes held such tenderness she nearly melted.

"If you truly mean that, then this is the moment I have saved this for." He handed her the scroll. "Read and believe."

Eloise opened the scroll and skimmed down through the listing she'd provided Geoffrey. Toward the end, above the myriad signatures, a clause had been added in unfamiliar writing.

As bride price, Sir Roland St. Marten, knight in service to King Edward of England, vows to hold safe and protect Eloise Hamelin of Lelleford. Possessing nothing of material value with which to gift her, he bestows upon her all that he may, being his oath to love and cherish her all of his days and beyond, no matter what life may impose upon them both.

Love and cherish.

Her throat closed up. Tears welled up and blurred her vision, preventing her from again reading those precious words.

"Oh, Roland." She collapsed against him and cried out her joy, held upright by strong arms and his balance.

"I love you, Eloise. As I told your father, my love for you was the only reason I considered the marriage. 'Twas my fondest wish that someday you might find it in your heart to return my affection."

"Why——" She cleared her throat and tried again. "Why did you not simply tell me?"

"Because I wanted you to believe." He brushed a palm across her cheek, coming away wet. "Do you remember telling me that gallant utterances from a suitor were not to be believed, that professions of adoration were all chivalrous nonsense?"

She remembered saying something similar on the day they'd passed by the village church, when they'd discussed Hugh's death and his infatuation with his bride.

"I remember."

"That is why I put my professions in writing, so that if you ever doubt that I mean it when I tell you I love you, you have only to look at the bargain which cannot be broken or set aside."

With irrefutable proof of Roland's love in hand, Eloise pulled him down for a long, heartfelt kiss. He'd given her all he had to give, his heart.

She'd keep it safe, guard it well. Beginning now.

Eloise set the scroll on the table and reached for the laces of Roland's tunic. "Now are you ready to celebrate?"

A wide grin spread across Roland's face——and lasted most of the night.

About the Author

SHARI ANTON'S secretarial career ended when she took a creative writing class and found she possessed some talent for writing fiction. The author of several highly acclaimed historical novels, she now works in her home office where she can take unlimited coffee breaks. Shari and her husband live in southeastern Wisconsin, where they have two grown children and do their best to spoil their two adorable little grandsons. You can write to her at P.O. Box 510611, New Berlin, WI, 53151-0611, or visit her Web site at www.sharianton.com.